DEEP ROOTS

ALSO BY RUTHANNA EMRYS

Winter Tide

RUTHANNA EMRYS

DEEP ROOTS

A TOM DOHERTY ASSOCIATES BOOK

NEW YORK

DEEP ROOTS

Copyright © 2018 by Ruthanna Emrys

Edited by Carl Engle-Laird

A Tor.com Book
Published by Tom Doherty Associates
175 Fifth Avenue
New York, NY 10010

www.tor-forge.com

Tor® is a registered trademark of Macmillan Publishing Group, LLC.

The Library of Congress Cataloging-in-Publication Data is available upon request.

ISBN 978-0-7653-9093-6 (hardcover)
ISBN 978-0-7653-9092-9 (ebook)

Our books may be purchased in bulk for promotional, educational, or business use. Please contact your local bookseller or the Macmillan Corporate and Premium Sales Department at 1-800-221-7945, extension 5442, or by email at MacmillanSpecial Markets@macmillan.com.

First Edition: July 2018

Printed in the United States of America

0 9 8 7 6 5 4 3 2 1

This book is dedicated to:

MAX GOLDSTEIN—*arrived in New York City from Russia, date unknown*

IDA HACKER GOLDSTEIN—*arrived in New York City from Russia, date unknown*

GUSTAV FISCHER—*arrived in New York City from Germany, date unknown*

EDWARD ROSENBAUM—*arrived in New York City from Bavaria, Germany ~1850*

ROSETTA HIRSCH ROSENBAUM—*arrived in New York City from Bavaria, Germany ~1850*

HANNAH PLAUT STERN—*arrived in New York City from Germany ~1852*

AARON STERN—*arrived in New York City from Germany ~1853*

MORRIS WEISENFELD—*arrived in New York City from Roumania sometime between 1897 and 1899*

RACHEL FRIEDMAN WEISENFELD—*arrived in New York City from an unknown origin, 1899*

SOLOMON NEDELMAN—*arrived in New York City from Chernobyl sometime between 1900 and 1906*

ROSE ELMAN NEDELMAN—*arrived in New York City from Russia sometime between 1904 and 1906*

. . . and all my other immigrant ancestors.

His solid flesh had never been away,
For each dawn found him in his usual place,
But every night his spirit loved to race
Through gulfs and worlds remote from common day.
He had seen Yaddith, yet retained his mind,
And come back safely from the Ghooric zone,
When one still night across curved space was thrown
That beckoning piping from the voids behind.

—H. P. LOVECRAFT, "ALIENATION,"
Fungi from Yuggoth

Why fades a dream?
That thought may thrive,
So fades the fleshless dream.

—PAUL LAURENCE DUNBAR,
"WHY FADES A DREAM?"

The shadow of the half-sphere curtains
down closely against my world, like a
doorless cage, and the stillness chained by
wrinkled darkness strains throughout the Universe to be free.

—YONE NOGUCHI, "AT NIGHT"

DEEP ROOTS

PROLOGUE

Nnnnn-gt-vvv of the Outer Ones—May 1949:

There is a world—a planetoid, chosen for ease of camouflage among thousands like it—where wind whispers through air cold as the vacuum. The nearest star is a distant candle. Radar, radiation, subtle folds of gravity: these are the best ways to perceive the cities tucked into crevasses, the spiderweb bridges spanning jags of icy mountain.

The bridges, aeons old, were here when we arrived. They offered omen and reminder: Life persists everywhere. Life vanishes everywhere. Find it and listen, or it will pass unknown. I spread my wings, furl my claws, and spring from Yuggoth into the void behind and between worlds.

Here is neither cold nor heat, only form. Shimmers of color, more perfect than any permitted by surface physics, mark direction; bubbling shapes carry messages left by travelers past and yet to come. From deeper still drifts a faint fluting. The pounding, pulsating trill wavers on the edge of understanding. Pay too close attention, and the friction will wear your mind smooth.

Conversation between winged and wingless is our best distraction from that distant melody. Embodied travel-mates fly beside me. The disembodied, in their canisters, come encircled in our clasped limbs. Amid reality's foundations, we speak with equal ease of the deepest philosophy and the most immediate gossip.

We break through the dimensional membrane on the edge of atmosphere. Through heat and wind I plummet, extending just enough of myself to enjoy the physicality of speed, before landing lightly on a granite cliff shadowed by *pines. Here, on a hill that humans avoid as much from habit as from half-remembered fear, I feel the mining colony shifting beneath me. Travel-mates and cross-mates and offspring and research clusters, the ever-changing rivalries and friendships and political debates through which we adapt to this place as to a trillion others.*

Soon there will be a shorter journey to our new-delved mine, in a city richer and denser than any human habitation we've dared before. Soon there will be new recruits who can help us understand what's happening on this world we've adopted, and unwelcome insight into what we must do about it. But for now, I am in Vermont, and I am home.

CHAPTER 1

June 1949

Grand Central Station stretched beyond human scale, and the crowd within matched it. Amid the swift current of travelers Neko held tight to my hand, even as she craned to glimpse columns and golden statues. Trumbull and Audrey and Deedee took the lead, a confident vee to navigate the turbulence. I trailed in their narrow wake, overwhelmed by the stench of a thousand perfumes, a thousand joys and worries and attractions, a thousand bodies flavoring New York's overpowered air.

"This way," Audrey called back. She led us toward an archway.

"How can you tell?" Caleb muttered.

"Let's hope she knows," said Charlie. "We can't very well stop to check." His cane thumped the marble floor as he worked to keep up. He was right—Audrey's speed merely kept us in pace with the crowd.

"You have to know," she called back cheerfully. "Otherwise, you get lost."

After the first shock, the crowd began to resolve into people, variety too great to seem truly monolithic. There were pale-skinned women in well-fitted dresses and neatly jacketed men like those who dominated Arkham; others whose features reminded me of Morecambe County's Polish communities. Such immigrants, I'd been told as a child, would make signs against the curse they saw in our faces, but it was the long-settled descendants of Puritans whose superstitions were most dangerous.

Beyond these familiar types, I saw every kind of face and dress I'd encountered in San Francisco and a few I hadn't. Scandalously short skirts and faces hidden by scarves, eyes heavy-browed or framed as neatly as my Nikkei family's, fabulous beards and unlikely hats. A woman who barely came up to my shoulder carved a determined path with a pram, cooing at her child and glaring at all who brushed too close. Two clean-shaven negro men in brown robes backed against a pillar, bent over maps they protected with jutting elbows. A rotund white man carried a trombone under one arm and hoisted a bag of papers with the other. He checked his watch, and hastened his step.

In Arkham and Boston, we'd drawn stares—for my face or Audrey's magnetizing effect on men, or for the variation within our group. Here we received only the scant attention needed to avoid collisions. I began to believe that we might really, after so many false leads, discover some distant cousins overlooked by the government during Innsmouth's destruction. Our expatriates could easily have settled here unremarked.

And so they might remain, if the press of the station gave any taste of what awaited us outside.

"There it is!" Audrey pointed above the sea of heads, and when I stood on tiptoe I could see the pillar of the station clock where Spector had promised to meet us.

In the grand hall surrounding our landmark, I pulled even closer to the others. Trumbull glanced back. "Look up."

I drew breath: above, across the vast ceiling, stretched a painted sky. It was stylized, constellations imposed on line drawings of Pegasus and ram and skittering crab. These stars were trod by the comprehensible, human-image gods to which the station was a temple, not the distant suns that birthed mine. And still, it was holy.

Caleb glanced at Professor Trumbull. "Are *their* cities like this?"

She smiled. "This is as close as humans come to the Yith's capitol." I wondered how close the comparison came, what remembered glories she now excavated from her mind's sojourn among that ancient, inhuman race.

The clock topped a ring of counters. Behind them, harried clerks dispensed guidance to equally harried travelers. Charlie tensed; through our confluence I felt him shiver with fear or joy, or both. I followed his gaze to where a thin, black-clad figure waited, a branch parting the current. That perfection of stillness melted as we approached, and quick strides brought Ron Spector easily through the press of bodies. Spector's decisive movements and energy, startling in San Francisco or Arkham, seemed born of the station's rhythm. He clasped Charlie's hand and Caleb's with equal apparent pleasure, offered to take Trumbull's suitcase and slung my shoulder bag across his chest as well. The rest of us fell into step behind him, save for Deedee, who kept pace by her old colleague's side.

"You find us a place near this doctor, the one who thinks he's found Caleb's wayward cousin?" she asked.

He shook his head. "There's a boardinghouse that I trust near my family in St. Mary's Park. Clean, and good food, and willing to put up with people coming and going at odd hours. And cheap enough not to scare Miss Marsh." He glanced back only briefly, but his voice was teasing. "It's a quick enough ride to Brooklyn on the IRT Lexington Avenue line, and who knows where you'll have to go once you talk with your doctor."

"That's fine," I said, though I wondered at the way Deedee pulled herself straighter, the hint of shortened breath that passed sudden and vivid through the confluence. It might be better not to ask; for all the intimacy of our connection, Deedee preferred to keep her distress private.

A newsstand halted Spector's momentum; he swung aside to examine the headlines. I wasn't surprised: they were full of the Hiss trial, Soviet spies infiltrating the American government through mundane stealth. Spector likely knew the agents who'd tracked the man down. He must be immersed in both the rational fear of further collaborators and the hysteria that President Truman warned against at the bottom of the page.

There was an edge to the headlines that I didn't like. Even knowing a fraction of what Spector's masters feared, I could guess at the tensions swelling. Frightened people would look for enemies, and find them.

Spector straightened, shook his head, and led us down to the subway station. Tiled walls created an echoing cave of footsteps and muddled conversation, but the crowd was sparser. I was relieved to see signs forbidding cigarettes and pipes; my throat still stung after the ride from Boston. Even so, the platform air was a stew: half-spoiled food, urine, sweat, faded perfumes and musks. It cloyed and teased, wavering curtains of rot blowing aside for a moment to reveal hints of lust and roses.

"We'd better move farther down the platform—more room for your luggage near the front of the train." Spector's voice recalled me to practicalities. I followed, watching his confident stride. This was why, despite all my doubts, we'd asked for his help finding our way around New York: on his native soil, he offered the best chance of finding what we sought. That, and the pleasure his company brought Charlie, were sufficient arguments for his presence.

Still it rankled. I'd come to like Spector the last time we worked together. But until now I'd never gone to him for help—he'd always approached me first. And while he'd proven himself largely trustworthy, he was an agent of the state, and some of his colleagues were far less honorable. He was here with us now on his own time, but he could not be counted on to offer help alone, even if he wanted to.

The state had destroyed Innsmouth. Asking for Spector's help as we tried to rebuild came perilously close to suggesting they could make up for that crime.

The train cried its arrival: a long piercing scream like a monster in mourning. Inside, bodies pressed close. The smell was worse than any-thing in the station. It was nothing like the ticketed train up the coast, one passenger per seat, nor like the open cable cars in San Francisco. I held my breath and clutched my valise. Far better to think of the train from the camp to San Francisco, full of familiar sweat and freely mixed Japanese and English chatter—and not of an earlier trip in boxcars smelling of rotted fish. I closed my eyes, listened: around me voices rose in a dozen accents of English, some Eastern European tongue, the unmistakable weaving rhythm of Chinese. My ears rang painfully, but my breathing slowed: it sounded more like San Fran-cisco than like anywhere else I'd lived. Eventually, I opened my eyes.

The train shook and rattled. Spector shifted easily with the move-ment, rocking slightly as if on a boat. Deedee kept a hand lightly on the back of a nearby seat; she too adapted easily to the ragged sway. A pale young man gave up his seat to Charlie, who settled in with a nod and pulled his cane close to avoid others' legs and ankles. The rest of us gripped poles and handbars, trying our best not to trip into the sea of strangers. Neko caught my eye and nodded, wan smile be-traying her own nerves.

The press eased as we left Manhattan. The remaining riders wore darker clothes, more mended, with scarves or strange small hats pulled tight against their skulls. Finally Spector led us out onto a smaller platform, then up to the street. For the first time I tasted the city's open air.

"Welcome to the Bronx." Spector sounded uncharacteristically shy.

San Francisco, the city I knew best, stretched over ancient hills and endless fog. It was easy to imagine its topography stripped of human habitation, grown wild with the strange plants and stranger animals that would cover it through aeons without witness—and to imagine it reborn long after humanity was dust, hills only a little eroded, as a new city for another species.

Not so, New York. I knew we stood on an upthrust of bedrock, scarcely five miles from the open water of the Atlantic. But the honking cars, the grocers and delis and hardware stores and veterinarians squeezed together with no apparent pattern, the sidewalk crammed with food carts and families—all seemed crafted on a foundation of human whim alone. Newsstands blared civilized horror: bloodshed in China, Soviet spies in America, magazines speculating about "push-button warfare." Exhaust mingled with tobacco smoke and the scent of hot dogs and pickles, sweat and aged dirt and oil and disinfectant. No hint of salt water could wind through that tapestry.

And yet, Spector relaxed into this rhythm. The street *hummed*. Its shifting vibration made me want to pull off my shoes and let the energy course through me. I wanted to ride and gentle it as I might a thunderstorm, or drink from it like the ocean. It made its own topography, seductive as it was terrifying.

"Thank you," I said to Spector.

Neko stretched her fingers to catch the air. "Does your family live around here?" she asked.

"Five blocks north," he said. "But Tante Leah's boardinghouse is closer."

"Are you going to introduce us?" asked Charlie. His voice had grown tight. Caleb too looked nervous; his neck twisted, owl-like, at every surge of sound.

Spector ducked his head. "I'm sure you'd get along with them, but Mama and my sisters . . . they aren't the most discreet people in the world. Downright nosy, really. Leah's more likely to let people keep to themselves."

Caleb humphed, and Deedee brushed his elbow. People hurried around us, seeming too caught up in their own worlds to care about anyone else's business. Then again, each pause to buy a hot dog or read a flyer must rub against five others doing the same; only gossip would make the friction bearable.

My throat stung. If I let myself start coughing, the fit would bring me to my knees. I swallowed, forcing saliva, and focused on the tantalizing hum. It seemed blasphemous to treat it like anything natural, but when I pushed past my reluctance I found it easier to navigate the breaks in the crowd, and to catch miserly breezes that eased the tightness in my lungs.

We turned onto a side street. The mosaic of signs and awnings gave way to simple row houses of worn brown stone, each narrow facade flush with those on either side. Tinny music wafted through open windows. Trees stood isolate in sidewalk grates; herds of dandelion and grass pushed tendrils through every crack.

Spector led us to a house fronted by steep concrete stairs. Inside, I blinked against suddenly dim light. The lobby reminded me, painfully, of the old Gilman House hotel: the tiled floor and cool shadows, and folk looking up curiously from card tables to examine the newcomers. Gilman House had always been as much local gathering place as residence for Innsmouth's occasional out-of-town visitors. The people here—bearded men in dark hats, women in shawls and scarves—seemed thoroughly settled, and I wondered if they lived at Tante Leah's or simply accreted from apartments nearby. Stale cooking oil and old smoke permeated the air with a peculiar, almost plastic smell, bearable largely by comparison with the miasma outside.

An elderly woman rose from her chair. "Ron, zenen di deyn gest?"

"Ya, zey . . . zenen." Spector spoke more slowly, hesitating over his words. "But they only speak English."

She looked us over. She was short—barely past my shoulder—but she had an air of hospitable authority. "Well, I figure that. Shvartse girl, a couple of shiksa . . . doesn't matter. You have strange friends, I have rooms, I have food. Just tell me, your mama asks, you have a Jewish girl somewhere?"

He grimaced. "I don't have a girl anywhere, Jewish or otherwise. She knows that."

"She worries about you."

He sighed. "I have two brothers and two sisters, all married but Sadie, and Ira and Rivka have kids. She should relax."

"Oh, Sadie. She's a mashugina. You should be grateful, you give everyone less worry than her. Well. You need, looks like one room for the boys, maybe two for the girls?"

We moved swiftly—and to Spector's clear relief—from familial imprecation to the process of getting settled. Tante Leah bustled us upstairs, distributed stacks of fresh-pressed towels, and divided us among our rooms.

I could stretch my arms and touch both bunk and opposing wall; we couldn't stand at all without stacking our two valises. A slit window admitted a warm, fetid breeze and the view of nearby bricks.

"It has a lock," said Neko, and I allowed that this hadn't been a virtue of all the rooms we'd shared. The sheets and mattresses seemed clean, and burying my nose in the pillows offered a respite from the city's scent rather than a magnification.

When we came back downstairs we found Spector talking with a newcomer. Spector shifted, seeming dissatisfied with every attempt to fit in his chair, while the other man leaned forward intently. The newcomer shared his long broad nose, the slender frame that folded to encompass available space. Spector saw us and gave a little embarrassed shrug. He rose.

"Miss Aphra Marsh, Miss Neko Koto, this is my brother Mark. Mark, these are some of my friends from Massachusetts. And here are the rest." This last as Caleb and Charlie, Professor Trumbull and Audrey, appeared on the stairs.

If Spector had truly wanted to keep us from his family, as he claimed, he wouldn't have brought us here. I hung back, uncertain what was expected.

"Always good to meet Ron's friends," said Mark. "He doesn't bring them home very often."

"And have Mom fuss over everyone?" said Spector.

"She has been, anyway. Someone"—he waved a hand at the common room—"told her you'd been here to set up a room, and you hadn't said you'd be bringing anyone by, so of course she sent me to invite whoever it was for dinner."

Mark's eyes lingered on each of us—no. On the women, with a little frown completing his assessment of each.

Spector let out a breath. "If their plans permit, I'm sure they'd be glad to . . . they didn't come here to visit *me*. I'm just helping. A mitzvah."

"Mm. It's the first time you've been here for years, outside of holidays."

Spector shrugged. "She's always asking me to visit more often. And my friends needed a tour guide."

Another glance. "You make interesting friends."

Caleb put his arm around Deedee and frowned in return. Mark's eyes darted between me, Neko, and Audrey.

Trumbull took Mark's hand and smiled, all Arkham upper-crust confidence. "Thank you for your kind invitation. We'll be glad to come by for dinner, of course—just as soon as our business allows."

Caleb Marsh—May 1949:

Deedee takes another leather-bound volume from the pile. Mottled calf-skin has worn thin, ink fading over embossed runes. She squints at the ornately lettered title. "The Meeting of . . . Words?" A few months' study, and our languages already come more easily to her than to me. But I'm not envious. I enjoy watching her learn, the way concentration interrupts her usual performance and lets her thoughts show on her face.

She surrenders the book to Charlie, and he traces the line with his finger. "Zhng'ru Gka Lng'rylu . . . but 'words' is 'lghryl,' right?"

Aphra nods. "Lng'rylu is what you feel with, in your mind or on your skin. Especially pain or discomfort. I've seen an English version translated as The Parliament of Nerves. *It's about healing; we had a copy at home." But not this copy, I think. Parliament's not the kind of book where families used the inner cover as a record of births and metamorphoses, but there would have been a name plate. I remember going with Father to pick up a new stack from the printer—trying to follow the labyrinth coils of the sea serpent on the family seal without losing my place.*

"Healing," I say. "That sounds safe enough for the open collection."

Audrey's already shaking her head. "If it can be used for healing, it can be used as a weapon. Ask a surgeon how many uses he can think of for a scalpel."

Aphra sighs, and Charlie puts the book on the "restricted" pile. "You're probably more imaginative than most surgeons," I tell her.

"That's what I'm here for."

I hate this work, and I know Aphra does too. We're sorting sacred texts into scalpels and swords: the tools that might help people accept us, and the weapons that air-born men would misuse for their petty wars and political ambitions.

At least sorting books gives me a chance to practice my still-pitiful Enochian and R'lyehn. And it's a distraction from my failure at what I should be doing to rebuild Innsmouth—reclaiming our land from the developers who want to crowd our beaches with G.I.s and their pretty wives and children. Strangers have already paid well for the new clapboard cottages on the outskirts—and for a few large houses boasting seaside views. They have that—and easy access to the beach where we ought to meet freely with our elders.

Even the homes we've successfully bought stand empty.

Audrey takes the next book from the library cart. "Tald'k—that's 'song,' right? Tald'k Ka R'drik Gak-Shelah—" She stops and leans back, narrowing her eyes. "You blush on a dime, Aphra. What's a R'drik Gak-Shelah to make you go all red in the face?"

"Who," I say, grinning. It's a thorough distraction, at least. "Who are R'drik and Gak-Shelah?"

"How the void do you know?" Aphra demands. "You were six." I flinch. It feels like a strange moment, her amused indignation a flash of the snotty older sister I knew before the camp.

Deedee touches my arm. "Six is old enough to wonder what the fuss was about."

"So is thirty-five," says Charlie.

"I'll bet I can figure it out," says Audrey. She pages through the book. "There are pictures."

Aphra sighs. "It's an old romantic epic. It's a common sort of story, but more . . . detailed than most. It has a reputation."

"I'll say. This is the kind of book you find locked in your mom's bedside table." Audrey peruses the illustrations with a thoughtful look. "What's the story about? Aside from the obvious."

Watching Audrey tease Aphra awakens my boyhood self as well, smirking at my sister's discomfort. I don't think Aphra even notices the flirtation behind the teasing, but she gives in first. "I know you think we're more permissive than men of the air—and we are, in some ways. But our duties can be as rigid as any Christian marriage. On land, when we're fertile, we must find good mates, produce children, raise them and support them, regardless of whether that's the work—or the mate—that touches our hearts. And most people accept those strictures, because once we go into the water we have aeons to love whomever we please, or turn inward and write poetry without stopping to feed a family . . ."

I try not to flinch again. Our parents didn't get those chances, nor our neighbors. And yet Aphra still believes in duty first, always.

She goes on: "But we're human, and we enjoy stories about people who break through even the most vital boundaries. R'drik and Gak-Shelah are lovers who can't breed together, and so their duty is to keep apart until their metamorphosis. Instead they take ship, traveling a trade route and trying to hide their relationship, and putting off the families who'd have them marry others. And then R'drik goes through metamorphosis young, which makes it even harder to hide." She's blushing now; it's not a book she ought to have read at eleven.

"It would be hard for them to enjoy each other's company, under those circumstances," says Charlie. He makes it sound like a casual literary observation, but I know he speaks from experience.

"It's not that realistic," Aphra says. "When it's not, um, explicit, it's full of long poetic passages about how their love engulfs them in the glories of the deep water, and their joy is only to drown in each other."

"It's not a book of magic, anyway," I say, considering the slender "unrestricted" pile.

While we hesitate, our table is graced by the unwelcome arrival of Irving Pickman—against our objections, the head librarian for the Kezia and Silas Marsh Memorial Reading Room. He beckons Aphra to his desk; I follow close behind. Something's pleased him, adding a smug edge to his usual placatory smile.

"Have you found something?" I ask reluctantly. I still don't think Aphra should have asked for his help. Bad enough that Miskatonic forced the smirking bastard on us. Worse to admit to him that all our attempts to track down Innsmouth's lost children—mistblooded who carry a hint of our strength from generations back—have failed. But he is an expert in genealogy. And Aphra is eldest-on-land; it's her right to admit our shame.

"I found something," Pickman confirms. "Though not what I originally expected. The names you gave me—I haven't tracked down anything on those yet, other than the false leads you mentioned yourself. Old trails and poor record-keeping." Amusement creeps into his voice. I grit my teeth at the implication that the record-keeping is our fault, with some of those records still likely buried in his storerooms. "But I had a thought." His eyes slide to me. "I've a friend who moved to New York a few years ago, a doctor with an interest in anthropometry. You'll excuse my saying so, but what they say about . . . that is, Innsmouth families do have a distinctive skull shape. I thought that if someone had passed his way, he'd be likely to recall it—to recall them. And any family that moves frequently enough almost has to end up in New York eventually. Sheldon loves it—a wonderful place to study mankind's full range. Everything from the most advanced academic minds to the coarsest specimens, all crowded in a few square miles."

He pauses, gives a deferential chuckle. "My apologies. Sheldon does go on in his letters, and I suppose I'm passing on the favor. In any case, I described the type as well as I could, and he told me that a few years back a woman came to him, one of the coarser types, worried that her son might be sickening. He'd been born perfectly normal. But by five he showed deviant growth patterns, especially around the eyes. Sheldon wasn't familiar with the type, but

*he's continued to track the family in the hopes of learning more and improv-
ing his records. The family—Laverne was the name, and I've no idea which
of your list they're descended from—lives in an apartment in Red Hook. The
boy's about seventeen."*

I swallow, aware that I should be grateful. But for the most part I'm
annoyed that we didn't think of this first, that we had to depend on someone
who thinks we're "deviant" to think of asking around for others with the
so-called Innsmouth Look. And I imagine what it must have been like for
this boy, raised to think our looks a disease. At least I knew, growing up,
that it was something to be proud of.

"Thank you," says Aphra. Sounding perfectly calm.

"Sheldon says he'll happily direct you, but he hopes he might be able to
take casts of the original type, perhaps run some tests . . ."

"The hell—" I start. But Aphra catches my eyes, the faintest shake of her
head cutting off my suggestion of what Sheldon can do with his casts.

"No experiments," she says. "But we'll talk with him."

I ask, voice neutral as I can make it: "What recommendations did he
make? About the boy?"

The pale angles of Pickman's face redden. "As I said, he didn't have many
similar cases to draw from. I told him that Miss Marsh and you both seemed
somewhat intellectually minded. And certainly the town seems to have
produced an extensive body of scholarship."

"Thank you for your estimate of our mental capacity," says Aphra. "I do
appreciate your looking into this. It's not an avenue we would have thought of."

We make our excuses, and leave before either of us can say something more
pointed.

That night, Neko drooped her head from the top bunk. "He thinks
Mister Spector is dating one of us. He's trying to decide which one
he'd hate least."

"I saw. I don't know whether to be offended. Spector needs to have
kids to preserve his people, the same as I do. I've seen it in the

papers: the Germans killed a full half of them during the war. But his brother should have just asked. I don't like anyone looking at me that way—at any of us." The idea had been echoing in my mind since before we arrived. Rebuilding Innsmouth must, ultimately, mean children. Children who might show a hint of my long fingers and protuberant eyes, who with luck would carry out that promise in aeons to come. Children, perhaps some of them with the man we'd come here seeking.

She grunted. "I suppose. You know what Mama said to me before I came out east?"

"A lot of things, I assume. She was full of advice for me, most of it good." I found reassurance in Mama Rei's fussing, and heard the lullaby in its rhythm. But I'd come to her as a lonely adult, exhausted by endless waves of mourning.

"She said, 'It's all very well for Caleb, he hasn't any choice in the matter. But you come back here when you're ready and marry a Nikkei boy.'"

"Parents want to see their blood carried on. It's only natural. It just isn't right to hold it against people of different bloodlines. We used to do that, and look where it got us." I'd made the same mistake: I'd dismissed Sally's air-born ambition as less than my own, and she'd died because of my shortsightedness.

"You think I should marry a Nikkei boy too." Her inverted face disappeared; her mattress springs sagged with a chord of creaks.

"Neko." I pulled myself up over the rim of her bunk, but she turned toward the wall. "I'm sorry. I'm worried about how I'm going to find a mate; I didn't mean to say anything about yours."

"Good—don't."

"You've got the excuse to travel with me—"

"And I need it. Because when it ends, I go back in my cage."

"Neko——" I wanted to tell her she could have both, children and freedom, that she didn't need my protection to choose her own life. "I love you. I'm sorry for fussing."

"Love you too. Go to sleep."

I patted her shoulder awkwardly, swung back down to the ragged choir of my own mattress.

I lay there for an hour or more, unable to set aside Neko's resentment. When she followed me back to Massachusetts and my confluence, we'd both expected her to serve as an emissary to newly located mistblooded. Our findings had justified a few day trips—far less than I'd meant to offer her. Far less than she seemed to need, as assurance that she was forever beyond the barbed wire and equally barbed rules of the camp. I balmed my own scars with ocean air and long walks, proof that my body was whole and free, but Neko found Morecambe County as restrictive as San Francisco. Even so, she wouldn't take the bus to Boston or Providence for her own sake. She needed a practical excuse. Whatever track my own fears followed, I shouldn't have let them overwhelm her delight in this rare opportunity.

My worries blurred at sleep's edge: from Neko's anger to Spector's family, Spector's hazardous romance with Charlie, Deedee's brooding on the train—and behind everything else, the question of the lost family we came here for, and what they'd do when we found them. *If* we found them.

Every time I began to drift, a car horn or a shout or a muffled snore pierced the cushion of fatigue. Less identifiable noises insinuated themselves from every direction. The city stretched above me and below, and far around, and I felt suspended in some alien dimension. It was tempting to ignore the disorienting sensation, and return to the familiar turmoils that had kept me awake to begin with. An ordinary tourist might lock a door and hold the city at bay. But the confluence had been studying dreamwalking. I'd earned just enough skill to make myself vulnerable: I could stretch my mind into the worlds that lay sideways from our own, and explore for a few precious minutes, but I hadn't the finesse to avoid wandering in accidentally.

I would have preferred to set aside my studies until we returned home—but I couldn't count on staying tightly tethered to my own thoughts while I slept. I needed to deliberately inspect the shallows of the local dreamlands before I faced them unwitting. Charlie, whose skill was close to my own, would need to do the same.

Dreamwalking was a matter of tightrope-slender balance—much, Charlie had said wryly, like the physical world. The balance was written into the spells: symbols of rest set against those to ensure eventual wakefulness, and symbols of the mind untethered measured against those to strengthen life's most necessary bonds. It was there in the mindset: drifting out into Earth's neighboring dimensions, we had to imagine our bodies well enough to hold selfhood coherent, yet still take advantage of our minds' newfound freedom. And it was there in the space itself, and the knowledge that if you forgot yourself in wonder at the vision before you, you could forget yourself forever.

I didn't intend to reach that far tonight—only to know my surroundings well enough to ensure a modicum of safety. And so my symbols were simple, a bare reminder of the world-piercing lullabies that marked the full rite. I sketched them in my notebook by the city's luminous glow, and whispered the words of an old song. Comfort and magic twined, and I remembered my mother singing the same evening blessing.

I breathed, cautiously letting myself drift. Neko's familiar dreams lay open above me. Twists of color, scattered images: buildings, imagined cities, the people on the subway. She twitched among incomplete ideas. They spilled over the edges of everyday reality, coloring directions that she wasn't able to travel. Other sleeping minds lay close, and beyond them I could vaguely sense the depth upon depth of near-earth dreamland, realms half-shaped by sapient imagination and half by physics increasingly distant to the laws that made life possible.

Here, so close to waking, I'd expected an extension of the street's chaos of scent and sound. Instead, after a vertiginous moment, I found the humming vibration that had tempted me earlier. It pulsed in quavering harmony—then resolved with alarming abruptness. It was a heartbeat. It was a million heartbeats, rising and falling steadily. It swept me up with the others and made no distinction between native and visitor, air and water.

The vibration was a wakeful thing, and yet my own pulse slowed in response. My breathing evened and my nostrils, clogged with smoke and soot, cleared. I began to withdraw into my body, pulling a thread of that dreaming rhythm, ready at last to relax into ordinary and comfortable sleep. Then the thread snagged on something.

I stilled, mind suspended between states, while I tried to work out what had so disturbed me—without attracting its attention. An off-note had entered the shared human rhythm, a dissonance that threatened the whole pattern. Further into the dreamland, I might have been able to sense it more clearly. Here, shivering between states, I could tell only that it wasn't any of the predators I knew. When the full moon rose above Innsmouth in our native dimension, nightgaunts wheeled the dreaming skies like starlings, and shantaks cried in the distance. Their songs could freeze prey from a thousand miles away, but the wards against them were sketched in elementary textbooks. They were familiar, dangerous but natural. This asynchrony, whatever it was, didn't belong to any of the realms I could touch.

It seemed to come closer. I concentrated, unmoving, hoping to catch a glimpse but hoping more to remain unseen. There, amid the city's oscillating pulse: a discordant buzzing hum that refused to resolve. It grew louder until it drowned out thought, until it overflowed the bounds of hearing and filled scent and sight and touch with its droning power. Then, at last, it began to fade.

While I strained my senses to understand, the thing vanished. Its whole passage could not have taken ten seconds. New York's native rhythm rushed in to fill the vacuum, covering the trail as if it had never been.

Disquieted, I pulled back into my body and my own private dreams. I slept fitfully, waking with leaping heart whenever I felt my mind slip. And between these moments of fear, I dreamed of Trumbull standing at a chalkboard, sketching ever-wilder shapes of tooth and tentacle to explain what I'd encountered.

CHAPTER 2

I woke with gritty eyelids, mind still probing the fierce cadence that drowned out any hint at last night's mystery. Within the city's lulling heartbeat, millions of real people traveled in a swirl of hunter and prey, con artist and wary mark, and all the mundane desperation born of the press of ordinary bodies. Whatever dangers lay beneath the surface—hazards in their own right—I had no way to see them.

The dangers I knew were bad enough. If I hadn't feared the consequences, I'd have brought the whole confluence to stand between me and Dr. Sheldon's curiosity. But I didn't wish to scare him off, make him think we were reneging on our end of the agreement. And if he felt some possessive obligation toward our lost relations, as Pickman had suggested, I didn't want to suggest any threat against them.

So Caleb and I went alone, following Spector's direction to the doctor's well-trimmed Brooklyn neighborhood. Alone, we climbed the polished stairs to his waiting room.

When I pictured the man we were about to meet, I'd imagined a twin to Irving Pickman. The man who'd sent us here was tall, bone-thin, with a long, sharp face: in every way typical of the old Morecambe County families that dominated Miskatonic. Instead a ruddy, round-featured man, thickset enough to prove he'd never gone hungry, surged past his secretary to welcome us. His handshake engulfed my long fingers.

Dr. Sheldon settled us in his office, a place of well-cushioned chairs and mahogany furniture. He offered scotch, which Caleb accepted and I declined. I perched on the rim of my seat in an attempt to maintain a dignified posture, unnerved by his effusive hospitality.

"Well." He settled back on his own cushion, sipped his drink. "Ivy Pickman says you want to know about Miss Frances Laverne and her boy Freddy. He was barely a year old when she came to me. She was worried about how the boy was growing—her regular doctor thought he might have some defect that hadn't been obvious at birth. No father in the picture, I'm afraid. Freddy was a fascinating case. I'd never seen the type, though Miss Laverne admitted that her own father'd had some of the same look. The eye sockets in particular, most unusual, and some interesting anomalies in the neck bones."

He beamed at the two of us. "Rather an unexpected pleasure, to encounter the adult version of the form. I do hope you'll let me take measurements later."

I tried not to grit my teeth. We needed his help. Caleb's eyes narrowed, his lips parted, and I forced myself to conciliation: "If you like."

"I'm sorry, Miss Marsh. No offense intended, truly. But the theoretical and practical implications are urgent. My diagnosis of the boy was quite inept, you see." He chuckled, humility either false or strangely comfortable. "I'd never seen his like, of course, but I generalized from the closest types I knew, and I felt I ought to give Miss Laverne a realistic idea of what to expect. He looked like a coarse specimen, with little capacity to benefit from any deep education. Such types are steady physical workers at best, given a firm hand in the raising, but prone to vice and laziness. You needn't frown so—as I said, I was quite off the mark. Freddy proved himself extremely bright early on—learned letters and figures quickly, and fast on the uptake with ideas. Miss Laverne kept bringing him in as he got older, and he'd pull books off my shelves and ask all sorts of questions." He leaned forward. "Is that typical of your family? Do you tend towards high intelligence?"

"We like to think so," Caleb said blandly.

I'd sunk back in my chair despite my best intentions, distracted by this chain of confidences. My unrestful night was beginning to tell on me: fatigue made every insult more alarming, every new drop of information more portentous. Hoping to encourage him to share more of the latter, however upsetting his attitude, I proffered more detail: "We've always valued education from a young age. I knew three languages well by the time I was twelve." I regretted that last as soon as I said it, and hoped he didn't ask me which three. I supposed I could count my shoddy Latin, though my parents certainly wouldn't have.

Sheldon nodded enthusiastically in the face of a theory confirmed. "That sounds like Freddy. Always eager to learn—a little brusque, like your brother here, but that's understandable, really. I didn't think the intellect could come from his father's side. Miss Laverne admitted that the man was a negro, obvious enough from the boy's skin, and they're hardly known for intellectual pursuits."

Caleb stiffened, then took a slow swallow of scotch. "Actually, my fiancée is negro. And she speaks five languages—I saw her pick up the last two in about six months, at the same time."

"Well, there are always exceptions. I don't suppose she'd be interested in coming in? In any case, if Freddy is any indication, I commend you on what's likely to be a profitable match." He smiled and put his glass down. "And an unusual one, I imagine. Your skull structure is really extraordinary—whatever lineage you come from must be relatively isolated. A small group?" He tilted his head invitingly.

Caleb turned to me, teeth bared in a not entirely friendly grin. "He wonders if we're inbred, sister dear."

"Caleb . . ." I said warningly.

Sheldon held up his hands. "I don't mean any offense. It's as common in the highest lineages as in the low. Look at any aristocratic family, and you'll see an astoundingly similar conformation—perhaps two noses or chins to choose from, but the skull shapes will be almost identical. Weak hearts may take them down young, but the advantages of their lines are still clear. I only meant that your bone structure is so very unusual—and in all my practice Freddy and his mother are the only examples I've seen. So it's clear you keep to yourselves."

"We've tried." I breathed in sharply, out slowly. "Please forgive my brother. Our neighbors in Massachusetts used to accuse us of incest." Caleb and I had spent hours debating how much or how little we could tell him—and before Caleb brought it up, I thought we'd agreed to avoid this part. Now I had little choice. "Nor was that the worst of the libels. Eventually, those lies reached the government and brought soldiers down on Innsmouth in a massive raid. I don't care to discuss the details, but they treated us harshly. Only my brother and I survived." No need to add: *on land*. Though the image of Sheldon meeting our grandfather and asking to examine his skull made me suppress a huff of amusement in spite of the tension.

"That's why we're here," I continued. "To find any distant relatives who may have survived. The Lavernes are the first lead we've found."

Sheldon's eyes had widened. He started to raise his drink, shook his head, put it back down. "I'm sorry for your loss. I didn't mean to pry into a painful subject. Of course I'll put you in touch with Freddy and Miss Laverne. And surely you'll want a better understanding of your type—with proper measurements, sketches, an understanding of developmental courses, it will be far easier to find more of your cousins."

"I know," I said. I ducked my head, shoulders stiff against the surrender. Caleb, his anger withered, looked at me anxiously.

We sat rigid while Sheldon bustled with rulers and measuring tape, a gridded notepad, and various oddly shaped metal contraptions. He seemed not completely oblivious to our discomfort, and filled the silence with murmured numbers and expressions of pleasure in our bones.

"Well, there," he said at last. He traded the pad for a larger sheet of thin paper, and began sketching. "Thank you—I hope I'll be able to find more of your kinfolk. At the very least, there are the Lavernes. Give me a moment to get this down, and I'll write out a letter to assure her of your relationship."

"Thank you," I said, trying to sound grateful. I knew gratitude was warranted, for he offered a true gift, but I couldn't bring myself to feel it.

He frowned. "I should warn you, though, the boy's fallen in with poor company recently. It's not his nature, I think—not everything comes down to caliper measurements, after all. It's a lesser form of the trouble you've encountered. Your average untutored citizen, he sees someone odd-looking, and he doesn't try to understand what that oddness truly means. It's only natural for the boy to seek friends who can't afford to be discerning. A real pity—I hope his better instincts tell in the long run."

I blinked at the unexpected nuance and wondered what he might think of the Kotos as "company." We knew what he thought of Deedee, I supposed. "Poor company? What sort?"

He shrugged, frowning. "His mother hasn't been forthcoming. But I know she doesn't approve, and her discernment—well, except for the boy's father, clearly . . . a man of good character would not have vanished on her, I mean. Perhaps you'll be able to provide Freddy an alternative."

He finished his thankfully rough sketching, and scribbled a note. "There you are. And their address as well. I wish you much luck."

"Thank you," I repeated.

"I'm glad to help." He stood, shook our hands with somewhat more sedate enthusiasm. "I'm sorry for what happened to your family. The human race benefits from having many types, even—perhaps especially—the more obscure ones. Few people appreciate that we need a great range of talents and predilections—it's a big, complicated world, after all."

Outside, my eyelids felt tight and gritty. I looked at the papers he'd given us: the note and the address.

"Sister dear," said Caleb under his breath. "He's better than half of Miskatonic, but I'd still like to snap his neck. Void take his 'coarse specimens.'"

"Thank you for restraining yourself." I rubbed my forehead where the measuring tape had pressed, and pushed away an image from my mother's file: her corpse laid out, chalk marks showing the difference in height from the start of her metamorphosis. Halfway through her transformation, skin flaking in great patches around nascent mal-formed scales. Eyes blind and bulging in shrunken sockets. Caleb, mercifully, hadn't seen the file.

We ought to have taken the train across Brooklyn. Unless we failed entirely the cipher of subway signs and announcements, it would be far faster. But we were both shaken, and needed urgently shed some of the anger raised by Dr. Sheldon's casual arrogance. So instead we walked for three hours—roundabout, and losing our way twice—to find the scribbled address.

Miss Laverne's neighborhood was shabbier than Dr. Sheldon's, her building more poorly kept. A thin strip of straggling grass stut-tered against the front steps, setting off red brick and dirty win-dows. The tiny foyer smelled of garlic and melted wax. Black and white tiles, faded by grime, mosaicked the floor.

My ankles ached, less from the length of our walk and more from the unfamiliar dance of threading the crowded sidewalks, the ten-sion from dozens of momentary frights and flinches. Four flights of stairs spread that ache up my thighs and back and into my neck. I wanted some safe place to rest, and knew that sanctuary a long way off. Outside the door, Caleb and I caught our breaths and exchanged glances. It seemed unnecessary to speak of our shared fears, of the irrational reluctance to give them a chance to take form. I flexed my toes against well-worn soles, imagined digging them into cool sand. I knocked before I could lose my nerve, three swift raps.

A woman answered the door in seconds, breathing hard. She gripped the knob as if she too had been bracing herself, and blinked rapidly.

"Hello? Can I—" She swallowed the remainder of the sentence.

If I hadn't known to look, I might not have seen it. But her chin and neck were wide and strong, her light brown skin uniform enough to suggest veins buried deep below the surface. Her large eyes sat high in her face, and her waist was thick with muscle and insulating fat.

"Cousin," I said, the word spilling from my mouth. I held out the note. "I'm Aphra Marsh, and this is my brother Caleb. Dr. Sheldon sent this. To testify to our likely relationship, and as an introduction."

She tightened her grip on the door, as if it were all that held her upright. I watched her force breath and movement. She stepped aside slowly. "Frances Laverne. Of course, you know that. I'm sorry. Please come in."

She offered us a couch upholstered with red corduroy, worn to the quick and smelling of ashes. She brought two glasses of water and set them on the coffee table as if every motion were rehearsed. She sat at last in an overstuffed armchair. Cotton spilled through its seams where her elbows rubbed against it. She reached for a pack of cigarettes on the table beside her, then pulled back and folded her hands in her lap, clenched tightly together.

"Will you tell me where Freddy is?" she asked.

Caleb and I looked at each other. "But we came here to meet him," said my brother.

"And you," I added.

"But you're—" She dropped her gaze to her knotting fingers. "I haven't seen him in a week. Grandpa told me stories about our family. How can you show up now, and not know where he's gone? He didn't hear—the call?"

"The call?" I echoed. But even as I said it, I imagined her family, with the trickle of water in their blood, understanding only that they were different from other people. If that water welled to the surface in a rare few, the rest of the family would see only that they suddenly abandoned their lives, perhaps leaving some cryptic explanation. "He'd be very young for it."

She looked up. "You know what I'm talking about."

"Yes."

"My grandfather said you hunt the ones who leave, and make them come back to the sea." She sounded frightened, yet strangely hopeful.

"We have, sometimes," said Caleb. His voice was gentler than usual. "We don't anymore. Though there's a home for you in Innsmouth, if you want it. We just wanted to meet you—to meet others of our family."

"Oh." She took a cigarette, looked around anxiously, patted her pocket. Caleb pulled out a matchbook, leaned forward, and lit it for her. "Thank you. I shouldn't—can you tell me about us? You must know more than I do."

"Probably a lot more." I smiled, trying to look reassuring and not foolish or alarming. Still she flinched. It was years since I'd last seen a young person of the water other than my brother; she was the first I'd ever met whom I hadn't known from childhood. My every expression and posture felt inadequate. To Miss Laverne, I was a monster from half-believed stories, and I didn't know how to break through that barrier of unreality. "Tell me what you know, and I'll add what I can. And then perhaps we can figure out how to find your son."

She took a deep drag, let out a long breath of smoke. Here too, she was different from us: lungs unscarred, fears and reactions shaped by her own troubles. She must have been haunting the door and the phone, waiting for news. "If that's what you need, I'll make that trade. But all I know is what Grandpa told us. And half of that was just boogeyman stories, to scare kids for fun or keep us in line."

"Boogeyman stories are important too," I said. There was no way to explain that I hadn't meant it as some cold exchange, her stories for her son.

"Okay. Just remember that you asked." She put the cigarette to her lips again, then let it dangle between her fingers. She was trying to look casual, I realized, a mask stretched thin over her fear of us and her fear for Freddy. "This is all family legend, really. The story goes that Grandpa's own grandfather was seduced by a sort of a mermaid." She paused, waiting for some reaction. I nodded and gestured at her to go on. "Maybe not exactly a mermaid. You know what a selkie is? She looks like a woman, but she slips on a skin and turns into a seal. If you hide the skin, supposedly, she has to stay with you till she finds it. She was something like that: a woman from the water. When she found out she was pregnant, they ran away together. It's all a story, of course." She watched our reactions from behind lowered eyelids. She was looking for our belief, I thought, or expecting our doubt.

"It sounds reasonable so far," I said.

"Really?"

"Really. What happened to them?"

"Grandpa said his grandmother eventually got lonely and wanted to go back to her family. Maybe she heard the call herself. But his grandfather didn't want to go, and wouldn't let her take away his first-born son. She left swearing her family would track them down. He must have believed her, because he spent the rest of his life moving from town to town, dragging his kid along. It didn't work, because his son—my great-grandfather—disappeared when Grandpa was little. Or that's how Grandpa always told it. Honestly, I think—thought—it was just a way to explain his dad running off. Men do that, after all. But Freddy . . . where *do* we go, when we disappear?" She glared, as if defying me to refuse an answer.

It took me a moment to respond to her challenge. I imagined the scene: a woman of the water, not yet come into her strength, trying to take her child home, forced away by the man she thought she'd loved. Coming back with a posse of elders to discover them gone, following them for years . . . I glanced sidelong at Caleb, wondering if he sympathized with the woman of his own race, or the man unwilling to give up his child. I shook my head, pulled myself back to the present. "Your family legends aren't far off. We are Chyrlid Ajha, the people of the water, and those of us with enough water in our blood go into the sea when we're older. No seal-skin required."

"Huh. That sounds pretty crazy."

"So did your story. I'm just telling you that it's true." My shoulders trembled. I wasn't at all sure how this should go. "That's probably not what's happening to Freddy, but it's not impossible. Even—" We had few polite ways to describe someone with so little water in their veins. "Even mistblooded, like you and him, sometimes undergo metamorphosis. And when you do—when we do—the ocean protects us from age and illness. Your great-grandfather and your great-great-grandmother are likely alive in the deep cities. You could meet them."

"If Freddy's changing, is that where he is? In the ocean? Could one of *them* have come for him?"

I shook my head. My voice caught on the ashen air. I coughed, trying to make my words come clear. "We're the only ones who know about Freddy, and we expected to find him with you. The change takes weeks. But if he didn't know what was happening, it would be frightening. I can imagine him running away, going to ground."

"Have *you* noticed him changing?" demanded Caleb. "Hair falling out, eyes growing more prominent, folds in his neck?" He ran fingers along his own thick neck to illustrate. Minuscule wrinkles, barely perceptible, lined the skin beneath his ears. I touched my own, unthinking. They were more prominent, but not yet tender. I remembered my father wincing as Mother pressed wet cloth to burgeoning gills.

Frances's eyes widened. The tip of her cigarette flared. "Nothing like that."

We watched each other a long, silent minute. Suspicion sharpened her regard. I'd imagined sharing with her and her son the secrets of their past, a taste of our treasure. But the explanation of her birthright seemed inadequate. Her glare carried silent accusation: *You're here. He's gone. Why can't you explain? Why* won't *you explain?*

In my own desperation, I reached for things I *could* explain. About life in Innsmouth, about the schools and families and the rituals. About R'lyeh and Y'ha-nthlei, Lhadj'lu and Mach-richyd. All the things her great-great-grandmother would have wanted for her child.

She allowed me to change the topic, even asked questions. When do people change? How many cities are there in the ocean? But not infrequently, she glanced at the door or the phone with prey-quick eyes. I suspected that she tolerated us not because of the benefit of the doubt, but out of a desperate conviction that we could still help her.

I wanted to offer that aid, however little it might be worth. To understand what we could do, though, she needed to know the full truth behind our presence. So I told her about the camps. About why we were here, now, looking for distant relatives.

"And what do you want from me?" Her tone was nervous, perhaps a bit curious. She lit another cigarette. "From Freddy?"

"What we want . . ." I said. "If you came back to Innsmouth with us, you'd have a place with your own people. You could help us rebuild. You'd have a house of your own, and all your share from our family's wealth. We could offer an education for Freddy, and for you if you wanted it, from people who've been teaching for a thousand years—who've seen firsthand the history glossed over in books, and invented arts half-remembered on land." I caught back my eagerness, mindful that she'd just met us and didn't trust us. "If you don't want that . . . then talk with us. Get to know your family, on land and in the water. Don't stay lost. And we would still have resources to offer you. No one of our blood should go hungry, or want for shelter. We agreed on that, before we came here." Caleb nodded firmly, and gripped my hand.

The ember between her fingers glowed brighter. "There's a catch."

Caleb shrugged, letting go my hand. "You'd be admitting a relationship to people the government tried to kill a decade ago. Our neighbors think we're monsters. And we're trying to build a town from the ruins up, when developers want to sell it all to war vets. That should be enough catch to satisfy anyone's cynicism."

She frowned and puffed. "If you can help find Freddy, maybe I'll think about it." She stubbed the cigarette into the ashtray, and leaned forward empty-handed. "I haven't gone to the police. I don't want to get him in trouble. But I asked around, tried to get the neighbors to keep an eye out for him. No one's seen anything. Though I suspect most of them aren't looking very hard."

"Dr. Sheldon said he was spending time with a 'bad crowd.'" Caleb's voice took on an ironic lilt.

"I . . . yes, but not how you'd think. They didn't seem like a gang. Or mobbed up, or anything like that. Just—off. They all look smug about something, and don't have any time for anyone who doesn't know their secret. Freddy started acting the same way, dropping hints that he'd learned something big. A couple of weeks after all that started, he just disappeared. And then you show up."

Something about her description of Freddy's new crowd tensed the muscles in my neck. They didn't sound like a gang—they sounded like a cult. I wanted to think I was being paranoid, but I knew from my own experience that such people could be dangerous companions, especially if they knew less about their "secrets" than they thought they did.

I glanced at Caleb. Our efforts at genealogical research proved our ineptness at tracking people down. I hoped we'd find it easier to look for a specific person, one who'd vanished last week instead of decades past. And perhaps his new friends had left other traces. The alien presence I'd felt the night before could have been the sign of some working gone wrong—or right.

But it was *our* arrival that Frances had latched onto. "Us being here now—that *is* a coincidence. I wish it wasn't—that we'd come with the news you were waiting for. But we'll do our best to help, if you'll let us." We could try a summoning. If magic didn't work, we had other resources. I hated the thought of asking Spector for more, but wasn't finding lost people supposed to be one of the things FBI agents were good at?

She bobbed her head, half nod and half unnerved twitch. "Help me find him, and we can talk about the rest."

Nnnnnn-gt-vvv of the Outer Ones—June 1949:

"Here, look at this." Pleasure thrums in Kvv-vzht-mmmm-vvt's voice, cutting through my disorientation. The new-delved mine is an opportunity to change everything about the old that subtly grated—even if I had adapted to the mistuned electromagnetic generators, the imperfect proportions of the guard console. It was wrong to forget the possibility of improvement. To accept, without trying to change, the errors of the universe.

Worse, though, to let our haven enforce the illusion that the universe can always be altered. Architecture as debate. Very much my thrice-mate's style.

"This," at the moment, is the new conversation pit. The broad steps are comfortably lit, and elegantly sculpted to encourage intimate interaction within the larger shared space. Perception still warps where that space was pulled in tight for easier construction. Dust leaps in microscopic whirlwinds as newly cooperative planes unfurl into their final configuration.

Kvv-vzht-mmmm-vvt brushes the floor with its cilia. Limbs vibrate, and topology suddenly shines clear.

"Oh, that's perfect." The steps have been marked with small depressions, each precisely shaped to stabilize the base of a canister. Our wings brush affectionately.

"Shelean's idea," it says. I'm not surprised—she spent our most recent flight enthusing about these designs to our newest travel-mates. The surge of

recruitment, of new minds and ideas, has been one of the pleasures of this move. And one of the goals. Vermont's vein of humanity was close to tapped out—another place where we'd grown complacent. New York is rich, un-plumbed. If there's anything about Earth's minds that we don't yet under-stand, we'll uncover it here.

Our new travel-mates, and the older ones who originally hail from this area, have been vital to our delving. I'm not old enough to remember the first construction on this world, but I remember when the Vermont mine was the Hoosac mine, and I remember the constant flux of new growth and as we adjusted to human settlement. Back then, we were the first to claim our hills. Here, our foundations are laid beneath a bedrock of deeds and permits, every-thing skimming close to the membrane of the city outside.

I think about the argument immanent in these choices, as Kvv-vzht-mmmm-vvt shows off the chapel, brightly worthy of its gods, and the upgraded corporeal monitors. Beneath the surface shimmer of new equipment, we came here to argue. Only the argument's importance—not only to the survival of the species among whom we dwell, but to our own integrity—makes such close quarters worth the risk. Here we'll contend, reason against reason and perception against perception, until we grasp each other's philosophies in full and gain the consensus on which our own preservation depends. It's working: I'm starting to better understand Kvv-vzht-mmmm-vvt's convictions. And they worry me.

CHAPTER 3

The summoning failed. Caleb and I crowded into the boys'
room with Charlie, late enough that Spector's "aunt" wouldn't
hear about it. We sketched a diagram, and laid on it hairs
Frances Laverne had given us from her son's hairbrush. Blood would
have been better, but Freddy wasn't accident-prone enough to have
left any bloodstained bandages behind in their trash. Frances's look
of revulsion, when I'd asked, had made me regret bringing it up
at all.

The problem, of course, was that Freddy was mistblooded. Easy
enough to calculate the precise degree of mixture—if the star-crossed
affair of Frances's story was unique in his ancestry. More likely, though,
his father's family had carried a trace of the water or his great-great-
grandmother had a wisp of air in her veins. If we'd been trying to
find either of *them* it wouldn't have mattered, but the combination
made a difference.

As we chanted the words that should have shaped the call, we hit
another barrier. The city itself clung to our spell like mud. It sucked at
our magic and slowed our speech. I found myself short of breath, my
heart speeding and voice cracking with smothering memories. The
rhythm that had reassured me briefly in the night now pounded so
loudly that I couldn't hear my own words, and couldn't imagine our
target hearing them either. I tried to push against that pressure, but

my chant stuttered into silence. While I gasped, the others closed off the abortive spell, avoiding the risk of true disaster.

"What was that?" I whispered hoarsely. I thought again of the strange disruption I'd sensed on the edge of the dreamland. Could the strength of the city's rhythm today be backlash in the wake of that passage, or even the disruption's purpose? But I'd sensed no such compensation last night.

"I was going to ask you," said Charlie. "I wish we'd brought more books."

I had to know whether he'd felt the same thing. "Did you pick up anything odd last night, during your meditations?"

He shook his head. "The dream realm feels more intense here than at home. But so does the waking world."

"I thought I felt something strange go by, just at the end. But there are so many natural hazards there that I don't know if it was really out of the ordinary."

"I don't think what we just hit is all that extraordinary, either." Caleb stood, stretched awkwardly, and leaned against the narrow window, forehead pressed to forearm pressed to glass. He looked out on brick, but I could still feel that dangerous pressure behind the stirring rhythm I'd sensed before, simultaneous and contradictory.

"Well, go on," I demanded, my voice harsh with fatigue.

"The city is so big, bigger than any place we've worked before. If there are a million people between us and what we're trying to summon, and some of them have a little air, or water . . ." He trailed off, glanced over his shoulder.

"Then you get too much that's *almost* like what you're looking for," I finished. It was, in fact, a plausible explanation for our failure. "And any of that could be ten people, or a hundred, who together have enough of the water's blood in them to trip the spell."

"That's interesting enough," said Charlie. "From the perspective of magical theory. But how does it help us get around the problem?

Those million people aren't going to make it easy to track down your cousin—or his friends—the ordinary way, either."

"We have to find him," I said. "For his own sake, as well as his mother's. And for ours." Fail Freddy, I was sure, and we'd lose them both. Frances would refuse to have anything to do with us—or worse, decide that we'd stolen her son and call down authorities to destroy Innsmouth once again.

Caleb gave up on the window, and slouched back against the sill with arms crossed. "If we've compromised to get this far, we may as well keep compromising. I imagine Mr. Spector, unlike us, actually has experience with this sort of thing."

"I know he does." Charlie's cheeks flushed, barely perceptible in the dim light. I smelled an edge of sweat. "He's told me some stories. From Europe."

Which would make it during the war. He wasn't normally prone to boasting of his exploits. I wondered what he'd confided in Charlie.

I was eldest-on-land, and it was ultimately my decision who to trust with our weaknesses. But I could see no other options.

"I'm sorry," Spector said. We sat in a corner of the lobby, voices soft, and I wished we had more privacy. "I can't."

"Freddy Laverne is just a boy," said Charlie. "He needs help to get out of whatever stupidity he's gotten himself into." His intent gaze, focused on Spector, seemed to carry more signal than his words. Knowing what they risked with their affections, I thought they might have particular troubles in mind, narrowly avoided in their own boyhoods.

"I know. But I still can't do it. You'd be better off with the police—and they might be more sympathetic than you'd think. They were all boys too, after all."

"Mister Spector." My voice barely rose from a whisper. "Freddy's disappearance might have nothing to do with his 'bad crowd.' He could be starting his metamorphosis. Even the FBI coming in officially—at least they'd know what they were looking at."

He ducked his head, not meeting my eyes. "I'm sorry. I can't. Officially or unofficially—I'm not sure which would be worse."

"Why the hell not?" asked Charlie. I was glad for the heat in his voice—he could risk letting it show more safely than I could.

"Because we need to keep working in New York!" Heads turned throughout the lobby, then bent to murmuring. An older lady cocked her head and started to push herself up. Spector shook his head at her and forced his voice low again. "I'm sorry. But you don't know what we go through to convince local police that we're worth calling in—to convince them that we're not going to tread on their toes or steal their cases, that they can cooperate with us and not lose anything. I come in officially, and I go over their heads exactly the way we swear we'll never do. I come in unofficially, and it looks like we're going behind their backs. Either way, next time some asshole decides to kill half a dozen women in Manhattan and then hide out in New Jersey, they'll wait twice as long before asking the FBI for help. Excuse my language, Miss Marsh. I wouldn't pay that price even if it were mine to pay."

"Oh," I said. Still tired, I let slip anger that I should have kept bound and hidden. "I should have known better. It may look like the state goes wherever it wants, but it's only *we* who have no say."

Spector took a deep breath, put his hands on the table, one hand cupped over the other. Met my eyes. "I'm sorry. Even within the Bureau, anything I do requires layers and signatures and dividing tasks just the right way to salve egos. Between state and federal is much worse. The raid—you wouldn't like to see how many people signed off on that."

"Oh," I said again. I imagined a file, thick as the one that held my mother's remains, full of approvals preserved in cold ink.

Spector frowned at the table, at his drumming fingers. He shifted in his chair. "I don't like it either. Boys run, but this doesn't sound right. Sometimes when a mother doesn't like a kid's friends, it's harmless enough, but the way she describes them . . ." He frowned again. "You really think something is wrong."

"I—yes, I do." Under the intensity of his demand, my responsibilities pressed in around me. "He *could* be starting to change. But it would be sudden. And I agree with you about his mysterious 'bad crowd.' Maybe it's my imagination, but the description reminds me of . . ."—I hesitated, knowing my fears could raise the stakes of Spector's involvement even further—". . . of Oswin Wilder."

Spector flinched at the reminder. The cult leader wasn't a pleasant memory for either of us. I waited while he bent over clasped hands, knuckles rubbing against temple until some decision was released. "I can't intervene directly. But my bosses are smarter than you might think. They know to trust our hunches, and there are ways we can ask around. Delicately. If I find the right sort of pattern, the city might agree to let the Bureau in."

"We don't want 'the Bureau,'" said Charlie. "We want *you.*"

"I'm sorry. The Bureau's resources are what I've got. And once I start asking, the Bureau is what you'll get. If something really is wrong, it won't just be me looking into it." Left unspoken, that many of his colleagues were threats in their own right.

Also unspoken: the worry in Spector's eyes. He wanted to help. He might refrain, if I insisted. Standing by went against his nature, but he'd do it to soothe my fears and his own shame over their cause.

On our own, the confluence barely knew where to begin the search. Frances's leads were too tenuous to grasp. She didn't know the names of Freddy's new friends, she didn't know where they lived, she hadn't even been able to describe their faces. The task rose before me, daunting as our genealogy search, and with no one left we could beg for help.

I wanted to refuse Spector's offer. But Freddy, and Spector himself, deserved better.

~~~

Sometime after Spector left, Caleb found me alone at the table. "Well. Is he going to help us, or does he have some entirely reasonable excuse for sitting on his hands?"

"You hate asking."

He shrugged. "It makes it all the more frustrating when we don't get it. And yes, I know I'm the one who suggested going to him. Doesn't mean it makes me happy."

I sighed. "He *may* be able to help. He's finding out." I should have said more, but Caleb's bitterness would only exacerbate my own worries. "I need air. Do you want to come with me?" He nodded, and pushed his chair back. In truth it wasn't air that I needed but water: rain, mist, a thousand forms and none of them at hand now.

When I imagined my metamorphosis, I imagined diving into the ocean: a sudden shock of cold and silence and salt. I imagined my gills flaring to pull in oxygen, and the welcome simplicity of becoming fully part of something older and stronger, something that could bear me up without effort or notice. New York was a bright mirror to that inhuman power. It was loud and hot and my every sense breathed in people as gills would draw oxygen from water. I wanted to flee. I feared drowning. And yet, the city reflected my nature as well as the sea. I could not demand to be recognized as human and deny this connection—much as I might want to.

"I'd been thinking," I told Caleb as we made our way through the crowd, "about observing Summer Tide this year."

He glared, and I could see that he wanted to pick up the thread of his objections to Spector. He let it lie, though, and I wondered what he guessed. "Of all our traditions, don't you think that one deserves to be put to rest? It was a lonely holiday even when we had the whole town alive around us. Why seek more loneliness now?"

"There's a reason I put it off. But it's different now, when we can return to the elders in the evening." For the Winter Tide, I'd needed to learn control over cloud and rain, and find the courage to share my past with Charlie—hard, but the rewards had been worth the fear. Summer Tide didn't call for any magic at all, but it would be even harder to observe.

He shook his head. "I remember the last one before the raid. All I wanted was a whole day without adults telling me what to do. I ran straight to that spot in the bog with the striped tadpoles; I was afraid you'd claim it first. I didn't think once about the value of community and family, or any of the things you're supposed to meditate on in your solitary wanderings.

"You know, I felt so mature for finding a place by the ravine to sit and think, instead of going to play in the bog. But I thought more about how serious and grown-up I was than about any of those things, too. Now I think I might like to spend the day alone and *know* it was only temporary. But I can't imagine trying that here, with so many strangers around. Even if none of them spoke to me, it would be because they didn't care, not because they chose the silence."

We walked a long time, speaking occasionally but for the most part choosing silence. I hoped the city would jar something loose, provide a serendipitous clue that would let us find Freddy without aid, but in the end we only exhausted ourselves.

That night I slept heavily in spite of my fears. I half-woke when Neko rose; I rolled over and clutched my pillow. Somewhere deep, I felt myself gnawing at the problem of the search. I let sleep reclaim me.

Someone pounded on the door, jarring me awake. From the light outside it was mid-morning. I pulled a shawl over my nightshirt, and found Charlie in the hall.

"Sorry to wake you up—it's Caleb. He won't come out of the bath, and the other guests are getting upset. He won't talk to me."

The line stretched down the hall, muttering and glaring. Propriety already seemed broken; I excused my way through the small mob, knocked symbolically, and went in. Thankfully no one else had yet dared that barrier.

Caleb hunched in tepid water, scrubbing his arms and crying in silent gasps. The back of his neck was red and raw. I dropped to my knees on the damp floor and grabbed his hand before the sponge could do more damage. He struggled briefly, then collapsed shaking, curled around his knees.

"Caleb, what's wrong? Caleb, it's okay." Through the confluence, pulse and breath surged in a flood. I forced my own to slow. I held him until, still shaking, he slapped the side of his neck and shoved it against me.

I took his shoulders; he twitched beneath my touch. Where he hadn't scrubbed himself raw, I saw that walking in the sun had burned his fair skin—the sort of flaking and peeling that most of Innsmouth once bore half the summer, inevitable despite constant applications of aloe and beeswax salve. How I'd avoided it so far I had no idea, but I didn't expect my luck to last.

"You've got a sunburn," I said inanely.

"The ocean is right here," he whispered. "It's right here, we're no-where near the desert. Please, Aphra. It's not right. I can't make it go away—" He pulled out of the whisper into a single sob, turned, and flung his sopping arms around me.

"Shhh . . . shhh . . ." I rocked him, wishing I had salt. He'd been six, when we came to the camps. Too young to recall the ordinary pains of ordinary life. "We've always burned easily, Caleb—not only in the desert. Out here it heals quickly, I promise. I promise . . ."

At last, the rigidity drained from his muscles. I became aware, again, of muttering in the hall. I handed him a towel. "Come on. Men of the air need their time in the water too."

"Oh, no. Could they hear me?"

"I don't think so." He'd been near silent in his distress. "But we're not making friends among our neighbors."

"We never have." But he pulled his shirt over his head, shuddering as it brushed his neck.

Audrey met us in the hall, flashing a smile that neatly disrupted any complaints Caleb might otherwise have received. She pulled us toward the stairs. "Mr. Spector's here. He doesn't look happy."

Ron Spector—January 1949:

The trick with strong drink is moderation. Then, when you truly need it, alcohol numbs quickly and easily. The flask has been sitting in my jump bag for a year and a half untouched, and its scotch tastes of rubber and metal.

Wooden bunk, plain mattress, thin sheets, and a scratchy wool blanket. Miskatonic students doubtless bring their own linens. I've slept on worse. To be fair, so have some of the students; enough here on the G.I. Bill who're grateful just to sleep safely, regardless of what luxury they were raised in.

Blessed art thou, oh Lord, who has sustained us and brought us to this season. Blessed art thou, creator of the fruit of the vine.

As I mumble the prayers, Charlie Day walks into our shared bunkroom. Forestalling my apology, he reaches for the flask, eyes locked on it like a man climbing from a trench. He swigs, closes his eyes. I'm surprised to find myself grateful for the company.

"Thank you," he says. "Best thing I can think of after the day we've had."

"I'm sorry. Barlow's a bastard." George Barlow's more complicated than that, but I'm not inclined to be charitable right now. This afternoon he accused Day of being a Russian spy, tied him to a chair, and threatened him with some sort of magical interrogation I'm only half-convinced was a bluff. And then I had to dine with him. He still claims Day must be a traitor, even knowing he's one of my irregulars. They'd be regular, of course, if only they'd take the job.

"Barlow." Day sits heavily on the mattress. He's shaking. "Human politics. God. Gods. How are we supposed to deal with this?"

"Ah." Not Barlow, but Trumbull, or the thing that passes for her. I shouldn't have left them alone with that thing. "She didn't try anything, did she?"

He snorts, breaking into laughter that threatens hysteria. Alcohol buzzing through my system, I feel almost as aware of his reactions as of my own. I realize I'm staring, and look away hastily. I hand back the bottle.

"She wanted to see us closer up, find out why people keep guessing she isn't . . . the person who belongs in that body. Promised to teach us things we need to know, so we let her. I got a close-up look, while she was looking at us. While it was looking." He swallows again, looks at me with eyes not numb. "Oh god, did you see."

"I saw." I couldn't shake that moment, when I saw through a woman's eyes, gasped with someone else's lungs. Or the moment before. Passing the thing—the "Yith"—that wore those eyes now. "Hot and cold and jagged. I don't believe they're monsters. They can't be monsters."

"The Yith? They steal their children's bodies to keep living. To preserve their memories, it said. It's all they care about."

"Oh." I swallow more scotch, trying to feel human.

"I met Aphra's family this morning."

"Aren't they all—oh." I've seen the file on Aphra's mother, seen the photos and the autopsy report. Seen the files I haven't shown her, the bodies after the raid. I can imagine, then, what the living ones would look like.

"I love her. She's the best friend I've ever had, the best employee, the best teacher. And I don't want to think of her growing scales and claws and diving into the water to live like . . . and she wants it, of course she wants it. My back hurts every day, my hair's getting thin, and my damn knee, and she just grows stronger. Who wouldn't want it?" He's getting more animated and emotional, not less. It makes it hard to hide in the comfortable fog.

I pat his back, awkwardly. His body is warm, flush with fear or magic. I should pull away: this isn't the war. Men are cautious, in peacetime. Or whatever this is. I have to be more careful.

He looks up, his smile drawn. Still shaking. "Just when you think you know how terrifying the world can be. There's always something worse. Sometimes I think humans should just crawl back into our caves, leave the rest of it well enough alone." He laughs. "Of course it gets dark in caves, too. Probably all sorts of horrible things in there. I just want—"

He moves closer.

Relief, then, to be ordinary and human in our own bodies. Away from impossible creatures, of all species, who would not comprehend or approve of our relief. Fear ripples beneath our drunkenness, but it's easy to ignore.

As soon as Spector arrived, Tante Leah pushed on him a potato casserole and a bowl of chicken stew. He ate swiftly, unspeaking. As soon as his last bite had mollified our hostess, he urged us out onto the sidewalk. Caleb and I, Charlie, Audrey, Deedee, Trumbull, and Neko spilled out into the sticky air. Caleb hovered close to me, and kept touching his neck until Deedee offered her scarf.

New York's public bustle gave as perfect privacy as we might desire. Every shout on the street drowned out every other; if I focused hard and watched lips, I could make out most of what was intended for my ears. Weaker hearing might make the experience more comfortable, but would be no more conducive to eavesdropping. Spector threaded his way neatly through the morass, glancing back to ensure we kept up.

"I've got bad news," said Spector, "though you may like it better than I do."

"Well," said Audrey, "that's reassuring."

I watched him intently, afraid to miss some nuance. Spector so rarely hedged. At least he hadn't yet apologized or, worse, preceded his announcement with some personal revelation. I swallowed my first instinct: *say what you have to say.* He'd earned my patience.

He stopped to examine a store window full of multi-hued candles. I tried to catch the reflection of his lips. "I asked around, and we found a few connections. Laverne's not the only person missing."

"That's not good," I blurted.

"But does that mean you can help us after all?" asked Caleb. Something in me eased, cautiously, at the thought of Spector's abilities brought to bear on our search.

He nodded. "Have to, in fact—once we started asking, we found a lot more than the two or three people who'd been reported already. And the Bureau wants me on the case. Which should tell you something about the case."

Deedee crossed her arms. "It's no coincidence that a Marsh cousin's gone missing."

He shrugged. "It could be. We've no reason to believe the others are unusual—though we wouldn't have picked out your Mr. Laverne, if anyone had called him in. A couple dozen people have disappeared, all abruptly. Most after falling in with 'bad crowds,' or other odd behaviors. New York is at the southern tip of the pattern of disappearances, and the densest concentration; they trail out west into the Catskills, and up into Vermont and New Hampshire. On those outskirts, the disappearances have been correlated with . . . sightings."

"Sightings?" Audrey asked. She beckoned impatiently with her fingers. Neko shaped her lips thoughtfully around the word.

Now Spector looked apologetic. I braced myself. He was too polite, knew us too well, to do so without cause. Charlie drifted toward his lover, then checked himself and shifted in my direction instead. I touched his elbow as Spector went on. "There are longstanding urban legends throughout New England's rural mountains—the details are consistent, and there are some suggestive photos and artifacts in our files. The stories are about monsters from another world."

"Ah." He expected shock, I thought, either out of reflex, or because of our shared experiences with unearthly dangers. I pushed away sense-memories of the ice-cold outsider that had nearly killed me, chasing the niggling memory of a story from long ago. "What kind of details?"

"Claws like crabs, and wings like bats. They're supposed to live deep below the mountains, and fly out on moonless nights. There are local stories going all the way back to the Abenaki and Pennacook."

I'd heard that description before—where? Beside the mahogany bookshelf in my parents' living room? In temple, a priestly warning from one of our many canons?

Audrey leaned forward, bouncing slightly on her toes, and Neko's forehead creased in concentration. Her eyes grew unfocused. Caleb sucked on his lower lip, perhaps trying to track the same half-image I did.

Creatures from the depths between stars, who claim territory in the hills. A phrase rose to the surface: *they have no bond to earth or air or water.* And an image, whether from an illustration or my own childhood imagination, of dark wings shadowing long, insectile limbs.

"I've heard of them," I said slowly, and then blinked at Trumbull, who'd said the same thing in the same breath.

Neko released a huff of bemused surprise. "Of course you have."

Spector interlaced his fingers and considered us. His tension shifted, braced against his own reactions rather than ours. "Miss Marsh, you first."

"I don't remember much—Caleb, if any of this rings a bell, join in. They've got claws and wings and antennae. They do live in hills, underground—I think we have some sort of territorial treaty with them. I remember the priests saying that they didn't really care about that land—about their part of the earth—the way that we do about ours. That all worlds were the same to them. And that they wanted everyone else to be the same way."

While I spoke, Trumbull held very still. She gestured strangely with her hands, touching bunched fingers to thumbtips in odd rhythms: mnemonic fragments of the language she'd spoken long ago, in another body. At last she shook her head sharply. "I can't remember much more than that—except that I seem to have picked up incredibly strong opinions about the . . . the Outer Ones?" She closed her eyes, and her voice turned a strange mix of harsh and dreamy. "Disgusting creatures, colonists and miners who travel a million worlds and dabble with a trillion species. They boast of all they've learned, but write nothing down and call their work finished when all they've done is talk. They see everything and learn nothing; they are an embarrassment to Nyarlathotep." She opened her eyes, and her channeled anger twisted into amusement. "Now you know what I know."

On the streets of Arkham, our urgent postures and the invocation of a slandered god would have drawn dangerous attention. Here, it mattered only that we clustered by the shop window, blocking neither sidewalk nor door. The crowd surged past.

Spector seemed equally oblivious to the crowd. His clenched hands rose and fell again. "Miss Marsh, Miss Trumbull . . . I don't wish to distract from our immediate problem, but are there any *other* races on this planet that you've failed to tell me about? That I should maybe consider as possibilities next time I hear about a mysterious disappearance? That you never bothered to mention because it never came up?"

Sometimes it was easy to forget how little access he'd had to Aeonist texts. Or how much of their content he'd considered myth, inventions that might motivate crimes but could not commit them. "Mister Spector. Such creatures have always visited this world. I'm sure some of them are here now. The universe is large and varied. I might as well demand that you name all the human races, of the air alone, who live in this city. And my education ended at twelve—even now, I'm still learning about my own kind." He flinched. But hearing my own words, I wondered whether one of these creatures, swift and alien, could explain what I'd seen in the dreamland.

Trumbull nodded. "I only remember these things when I'm reminded. I'm sorry."

Spector sighed. He separated his hands, unraveling finger from finger. Into his trouser pockets they went, breaking the lines of his suit and effacing his irritation. "Well, it's good to confirm that our suspects exist, even if you can't tell me why they might suddenly make off with twenty-five humans."

I didn't want to ask, but: "Is that what you thought would upset us? Creatures from other worlds going after our cousin? They might make kinder captors than ordinary men."

"Not that. Or not just that. I'm sorry." And there was the apology. "With over two dozen missing, they won't let me handle this case alone. And there are only so many agents with this particular specialty."

Candles filled the window display, hanging on hooks or rising from brass sconces. Laid out in patterns, they might delineate the space for a ritual. In a large classroom, in the basement of a university building, chairs pushed to the side, they'd outline a sizeable spell. They'd cast a cold light, summoning cold things.

Charlie gripped his cane. "You mean to tell me that after everything that happened, they not only didn't fire your pal Barlow, they're sending him to trip you up again? He got a girl killed!"

We'd all contributed to Sally's death, even Sally herself. But George Barlow had started it, along with his stooge Peters, and his secretary-going-on-collaborator Mary Harris. Mary had worked with us willingly at the end, too late for Sally but soon enough to save myself and Audrey. George Barlow, so far as I knew, still thought the rest of us disloyal to the country—or to the species, if his allegiance extended that far.

My demands had brought him in. Any blood he spilled this time would be on my hands.

Spector looked at his reflection. "There are only so many of us with this particular specialty." He shook his head, and pulled away from the window's alluring distractions. "George has more experience with missing persons than I do. So does Peters, for that matter. They're not incompetent—they're just very willing to gamble. One of Barlow's gambles saved my life a while back."

Audrey adjusted her hat, casual as a crouching cat. "So you approve?"

"If I approved, I'd get along with them a lot better. But George's supervisors appreciate how he rolls the dice for them, and he's not going anywhere. I'm just as dependent on the people who go to bat for me and defend the risks I take."

"Risks like us," I said.

He shrugged. But there was frustration in his voice. "They don't trust you, Miss Marsh. You've every reason to hate us. You work with the government, but you won't work *for* it. If you'd sign something, it would make it a lot easier to explain that I'm not just dragging in a bunch of civilians—because I wouldn't be. It would sure as hell make this case easier, because we're going to need your experience and—you know how George is. Miss Harris may have learned better, but don't count on that making a big difference."

"She's still with them," said Trumbull. It was a reasonable statement, but her voice was so unruffled that it sounded like a non sequitur.

"I've got no quarrel with Mary Harris," I said. "But I'm not going to bind myself to you just to ease Barlow's mind. Or for any other reason. I'm doing this work for my people, not the state."

"For your people's sake, then. For your cousin's sake. Give me some leverage to make them listen to you. It's not just about Barlow. Miss Marsh, you've seen in the papers what we're dealing with. We may not have found any Russian spies borrowing our people's bodies, but we've found spies. People working with our agents off the books, without so much as an oath—it scares them."

"I'm still on the books," said Deedee. Her arm brushed Caleb's, a touch that might seem accidental unless you knew them.

Spector flushed and looked down. "I know. That ought to make more difference than it does." I wanted to ask why he thought his fellow agents would respect *my* signature, but I knew: not only the paleness of my skin, however ugly they might find it, but that I'd never seduced anyone on their orders. Her remaining connection to the FBI was the most tenuous possible, just short of quitting entirely. It occurred to me—I flushed myself—that some of her colleagues might well assume her relationship with Caleb a new assignment. Or they might look at the ugly man with a beautiful woman on his arm, and suspect she'd returned to her previous profession.

Caleb glared and took her hand. "The promises you want work both ways. We'll do without it, thank you."

I agreed. The thought of giving the government even a slender leash parched my lips and tongue. But another thought, treacherous, whispered that Spector knew his people well, and knew me well enough to realize the magnitude of what he was asking. He wouldn't bring it up unless his own masters had pressed him hard. Yet I couldn't countenance so great a sacrifice, not even to protect our cousin.

CHAPTER 4

Virgil Peters—January 1949:
   In the private reading room on the second floor of Miskatonic's restricted section, George Barlow paces. I can tell he's thinking hard; I hope he thinks up something useful. I'm turning over last night's failed inventory equation—last night's sabotage—for the tenth time, trying to find the flaw. Amnesic shadows occlude the whole evening. I can't recall enough to make a difference, no matter how I struggle against the fog. There's little I can do for Mary until my turn to read aloud.

Sally Ward, the kid who begged to join us, is up now. She stumbles over words as she reads, face ashen—her first taste of the eldritch has become a trial by fire.

Eldritch, that's Barlow's term. Stranger than strange.

I've always known we needed Mary. I could tell she had smarts from the day Barlow brought her on: a secretary who could tidy up a calculation as well as a letter. But it's hitting me now just how much our work relies on her. We'd all be happier with that skill intact and unspoken, her most of all. Whether or not Spector's irregulars gave her this impossible wound, I'd gladly strangle them for it. Or better yet, strangle a cure out of them. I remember moments out of context, ghost-like: the lot of them standing amid our sketches and figures, shouting.

She wasn't crying, when we found her in the office this morning. She was meticulously examining every book, every page of notes she could find. She asked *us so calmly, for each one, whether we still saw letters, whether the nonsense chicken scratches were on the page or in her mind. She looks calm now, holding up a hand to silence Sally, dictating notes to the girl's callow boyfriend. The hand goes down; Sally's strained voice goes on. Barlow drops into a chair to scribble notes of his own.*

Rustling at the doorway. Goddamned Spector standing there, bland as you please, his "irregulars" crowding behind him. George jumps to his feet, already reaching for his gun.

"Ron," he says. "I can't believe you'd bring these people here now, of all times." I can believe it. The man has no shame, no true loyalty to keep him in line. He does what he pleases, and sticks his big nose in everything. It'd be fine if he knew what he was doing, but he's never understood the things we study. The laws that folklorists are pleased to call magic, he sees only as myths to motivate fascists.

"I'm here to help," says Spector, as if he hadn't dragged along the people who caused the problem in the first place.

For once, George doesn't put up with his bullshit. "You've made it clear, you won't even admit to yourself that you're harboring saboteurs. And you," he adds to the bitch of a professor that Spector's added to his stable. "I'll have your head for however you convinced the guards to let you by."

(I try to be a gentleman to women, even in the privacy of my mind. I make an exception for the ones who've tried to violate that privacy and control my thoughts—yet another time Mary's work protected us. If Dr. Trumbull pushes her way in today, she'll get an earful.)

"We came in the back door," says Miss Marsh. Speaking of women it's hard to think well of. I've seen her family's files. I don't believe for a moment she counts herself as American, and Spector's a fool to trust her. "And we came now, of all times, to help. As Mr. Spector said."

George jerks his chin at me, as good as a direct order. I pick a target as I start to move—Miss Marsh is the ringleader, and by how she stands she's no trained fighter. I twist her wrists behind her back, and shove my free arm against her thick neck. Muscle tenses against me, where I would've expected a pad of fat; her pulse pounds against my skin. As my thinking mind catches up with my fighting mind, I remember more about her family and realize she's stronger than I credited.

And there's her brother close by, deceptively lanky as she is thick, looking terrified and murderous. Her head moves fractionally against me, a gesture that might carry as much menacing authority as George's nod. I drag her back, glaring, hoping her followers don't call my bluff.

Spector raises his hands. "Don't make this mistake again, George. My people aren't responsible for your problems, and you have two women hurt."

And all I can think, too busy to look at either Mary or Sally—Sally, who I assumed was just feeling the strain of her first working gone sour—is: two?

Until Barlow's arrival, there was little to do but fret. I would have preferred to fret at the elders, not to mention give them warning, but while we'd traveled by train they had only their own muscles and seamounts to carry them up the coast. They wouldn't be in summoning range for at least another day, even if the currents ran fair.

Spector, under no such limitation, disappeared for the day to appease his own family for the vacation cut short. The rest of us found a nearby park, away from the gossips at Tante Leah's, and tried to unearth recollections of the hill-dwelling aliens. Neko and Audrey played interlocutors, asking questions that they hoped would prompt me or Trumbull to come up with more detail. For the most part this was entirely unsuccessful. After a while, Neko began keeping score, marking in her notebook a point for every query that drew a real answer, but if it was a game we were clearly losing. Charlie and Caleb speculated fruitlessly as to what the Outer Ones might want with the missing. I swore that on our next genealogical expedition, we'd leave someone at Miskatonic who could be telegrammed with urgent research tasks. Trumbull disparaged the city's collections. Apparently nothing from NYU to the massive public library with its guardian lions held so much as a *Necronomicon*.

Late that evening, Caleb caught me alone in the corner of the common room. "Did you know he'd bring them in?"

I closed my eyes. "I knew it was a risk. I didn't see any other way. Are you going to castigate me for it?"

"No." He voice sounded too even, strained over some unreleasable emotion. "I want to know if you think we should leave."

"Leave New York?" I searched his face for despair or anger or a shift in his ordinary background of bitterness. I found, instead, doubt.

"Of course not. This boardinghouse of Spector's. Deedee and I could take a draft from the bank, and stay at any hotel we cared to, without anyone squinting and trying to eavesdrop whenever we walked through the lobby. We could pick a place at random; that would make it harder for them to find us. We could try to track down Freddy before the feds do—maybe even get these aliens out of the way before that ass Barlow decides they're Russians in rubber suits." The plan fell from his lips in a rush, his breathing at the end short and shallow.

It was tempting. The thought of meeting Barlow and Peters again made me shudder. I carried enough painful memories that I couldn't afford to flee for shudders alone, but these people were a real danger to our family. At best, they thought us an artifact of another generation's threats—the last remnants of the deadly cults that had supposedly plagued the '20s. At worst, they believed us an ally of this generation's threats. And whatever we did, they saw as proof.

Yet the thought of investigating on our own frightened me as well. "If we hide from Barlow's team, they'll be hidden from us as well. And they'd find our cousin first. We're lost trying to find him on our own, we've already said so."

"I know. Oh, void, Aphra, I don't know at all." He pulled a cigarette from his pocket, twitched the unlit stick between his fingers. "They're dangerous to work with, and dangerous to hide from. If they get to the Outer Ones before we do, they could start a war. I don't know how we could stop one even if we were there. And what they'd do if they walked in on Freddy with gills half-formed, I don't want to think about. It might be worth staying close, just to be first in that door by half a second."

"I . . . yes. And if they try some spectacularly stupid spell, there's a chance we could talk them out of it, or warn Spector. New York's . . . there are a lot of people here. I don't think Mary would make the same mistake twice, but even she seems attached to looking for new ones." And the kind of cold, unearthly creature that had tried to consume us at Miskatonic would find richer and denser prey in the city. "I hate to say it, but let's work with them for now. Cautiously. We can strike out on our own if things go really sour."

Late in the afternoon the following day, Spector reappeared. Today's suit was darker, crisper, and more clearly armor. "They're here," he said. "You should come meet them."

On the train, I spoke to Nyarlathotep. You can pray to any of the gods, but with Nyarlathotep, traditionally, you also converse—and you prepare not to like, or understand, the answers.

You offer people what they ask for, however dangerous. I begged for help in our search, and you sent it. If you are the one who tempts Barlow with dangerous knowledge, if he is your fool, so be it. But please, lead him to dance the cliff's edge as far as possible from my family.

I might have been less selfish, and asked the Thousand-Faced God to guide Barlow away from *anyone* who might be hurt. I might have begged for Freddy's safety. But It rarely rewards broad altruism. Nyarlathotep is patron of forbidden knowledge and dangerous journeys and many other things, but self-love and specificity run through all of them.

Barlow's hotel reminded me not at all of the Gilman. The lobby was velvet and crystal, the staff uniformed and vigilant.

"Don't you have a local office?" asked Caleb.

"Not where we could talk freely about this case," said Spector. "And while George isn't afraid to sleep on the ground, he doesn't turn down luxury if it's on offer, either."

In the elevator, I braced myself. The young negro man in his gold-buttoned scarlet flicked cold eyes across our motley group. I sent another quick prayer to Nyarlathotep, that this test might not be too onerous—and then, thinking better, prayed instead to Cthulhu for patience. The Sleeping God rarely offers help, and so offers the most reliable comfort.

Mary Harris answered the door, of course: still playing secretary on a cursory level. She greeted us politely, but reserved a brilliant smile for Trumbull. "Catherine! I hoped you'd be along."

The two exchanged an enthusiastic handclasp, and were already deep in mathematical esoterica as Mary led us to where the others sat. The absurdly large room gave them time for such equationing. Abundant open space framed the carven and upholstered furniture. Doors suggested private bedrooms discreetly tucked away, but Barlow's team seemed to have unpacked most of their materials in the common area. They'd hung a map on the wall, and a chalkboard. Another slate lay on the floor, marked up with unfamiliar symbols, but no magic seemed to be in process. I let out a breath I hadn't realized I'd been holding.

Despite Mary's enthusiastic greeting of her one-time collaborator, I noticed that their descent into technical camaraderie gave her an excellent excuse not to meet anyone else's eyes.

Nor did her own enthusiasm cover for her teammates' lack. Barlow nodded at Caleb, a bare civility. "Ron tells me your cousin is among our missing."

Caleb glanced at me. "Frederick Laverne," I confirmed. "His mother didn't report his disappearance."

"Why not?" asked Peters. "Is he involved with something?"

Barlow put his hand out, palm down, discouraging this line of questioning. "Mr. Marsh. Miss Marsh. We'll be glad to hear what you know about the boy, but there's no reason for you to take part in our investigation. And plenty of reason for you not to."

"George, I've already told you—" began Spector, but subsided when Barlow made the same gesture at him. The reflex of their past collaboration showed.

I swallowed both the fear Barlow's presence raised and the instinct to defer, or to defend myself. He had no right to judge us. "Mr. Spector works with us for a reason, Mr. Barlow, and we with him. He assures us that you're good at finding people, and I'm willing to take his word for it. Why won't you take his word for our skills?"

"It's not your skills that worry me."

Mary put a hand on Barlow's arm. "Mr. Barlow. I trust both their skills and their willingness to cooperate when they say they will. And really, would you rather have them running around investigating *independently*? You know they will."

Peters snorted. "If you're worried about another Detroit, that's a pretty poor recommendation."

"I'm not saying that." She smiled, ducking her head. "Just that you can't ask people not to help their own families, not and have it stick. I want to hear what they think about these Mi-Go."

Deedee pulled out a chair, sat gracefully. She smiled at Barlow, eyes downcast, and I saw the choreography plain in her movements and Mary's. "Mi-Go?"

"That's one of the names they're known by," said Mary. "Outer Ones is another. Old Folk. They're supposedly behind the legends of fairies, but they don't look much like Elsie Wright's photographs. Mr. Peters, would you mind finding one of the illustrations?"

Peters didn't look pleased, but he took a clothbound volume from one of their stacks, and opened it to a marked page. There lay sketched my childhood recollection: crablike claws, overarched with bat wings fading to fog at the edges, and an eyeless head covered with irregular protuberances like some exotic fungus. Barlow retrieved a folder from across the room. Inside, another drawing in a more formal style: where the book showed the creature poised for flight and clutching some device in its foremost claws, the folder showed it splayed as if ready for dissection. I suppressed a shudder. The two figures could have been drawn from the same verbal description, but the details were all different: the folder showed the head rounder and the protuberances more varied, the placement of the claws completely different and more lobster-like than crab-like.

"This one's a composite," said Barlow, tapping the folder. "From reports a few years back of bodies seen in a flooding river. No corpses were found, of course, and it was dismissed at the time as mass hysteria." Mary's eyes tracked his finger. Her gaze passed over the drawing and back to us.

"Mass hysteria," she said, "usually means someone's worked hard to convince people that they didn't see anything."

The scene in front of me slipped further into focus: Barlow, trying to pretend that he and Caleb were in charge; Mary and Deedee, trying to let him. That might be the best way to get work done, but I couldn't imagine keeping up the pretense. Innsmouth women might deck themselves in gold for a man's pleasure, recite passages of lore to show off their learning, or cultivate an interest in stories about fishing expeditions. But my mother had never taught me how to efface myself to bolster male self-importance—nor had my father taught any need for it. Kezia Marsh was born from one of the family's foremost branches, and Silas Marsh's branch, though distant, had honor of its own. When one of them deferred to the other, they gave precedence openly and honestly.

"We've had an uptick in sightings over the past couple of months, all along the Berkshires and White Mountains," said Barlow. "Clusters in the vicinity of disappearances, cutting off after each one. Even a few possible cases here in New York, though they're pretty vague."

"I hate this city," added Peters. "One of these monsters could walk down Fifth Avenue, and people would only report if it stopped traffic."

Barlow shrugged. "Once we dig a little, we'll find more. Speaking of which, Mr. Marsh . . ."

Again, Caleb bent his head in my direction—this time with the slight smirk that suggested he was on the edge of swooning against me and calling me "sister dear." So he'd seen it too. I toyed with the idea of explaining the concept of "eldest-on-land" to Barlow's team, just to forestall my brother's mockery. But then, Caleb's way of playing into assumptions might be safer than forcing them to see their error.

"I'll tell you about our cousin," I said. "And what little we know about these creatures."

I spoke, balancing safety and the need to share our knowledge with every word. Some judgments were easy: even Spector acknowledged that it would be disastrous for them to know about the Yith, so I glossed over the source of Trumbull's insights. The Lavernes were harder. Spector had already mentioned their existence, and I couldn't blame him. Their situation might offer clues to the other missing people. It seemed less likely, now, that Freddy had holed up somewhere to let his gills grow in. But his family's history, as much as we knew, cast Innsmouth in poor light. We'd bled for such stories.

Among my own people, I'd happily criticize the ill treatment of air-born lovers. But I said only that the Lavernes were long-lost cousins. And that we wanted, very badly, to bring Freddy back to his mother.

Then there were the Outer Ones themselves. The Yith were legends to my people, something close to gods. Their archives would preserve Earth's memory long after the sun burned out. And for the sake of that preservation, they destroyed entire races and stole their own children's lives. They cared little for the petty politics of centuries, but would casually wipe out anyone who tried to restrain their field expeditions—or who simply made themselves inconvenient. Barlow's team, though they didn't recall it, had escaped with relatively light wounds.

But the Outer Ones were sketches and rumor. I didn't know what they held sacred, what goal could have motivated these disappearances, or whether the creatures would care about attention from human authorities. I had no idea what kind of threat they might pose. And so nothing told me whether the greater danger came from Barlow knowing less, or more. I shared what I could, and hoped it wouldn't bring disaster.

As I finished, Barlow tapped an arrhythmia on the table, frowning. "Is that all?"

"That's all any of us can recall right now. If we were at Miskatonic, we could do better research." And in a day, two at the outside, we'd consult with our elders. But I hadn't mentioned their impending arrival.

Peters prodded the book. "This says they're from 'space that is not space.' I suppose we could ask Dr. Einstein what that means. But it's probably why they don't show up in photos—unless they just break cameras to avoid anyone getting a clear shot. They supposedly have outposts in deserted hillsides and mountains around the globe. And somewhere called 'Yuggoth' on the outskirts of the solar system, which everyone assumes is Pluto."

"I've heard of Yuggoth too," I said, and then wished I hadn't. I knew Yuggoth only from poetry and mysticism, irrelevant to our search and inappropriate to share with this company. But they looked at me expectantly. "Just stories. It's where the gods first came to our solar system, before settling on Earth." *Strange towers and curious lapping rivers, labyrinths of wonder and low vaults of light, and bough-crossed skies of flame . . .*

"We don't need legends," said Barlow. "We need descriptions of what they're made of. Something unique, like blood type or chemical composition."

"I still think I could track them without that," said Mary. "We could tailor a talisman to search for anything outside the normal material range for this area."

"I've seen your 'general' spells," said Caleb. "You're not trying that again with our cousin in the way."

To my surprise, Barlow nodded. "Mr. Marsh is crass as usual, but we still don't know what went wrong with that inventory, or how vulnerable any generally targeted equation could be to interference." He cast a perfunctory glare across Trumbull. "Leaving aside, for the moment, the question of where such interference might come from."

Peters followed Barlow's gaze, and his expression turned predatory. "Ah, Professor. Maybe you could find a creature from another world with one of your mental tricks? Compel them to cooperate?"

"That's not how it works," said Trumbull. She kept her expression bland. Yet another thing I hadn't considered: of course Barlow and his team would want to make use of her demonstrated abilities. Or rather, the abilities her Yithian guest had taken back to the Archives when they left. Barlow's team still didn't know, and would hopefully never know, that the woman in front of them wasn't the person they'd sparred with at Miskatonic. I sought a distraction both from the question of Trumbull's mentalism and from Mary's dangerous taste in spell design.

Our own magic was rooted in self-knowledge—good for understanding and affecting others, but not for finding people yet unmet. Summoning without a clear target, in addition to being wildly dangerous, was useless against an unfriendly subject. An unwelcome call could usually be refused. Even an irresistible call couldn't prevent friends and allies from following behind to firmly discourage future summons.

I thought again of the cryptic presence I'd encountered my first night in the city. I still had no evidence that it was an Outer One— but if it was, it meant that they made their mark across dimensions. Even if I was wrong, anomalies well-camouflaged in the waking world might still be easier to track in others.

"Do any of you know how to dreamwalk?" I asked.

CHAPTER 5

Mary did know something about dreamwalking, it transpired, though it wasn't an art she'd practiced with her team. Barlow and Spector disagreed about whether the two of them had ever done so; after listening to their description I couldn't judge whether the drugs forced on them by a German captor had facilitated and shaped an astral journey, or merely caused vivid and coincidentally informative hallucinations.

But they liked the idea, and their files offered at least speculation that Outer Ones traveled easily between dimensions. Mary and Trumbull quickly fell into a reverie of mathematical discussion, with Barlow and Peters throwing in occasional questions and suggestions.

I listened for a few minutes, following only a little, before saying, "But picking out something strange in the dreamlands—we already know how to do that. You don't need anything new to make this work."

Mary tapped the edge of a pile of papers, absently straightening them. "How long can you stay out? It sounds like you have more experience than me."

"I've done about fifteen minutes, so far. I could probably go a bit longer if I were careful."

"Travel is easier, dreaming—but could you scan the whole of New York City in twenty minutes?"

I felt foolish. I could probably cross Innsmouth, small and well-known, in that time and miss little. New York was on a different scale.

"I'm not trying to find a way to stay out longer," she assured me. "Though it sounds like an excellent area for research. We need to focus our search, and make the best possible use of the time we have. Virgil, I think that mahogany box with the knot on the cover has what we need."

Peters brought her a case filled with tiny cloth-wrapped bundles. I'd seen the teams' talismans before, and wasn't thrilled to be in their presence again. This batch, at least, felt relatively benign.

"Who should go?" asked Mary.

The dreamlands have predators, and the best way to survive them is to avoid attracting their attention. A large expedition, full of scent and weight, would be lucky if it drew only a flock of nightgaunts. Two or three people could slip through the shadows unnoticed.

"It sounds like you and I have the most experience," I said, cringing inwardly. Mary's designs had both put my life at risk and saved it, and I did not want to face the dreamlands with her alone. And the idea of leaving my unconscious body here, no matter how many friends stood guard, made me queasy. I didn't want Barlow and Peters seeing me so vulnerable, but there was no way around it. We needed to find Freddy, and this was the best chance we had.

"Charlie should go too," said Audrey. "He's worked with you longest. I can stay on the edge and help anchor." I nodded; Audrey's awareness of my fears eased them, if only a little.

"I don't like you going out alone." Barlow told Mary. He sounded tentative, in a way that surprised me. No, not tentative. He was asking her rather than ordering: sometime in the past five months, he'd learned to respect her skills.

"I need their experience," she said.

"More than you need someone you trust at your back?" demanded Peters.

"Yes," she said firmly. "Watch my body. Let Miss Winslow know if there's a problem with my heartbeat or breathing. I'll be careful."

I drew the diagram with special care. This was no brief foray to ensure a safe place to sleep—we needed guidance and support beyond the structures of our own minds. And Mary must *see* that I was working in good faith. She checked my preparations, then Charlie and Audrey did the same. Neko watched, arms crossed, frank curiosity on her face. She rarely participated in our spellwork—more often doubted our sanity in pursuing it so deeply—but took advantage of opportunities to observe. And I saw, gratefully, the way her eyes turned cold as they passed over Barlow's team.

Fear scars, and I knew full well that my stomach turned as much from remembered vulnerability in the camps as from my unpleasant experiences with the present company. Neko knew every ridge of tissue beneath those scars, all the half-healed wounds. She might well be the weakest person in the room, but her quiet watch reassured me most.

Mary handed me a talisman, strung on thick silken string. Running my fingers along the cord, I felt a brush of static and smelled warm beeswax. Touching the cloth bundle itself released a puff of frustrated avidity. I imagined a shortfin mako shark, like the ones elders sent leaping after prey, and felt a burst of irrational affection.

"What's it hunting?"

"I do think of them as hound-like," she said. "It hunts whatever seems furthest from the local physical norms—within bounds. Assuming the safety protocols work, it shouldn't pick up anything like the creature that killed poor Sally. I did learn something last winter." While I tried to figure out how to respond, she added, "I *am* sorry. I know that was my mistake." Peters looked at her sharply, and Barlow patted her hand. It was clear that they neither agreed with her culpability nor acknowledged any in themselves.

Mary's magic was a thing of equations and geometries. She inferred new methods from half-guessed principles, and tested them at great risk to life and sanity. Whether because of her newfound caution, or her recent interest in learning about older and more stable ways, she let us take the lead this time.

I cut my hand and traced blood into our symbols. The familiar sting of the knife was a comfort by now; my breathing slowed, body ready for ritual. My travel companions, in their turn, offered their own sacrifices to the pattern we were about to enter. I began singing. Charlie joined in, and after a moment Mary hummed along with us. I was glad the lyrics were in R'lyehn, which she understood only a little. There's something intimate about a lullaby. In the words, I imagined my mother's hopes and anxieties for her infant children, and my grandmother's before her, back to the oldest Chyrlid Ajha in the depths of R'lyeh, waiting millennia to meet their descendants.

Dreamwalking is an old practice, simple and powerful. I lay on the chemical-scented carpet, surrounded by people I could not trust, and I slept.

It was late morning, but the hotel must have harbored patrons sleeping off midnight business trysts. Around me swirled the scraps of a dozen ordinary dreams: faces dimly recognized as lovers, an emerald green sink that invoked visceral fear, a cat butting my ankles fondly with miniature goat horns.

Charlie bent to rub its forehead. He looked much like he did in the waking world, save that he didn't carry the cane. Mary, hair loose but primly dressed, appeared beside us.

"One layer deeper?" she suggested. I nodded, and let go my hold on the fringe of our own world's thoughts, letting the current pull me through to our neighboring dimension.

We stood on a marble balcony. A city stretched before us: not New York itself, with its close-crowded townhouses and skyscrapers, but its mirror in spiderweb and fairy-light, classical columns and domes and narrow needles of steel that seemed to pierce the sky rather than scrape it. Thunderclouds gathered, a comforting shadow beneath which the city glowed like a hearth. One sunbeam knifed through a gap in the cover. In its spotlight I saw the spark of driving rain; dark shapes flitted among the drops. I smelled clean wet rock and ozone. From far away, I felt the gentle tug of my connection with my body, reassuring but easy to resist.

"Good boys," said Mary approvingly.

At our feet, the talisman hounds had taken on further form. Iridescent swirls of mist, vaguely bestial, twined around her ankles. Something about them suggested tongues and teeth, and nostrils straining for a hint of prey. One of them brushed my leg, ghostly cold, and I flinched unthinking.

They unwound from their mistress, and slipped toward the insubstantial-looking bridge that stretched from the balcony's far end.

"This way," said Mary.

"It doesn't look like there's any other," said Charlie. He looked out over the view. "I can see why the first people to come here thought they must be traveling in dreams. It's . . . impressive. And seems tailor-made to make anyone worry about falling."

"Or flying," she said. "Dreams are as good a metaphor to start with as any, I suppose."

I stooped to examine the bridge before I dared step on it. The material was impossible to discern: woven of a thousand narrow strands like a massive fishing net, glossy black as onyx. Touching it produced a shock of bright and undifferentiated emotion; after the first prod I tried to avoid skin contact. As I followed Mary onto the expanse, it felt as if I struggled for balance on a great cat's cradle. It drooped and swung beneath my weight.

The hounds led us swiftly; distance here did not seem to work according to familiar laws. The landscape beneath our feet shifted with every step, giving a new glimpse of the glittering alleys below. It was convenient, but a reminder that we walked the boundary of the rules permitting our own blood and breath. In further dimensions, physics became even stranger, and human minds and bodies would both fail.

The bridge led to another building, a needle of sky-blue stone. A narrow ramp spiraled its outer wall to another arch, slick and steep. I couldn't help but lean toward the safe inner wall; where my fingers brushed I felt again that shock, and this time the pounding behind it, the rhythm that Spector rode in the waking city. Perhaps the shock was the myriad emotions of millions of New Yorkers, cascading over their manmade cliffs into the dream city. I shrunk from every unintended touch. More than a moment of that torrent and I would have been washed away, my own petty thoughts crushed.

Yet creatures lived here. They scuttled along the canyon streets below, too distant to make out forms. Something butterfly-bright landed on the lapis wall and dug its proboscis into a crack. As it drank its wings sparked tiny blue lights, faster and faster until it leapt away into the air and its flicker became a steady glow. Charlie stopped a moment to watch, lips parted.

Farther we went, following Mary's hounds, and slowly we wound closer to the streets. I tried to track my heartbeat, to focus on my distant breathing body, but the city's rhythm began to seep through the soles of my imagined boots and confuse my senses. Our walk so far could not have taken less than a quarter hour. I felt the vital connection to my body, taut with the distance we'd traveled. If we didn't give up now and retrace our perilous route through the dream city, we'd have to risk returning to our bodies from wherever we found ourselves, releasing all that quivering tension at once.

I said nothing. Wherever they were, the Outer Ones controlled the fate of dozens, including my still-unmet cousin.

The last bridge devolved into a staircase, its steps so narrow that I had to descend sideways like a crab. The hounds swarmed down and hovered at the bottom, panting with amorphous tongues. By the time we reached them, I knew we'd found the place.

After the squeeze of the stairs, the open plaza beyond made my ears buzz with vertigo. The scent of green decay rose into my nostrils, incongruously swamp-like. As I caught my balance and looked up, there could be no question. Amid the needles and domes, a squat concrete building sat in isolation. Fungus spread across its surface in a thousand unlikely colors. It wreathed the walls in vining stalks and broad caps, magenta growing into sea-green and royal purple, blood red fading to venomous yellow.

Mary darted forward, hounds at her heels. She tugged her sleeve over her hand and plucked one scarlet cap. She ran back panting. At the same time I doubled over, retching. My vision wavered, and I swallowed hard against the surge of nausea. Charlie put out an arm to steady me, but instead he sagged against my side.

"Too long," I cried as Mary arrived beside us.

She nodded urgently. "We have to go back *now*." The hounds swirled around the clutched fold of her skirt. She unwrapped the fungus with shaking hands. One of the talismanic creatures sniffed the cap, then surged over it. Her hand shook harder and the air around it seemed to warp. I turned away, nauseous beyond the strain of my desperate need for physicality. When I looked again her prize was gone.

I gave in to my body's pull, cast my mind toward it with all my will. Leaving from the balcony where we'd entered, I could have controlled my passage. From here, I could do little more than pray that the force of my return would leave my mind intact. I curled myself against burning wind. The world stretched and tore around me, and the torrent of emotion spilled into my lungs and mind. Out of the undifferentiated swirl, mourning and fury and lust lurched like twigs in a flood.

I came to on the hotel floor, and it took me a moment to remember how to breathe. I was drowning in fear. I gasped and coughed, and nearly blacked out again as the coughing became a fit, ragged hacks through which I couldn't draw breath. I felt Caleb's long arms around me, his hand stroking the paroxysms from my chest and throat, and then the precious touch of water against my lips. Fear subsided into relief and a well-earned headache.

Charlie sat beside me, breathing ragged. He rubbed his temples and winced. He opened his eyes, and froze. I followed his gaze—my own vision still wavering—and scrambled to my feet, clinging to Caleb to stay upright.

Mary convulsed on the floor, eyes wide and unseeing, hands clenched and muscles locked. The smell of decaying foliage permeated the room. Peters grabbed cushions from the sofa to pad her movements; Barlow knelt and turned her on her side, hands gentle on her shoulders. He murmured reassurance, but glared when I approached.

"It's the mushrooms," I managed, voice still hoarse. "She took a sample; that's what's doing it."

He shook his head. His glare turned, unprovoked, on Spector. "This doesn't go in your report. I'll put up with your irregulars just as long as you can keep them reined in, but don't you dare get Mary pulled off duty."

Spector took in Barlow's anger, and his tender and practiced movements. "This isn't the first time."

"If she's got any chance, it's with our research." Mary's convulsions stilled, and Barlow eased her head into his lap. "Whatever happened in Arkham, she won't get better locked up in some hospital. We've already had a doctor look at her privately—this is going to have to be our way. Promise me, Ron."

Spector's Adam's apple bobbed. "I won't mention it."

Vulnerable to later lesions. That's what Trumbull's guest had said, dismissing the trivial sequelae of the mental surgery that had sliced away Mary's ability to read. Necessary, in the Yith's estimate, to prevent her from endangering the records at Miskatonic. We couldn't trust her partners to treat the Yith with the caution they deserved, so we'd never told her what happened. Their tender choreography stung my conscience, but I still thought that choice right.

Vision returned to Mary's eyes, and on her lips a pleased smile overcame the rictus. She reached above her head, patted Barlow's hand awkwardly. He supported her elbow as she levered herself to a sitting position. He started to get her a pillow. "What are you all doing? We need a sample talisman, now!"

"Right here." Peters squatted and dangled a pendant: a deep blue stone with black veins running dimly through. Gold wire wound it in ornate patterns. Mary tugged clumsily at the hound amulet, and Barlow lifted it from her neck, wincing.

"You caught something there, all right." Barlow laid the cloth bundle and the stone before her. Peters sketched a diagram, and helped her make the shallowest of cuts in her palms. She braced herself even for that. I tensed as she laid hands on the two talismans and spoke her "equation"—but I felt no chill, and no change in my own impulses. She spoke each syllable distinctly and slowly, as if she too feared the consequences of mispronunciation.

The swamp smell grew overpowering, then began to fade. I felt a brief pressure, as if something contracted around me. Then the smell vanished, and Mary lifted the pendant in triumph. Barlow passed his hand close by, then laughed, squeezed her shoulder, and moved back to give her the professional distance absent for the past few minutes.

Peters slapped Barlow's back, and to Mary said, "Nice work!"

"It'll be useful," she agreed, running the back of her arm where sweat shone on her forehead.

This time, no one gainsaid me as I approached. The blue stone had grown a veil of dull gray lace, fungous. The green smell was still perceptible, merely constrained.

Mary smiled at me, expression tight but pleased. "Since January we've been working on more efficient ways to separate earthly and esoteric energies. Our target's dreaming effluvia isn't the same as an outsider, and the hound talisman's a poor proxy for a human, but it's a good proof of concept."

"Oh." I felt torn between horror that she would casually plan for another incursion—the last caused by her own team's carelessness— and startled gratitude that, in the face of her other duties and wounds, she'd cared enough about Sally's loss and my own pain to develop a better solution.

"Enough admiring my necklace," she told her team. "We need to track where this connects in *our* plane."

"You should rest," said Barlow. "Your skin looks like chalk and you're still shaking."

"I should," she said. "But these prototypes aren't stable, and the sample will leak back into the fringe within hours. Catherine, I'm afraid this will require less of your creative insight than the last time we collaborated, but we could still use your help."

Trumbull joined Barlow and Peters in sketching interlinked diagrams on their slate and looking up details in a dozen books, punctuated by frequent consultation of a city map. At the center of the controlled chaos, Mary consulted and directed and argued, propped against cushions and fortifying herself with an orange that Barlow had provided.

The rest of us crowded around to watch. I wanted to flee, and I wanted to interrogate every line of chalk for potential danger. But this was the first time I could observe their work without my own life at risk, and I had to admit that their methods were fascinating. They thought of magic in terms of equations, clear descriptions that could force the universe itself to come clear. It wasn't cold, but full of admirable curiosity—and a mad lack of fear—about how the universe would answer a perfectly delineated question.

After a few minutes Barlow abruptly set down *Flora of the Seventh Path.* "I swear to you all, the tracking equation we're working through now isn't the least bit experimental. We've used it dozens of times— Ron, you saw an early version in Krakow, even if you insisted it was just luck. But it takes several hours to do right, *even without distractions.* Is there any way I can talk you all into clearing out until dawn? Or even some of you? I will get you an extra room, or pay for dinner and dancing, or you can go play pinochle back at your boardinghouse.

We're a lot more likely to burn the city down with a dozen people jostling our arms."

Spector scanned the crowded room and nodded. Then he said to Charlie, casually, "Buy you a drink before you head back?"

"Sounds good," said Charlie with equal aplomb. No heads turned and no eyebrows rose as they made their way out.

"What about you?" Peters asked Deedee. "This isn't exactly your specialty, is it?"

She put her hand on Caleb's arm. "And what exactly is that supposed to mean?"

Peters frowned at the touch, but then a glint of amusement came into his eyes. "I suppose if you can't seduce the location out of anyone, it's a good thing you brought your current target. Why don't you take him out dancing?"

I stood, ready to get between Caleb and Peters, or between Deedee and Peters, and trying to resist the urge to let them do exactly as they pleased. But Caleb simply said, "Why don't you rephrase that?"

He shrugged. "Because I've seen her file. And yours. Looked you both up, after last time. I like to know what people are going to try behind my back."

"I don't need your file to know *that*," said Deedee. I could hear the fury in her voice, banked into false gentleness. "Caleb, honey, how badly do we need these jerks at *our* backs?"

"Not badly enough." He deliberately turned away from Peters. He looked at me, and at Neko and Audrey. "You all stay here. Someone has to watch them—but Miss Dawson and I will make our own way. We'll catch up with you later."

Deedee stalked out, Caleb at her heels. I wanted to follow—but I didn't believe that had been an unthinking insult. Peters had known exactly how to goad them past their breaking point. Barlow might want to keep us in sight; Peters would do his best to drive us away.

CHAPTER 6

Deedee Dawson—June 18, 1949:

I try to shake off the anger. You can't let people play you like that, and Peters's offense was no accident. I should've stuck around. I'm glad I didn't.

Caleb trembles. Such strange intimacy—I can feel his pulse as if it races through my own chest, the pain as it pushes blood too fast beneath his skin. But when I touch his shoulder, I can still sense the masks between us. Friction, thrill, and the comfort of two people who respect each other's stupidly overgrown shields.

"So, bank?" I ask.

"Bank. And a decent hotel. I want a place where they can't find us. Let's figure out how we're going to keep up the search without them, and keep in touch with the others. Oh gods, I want to strangle that jackass." His fingers flex, full of violence decades suppressed.

"So do I. But it would upset Mary."

He snorted. "If she wants to work with that kind of man, she deserves what she gets. Spector offered her the chance to leave."

My shoulders lift. "I guess she likes knowing where she stands with them. Maybe it's fun to be the only person in the room who knows what she's doing." I'm not being fair, but I don't want to be fair right now. "Bank. Then get ourselves a big room with a big bed. Then—" I don't know if it's his twitchiness or mine, or if there's a difference. My nerves jangle with unspent tension, *fury with no outlet.* "—*Do you have a brilliant idea for what we should do tonight?*"

He slumps, sullen. "*No.*"

"*Good. Neither of us is going to come up with anything useful until we blow off some steam. You know how to dance?*" *I know damn well he doesn't.*

"*I can waltz, a little.*" *He ducks his head. I imagine decades-past lessons in deportment. Little Caleb, concentrating hard on stepping in time,* one-*two-three* one-*two-three, with a roomful of bug-eyed five-year-olds. It's hard to picture him so young.*

"*I'm not thinking about a waltz. Don't worry, you'll pick it up.*" *In R'lyehn I add,* "*I've seen how fast you learn.*" *I earn a fleeting smile.*

We find a bank, and an absurdly glitzy hotel, and a department store—three reassuring reminders that we're still far enough north that money can buy obsequious politeness. I start to relax, and see Caleb tucking his tension deeper below his skin. Nothing's going to make him pretty, *but in New York we can find a proper suit for his lanky frame, and I know how to look at him right. A proper dress for me, too, picked to suit my own tastes rather than some assignment.*

Taking my pasty-skinned Deep One boyfriend to a Harlem nightclub may not be the subtlest thing I've done all year. But I want, for once, to be the one who fits in. The desire to see people I used to know churns in my belly with the terror that someone I knew will see me and ask where the hell I've been.

Massachusetts has been safe, after a fashion. Morecambe County's lily-white, and I've rarely dared socialize with the other negro servants from the university—or better yet, sneak off to Boston to relax with people who wouldn't ask why the dean's floozy can swear in Russian. This isn't safe: the painful pressures and stupid choices of my childhood lurk far too close.

The music's loud, just on the edge of what I know Caleb can handle. The crowd flashes. We get drinks; he watches the dancers. I watch him—when he catches the rhythm, starts nodding and tapping his feet, I pull him out on the floor. He's new to it, but he knows his body and mine.

We're outside for a breath of air, sharing a cigarette, when a girl with curls spilling past her shoulders and a grin a mile wide comes through the door trailing the soaring notes of a sax solo. She stares at me and her grin widens.

"Thea—is that you?"

Every bit of FBI training rises in the moment when I don't flinch, when I look up with my arm easy around Caleb's shoulder and ask, "You looking for someone?"

Carrie Waters, who I swapped notes with all through grade school, loses the edges of her smile and says, "Sorry, I guess not."

"Need a light?"

She doesn't, thankfully, and goes off down the walk.

"You okay?" Caleb asks when she's out of sight.

"Yeah. She was just confused."

He rubs my back, and I lean against him. He doesn't pry, doesn't reassure me that I can tell him anything. "Do you want to go back?"

"Sure. I'm getting tired, and we've got a long day ahead." My feet still itch to dance, but I'd just keep looking over my shoulder. "Whatever we do with it."

We walk slowly. He flirts in two languages; I flirt in six; he almost distracts me from worrying.

I've never been as close to anyone as I am to Caleb, or for that matter to Aphra and Charlie and Audrey. Unlike the rest of them, I came to that closeness with my eyes open. I wanted magic that no one could take away, and intimacy was the price. I've been surprised by how easy it is. The confluence slips around the walls that have plagued family and lovers my whole life. Maybe it's the certainty. With them, there's no doubt and nothing to prove; our connection is tangible as a held hand.

But secrecy's a long habit, and lies told long enough become real. The confluence doesn't care about the shameful secrets they think I hide, the wounds Peters imagines he can tear open with his insinuations. Now, too close to home and yearning for its taste as much as they yearn for their own, I wonder what they'd think of my true past, duller and realer than what they assume.

≈≈≈

I settled on the floor an acceptable distance from the slate, with Neko beside me. Audrey prowled the boundaries. My fascination and pent-up anger eventually mixed with reluctantly admitted boredom. It was slow, painstaking work. A little over two hours after they began, they gathered around the slate. Mary still leaned on Barlow's arm. They lit candles much like the ones in the shop window. Mary spoke—no chant, just a string of equations and unfamiliar words—and if there was blood I didn't see it. Only two of the three ingredients I'd always thought necessary for any spell, but the diagram glowed briefly and flowed into a new configuration, and the candles guttered out.

Peters stood, stretched, flicked on the light, and described the configuration to Mary. Based on her answer and an apparent correction from Trumbull (neither of which I understood), he drew an arc on the map around one edge of the Bronx.

The cycle began again. They drew, and read, and argued, and at midnight made another mark on a different part of the map. And again. My eyes were dry and drooping by the third round. Exhaustion made me almost willing to trust their judgment—or at least to trust that if I napped on the couch, someone would wake me for any deviation from the earlier working. Audrey tucked her legs up and dozed on a cushioned chair. Neko draped her arms across the couch's spine, on watch and vigilant.

I fell asleep thinking about new men of the water, and dreamed fields of mushrooms. When their light waxed, I half-woke to count candlelit map-marks, then dropped back to sleep.

I woke fully when Spector and Charlie returned. The windows showed a sky bruising purple, and concrete rising bright out of sunless streets.

"Where are Mr. Marsh and Miss Dawson?" asked Spector.

"They decided not to work with us," I said stiffly. If he followed the track of my glare, he could draw his own conclusions.

Three arcs lined the map's edges. Within their intersection, three smaller arcs converged on a space of a few blocks. Barlow promised we'd find our quarry there.

"Hunts Point," said Spector, looking over his colleague's shoulder.

"Your stomping grounds, right?" asked Barlow.

"Maybe they hide their wings under those scarves," said Peters. He mimed the head coverings I'd seen on women around the boarding-house, tying an imaginary knot under his chin. My hands clenched, unseen. *How long can I keep an eye on him before I lose all self-control?*

Spector drew back from the map. "It's next to St. Mary's Park, sure. But there's a stretch of old factories in between, and it's full of aban-doned buildings. You could hide anything in there."

The area where we came out of the subway wasn't quite as Spector described. In an ordinary town, the traffic by foot and car would have seemed ordinary; it was only in contrast to the city around it that Hunts Point could be described as unpopulated. The map led us not to abandoned warehouses, but to low buildings with flat roofs and shuttered or boarded windows. People spoke with animated gestures, laughed raucously on stoops—but even so the city's energy felt muted.

Here in the waking world, the Outer Ones' abode wasn't obviously marked. I lifted my nostrils, trying to catch a whiff of green, but smelled only New York's pervasive dust and smoke. Nor did vining mushrooms announce the presence of something wondrous and alien. But on the stoop of one clearly uninhabited building—windows shattered on the first floor, empty even of cheap boards—loiterers looked not at each other but at the street. And they stood out just as we did. An Asian man and a white woman bent their heads together; two black men sat on the step below them, one older and bearded, the other young and clean-shaven.

A fifth person sat beside the Asian man, reading a book. I couldn't see his face clearly. But the Asian man—Chinese, I thought, though

I couldn't be sure—elbowed the other's side. "Hey, I didn't know you had littermates!"

The man looked up. His skin was darker than his mother's, the far end of Innsmouth's spectrum from my own. It padded his bones well. Long fingers wrapped his book. He had large eyes set high in his face, a thick neck, and a wide mouth just now gaping open. He was unmistakable. Freddy Laverne elbowed his companion back and said, "Of course I do. Too smart for anyone to drown us!" But he stood when I came over. My companions waited across the street, even Spector's colleagues giving me this moment on my own.

If I'd been unsure how to talk to Frances, I found myself utterly tongue-tied with her son. He stared back, seeming equally uncertain, equally fascinated. Eventually he asked, quietly, *"Are* we related?"

"Yes. Distantly." I hesitated. At last I said, "Cousin. We've been looking for you."

"You brought a lot of company," said the white woman. She was thick-set with graying hair, and clearly none of our kin.

"Did you, um, come looking here last night?" asked Freddy.

"Yes," I said again. "It seemed like the best way to find your . . . hosts?" *Do you need rescuing?*

"They detected an intrusion." He turned the book over, and over again, passing it hand to hand. Science fiction pulp, I noted, the sort we'd sell for a penny at Charlie's store. "That's why they sent us out. I'd better take you to meet them."

"We'd like that," I said. "But why don't we talk first?" I tilted my head toward a spot on the sidewalk a few feet away, within sight of his friends (if friends they were), but out of earshot if we kept our voices low.

He glanced nervously at the others on the stoop. I couldn't tell whether he sought their support, or feared their interference. If they were captors, I might be grateful for the gaggle of FBI agents at my back. "I can talk right here."

I wanted to press. But a confrontation could easily blossom out of control—some of my own companions no more trustworthy than his. "Your mother's looking for you, and those people back there say a dozen others have gone missing. What's going on?"

"Mom doesn't get it. She doesn't think much of me when I'm home—anyway, it doesn't matter. You went looking in the near spaces, so you've got to know what's below."

"The Outer Ones," I said. Mindful of all the witnesses looking on, potential interference as well as backup, I continued: "I've heard stories about them. If you *don't* want to be here, we can help, in ways no one else could."

That earned glares from his companions, and he shook his head vehemently. "All of us 'missing' people, we're here because we want to be. There's so much wonder and glory in the universe, why would we stay in the neat little holes our families make for us?" He peered over my shoulder. "Those guys look like a bunch of cops. Can you get them to go away? I tell you we're not 'missing,' we're just not where we were."

"They're going to want to see that for themselves, I'm afraid," I said.

"I can't introduce them to everyone," said Freddy. "Not everyone's here in the mine. Not everyone's even on *Earth*." He announced this last with whispered relish. "I've heard stories about *you*. I always thought Mom made them up. If you try to make me go back or take me into the sea, they can stop you."

"We're not going to force you to do anything." His fervent enthusiasm for the Outer Ones made my skin prickle, seeming to confirm my worst suspicions. I couldn't fully articulate the sense of danger, but I wanted to stay out here, with friends and backup close to hand. But I could already tell that I'd learn nothing that way. Another push, and he'd retreat behind that boarded-up door. I held out my hands. "If you can promise our safety, we'd like to meet your new friends."

"That would be great," he said. Another glance across the street, pupils wide and eyes narrow. "How many of these people do you need to drag along?"

The answer to that question took extended negotiation. It would have stretched longer if Barlow had been willing to look indecisive. He wanted to bring his whole team, but I feared what he—or worse, Peters—would say to these creatures we barely understood. I didn't know what we'd meet below, but I didn't expect anything as simple as violence. Barlow and Mary had an argument that never rose to the level of words. In the end, Mary and Spector were chosen to represent the state's first deliberate contact with creatures from another world.

I was grateful for Caleb's absence; I knew what Grandfather would have said if we both descended into such unknown territory. Trumbull wanted to see for herself people who could so distress the Yith. I didn't want to do without either Audrey or Charlie, but reluctantly delegated Audrey to stay behind and ride herd on the FBI agents.

"If you think I'm coming all the way to New York and then hanging out on the street while you talk to people with wings, think again," said Neko.

The deliberations kept me from thinking too carefully about what I'd agreed to. Like Neko, I could hardly imagine finding our cousin allied with otherworldly creatures, and then avoiding them. Even if that might be the wiser course. We knew that they were old and powerful, and that the Yith despised but had not destroyed them. We knew very little else.

All this, to gain the trust of a boy we'd just met. He couldn't possibly understand how valuable he was.

Freddy led us inside. The hall was dingy, scattered with plaster pebbles and broken glass. Rickety wooden stairs descended into barebulbed shadow. His fellows stayed behind. I could only guess what messages they'd sent ahead, and what powers might now watch over him, invisible and immanent.

"It's a long way down," he warned. Then, shyly, "Tell me about our family. Are there a lot of us?"

I was grateful anew that Barlow and Peters remained above. Mary had already met my elders, and seen us vulnerable. "In the water, there are. On land, I know of none except for my brother, and you and your mother. You'll meet Caleb later."

He listened as I told him about the raid, and about what it meant to go into the water. Where his mother had twitched, questioned, doubted, Freddy soaked up these ideas in stillness, even as he directed us down a labyrinth of increasingly clean and well-lit corridors and stairs. We were beyond the building above, I thought; these must be new excavations.

"Is Mom going to do that?" he asked. "Grow scales and gills? Am I?"

"You both might," I said. I wanted to give him a more certain answer—no. I wanted the more certain answer myself, to know whether this new relative might someday dive beneath Union Reef and swim Y'ha-nthlei's carven streets, or stand with intimidating confidence born of centuries' experience. "Anyone with even a little of our blood has a chance. But the more generations that blood's been diluted, the smaller the chance."

"Well, I suppose if I really want scales, I can ask *them*."

"It's more than scales," I said. I ran my hand across the whitewashed wall beside us, reassured by its cool solidity. We were deep underground. "It's more than the metamorphosis. You've always stood out, I know. Men of the air think we're strange and ugly. Getting our heads measured is about the best we can expect. Imagine living surrounded by people like you. People who think you're normal and reasonable, and who won't judge what you can do based on the shape of your eyes."

He stopped at a door more solid than any we'd come across thus far. "I have imagined that. All my life. And I've finally found it." The certainty in his voice, the confident awe, were things I'd heard before—and they confirmed my premonition of danger. For I'd heard them from a woman shining with faith in Shub-Nigaroth's love, eager to walk into the ocean and drown herself for an imagined immortality.

Freddy looked over the party that trailed behind us. "They're through here. Show respect." And he opened the door.

CHAPTER 7

The room within was dim, lit by panes that glowed violet and indigo on counters and walls. Humans, working at some of those counters, barely glanced up at our arrival. I smelled the now-familiar swamp-scent, but with some putrescent gas mixed in, as if bodies decayed amid the rotting greenery.

A low-pitched buzzing stung my ears. That too, I recognized: it was the sound that had assailed me on my first night in New York. I'd been right, then. Whatever else about them might be rumor, the Outer Ones passed easily across the barriers between worlds.

As my eyes adjusted, I saw that the light silhouetted inexplicable shapes—equipment with unknown purpose. It took long seconds for me to process some of the shapes as living beings. Then they moved. I flinched, would have stepped back if there had not been so many people behind me; the movements looked wrong in a way I could not describe.

Two of them *moved* around the purple-lit tables toward us. They didn't look like Peters's illustrations, but I could not imagine drawing them more accurately. Their claws were long, tipped with pincers, glossy as a beetle and mottled with wartish bumps. I thought they had at least two fore and one at the rear. Above the claws bent unlikely joints, shadowing their torsos (if torsos there were). Their heads were masses of gently waving tentacles like anemone stalks, studded with narrow spikes that flexed as they moved.

Worst of all were the wings. I could not bring them into focus. When I tried to force shape on them I saw membranous shadows, bat wings with too many joints, mist strung on an ichorous skeleton. My stomach clenched and turned.

But I could find a dozen people at will who would swear my own looks a nauseating justification for distrust. I'd come here to speak with Freddy's allies, and speak with them I would. As always, in the face of strangeness I fell back on etiquette.

"Hello," I said. "I'm Ghavn Aphra Marsh, and these are my friends Charlie Day and Neko Koto. Professor Trumbull of Miskatonic University. And Ronald Spector and Mary Harris of the FBI." Proper even to my full title. Normally I avoided the uncomfortable reminder that I was the youngest senior-on-land in history; now it seemed best to wield every sign of authority at my disposal.

Freddy approached the nearest Outer One, and I repressed a shiver. Fortunate that I was working to keep my face impassive, for the thing bent its head and engulfed his hand in those worm-like tentacles. He smiled and his whole posture relaxed.

"Aphra is my cousin who I just met," he said. "These are the guys who set off the alarms last night. Aphra, these are Kvv-vzht-mmmm-vvt—" He spoke the names with a clear effort of concentration, each a humming, buzzing concatenation clearly not intended for human tongues. "—and Nnnnnn-gt-vvv. They're sort of ambassadors." I repeated the names to myself, to master them as well as I could on one hearing.

"Emissaries and miners," said Kvv-vzht-mmmm-vvt. Its voice was carried in modulations to the constant buzz that, I now realized, came from the Outer Ones themselves. "We seek like minds among the races of Earth. If you come to share company in peace, we welcome you."

"We do," I said, glad anew for Peters's absence. I pulled over myself, shield-like, the dignity I still thought of as my mother's. "We also come to check the safety of people who've vanished. My cousin assures us he's well, and we hope the others are also."

"They're our willing travel-mates," said Kvv-vzht-mmmm-vvt. "Is this why the American government is here?"

"Yes," said Spector. I heard the quaver in his voice, but it was subtle. He fumbled belatedly to show his badge.

"I told you," said Nnnnnn-gt-vvv. "New York is different from Vermont. The comings and goings of most inhabitants are attended to by only a small fraction of the city, but that's many more than in the hills."

"And yet," said Kvv-vzht-mmmm-vvt, "this is no time to stay safe underhill. Mr. Spector and Mrs. Harris—are those the correct titles? I hope we can ease your minds about our companions."

"I'd like to speak with them," said Spector. A sidelong glance as he considered whether Mary's title was worth correcting; she shook her head and waved him to continue. "Maybe you can tell me a little about what they're doing here?"

"We're traveling," said Freddy. "And talking, with the most amazing people from everywhere in the universe, and some from outside it. You have no idea—Miss Marsh talked about fitting in with people just like you. I fit here, even if some of my friends look less like me than the Outer Ones do."

A sharp inhalation behind me, Trumbull's only reaction.

"Traveling where?" asked Neko. "How?" She craned her neck, as if some pulp-cover rocket might be hidden in the room's shadows.

"Only our minds travel," said Freddy. "They have wonderful machines to hold them while our bodies stay safe here. You can see, and hear, and talk, and go places that would be too dangerous otherwise."

"It's dangerous anyway," I said. I should have been more diplomatic, but the excitement in Neko's voice frightened me. It echoed Freddy's, and reminded me how little I'd provided to sate her wanderlust. "Mortal minds can't travel the voids without losing themselves."

"I can," said Freddy. "I've done it. I've been to Yuggoth and seen the cities of ice, and water that flows like lava. I've seen Outer Ones dance to the music that fills the space between. I've talked with people who are colors, who don't have our sort of bodies at all. And I'm still me—more me than I've ever been."

Nnnnnn-gt-vvv drifted toward me, claws soundless on the tiled floor. I took a step back, then forced myself still against the charnel breeze of its wings.

"I know your superstition," it said. "Clinging to this rock and claiming that humans can never live beyond it. You've learned to fear the universe outside this one little globule. Those who taught you had their own purposes for instilling that fear. Doesn't Nyarlathotep tell even you to ask the most dangerous questions, and travel as far as you need, wherever you need, to find the answers?"

"I'm of the water," I said. "So is Freddy. It's not superstition to say we need that water to survive. A planet's a big place. We've found all the danger we need to satisfy Nyarlathotep's purposes."

"If being of the water means staying on Earth, I'm not interested." Freddy gripped Kvv-vzht-mmmm-vvt's limb. "I want to know my family, but I won't trade the stars for some hick town in Massachusetts."

"You don't have to," said Nnnnnn-gt-vvv. Cilia rippled in Freddy's direction. "She's parroting what she's been told—you're proof it isn't true."

Charlie put a quelling hand on my wrist. Mary swept between me and the Outer One. "We believe you that Mr. Laverne is fine," she said. "We'd still like to see the others, talk with them, make sure they're okay. And we'd like to learn more about what you're doing here. New York is full of immigrants and the United States is used to taking them in—we may be able to help you."

"Sweet youth," said Nnnnnn-gt-vvv. "There have been Outer Ones on this land since before North America was a continent. Humans lived among us long before the United States was a country, or New York a city. *We* are used to taking *you* in."

"We've no desire to cross the local authorities," put in Kvv-vzht-mmmm-vvt. Claws shuffled, and one limb snaked around Freddy's side. "You'll have the interviews you desire, and we'll come to an accord. Nnnnnn-gt-vvv, find out who can speak with them today. I'll show them why we're here, and then the stasis tables so they can see our travelers well cared for."

Kvv-vzht-mmmm-vvt herded well. Even frightened, I was impressed by how quickly it (He? She?) diverted the confrontational Nnnnnn-gt-vvv and shepherded us into the corridor, heading deeper into their complex. As we left I heard human voices murmuring elsewhere in the room, answered by Outer One buzz-hums.

Freddy let go of Kvv-vzht-mmmm-vvt's side and walked next to me. With his patrons near, he seemed more comfortable with my presence. "Tell me more about our family?"

"And our 'hick town'?" I asked, regretting my sarcasm at once. His dismissal shouldn't have stung so.

Freddy hunched his shoulders, and it came to me suddenly how young he was. "I still want to know."

"It's not just the town," I said quietly. Having found Freddy, I wanted him to understand us. More, I wanted him to *join* us, though his cultish adoration for the Outer Ones seemed a potent barrier. "Innsmouth is the edge of something vast and wonderful, even if it's an earthly vastness. Innsmouth is our spawning ground, the place where we learn what we have in common with the rest of our species, and learn what it means to be of the water before we grow into it ourselves. Beyond and below the reef is Y'ha-nthlei. The elders dwell in the city's crystalline caverns during the day, come up at night to teach and protect us and show us the forms we'll one day wear." I remembered this past winter, seeing my grandfather for the first time in twenty years. His scent and his scales reminded me that my life—my people, though we'd nearly been wiped out on land—were real.

"Y'ha-nthlei is built into and under the reef. It's a city of caves and crystal columns where stone drips like icicles, coral halls as grand as any palace. The elders breed giant sea turtles and sharks to draw their carriages, and jellyfish to light and ward their doorways. And for all its wonders, Y'ha-nthlei is only an outpost. The deep cities of the Atlantic outstrip it as a cathedral does a household shrine, and R'lyeh is worthy of the god that sleeps beneath it."

I paused for breath, and flushed to find the humans staring at me. Kvv-vzht-mmmm-vvt might have been as well, for all I knew. Trumbull's eyes were distant. Charlie smiled. "It sounds incredible. I wish I could see it."

"So do I," said Neko. "Kappa-sama. I wish you'd talk about it more often. You've never said much about how your people live in the water."

I laughed shakily, and began walking again so we wouldn't be standing awkwardly in a dingy corridor, discussing miracles. "You've never called Innsmouth a hick town, I guess."

"Have you seen those cities?" asked Freddy.

"No—but I will someday. After my metamorphosis."

"With our help, you could go today," he said. He glanced at the Outer One.

"It would take negotiation," said Kvv-vzht-mmmm-vvt. "Or dodging their border patrols. Cautious creatures."

"I'll go," said Freddy. "I may not want to live in Innsmouth, but I'd like to talk to the elders. We talk to everyone."

At the end of the corridor an archway loomed, so sudden that I suspected it had been cloaked by magic until the last moment. Blue lights glittered within the darkness, brilliant pinprick stars.

"Come inside," said Kvv-vzht-mmmm-vvt, "and see *our* cathedrals."

As we entered, the light shifted again. The blue lights grew brighter without seeming closer, and were joined by pale sparks of gold and scarlet. My vision layered with afterimages of other colors, as if fireworks had stung my eyes a moment before: these lights only the remnant sparks drifting groundward. Amid this disorientation, cushions circled a cylindrical altar carved from a single hematite block. Codices and manuscripts piled on a low shelf to the side.

Trumbull pounced on the books. Almost immediately, she found one that caused her to suck in her breath and open its cover reverently. My own watering eyes were drawn by the altar. It held only one object: a metal box glinting in the wisp-light, covered in raised images. Bas-relief Outer Ones and other, equally strange species engaged in incomprehensible acts. Within the box, narrow struts held a polyhedral stone, its many surfaces each a different shape and size. The stone was translucent blue-black, with inclusions of some deep red opalescent material. My vision cleared as I looked on it. But when I turned my gaze elsewhere, the blurring afterimages returned.

"Would you like to begin?" asked Kvv-vzht-mmmm-vvt. I couldn't tell who it was talking to, but Freddy said, "You want me to lead? Okay, I guess, sure. Thank you."

"You've traveled with us," said Kvv-vzht-mmmm-vvt. "You know our ways. And they *are* your family."

"Thank you," he repeated. He went to stand at the altar. Kvv-vzht-mmmm-vvt settled amid the cushions, limbs bending and bending again until it huddled in the shadow of its own wings, outlined in blue lights. I hesitated—but if I let Freddy show me what the Outer Ones had taught him, perhaps he'd be more open to learning our own ways. I sat, and the others followed my lead. Trumbull gave her book a lingering glance, but joined us.

"Nyarlathotep." Freddy stumbled over the name. I remembered hesitating so, as I learned to speak the prayers of fertile adulthood for the first time, preparing for a ceremony I never got to perform. I missed his next words. ". . . entreat us to learn from all who will teach, and to enter every unbarred room. You offer knowledge glorious and dangerous. You offer perceptions wondrous and fearful. We flee toward you, always. To you, mighty messenger, must all things be told."

"To you," buzzed Kvv-vzht-mmmm-vvt, "we shall tell all things."

"Ïa," I murmured, head bowed. This was not a ceremony of my people, but it was still reassuring, in the midst of strangeness, to hear my gods invoked. And if there was one most appropriate to invoke amid this risk and strangeness, it was the Soul and Messenger.

Freddy hesitated once more, and I had time to remember people who had invoked my gods without sharing my understanding of what they wanted. I should not let myself be so easily swayed. My cousin lifted the polyhedral stone from the box.

"Behold," he said, and I was lost.

I felt wrenching nausea, as if the most vile things filled my mouth. A smothering fog seemed to envelop me. I struggled to remember how to breathe. Then I felt no more, only saw and heard.

The fog had vanished, and my body with it. I could still tell that it was out there, somewhere, but I had no sense of direction or distance. I floated on the edge of a chasm, looking down. Far below, a cyclopean city curled inward like a many-armed galaxy. Countless stars glowed in and above the streets. Statues thousands of feet high topped temples whose foundations were lost in darkness. Striding Nyarlathotep, Shub-Nigaroth and her close-huddled brood, Cthulhu with claws outstretched, guarded the rooftops, carved in minute detail and limned with luminescent algae. I plummeted. Without any sense of touch or temperature or even control over my own movement, it took a moment to realize I was diving through deep water, no light above to suggest how close the surface might lie. Spires and rune-carved walls rose around me. Squid flashed past, and long fish with strangely shaped fins, all pulsing with light. Deep vibrations and high, fluting melodies emanated from the plazas below. And swimming up to meet me came a cadre of elders, bodies decorated with ochre symbols, spears drawn.

Then they were gone, and I seemed to stand—still without any sense of legs beneath me—in a landscape without color. A bridge stretched ahead, black columns streaked with gray beneath a sky of pure and depthless white. Flakes of white drifted toward the ground, snow cut from sheets of paper. Inexplicable terror overcame me as they slowly fell nearer.

The black-and-white world vanished, replaced by a blaze of color. A thousand unnamable shades filled me with awe and fury. They shifted like clouds, like ink, like fire. In that conflagration I still could not feel heat or pain, and I wasn't sure whether the emotions—wild and bright as the colors—were mine or belonged to the thing that surrounded me.

Then I stood on a balcony, and watched with casual curiosity as furry white animals writhed over and around each other at the far end. They were legless as snakes. The sky above glowed purple, and music like violins skirled behind me.

At last I felt my body again. A moment of shock, the brief vertiginous sense of falling, and I opened my eyes to the altar room. I took a shaking breath. I gripped my arm, scraped nails against flesh to confirm its existence. Amid the distractions of all I'd seen, the pain felt strangely dull. I wavered between exhilaration and revulsion.

Spector pressed his nails to the floor as I did my arm. Anger showed only in his downturned lips. I remembered that he always asked me, before joining a ritual, whether gods not his own would be named. He might be more distressed by Freddy's prayer than by the visions themselves.

Neko stared at Freddy and the altar, lips parted with pleasure. "Sugoi," she said with awe, and he grinned back at her. *Amazing.* Charlie looked much the same, but through the confluence I sensed his blurred perceptions and quickened pulse. He looked at me and mouthed: *are you all right.* I nodded, doubting my answer. Trumbull, of us all, was the only one who looked serene.

And Mary—between one second and the next, Mary went from still and bland to bent over retching. She gasped between heaves, shaking her head as if to try and clear the disorientation that still lay over my own mind.

Spector scooted to her side but then hovered uncertainly. Trumbull, with less reason for reticence, took her by the shoulders and rubbed them gently. She offered a stream of quiet, meaningless reassurances.

Kvv-vzht-mmmm-vvt skittered to the side table with the books, and pulled a matte black box from a drawer. "This isn't a normal reaction," it said. "Let me look; I may be able to help."

Spector stiffened and started to get between them, but Trumbull nodded. "Please."

Spector subsided, his reluctance obvious. The Outer One opened the box to reveal a variety of incomprehensible tools along with a packet of bandages and a set of vials. It opened one of these with dexterous tendrils. Vapors drifted around Mary's face. The odor was gentler than smelling salts, pungent and herbal. My residual nausea eased.

"Not—the problem," she gasped.

"It's her brain, not her stomach," said Trumbull. "She has these fits sometimes, and she can't read—backlash from a ritual gone wrong. Can you help?"

Whether from the medicinal gas or the natural passage of time, Mary's breathing began to ease, and her now-empty retching tapered off. Kvv-vzht-mmmm-vvt probed her head with a clawed limb, took various instruments from the box, ran them over her. I shuddered in sympathy, weirdly reminded of Dr. Sheldon's skull measurements.

"That's very focused damage," it said. "to surprisingly localized portions of the parietal lobe. What was the nature of the ritual?"

"Inventory equation," gasped Mary. "We were trying to gather a census of the powers in the area."

"It was a summoning," I said. "Overly general—it brought in an outsider." I felt the guilt of what I did not say.

"Sapients can maim ourselves with any tool," it said. "We may be able to give some small aid—perhaps better treatment for the spasms. But the injury has scarred over. To restore full function, we'd need to stimulate growth of large segments of the brain and mind. It could change your personality."

"No, thank you," said Mary. She rubbed her temples gingerly. "That's a remarkable device. Are the images real? Are they showing things happening now, or are they like a movie?"

Freddy had found a towel somewhere, and knelt to wipe her vomit. Now that the moment of crisis had passed, my throat stung with the mix of that stench and the Outer One's natural foetidity. I was grateful for his intervention.

"Usually they're real," said Kvv-vzht-mmmm-vvt. "They're always things we and our travel-mates see, or think we see. Sometimes they're things witnessed now, and sometimes they're older—between stars, the distinction becomes fuzzy."

"You said they'd explain why you're here," said Spector. Trying to care for Mary seemed to have calmed him.

"Yes. The visions are reminder and illustration of our driving mission. Nyarlathotep teaches that there is no species so abominable that it has no wisdom to share. Mad or parasitic or inimical to life from other cosmic reaches, you can always find someone willing to talk. We seek the civilizations capable of living with difference, who can look on the vast and variable universes without fear, who can recognize wisdom wherever it's found. And we seek wisdom among species who will never transcend those fears. We find individuals among them who *can* share that wisdom, and take joy in travel and vast strangeness and the company of cosmopolitan minds, and we teach them and learn from them."

"We go everywhere," said Freddy proudly. "We talk to everyone."

"Yes," said Spector. "But why are you *here*? In New York?"

I wished I could read the Outer One's body language. It shuffled its limbs, in ways that might have been fraught with meaning to its own kind, and perhaps even to my cousin who so easily included it in his "we." "Usually we prefer more private places. But humans are approaching a critical time—new discoveries, new weapons. What kind of species are you? Can you survive your own capabilities, or should we now gather who we can before your fears overtake you?

To answer these questions, we have to meet more humans, and observe your centers of power. Thus New York."

"Ah." Spector seemed uncertain how to respond, perhaps nonplussed by the answer's scale. Mary started to get to her feet, and he took refuge in giving her a hand up.

"We should report to our people outside," she said. "They'll worry if we don't come out soon. But we'd like to talk more—and we still need to speak to your other . . . new recruits."

We'd planned to do that *today*—but I could tell Mary was at the end of her well-masked limits. And I needed time myself. I kept seeing that great city, plunged deep in its ocean crevasse. *That was R'lyeh* tore into frayed threads of *Please let me look again* and *What were they doing there? Are they fighting the guards?,* and then circling back to the shock of seeing what I'd only heard about in sermon and story.

Kvv-vzht-mmmm-vvt blocked my way as I made to leave. "A moment, Ghavn Marsh." Freddy glanced at us and hurried out. I was all too quickly alone with it.

"Are you more comfortable speaking R'lyehn?" Kvv-vzht-mmmm-vvt asked in that language.

"Yes." It was true, I realized—I found the Outer One's curdling strangeness more tolerable when it spoke the tongue of my childhood.

"Comfortable words are best for uncomfortable discussions. I must ask: your people are beholden to the Yith."

My muscles molded into iron coils. "Not beholden, but we respect them and are allied to them. Why?"

"You deserve more than to be their tools. They'll use and dispose of you as easily as they did the shoggoths. But that's a longer argument. Mrs. Harris's scar is unmistakable—no one but a Yith would sear a mind in just that way. It's one of their favorite punishments. I believe you're lying to her—or she'd know. I don't share the Deep Ones' obsequiousness towards the Yith, or the Yith's ideas about what's worthy of punishment. Why should I keep your secret?"

I was used to fear in the face of immediate danger, and the cold, long terror of loss. This was something new: a shameful, angry fear that fell into my stomach like a stone. "I *am* lying to her. But not to protect the Yith; they're capable of that themselves. Have you ever met one?"

Limbs shifted; tendrils rippled. "They're among Earth's many known hazards. When they steal one of our bodies, we encircle their mind in a holding canister and put the body in stasis until they agree to return their captive. It upsets them, and yet somehow they never seem to have enough control over their . . . trades . . . to avoid us. I've been tapped for that argument thrice, and always convinced them to go home swiftly. They're arrogant, baby-eating homebodies, but they can be reasoned with when they have no choice."

If the Outer Ones could thwart the Yith, I needed to choose my words cautiously. "When they've a choice, they don't take kindly to people interfering with their work. You've met Mary Harris, who's a woman of reason and honor, but I had her colleagues wait outside because I didn't trust them to negotiate civilly. If they knew what the Yith were, they'd try to use them, or attack them outright. They have enough resources to cause real trouble. The FBI could make our whole species seem a threat to the Yith's mission—and the Yith would do what they needed to continue their work."

Kvv-vzht-mmmm-vvt bent to run tendrils over my hair. I bit my tongue and forced myself to hold still. Static tingled my scalp; the Outer One's skin felt strange and sponge-like where it brushed my forehead. "You stand between these poor examples of your species and anyone you fear would take their rudeness personally. That's charming and admirable. But we've walked this world for all humanity's time on it and longer. We have *thick skins*." (That last phrase in English.)

"I'm not worried that they'll insult you. Or the Yith." Though I had been. "I'm worried they'll threaten you. They underestimate people who they don't consider human, and overestimate them at the same time—assume they'll act against the state if not intimidated.

I'd really rather they keep thinking of the Yith as a legend in old books."

"You said they work magic. They must read a great many of those books."

"And yet, they respect no danger they haven't seen for themselves. That's how they decided to run an unwarded general summoning, and why the nearest Yith decided they were a danger to the Archives' local repository."

"And so they stole her symbols so she couldn't do it again. The others as well?"

"No," I said. "Miss Harris is the group's genius."

"She's worked around it, I assume. Humans don't find illiteracy suicidally shameful."

"The rest of them take it in turns to read to her," I confirmed. "And write down what she tells them."

"And these are the worst of your species?"

"They take care of their own. But please, don't point them at the Yith. The last time they met one, they never suspected her true nature, but they got it into their heads that she was a Russian spy. They tied her to a chair, blindfolded her, and threatened torture." Which, it occurred to me now, had probably increased her displeasure with their chancy spell later on. "If they'd demanded the secrets of the Archives instead of treating her as a thoroughly human spy, things might have gone much worse."

The Outer One's buzzing rose and fell, rose and fell. "We must meet these people, before we decide what to tell them. It worries me that they know about us at all, if their judgment is as poor as you say—but perhaps we can reason with them. For now, though, we won't tell Miss Harris who scarred her."

CHAPTER 8

Freddy waited in the dingy hallway masking the Outer One lair. He put a hand on my arm, but withdrew it almost instantly. Kvv-vzht-mmmm-vvt buzzed at him and withdrew down the stairs.

"Your friend's okay," he said. "I've never seen anyone react to the trapezohedron like that. But I want to know what *you* saw, what *you* thought."

R'lyeh glimmered in my memory, a stolen sliver of my rightful inheritance, joy and guilt and desire intermingled. I wanted to meditate and set the memory clearly where I could preserve it. I wanted to cry at its beauty where no one could see. I wanted to return and see it again. I didn't feel ready to put it into words for anyone—and especially not for Freddy, so obviously avid to learn whether my epiphanies matched his own.

"Among our people, visions are private things." I tried to sound gentle. It occurred to me—if not for the first time, then for the first time in full consciousness—that I would probably have to breed with this boy. I couldn't imagine it.

"They're more than visions. Please. I want—you want me to learn about your home, and I want you to learn about mine the same way."

"How can you say I've learned about your home, when you don't even know what I saw?"

"I'm learning to think like they do. Home doesn't have to be one place, or even one planet. It can be everywhere you go, and the people who go there with you. The trapezohedron shows a glimpse of some of those journeys. Some of what you might see and feel, if you came with us."

My first instinct was anger. An absurdity: why shouldn't he invite me into his life and community, as I'd invited him? Yet the idea not only repulsed, but frightened me. I sought a safer topic.

"Your mother's desperate to hear from you," I told him. "She's been waiting by her door for news."

His shoulders slumped. "You can tell her I'm okay. I shouldn't have left Earth without letting her know something—but Kvv-vzht-mmmm-vvt was heading out to Yuggoth right away and I just wanted to *see*."

"What's it like?" I asked reluctantly. "I've heard rumors of how the Outer Ones travel. I know Nnnnnn-gt-vvv thinks I've been fed nonsense."

The question made him relax a little. "It's scary at first. Like with the trapezohedron, you can't feel your body—you know it's somewhere safe, but far away. And you know that no one will judge you by anything except what you say. It's wonderful to be able to just talk, and never have to play those little schoolyard games of who's bigger and stronger. And in the space between worlds you find the most beautiful patterns. There's music like nothing on Earth."

"I've fought hard to keep my body my own," I said. "Everything I know says that untethering your mind isn't healthy for either part of you. Fatal, often."

"Well, the Outer Ones have ways around that, obviously. They've been doing it for millions of years. I trust them. You've met my mom, and you've met Dr. Sheldon. They aren't people you can really talk to. Mom is always worried about how I'll turn out, and *he's* always excited because it'll be interesting no matter what I do. Kvv-vzht-mmmm-vvt, all the people here, they're the first real friends I've had."

"I'm sorry." I couldn't think what else to say; my own experience of loneliness was so different from what he'd faced. And yet there was still that taste of poisonous delusion in his conviction. I wanted to believe it was only my own paranoid imagining. "You've gone too long without any sort of community. If the currents are good, some of our elders will arrive in New York's waters tonight. We'll be there to meet them; you could come with us. I can invite your mother, too; it might ease the reunion."

"Oh!" He seemed startled, but not displeased. "I'd like to talk with them; I said I would. Where are they going to come ashore? Or do you have a boat?"

"No boats required." A stab of memory, almost as vivid as my earlier glimpse of R'lyeh, showed me Innsmouth's marina on the first day of the season, sails rising hopefully to catch the wind. At some point we must rebuild that part of the town as well. Though first we'd need to find people who knew sailing—that skill had been lost on land with so many others. "We haven't decided where to summon the elders yet. No one in this city seems to sleep. I don't suppose— do you know a beach that would be deserted late at night?"

He thought. "Coney Island gets pretty dead after the park shuts down. Unless someone else likes sleeping roller coasters, you're guaranteed privacy. It's fun during the day, but in the dark, with the rides shadowed against the moon, it's like another planet." He grinned. "I wonder if it'll still seem as interesting now. Though I suppose your family will make it strange enough."

As I emerged into sunlight, Audrey caught me. "About time you got out. We've just about persuaded Mr. Barlow not to storm the place with guns blazing." Mary had clearly invoked her own infirmity, because I could now hear them arguing about whether she ought now to get the rest she'd missed in the night. That one, she seemed willing to lose.

"Caleb and Miss Dawson will be frantic," murmured Charlie. "Audrey, how much of that could you feel?"

"How much of what? You both felt a little nervous the whole time, and there was one moment where it felt like something startled Aphra. But nothing that felt like real danger—that's what I kept trying to tell Mr. Barlow."

"But I had a coughing fit," I said. "And there was a ritual . . . This doesn't make sense." I closed my eyes and focused on even breath, slowing heart. I could feel Audrey, breath quickened with confusion. And elsewhere, a more general sense of Caleb and Deedee, with no sign of panic to focus my attention. Away from the distractions of the Outer One lair, my skin itched all over. I found myself squirming as if I'd put on a dress askew. "I want to do the Inner Sea later."

"Of course." Charlie put a tentative hand on my forehead, priestlike, and I inhaled the city's sweltering potpourri. The day had grown warm. My stockings, comfortably thick farther north, chafed my legs. Somewhere a man's voice screamed about money wasted playing games; radios and horns and shouts blended into a background whine. Gratefully, I heard and smelled and felt all the physical world had to offer.

I wanted time alone to think about my visions, to settle in my memory that flash of my true home. I should never have seen it until decades hence; I shouldn't want to see it again now. But it was New York that I must think of. Frances, and how to explain what had happened to her son. Freddy himself, and what I needed from him, and what, if anything, he needed from us. The Outer Ones, and their purpose in the city, and what they were doing with my cousin, and what the state might wish with them. I felt the exhaustion of an overwhelming day, and most of it still to come. We had much to do before we could reconnect with Caleb and Deedee, or summon the elders. Dark and quiet, and time to think, were a long way off.

≈≈≈

Catherine Trumbull—Date not noted:

Time is hard, these days. Sometimes when I wake, I don't know the era or the century. More often, I forget the importance of minutes and hours. I set alarms in every room to remind me of meals and meetings and classes. I wear a watch on my wrist and carry another in my skirt pocket, quiet weights like strings around my fingers. After the first irritated student complaints, I write a note in big letters and place it on the lectern when I teach: "Look at the clock. Stop at 10:50."

The people I love most are dead, or unborn.

By the standards of their neighbors, Innsmouth's people are mad and strange and scandalous. With them I can speak about things that matter. They remain strangers, but they keep me from feeling too lonely.

Miss Marsh invites me to her house, half in fresh repair and half sagging beams. She greets me with a rare smile. An elder sits in her kitchen—new to me, I believe, though I have trouble distinguishing their froggish faces and varicolored scales. This one has an unusual crest, small and black and clinging close to the skull, which I think I would recognize. But sometimes I forget to mark appearance as well.

Before Miss Marsh can introduce us the elder rises, bows, grins with sharp teeth.

"Khur Catherine." Their voices are all deep, but this one is particularly resonant, with a strange accent that grabs my concentration. "I am Khur S'vlk. It is an honor to meet a fellow scholar."

It takes a moment to process the import of the words. I hear the title "khur" often from elders' lips: it's reserved for those who exchange minds with a Yith, adding their meager knowledge to the Great Race's prehuman store while their own bodies host one of the race's traveling researchers. Usually, though, I only hear it heralding my own name.

"You've been to the Archives?" I ask. In my imagination, humanoid form and scale and skin give way to a corrugated, cone-shaped body half again as tall, tentacular limbs tipped with grasping claws and drinking trumpets and one globe ringed with eyes and fine manipulators.

"Oh, yes. It's a great joy to meet another captive." Even through the accent I

recognize amusement; the respect of the elders contrasts notably with how the Yith themselves refer to us. "Aphra Yukhl says you are also a mathematician."

Later I bring books from my office. These hold precious marginalia in my Yithian guest's hand, half familiar and half alien. S'vlk translates what my scant Enochian cannot fathom. It's for these notes that the elder, whose ordinary work involves predicting the ever-changing topography of the ocean floor, has come from R'lyeh to meet me.

S'vlk's company is a precious echo of the Archives, collegiality unencumbered by physical form or Miskatonic's petty departmental cliques.

As with Xiùyīng in the Archives, I wonder whether my growing attraction is at all appropriate. I don't ask S'vlk, and when I hear Miss Marsh say "she" I resist the stab of absurd hope. It can hardly matter: even were my colleague interested, the people of the water hold relations between people of different lifespans taboo. Though circumstance forces the younger Marshes to ignore that restriction, S'vlk is under no such pressure.

"One day," I tell her, "we humans got to feeling homesick. We found a big balcony, a couple dozen of us away from the usual all-species mixer, and settled down to be melancholy with our own kind. Someone said they missed dancing—I couldn't imagine it; I hate going around in circles with men I can barely stand, tripping over their feet—but we decided that even if we couldn't dance in those bodies, we could make music. We borrowed a set of Yithian drums, or what passes for drums, and took turns trying to re-create rhythms from our own times."

S'vlk grins again. "I can imagine it. Those great wide cymbal things that their youth favor. Or did when I was there." We still have no idea how far apart our respective archival tenures may be. But I nod recognition.

"And the deep barrels with a sort of shark-like skin stretched over them, and the ones made of concentric metal rings. There was one of our fellows— someone who'd spent half his life migrating north with his tribe out of Africa into, I think, southern Europe. He could have had only the simplest instruments at home, but the rhythms he played were like nothing I've ever heard. They made me want to dance, and not care who I danced with."

S'vlk beats a tattoo on the kitchen table, slapping steadily with one thick hand while interweaving something faster and more intricate with the talons of the other. "Like that?"

"Yes! Not the same tune, but the same feeling. How did you know?"

Another sharp grin. "I'm older than I look. And we had better instruments than you'd think. I've always noticed how songs change as other kinds of thought shift. Mathematics and music are close kin."

"I never thought of it that way." Painting is the art that meshes with my studies, a different way of understanding space and distance and the things that inhabit them.

"You should explore their connection. I'm glad you enjoy our old songs—perhaps I'll play something, and you'll dance?" S'vlk leans forward and brushes a loose strand of hair back against my head. Her touch is light, claw barely shivering my scalp. I know that gesture doesn't mean what it would for a human of the air. Other elders use similar gestures for benediction, or quiet familial affection. Still I feel my face warm, and hope she doesn't notice.

As we return to our studies I think of Xiùyīng, my only romance that I didn't have to hide, the caressing slither of tentacle against tentacle. And I am lonely.

"I don't know what to think of this," said Frances. "People from another world—it's like something out of one of Freddy's stories. But you're from one of mine, so I guess anything's possible."

As it turned out, none of the city's seemingly ubiquitous trains approached the Lavernes' Red Hook apartment. Spector, after an uncharacteristically digression-filled discussion of our transit options, had determined that we should take the streetcar to a station whose stairs he thought wouldn't be too hard on Charlie's knee. At midnight, the 4th Avenue subway platform was sparsely populated, but New Yorkers' habit of not listening, or of not caring who heard, held even when the crowds dispersed. And though we were a crowd of our own, Frances's relief at learning that we'd found her son had averted any dismay at the additions to my entourage. We'd shed the FBI agents at their hotel, even Spector.

"The Outer Ones are strange to us, too," I said. "But Freddy calls them friends."

"If that's true, I wish he'd introduced them before he ran off. I'm so worried. You're sure he'll be there?"

"He said he would be." It was the third time she'd asked, but I couldn't blame her. I remembered the hints he'd given about their strained relationship, and hoped his curiosity would outweigh his reluctance.

The laughter of inebriated passengers and the hypnotic, painful roar of the tracks made the trip through Brooklyn surreal. Neko leaned back in her seat, watching the tunnel lights flash past, and Trumbull scribbled in a notebook. The city's rhythm was constant when I paid it mind, but fickle in its effects. It could buoy me with excess energy, then wear me out a moment later with the pace of its million heart-beats.

Charlie dozed on one of my shoulders, Audrey on the other. I felt very aware of their little movements, their exhaustion sharp from the morning's adventure and dull from the long day of preparation and explanation. Caleb and Deedee were vague impressions on the edge of awareness. Sleeping? Waking? I couldn't tell.

Audrey stretched and rubbed her eyes, shadowed with fatigue, as we slowed at Coney Island. She gave me a lopsided grin. "Does this count as one of our late-night raids? I've missed those."

I could have done without the reminder, since the "raids" she joked about had both been ill-fated. I was saved from responding by Charlie: "Maybe we should try the next one at noon."

Audrey shook her head. "Wrong ambiance."

We were the only ones at the station. Our steps echoed from tiled walls. In the train's wake, the shadowed tracks breathed up ammo-niac heat. Crumpled wrappers and scuffed floors told of greater traf-fic during the day; our destination was home to no one.

Outside, the breeze brought relief: still rich with sweat and trash, but topped with the remnant of sugared pastry and the homesick scent of hot dogs. Behind those, for the first time since we'd come to New York, I smelled the ocean.

Shuttered stalls lined the boundary road. Garishly painted signs promised delicacies and prizes. I could scarcely imagine what lay behind the shutters, yet it reminded me eerily of the little row of shops that once lined the street behind Innsmouth's dunes. The little buildings lay utterly lifeless. I caught myself shaking, and breathed deeply to bring my body under control. I was here to see my family, as I'd desired all day; it was foolish for a few closed stores to remind me of deserted Innsmouth. Perhaps it was Caleb's absence. Part of me still feared for him whenever I couldn't see that he was safe.

Frances led us down the broad expanse of Stillwell Avenue. I saw the name and imagined a stone well, mirror-smooth and dark as the reservoir west of Arkham where the hills rise wild around the water. Instead, crumpled wrappers and more signs: a card parlor, a fortune teller, a wax museum. Two gargantuan roller coasters swooped and twisted on either side of the promenade. They looked like castles of tracks. A tower rose amid the tangle to our left, pennants flapping and stuttering. I'd never seen anything built to such a scale for such a purpose.

Arched stalls lay in shadowed maws along the coaster's base. A figure slipped from one: Freddy, looking small against the outsized backdrop. He paused when he saw his mother.

"Hi," he said quietly.

"Hi?" She grabbed him into a fierce hug, then held him at arms' length to look him over. "Don't you ever do that to me again! I've always known how you slip out here at night, and I thought, let a boy have a little room to run around—but other worlds! I was scared stiff!"

"I'm sorry." He sounded at most half sorry. "I should've told you. But I thought you'd put me in the loony bin."

She snorted. "You think that's the craziest story I've ever heard?"

She shook her head. "Let's go meet the rest of our new family. But you're going to introduce me to these friends later, and do it right."

He squirmed from her touch, began leading us on past the roller coasters. "I don't know if you'd like them."

"Are they bad people?"

"Of course not! But they're not exactly *people*."

"I don't care what they look like. I care what they're teaching you."

The road spilled out onto a boardwalk—so wide that it might as well be a street of its own—looking over the beach. It covered the dunes entirely. The sand stretched wide and flat between us and the ocean. It was a palimpsest of footprints, scattered with detritus. Still the sight of the water dragged 'round an internal compass that had been whirling for days, pointing me firmly at my proper place.

"Look."

I followed Freddy's pointed finger back toward the land and down the walkway, and saw a gargantuan Ferris wheel looming over all. Gondolas dangled from both the outer rim and an inner loop, silhouetted by the city's glow. The contrast between the sea and this exuberant human construction reminded me strangely of San Francisco, where mountains pressed against ocean so that you could not, in the liminal space beside the waves, forget the immensity of either.

"There was a lot more here when I was a kid," said Frances. "The amusement park is dying; in a few years they'll knock it down and put up more houses like Levittown. That's what people want now."

"Not me," said Freddy.

"They're doing the same thing in Massachusetts," I said. "We're trying to buy up the Innsmouth land before they build over it, but . . ." Frances was right. In the shadow of the Ferris wheel I could see a couple of boarded-up bathhouses, and part of the walkway had either collapsed or was under desultory repair.

We descended to the beach.

At the base of the stairs I took off my shoes. Broken glass glinted among the pylons, but I needed the familiar sensation. Night-cooled sand slipped around my calluses. The susurrus of waves whispered beyond, achingly like home. Yet unfamiliarity shook me. It was the absence of dunes, or the inescapable city lights, or the alien colossi stretching behind. It was glass and crumpled paper. It was the sand itself subtly shaped by thousands of footprints, a change I could not describe save that daylight visitors had left some mark on the normally imperturbable beach. I flinched at what the elders might think.

Where the sand grew damp, I knelt to draw the summoning diagram. But my discomfort, the irrational shame at the land's encroachment on the ocean, slowed my hand. I also felt strangely shy about showing the Lavernes their first taste of magic. I felt instinctively that they must carry some vestigial understanding of what the thing should look like, enough to find me wanting. Utterly irrational: magic was no more or less natural to men of the water than those of the air, and Freddy's experience was so far removed from mine that he could hardly make the comparison. Still, I turned to Charlie.

"Would you like to lead today?" I asked him. He gave me a sharp look, but nodded at last.

Audrey tapped my shoulder. "Go wash your face," she said quietly.

She came with me and lowered herself at the water's edge, heedless of her dress. The tide was on its way out. Reluctant waves plashed against my knees. I dipped my hands and raised salt water to my lips. Audrey nodded and did the same. The taste cut through my self-indulgence.

The water had a sour bite. All manner of horrors had washed into it from the land above. But the mill run-off in the Miskatonic was worse. The elders would be able to make this last part of the journey with small hazard.

"You all right?" asked Audrey.

I nodded. "I think so."

"You're not normally unsure of yourself."

"I'm not used to this sort of strangeness. I don't know what to do with it."

She smiled. "Your instincts are usually pretty good."

"Not here." I shook my head. "I know how to deal with my own insignificance—with things that are bigger than me, that see my worst problems as trivial if they see them at all. But every building in this city is a testament to human ambition. It feels like it'll go on forever and like it's crumbling around me all at once."

She started to say something, but instead pressed wet fingers to my forehead. "New York is beautiful, but it lies. Just keep going like you usually do, and you'll be okay."

We returned to the others. Charlie was tracing the symbols with a steady hand. He drew the shape to call people of the water, and the inner glyph that would hold our blood and name us callers rather than called. He used the variation we'd learned from Trumbull's guest, the one that "invites but does not flatter." Whatever insecurities made me urge him to lead, I was glad to see him take the ritual on. It was a little foolish to take pride in his accomplishments when we'd learned so much in tandem—but he was still my student.

Freddy looked over his shoulder with curiosity, murmuring questions. This might be very different from the form used by the Outer Ones, but it wasn't his first taste of magic. But Frances's pupils rippled wide. Her lips parted. Would I soon have another student? It didn't seem right for me to take on so many. But of course there was no one else to do it.

My grandfather, on land, had spoken of the gods to sailors wherever he went, even men of the air. He'd sworn, rumor claimed, never to fear speaking truth. But *he'd* had no cause to spread our sacred arts beyond Innsmouth. Nor was I a wild-haired proselytizer, with a captain's lash to keep those who disliked my speech at bay.

To rebuild Innsmouth, I'd have to do both: teach about the gods, and keep teaching magic. The tasks daunted me. At some point, I could not afford to multiply the intimacy I shared with my confluence. Looking at Freddy and Frances, I felt again the premonition of mourning.

Ïa, Cthulhu, lord of the patient depths, let me take on this pain only when it's time. Let it wait, I beg you.

Charlie interrupted my reverie with a proffered blade. I pricked my finger and bled into the sand. I felt the summoner's diagram stir, a tiny sacrament of control.

At twelve, I learned that we honored the gods with such acts of anomalous order. Through ritual, we reclaimed a few precious moments from entropy. I had loved the flicker of candlelight, the taste of salt water, the moment of proud courage when the blood welled against my skin. But I had not understood.

With the call complete, there was nothing left to do but wait. Those familiar with the rite leaned back on the sand, or tucked up their knees to stare at the waves. Frances and Freddy followed suit.

"What are they like?" Frances asked me. "What will they want from us?"

That second seemed the real question. "The same things we do. Meeting you will be enough for now."

"Aphra's elders can be startling, the first time," said Charlie. "And not just the way they look. They don't hide what they're thinking."

"After you've been around that long," said Audrey, "why would you?"

"The Outer Ones are the same way." Freddy spoke quietly to his knees.

I chewed my lip. "Maybe they're honest with *you*. I still don't understand what they want." *And it worries me.*

He ducked his head, and said nothing.

"That," I continued, "the elders will ask for certain."

He sighed. Frances held very still, as if any movement might startle him off.

"They told you that they're not sure what's next for humanity. Whether the next war will be the last. And you have to understand that they *care*. Not just about humans, but about—" He laced his fingers, pulled them apart, looked at them as if some cryptic secret lay between. "They're connected with everyone they've ever met, every place they've ever been. They outlive most of those people and places, but they care what happens to all of them. So the question of whether humans are going to survive or not, and what they should *do* about it, matters to them. A lot."

Some unspoken implication hung on his words, and I still didn't understand. Frances said: "You mean they argue about us, the same way the papers argue about how to handle Russia and Germany."

He sat back on his heels. For the first time all night, he looked directly at his mother. "Yeah. It's more personal for them—everything is. The New York mine has people on all sides trying to prove their case. It gets pretty tense."

"What does Kvv-vzht-mmmm-vvt think?" I asked.

He hunched his shoulders. "Hard to explain. You should ask it yourself."

That brought up a more trivial question, but one that mattered if I intended to ask Kvv-vzht-mmmm-vvt such questions civilly. "Do they really like to be called 'it'? I can't tell their genders, if they have them."

Freddy relaxed visibly at the change of subject. "I know that sounds weird, but they seem to like it, and it's how they talk about each other. Their genders are complicated, and I think they change sometimes. There are a couple of people at the mine who just use 'he' or 'she' for everyone, and Rudolph—he's one of our travel-mates who used to teach literature—says 'they' was good enough for Shakespeare. But Kvv-vzht-mmmm-vvt treats that like . . . like the dirty jokes you think are really funny when you're twelve?" He looked at me expectantly, and I nodded vague understanding. I tried to recall what my friends and I had joked about during the brief part of my twelfth year when laughter was possible. Clever wordplay about our study texts, mostly, or sometimes not-so-clever, and rude stories about men of the air. The memory of those casual insults, and of friends who might have grown into more, brought doubled pain.

I let the conversation trail. I tried to meditate, seeking calm against the myriad uncertainties raised by my newfound cousins. On Innsmouth's beach, this would be easy. The hiss of incoming waves, the chirp of peepers in the bogs to the north, would make comfort of near-silence. Far from any city lights, clouds would smear the moonlight into a diorama of shadows. They'd give the sky a depth that human eyes could understand, where the far stars and the faint glow of the galactic disk could not. *The Milky Way,* men of the air said, trivializing it even more than the R'lyehn *V'hlchaja P'tych—the stream of night,* as if the vast spread of stars were merely a tributary of the Miskatonic.

In Innsmouth, I could stare upward and imagine the lives and deaths, civilizations blooming and fading, aeon-forgotten ruins and new-evolved limbs pulling through muck, which must exist in endless profusion throughout my field of vision. My harshest memories and newest fears, my people's desire for survival, humanity's ever-growing ability to threaten its own ambitions, would lie small against that backdrop. But now, starlight obfuscated, I found my gaze drawn to the Ferris wheel. I imagined how it would look in a few years or decades: a rusting edifice with spurs askew. Later still the sea would rise, eroding this coastline, and wash away these fragile structures. New York, for all its height and humanity, was a breath from the ocean, and would pass in a geological instant.

I knew Grandfather had argued hard, in Y'ha-nthlei, for Innsmouth's rebuilding. But to the watching elders, swords and muskets had spawned the atomic bomb in an eyeblink. They tasted the poisons washing into the Atlantic with every storm, and many thought humanity's extinction must come soon. In the deep crevasses sheltering R'lyeh, our remnant of the species could survive the sterilization of continents. The outposts and spawning ground, if left in place, would not be so fortunate.

Grandfather thought we should breed, and make new life and bring in new ideas, as long as we could. Not all agreed. On bad nights,

I doubted it myself. I wanted children to come after me and join me in the water—and feared children who'd inherit too much air from a mistblooded father, and sicken and age beyond my power to help.

Frances gasped, a single sharp indrawn breath. Freddy clambered to his feet and ducked his head, polite but wide-eyed. I turned from the amusement park in all its imagined ruin, and knelt to greet the elders.

CHAPTER 9

Tonight only three elders joined us, though they must have been accompanied south by an entourage carting goods and tending the nurse sharks. Frances, I suspected, would see only the elders' commonalities. Outsiders sometimes described them as hybrids of man and fish, or frog, or lizard. They were a head taller than any ordinary landsman, armored in slick scales that iridesced in the night's diffuse glow. Thick pads of muscle, webs spanning fingers and long toes, ears sunk into skulls, all told how perfectly they adapted the human form to the ocean's demands. Sharp talons and teeth told how dangerous those demands could become. And their scent, of oil and seaweed and the sea's own mix of salt and subtler minerals, told of home.

To me, their distinctions burned more brightly. Khur S'vlk, eldest by far, was nearly eight feet tall, her frame eel-slender by the standards of the depths. She moved with swift jerks or held sculpture-still, a hunter of ideas with patience honed by millennia. I'd only met her a couple of months ago, when she came up to study with Trumbull. It hadn't taken long to see that she'd earned the respect due her age and title.

Captain Obed Yringl'phtagn Marsh, my grandfather. The emerald and amethyst mottling of his scales was as familiar as my own raw skin.

Chulzh'th, Archpriest Ngalthr's acolyte, was less than a century old, and not yet at her full growth. But her midnight scales, shading to deep purple over palms and breast, drew the eye, and her bearing proclaimed the confidence of one who would someday be an archpriest in her own right. She put her hand to my forehead in a brief benediction. Her cool touch cleared my fog of confusion and fatigue.

"Your search has borne fruit," she said.

"More than we planned. I'll introduce you, but then there's danger elsewhere that we need advice on."

Grandfather twitched—he'd marked his grandson's absence immediately. And he'd none of his warriors with him, and went unarmed as an elder could be. An ill-considered attempt to protect me had cost him his spear, and though I loved him I wasn't sorry for that. There were other aspects of his penitence, I knew, that weren't discussed out of the water. Dark eyes scanned the amusement park and the city beyond.

"I don't expect the danger to find us here," I assured him. "Just . . . there have been complications. Caleb and Deedee are fine, but— They're elsewhere tonight."

"You'll explain that, of course," said Grandfather. But he relaxed from his defensive stance.

His attention released from the alien skyline, I introduced our newcomers, and told the elders what little I knew of their history. Freddy, unafraid, went down on one knee before them.

"I'm honored to meet you," he said.

Chulzh'th touched his forehead, frowned, and licked her fingers thoughtfully. "We welcome you back among your own."

Frances, at last, joined us. She put her hands on Freddy's shoulders, bowed her head. Her arms shook.

Chulzh'th started to reach out, then hesitated. "You need not fear us. We are your kin."

I spared Frances the burden of explaining. "Their air-born ancestors fled Innsmouth, and told stories of being chased down by elders. We *haven't* always treated such people well."

"I see from how you stand," said Grandfather to her, "that you would do anything to protect your child."

She straightened, and I saw a flash of the dignity I expected from women of the water.

"So would we," he continued. "That is what your ancestor feared, and I hope you will not hold it against us. You are *both* our children."

Some of the steel drained from her shoulders, but she asked, "And how do you plan to protect us? Why would we want your protection?"

Chulzh'th sat down in the sand beside us. Frances blinked and eased herself down as well. Freddy settled beside them, gaze lingering on his mother. Chulzh'th said: "Whether you want it is for you to say. But we have strength, and millennia of stored wisdom, and the words to the stories that flow in your blood. And gold, which is a pedestrian sort of protection but one that has always mattered a great deal on land."

S'vlk had remained still throughout this discussion, eyes distant. Trumbull had drawn near, but hadn't interrupted her reverie. Now the older scholar snapped into focus. "Tell us swiftly of this danger."

I rocked back on my heels, pinned by her attention. "There are Outer Ones in the city. They claim to be friendly, but I don't understand what they're doing. Freddy has been living with them."

"Ah," said Chulzh'th. She sniffed her fingers where they'd touched him.

"That's what I picked up," said Grandfather. He sounded relieved, an anomaly resolved. In R'lyehn he added, without rancor, "Voiddrunk vagrants. Aphra, there is a story I must tell you later. Trust their words, and never their actions. I expect your brother isn't with them, or you'd have said so."

"No," I answered in the same tongue. "He hasn't even met them yet."

"I can't understand you," Freddy said. "but I can guess what you're talking about. The Outer Ones are good people. I wish you'd stop acting like they're about to jump you in an alley or something."

"I met them too," said Neko. "I don't have any reason to think they're *better* than humans, but they welcomed us as Freddy's family."

S'vlk leaned in to take the boy's scent. "They hide in mountain mists and moonlit nights. They steal children and give nothing back. And they have always claimed some part of this world as their due."

Trumbull touched her shoulder. "Is that your opinion, or theirs?"

S'vlk blinked up at her. "Both. Though I cannot blame the cone-shaped young for sometimes choosing the underhill, I lost someone in my own youth that I still hold against them. Besides, they are obnoxious in negotiation, and they have little respect for others' territory."

"Excuse me," said Freddy. "I decided to travel with them on purpose. All their companions do. I'm not property to be stolen or bartered."

"Don't you realize how easily they can shape minds to their liking?" asked S'vlk. She looked around at the rest of us. "Do you understand what he means by 'travel'? The *meigo* flense mind from body with the most delicate tools. The *meigo* place these minds in metal baskets where they can see and hear and speak, but nothing else. Then the *meigo* carry those minds far beyond Earth—utterly helpless and utterly dependent. Their victims become accustomed to it. They grow loyal to the creatures who make them helpless, because they recall only being protected while they could do nothing for themselves." I shuddered; her description seemed to crystallize the fears that had gathered, awaiting form, since I first spoke with Freddy.

Freddy stood. "That's not—that's not even—it's not like that at all! They show us things we could never see if we stuck around safely on Earth! And we're only helpless if you think talking doesn't count as being able to do anything. Which, you're talking to me now, and you seem to think it'll do something, so don't treat me like a ninety-seven-pound runt because I spent a week debating philosophy on another planet!"

Grandfather stepped toward him. I rose, mindful of my ancestor's temper.

"Show respect, boy," he rumbled. "Khur S'vlk is fifty thousand years your elder."

Freddy glared at the sand. "Yes. But she's wrong."

"Be at peace, Yringl'phtagn," said Chulzh'th. "He's had no time to learn our ways, or our worth."

"I don't respect people who insult my friends," said Freddy. He raised his head defiantly. "I bet you wouldn't either."

Audrey stepped between Freddy and Grandfather, and Trumbull tightened her grip on S'vlk. "Respectfully," said Audrey. "I think everyone should sit down and cool off. You're all meeting for the first time and everyone's nervous. You don't want to pick a fight with your family when you barely know them. The biggest danger I see from the Outer Ones is how just thinking about them has your backs up."

S'vlk, thankfully, sat back. "Agreed. They are no greater threat than they ever were—nor any less. But I'll not lose another kinsman to them."

Freddy, at his mother's urgent whisper, ducked his head and said, "I'm sorry, sir."

Grandfather sighed. "Chulzh'th always says that I ought not rebuke my descendants for their likeness to me." He made to sit as well, then stiffened. "Khur S'vlk, am I confused about where that scent is coming from?"

The other elder leaned back and closed her eyes. Nostrils flared. "No. I smell something more than a mark left on a favored pet." She got to her feet, turned slowly. "If you intend peace, show yourself."

I heard a leathery flapping, but saw nothing. It seemed to come from every direction. Then the air twisted sickeningly. It was difficult to describe—no, it was difficult to perceive. The closest my mind would come was the image of water oozing through a wall I'd thought well-sealed against storms. But instead of water, it was a roil of eye-searing shadows.

Then the world snapped back into focus—almost. An Outer One folded impossible wings inward from the full extension of its other-worldly flight. Its bone-piercing hum filled the air.

Frances grabbed Freddy, muffling a cry. Charlie, Neko, and Audrey closed on me in a miniature phalanx. The elders drew together, and turned as one toward our visitor.

Freddy pulled away from his mother and ran to its side. "Nnnnnn-gt-vvv! You shouldn't have come."

Cilia stroked his hair. The Outer One's buzzing hum resolved into words. "Kvv-vzht-mmmm-vvt said as much. But we worried for you. I apologize for hiding—I didn't expect to be caught." Freddy snorted and prodded the creature's side.

"What harm did you fear we'd do him, to make you skulk in the borders of our world?" demanded Grandfather. "He is among family."

"He's among family with us as well." Nnnnnn-gt-vvv wrapped Freddy in an amorphous wing. "You hide too, when you doubt humanity's judgment. You didn't visit Coney Island among the daytime crowds, after all."

S'vlk stalked forward, pulling from Trumbull's grasp. "How dare you claim him as family?"

"Enough." Chulzh'th stood. "You two old hunters will find blood if you look hard enough. Our kin built lives without us—what else should they have done? We can't demand in an instant the loyalty of a child neither named nor raised under Dagon's eye. *Be at peace.* Let us discuss this like the civilized people some of us strive to be."

"Thank you," said Nnnnnn-gt-vvv. "Our peoples have long dis-agreed about many things, but rarely been enemies. Freddy was ner-vous, and we feared you might hold his friendship with us against him—as you did. That's all my reason for 'skulking.' "

I found my voice. "Now that you've shown yourself, what do you want here? We want to get to know our cousin, and teach him some-thing of our ways. The ocean flows in his blood—we want to show him what that means." But Freddy deserved better than my arguing over his head. "You have the right to know what you risk, traveling with them. What we have to offer, while you still have a choice."

He shook his head. "I know what I want."

"What *we* want," said Nnnnnn-gt-vvv, "is to save what can be saved of humanity. To help something survive and thrive beyond Earth. You remnants are satisfied to leave behind cold stories on stone; we want more."

"Humanity might do better than you expect," said Charlie. But he edged closer to me.

"Why?" I asked the Outer One. I hardly needed ask what Nnnnnn-gt-vvv thought we needed saving from. Even if it harbored no dark knowledge beyond the risks that kept me up at night, I could think of too many answers.

I'd spent my life knowing that humanity would eventually pass from the earth's surface. But I wasn't ready. Perhaps S'vlk, with all her years and perspective, would more easily accept humanity's extinction on land—or perhaps none of us were truly willing to face that inevitable burden of mourning.

Nnnnnn-gt-vvv's limbs writhed cryptically. "We've seen thousands of species learn how to grow and connect with others. We've seen millions collapse in the singularity of their own social incapacities. If you survive your weapons and wars, you're still beginning to change your atmosphere and soil and sea beyond the bounds most humans can survive. You remnants, with your wasted adaptive abilities, must sense those changes."

Chulzh'th rumbled deep in her throat, not yet a growl. "All species must pass, eventually. Even yours." I was glad that she left out the uncertain case of the Yith; that conflict seemed unwise to invoke. "What do you want of *us*, here and now? Because if you want to steal our kinfolk from the water, we *will* have blood."

"You talk about your relatives like property. They aren't yours, or the water's, or Earth's. There's a whole cosmopolitan universe out there, full of glory and wonder. If you don't want Freddy to experience that, it's him you need to convince. And you probably won't do it by yelling at him."

We were doing it again—not even yelling *at* Freddy, but yelling about him. And even worse, ignoring Frances because she wasn't under contention.

I turned to the elders. "This isn't what we want. Could you please back off for a few minutes? I promise I'll tell you soon what happened last night and this morning. You need to know. I just need a moment with my cousins." Through my connection with the confluence, as well as I could, I projected my gratitude for their nearness, the feeling of warmth and protection.

"Very well," said S'vlk.

Then it was me, and the Lavernes, and Nnnnnn-gt-vvv. The Outer One didn't seem inclined to give space as the elders had, and I hadn't the standing to ask. I chafed at the impossibility of getting him alone, of finding a place where he could listen to my offers without his patrons' whispering temptation. But with little other choice, I did my best to ignore it.

"Freddy. Too much has been happening at once since I met you, and there's so much I want to tell you. I told your mother a little, but—we keep circling into these arguments. You *are* your own person, and you *do* have a right to choose. But you must know why we're so passionate to claim you.

"Your travels frighten me, but I'm glad they give you joy. I don't want to deny you that, because my brother Caleb and I were held prisoner for seventeen years, for being what we are. All our people on land were taken to camps in the desert, and all except for us died in those camps. Under the water, our people are legion. But up here, where we can still breed and grow and have some sway over the rest of humanity's survival, it's only the two of us.

"We want to change that. But we need more people. And we need, eventually, another generation. That's why we sought you out. And that's why I'm frightened every time I try to show you what we are.

Because in 1928, knowing what I'm telling you and being what I am meant imprisonment and death. Today it means hard work and continuing to fight people who hate us. For all the joy of our stories and magic and history, it's a hard thing we're offering you. And perhaps it seems unimportant, or even desirable, that the Outer One arts could break your mind from your body and make you less that thing."

Freddy didn't immediately respond. In his silence, the ocean's endless growling choir broke against the rumble of distant traffic. The sickle moon brushed the edge of the Ferris wheel. A gull squealed, sleepless and asynchronous.

"You want to have kids with me?" he finally asked. His scrutiny evoked an unfamiliar self-consciousness. Even had he not learned to judge beauty from men of the air, I was closer to his mother's age than his. Nor did I have Audrey's art of making men feel handsome with a glance. In truth, I found him no more appealing than he did me—save that I wanted children whose blood flowed in whitewater torrents.

"I hadn't meant to bring it up so soon," I said. "But it's something I hope to ask, one day."

"You hadn't mentioned *that*," said Frances. She frowned protectively, and I didn't mention that she might as easily bear children by Caleb. The combination seemed all too much like the accusations once raised against us.

"I don't *like* it," I said instead. "It's as indecent by our standards as anyone else's, and I wanted to know you both better first. But every time we talk it feels more awkward and more forced—and now you're arguing with the elders. Honesty, however indecent, seems the only way." I looked at the sand. "And then you can reject us in full knowledge."

Frances pulled the cigarette box from her purse, glared, lit one defiantly. "I'm not running away. I want family again. I even think it would be good for Freddy—as long as you don't force it on him."

"I would never force anything." Did she see, as I did, the hint of force in the Outer Ones' generosity? Or did she only focus on imagined danger from her own kin, we villains of her childhood stories? "I'm not even *asking* right now."

"But I've *got* a girlfriend!" Freddy burst out. His eyes shifted. "Sort of."

Frances's cigarette dangled. "Since when? Is this one of your new friends? Who is she?"

I felt pressed between embarrassments. Somehow, though I'd caught the edge of Deedee's jealous arguments with Caleb, I hadn't considered that our newfound relatives might also have preexisting entanglements. Then there was that "sort of." *Sort of a girlfriend? Sort of a girl? Sort of* human*?* I tried not to imagine how an Outer One would romance a lover, or to see this as yet one more bond they'd wrapped around him. I caught a moue of disappointment on Neko's face, and wasn't sure how to feel about that, either.

"Shelean would not object to your siring children with other lovers," said Nnnnnn-gt-vvv. "She might even be pleased."

"She doesn't take her body back, even when she's on Earth," explained Freddy. "She doesn't like it—she'd rather stay encircled. So we mostly just talk."

I'd heard of elders who, though they'd sired children on land, called themselves women after their metamorphoses. Like Charlie and Spector, men of the air would have no such recourse in patience—they had only one short lifetime, in the form they were born with. I could understand why such people, or others whose bodies chafed the contours of their minds, might prefer the Outer Ones' way.

"I'd be glad to meet her," I said. "I'm not trying to get in the way."

"We could go tonight, if you wish," said Nnnnnn-gt-vvv. "By tomorrow your investigators will be crawling all over the place, trying to interview all our travel-mates to find out if they really want to be there. It will be quieter now."

Freddy jumped up. "Yes, let's!" He reached down to help his mother to her feet. "I want to introduce you!"

He was far more enthusiastic about this than about introducing himself to the elders. I'd wanted to bring Freddy and Frances into the community I knew: the histories the elders could share firsthand, the campfire stories I'd known from childhood, the rituals and beliefs that made Innsmouth more than a small town of strangely shaped humans. But the more I pressed, the further he retreated.

Frances frowned. "Where is this?"

"Hunts Point," said Freddy. "We can take the train, and Nnnnnn-gt-vvv can fly."

I went to retrieve the others, unsure how many of us should go. We knew the situation better than we had this morning, but what little knowledge we'd gained masked greater uncertainties. For all the Outer Ones' protestations of friendliness, they were not *our* friends, and knew it.

"I'll go along," said S'vlk.

"What?" said Chulzh'th, and "How?" dropped from my lips before I could forestall it.

"I've not seen a city of the air in full flower since Rome. And I want to understand this lair of danger for myself. It's the dark of night, and there will be shadows a-plenty. All I need is a cloak."

"We don't *have* a cloak," I said, gently as I could. "And modern cities have artificial lights—people would see you, and be more inclined to call police than a priest."

"Perhaps a talisman to draw the darkness around me."

"Have you gold and silver to work?" asked Grandfather. "I'd rather go with them too. But this city guards itself with barricades of light. See how the horizon glows?"

Nnnnnn-gt-vvv's teeth-jarring buzz came close. The elders drew themselves up to their full heights, and I wished again that I could read Nnnnnn-gt-vvv's body language. Even Earth's strangest native creatures lifted themselves against gravity to show strength, or bent to it for respect. But the Outer Ones treated gravity as a foreign custom, one they might follow or ignore as it suited them.

"I could carry you," it said. "I'll promise safe passage, if you'll keep your claws to yourself. And no humans will mark our passing."

"You're not scraping my mind into one of your jars."

"Neither necessary nor possible, here. I'm strong enough to carry your body."

Grandfather stepped forward, glared. "This should be my task."

S'vlk snorted. "We both dislike them, but you have no patience. And you don't know what to look for."

"My grandchildren are going into their lair."

"And so you'll take everything you see too personally. I know them better than you do."

Nnnnnn-gt-vvv chittered—laughter? "Listen to you people squabble, even when you agree. It's a miracle the people of the water so long outlive the air and rock." It darted forward, and my vision grew fuzzy where its limbs seemed to *flow* toward the elders. Chitinous legs fogged around scaled shoulders—and the Outer One was gone. And S'vlk. And my grandfather. I whirled, scanning land and ocean, as if I might catch some glimpse of where they'd gone.

Chulzh'th howled, low-pitched anger echoing from the boardwalk.

"Chulzh'th!" I said, now as alert for ordinary intruders as for our missing companions.

She looked around, recalled to herself but still furious. "I'll be back before dawn. Find them." She ran down the beach and through the waves. She eeled into the water, and it closed around her.

CHAPTER 10

W here did it take them?" I demanded. I peered anxiously down the empty subway platform.

"Back to the mine," said Freddy. "I told you, they'll be fine. It's carried me a dozen times."

"Yes," I said. "But through where?"

"The outskirts. It's sort of the space next door to Earth. It's a little strange, but it's perfectly safe with one of them there."

"Yes," I said. I breathed in, seeking a scrap of patience. "But what happens if one of the elders lashes out, and it drops them?"

"It wouldn't . . ." said Freddy.

"S'vlk knows better," said Trumbull. But it wasn't S'vlk, reflexes tempered by millennia mapping the ocean's ridges, who I worried for most.

"I wish we had some way to let Caleb and Deedee know what was happening," I said. If I felt frightened enough, would they be able to track my terror? Through the confluence I could tell only that they were alive and near enough to avoid nightmares. I was dependent on them coming back to find us, at Tante Leah's or perhaps at Frances Laverne's apartment, when they felt ready to do so. The helplessness rankled, and relieved: whatever I met chasing after the elders, they'd be safe.

At last the train roared in. During the day, surrounded by chattering crowds, it had been an ordinary vehicle. Now it seemed gargantuan, on another scale entirely from our little cluster of life. The car echoed with our entrance.

I gripped one of the overhead bars and swayed clumsily, unable to pace and unwilling to sit down. The train shook and whined. "What in the void are 'outskirts'? Are they on the edge of the dreamlands? Or is this a different direction? People who enter the dreamlands physically almost never come out—but they can; I've heard about it." Rumors and fictions, which I pushed to the back of my mind. Few places were safe for humans to travel without some tie to home.

Freddy slouched on the bench, shoulders hunched. "How would I know?"

Frances: "You let them take you somewhere without telling you where it is?"

"I've only known the outskirts existed for a couple of weeks, okay? I'll bet you don't know exactly where this train is right now, either. How many feet underground, or what kind of rocks are around the tunnel? But you trust the conductor to get you where you're going, and you've never even met him."

"Do you . . . ?" I asked Trumbull.

She shook her head. "I don't know anything about Outer One terminology, let alone how it translates to what your family or the theoretical physics people at Miskatonic would call any given fold of reality." She forced a laugh. "For what it's worth, S'vlk says the bedrock in this area is mostly schist."

"We've got another problem," said Audrey. She tapped her watch. "Chulzh'th said she'd come back by dawn. It's 2 a.m. now, and it's two hours by train to Hunts Point even if the transfer goes quickly. I love the elders, but I think their idea of distances on land is 'close enough to smell salt' and 'everywhere else.' What's she going to do when we don't show up?"

"Show the patience she always demands of Grandfather, I hope," I said. But Chulzh'th was better at preaching patience than practicing it herself.

On the empty train I swayed, and fretted, and begged the gods, for two useless hours.

There were no guards now outside the Outer One lair—though I assumed the alarms that first warned them of our attention remained in place. Without that initial acknowledgment, the corridors and stairs leading from the facade down to their true abode felt more disturbing. But there was no question of leaving anyone behind this time. They'd be too conspicuous on the street, and no one was willing to wait outside.

Our descent reminded me uncomfortably of sneaking into Miskatonic's Crowther library: the dim-lit corridors, the oppressive sense of being watched. And worse, the knowledge that something dear to us was caged within. The dingy labyrinth seemed endless.

"Freddy," whispered Frances, "are you sure we're supposed to be here?"

At last we reached the indigo-lit room where we'd first met Kvv-vzht-mmmm-vvt and Nnnnnn-gt-vvv. They, or other Outer Ones, attended their control panels even now. My bones vibrated with the hum of their presence.

"'Scuse me," said Freddy. "Nnnnnn-gt-vvv came through the outskirts with a couple of guests—do you know where they are?"

The tone of the buzzing shifted, and inhuman harmonics said, "They got here a while ago. They're in the conversation pit."

Freddy led us through a doorway into stark white light. The contrast with the shadows of the control room was a shock. I closed my eyes on pain, opened them on serene horror.

Rough-hewn altars thronged the room, arrayed in rows. Actinic spotlights blazed onto their summits. Under the glare of each lay a body, naked. Each appeared human. Each was deathly still. Each bore, on their face, a frozen rictus of terror.

Nothing moved, save for a human in a blue smock examining one of the bodies with a box-like instrument.

He waved at Freddy. "Going out again?"

"Not yet, Rudy. Soon!"

None of the rest of us spoke—despite the technician's casual manner, the tableau stifled my ability to find words. Neko stretched a hand toward one spotlight, but withdrew before I could chastise her.

Almost anything would have been a relief, after that. The chamber beyond was mercifully dim. A deep emerald glow thrummed from the room's edges. Shallow steps circled a central depression. Clusters of figures sat, or crouched, on the steps. The room was large, and there was plenty of room for many such groups to find a place; the arrangement appeared casual rather than deliberate. In the slow green pulses, I saw silhouettes of Outer One and human and something else: metal cylinders about half a man's height and a foot across, etched with unreadable patterns.

Two of the human silhouettes hulked larger than the others, accompanied by an Outer One and two cylinders. I nearly tripped in my haste.

"Grandfather! S'vlk!"

"Granddaughter. There you are."

My relief at seeing them here and whole overwhelmed me. And yet, something in their posture seemed wrong. "Grandfather, is everything all right?"

"Of course. As you can see, we're in no danger." His voice sounded uncharacteristically calm. Impossibly so. Even if he'd forgiven the Outer Ones for their precipitous departure, he'd expect my fear and respond to it.

Beside him, S'vlk sat serene, eyes distant, as I'd often seen her during ritual or scientific reverie—but likewise impossible in the house of those she called enemies. Trumbull knelt beside her. "S'vlk," she whispered, "are you there?"

A fractional nod was the only response.

"What did you do?" Even as I turned on the Outer One—Nnnnnn-gt-vvv, I hoped—I was aware of being deep in their territory. Of my dependence on their alien mercy. Whatever fight the elders had put up, I couldn't match; I and all my companions were utterly without meaningful protection.

Nnnnnn-gt-vvv—I assumed, for sanity's sake—extended a clawed limb. Chitin, mottled with coral-like ridges, glistened unnaturally. The limb oozed ichor dark as the creature's wings and as impossible to bring into focus. It was all I could do not to recoil.

"They struck me," it said. "I defended myself, nothing more. They'll recover their capacity for irrational anger in a few hours. In the meantime they'll be calm, and capable of seeing us clearly. No harm done, I promise."

"You call that 'no harm'?" demanded Trumbull. "You attacked her mind!"

Tendrils rippled toward the professor. "The Yith who once inhabited her brain left permanent scars. So did the one who took yours. What I've done is as temporary and harmless as putting on a blindfold—or removing it."

She sat slowly on the steps, putting down a hand to steady herself. "How do you know these things?"

Laughter trilled from one of the cylinders, high and wild. A voice, well-matched to the laughter, followed: "They're good at seeing what's in front of them, of course. So rare in humans! Freddy, are these your family?"

"Yes." He ran fingers along the cylinder, leaving faint trails of sweat, and watched our reactions with lowered eyelids. "Aphra, meet Shelean."

"Honored," I said. I tried to sound sincere, but knew I failed. I wanted to scream, to lash out, to spill more of what passed for Nnnnnn-gt-vvv's blood. But the freedom of all our minds, and the return of the elders' wills, depended on our self-control. My eyes watered with suppressed fury and fear.

"Fine conversationalists, aren't they? Come around here, let me see everyone. There must be more of you."

The other cylinder spoke—a more genteel baritone with strange echoes behind it. "They're upset, Shelean; it's a poor time to judge them. Guests, my name can't be vocalized, but you can call me Scarlet."

"What better time to judge someone?" asked Shelean. Her tone grew academic. "It's under the greatest stress that you learn who to trust, isn't it? Who'll turn on you to prove a point, or to feel more in control? Is that you, Aphra of the water? Like your elders, tearing bodies apart out of fear?"

"That is not me," I said. "And it's not Grandfather, either. He thought he was under attack, and he fought back."

Freddy elbowed Shelean's cylinder. "Maybe not the time for philosophical discussions on the nature of character."

"Why not talk about it when it's relevant? But I do want to see the rest of them. No, forget the rest, I want *that* one—the pretty girl with the blond hair. What's your name, girl?"

"I'm Audrey Winslow. Pleased to meet you, of course." She lifted her chin, all fearless insouciance. She hid her true emotions far better than I.

"So very pleased! Turn around, won't you? Let me look at your ears."

Audrey obligingly turned her ear to the cylinder. "Shall I dance for you as well? I'll need a partner if I'm going to waltz."

"Oh, bravo, no need. And your palms? Oh, I recognize those whorls, I do! Clear as any maker's mark, even after a few generations."

Audrey looked, if possible, even more self-controlled. "I don't believe in palm reading. Whatever you thought you saw, you're mistaken."

"Nonsense," said Shelean. "My sweet Freddy's not the only one to find lost relatives today. Give us a kiss, cousin! My family made yours, sure as I recognize their signature on your skin."

I pulled Audrey back and stepped between her and the cylinder. She didn't resist. Her palm was slick with sweat.

"Relax," said Nnnnnn-gt-vvv. It sounded like an order. "Shelean's no danger to you, or your confluence-mate."

"You didn't tell me," I said to Freddy, not daring to look away from the cylinder, "that your lover was a Mad One Under the Earth."

"I'd much rather you called me K'n-yan," said Shelean. "Name my family whatever you like—but I've gone to so much trouble not to be mad."

"I didn't see it was any of your business," said Freddy. "She's told me all about her people, and like she said, she's different. Besides, you didn't tell me one of *your* friends was K'n-yan."

"I'm *not*," said Audrey.

"Only a little bit." Shelean giggled. "Such a pretty cross-breed. Such an interesting experiment. Do your blood-guards work? Those seemed so clever on the drawing board, but I wasn't sure."

Audrey's voice grew cold. "They saved my life. And nearly destroyed me."

"Isn't that always the way? You needn't glare so. I was just my brother's assistant—I'd almost as little choice as his pet subjects. But I talked him into releasing a couple into the wild, for comparison. I gave your family sun and sky and a place to grow with no magic warping you. Our senior sisters were furious."

"That's how we found her," said Nnnnnn-gt-vvv. "We go even into the K'n-yan caverns, and wait on the edges for those who seek solitude—or who flee the hounds of their law. I told you: We go everywhere. We talk to everyone."

Shelean: "They'd have warped me for the arena. My aunts didn't like how my brother ran his experiments at all, and it was so easy to pin the blame on me. Oh Audrey, you've no idea how glorious it is to be free of our unstable flesh!"

"I'm doing just fine in my flesh, thanks," said Audrey. She remained behind me, clutching my hand tight.

"Of course *you* are—it's the magic that breaks us, after all. But it breaks the body and the brain, not the mind. When I travel I have no magic at all, and the reason of a child! And now I've met one of our freed experiments. Oh, you're splendid!"

I heard Audrey inhale slowly. Her nails dug into my palms. "Why did you do it? You and your brother?"

"Orders, of course! Study inheritance, find out what makes us K'n-yan and others cattle. But not like we did—going out into the air is far too dangerous, you know. The people of the air are violent and untrustworthy, and plague-ridden besides. But my sweet brother insisted. How else could we know what's really inherited, and what traits are gifts of where you grow? I was so excited. He never let me come up myself, of course. No adventures for me until I met our wonderful hosts."

The elders had opinions about the K'n-yan—stronger than mine, for I'd never met one before. Until I'd learned a few months ago what Audrey carried in her blood, the sum of my experience had been stories in books, and a bas-relief panel in the temple of Dagon depicting prisoners beneath the earth that had given me fascinated nightmares as a child. They were a tale of warning: humanity's third branch, driven mad by their own magical abilities. And dangerous in that madness, for they could transform flesh into stone and stone into flesh at a whim, or dissipate either into nothingness.

Archpriest Ngalthr, when he learned what Audrey was, had gone into a full defensive crouch. The *Yith* had recoiled. Yet S'vlk and Grandfather watched this exchange incuriously. That frightened me more than Shelean.

Nnnnnn-gt-vvv was capable of excising every reflex I had, every instinct to protect my family. And it counted among its allies someone who, if she were returned to her body, could warp our flesh with a thought. Someone who held a much more natural, if still dangerous, influence over my newfound cousin.

Movement drew my eye and startled my already tense muscles. I squeezed Audrey's hand. Another Outer One skittered around the rim of the bowl, and flowed down to us in a fall of clicking claws.

"Nnnnnn-gt-vvv, this place reeks of terrified human—what are you doing?"

The answer came in their own language, an incomprehensible oscillation of frequencies.

"Now they'll be arguing again," said Scarlet.

From Shelean's cylinder, a dramatic sigh. "So they will. Cousin, don't be frightened. Let's talk more—I want to hear what your family's been up to! We never got to *check* on our comparison group, after all. And I can tell you everything about how we made you. We have so much to learn!"

"I don't want—" said Audrey, and then shook her head. "It would have been good to know about the blood-guards before tripping them. But we're not your experiments anymore. Whichever ancestor was unlucky enough to meet your brother, it was a long time ago."

"Oh," said Shelean, "surely not that long."

"Do you *know* when it was?" I asked. Trumbull's guest had thought it no more than four or five generations; Audrey had been dubious. Perhaps, I thought too late, she would rather not know.

"After all the pale plaguey people showed up. *You're* not plaguey, we fixed that. But before they built that cute new building I've seen in the city, the one with the spire."

The Outer Ones paused in their argument. "Shelean has been Kvv-vzht-mmmm-vvt's travel-mate for a hundred and thirteen years," said Nnnnnn-gt-vvv, "and mine for nearly as long. We don't know how long she'd been hiding before that, or how recent her transgression—without daylight or seasons, the K'n-yan don't mark time well."

"Ah." From the twitch of Audrey's fingers, she was matching this to what she knew of her family history, and what she didn't. Unlike me, she couldn't call up her ancestors and beg them to fill those gaps.

And what did it mean, that Shelean *was* family to her? So often I mourned my family lost on land, and the narrow path for our future generations. But I still had the buoyant certainty of my ancestry to draw on—generations of elders living and available for question, and above all trustworthy in their witness of my history. I looked again at Grandfather and S'vlk, wishing for the power to do more than speak politely and wait out their recovery. A word misspoken, and my fragile protection would shatter.

"How long do your people live?" I asked Shelean.

Nnnnnn-gt-vvv answered. "Longer than men of the air, far shorter than those of the water. Almost a thousand years, if their own kind don't break them first. Which is the safest bet—K'n-yan are even worse than men of the air for turning on each other."

"What about me?" Audrey finally lost control of her voice; it came out in a rough whisper. She recovered, though, and added in ordinary tones, "But I can't have inherited that kind of lifespan. The Winslows all age normally—even if Gram is doing all right at eighty-nine. I don't have any two-hundred-year-old great-great-grandfathers hanging around."

"The blood-guards might help, now that you've used them," said Shelean. "They're paying attention now. But we don't really know how long the hybrids live—we never got to measure." She sounded petulant. Freddy gave her a worried look, and slipped an arm around the canister.

Neko, who'd been hovering behind us, came forward and touched Audrey's other arm. "It's almost dawn. Have any of you slept?"

"Dozed a little on the subway," said Charlie.

I wished she hadn't brought it up; my head swam at the reminder of fatigue, but I didn't want to leave Grandfather and S'vlk unguarded. Given an hour and a place to meditate, I could probably push my body to ignore the two lost nights.

"I have to let Chulzh'th know—" I said, and stopped. I could think of no way to do so, and she could leave no message that would survive Coney Island's morning crowds. I hoped she knew that, hoped she would understand that my failure to return was not—gods willing—a signal of disaster. It was easy to summon from a distance, but sending any message more complicated than "come now" was beyond my skill. I realized that I'd been silent too long, chasing the problem in circles.

"Those feds will be back later," said Freddy. "You can sleep here until then. We have beds." His eyes slid to Frances, begging agreement. She stared at her clasped hands, knuckles taut.

"Here?" Horror seeped past my effort to project calm. I could only think of those altars, blinding lights illuminating nightmare eyes.

But it would be far worse to leave anyone I loved here alone.

CHAPTER 11

The dusty room full of cots was the most ordinary thing I'd seen in the Outer One lair, but the incongruity destroyed any suggestion of comfort. The beds seemed a tissue of normalcy, likely to tear under the weight of our resting bodies.

No metaphor, that. On the other side of sleep waited a riot of swamp-scented fungi.

I led Grandfather to one of the cots; he sat at my direction. I knelt beside him. My throat closed every time I looked at him, but I did it anyway.

"The solstice is in two days," he said. "You should be careful walking alone."

"I can't walk alone," I said. "There's no place in New York to *be* alone. It'll have to wait until another year."

He rumbled thoughtfully, then focused on one of the cots. "I can't sleep here," he commented mildly. "There's no place to float."

"Are you tired?" I asked. "Maybe if you just meditate a bit, you can rest."

"I can sleep standing up," said S'vlk. She had drifted to the wall. "But not in this body. You have to . . ." She twined her arms in a way I recognized from Trumbull. The professor gently detangled her limbs.

"We can rest together," said Trumbull, and pulled her off into a corner. There, she chivvied her cross-legged and spoke to her in low tones. S'vlk leaned against her. They spoke of the Archives, in the rhythm of recollections shared more for the sake of companionship than to bring back specific memories.

Sleep ought to provide escape. Even camp-scarred nightmares might have distracted from my current problems. But I'd sacrificed that solace to my study of dreamwalking.

Ïa, Cthulhu, help me sleep in the shadow of others' dreams. Teach me patience in the shadow of frustrated desire. Teach me stillness in the shadow of ever-changing threats.

. . . I saw your city. It is very beautiful. Lord Cthulhu, forgive me my impatience in looking on it so soon.

The prayer gave me strength, perhaps enough to gird myself against mushroom-scented dreams. It occurred to me that I should also make obeisance to Nyarlathotep, whose patronage the Outer Ones claimed. Better to call to the Thousand-Faced God directly than have near only the face he showed the Outer Ones. But a warm draught stirred the air beside my cot, and I opened my eyes as Audrey sat heavily beside me. The air was warm, but she shivered. Charlie already lay on the next bed over, deep in meditation, but Neko joined us. She put her arm around Audrey.

"We're all monsters here," she reminded her in a whisper.

"What am I going to do?" Audrey kept her voice low. "I thought I had it all figured out—how I needed to handle my . . . my ancestry. I never expected to meet one of them, let alone one of . . . of our creators. I'm afraid to ask anything, and I'd be an idiot not to. Or maybe I'm an idiot to talk to her at all. Suppose she tells me how their magic works before I can stop her? If she says the wrong thing I could turn into . . . I could end up as mad and cruel as them, just from hearing the wrong thing." Her head drooped over her knees, and she wrapped her arms around a pained laugh. "Oh Aphra, your cousin has the *worst* taste in girls."

I should have been able to sense Audrey's heart and breath as they followed the rhythm of her anguish. Should have been able to share with her the little comfort I'd gained from praying. But in my exhausted state, the threads binding the confluence echoed distantly. Even my control over my own body was frayed.

"I know you," I told Audrey. "And you know yourself, better than anyone else I've met on land. Even when the black rose in your blood, you saw it coming, and we had time to react. I don't think she can force you to become anything just by talking."

"Did you listen to her?" asked Neko, her tone strangely gentle. "She may sound frightening—but from what you've said, the K'n-yan are crueler to each other than to any outsider, and it sounds like she got pretty close to the bottom of the heap. Everyone else joined the Outer Ones because they want to travel. She's here because she wanted to live free, because she wanted to control her own mind—same as you. Why would she take that from you, when she said you should be grateful for it?"

"I did listen," said Audrey. "She may say she likes being sane. But she doesn't *sound* sane."

"When I'm scared my English gets very precise and I add Nihongo no tango, like Mama. And Aphra sounds like a Victorian lady who gargles when she swears. If Shelean grew up around people who talk that way—if madness is her cradle tongue—she's going to sound mad even if she learned sane dialects later."

"Huh," said Audrey.

"I think," I said with effort, trying not to sound Victorian, "that Audrey and I should take a quick look together at the local dreamlands, see whether Charlie's started on the wards we need to sleep here safely, and help him finish up. And then we should all sleep. This is a terrible place for it, but these are the beds we have."

"We've slept on worse," said Neko.

Audrey Winslow—March 1948:

"Secrets passed down from ancient civilizations," says the boy. He pauses dramatically, and shifts his hand from my arm to my thigh. The pause lingers anticlimactically as he waits to see if I'll object. Finally he continues: "Pre-human civilizations. Even some of the professors believe it. Researchers in math and physics—they find insight in old texts that are supposedly folklore."

I lean into his touch, and run my fingers down his arm. "I heard that the Pnakotic Manuscript drops hints about atomic warfare. But our librarians at Hall claim the book doesn't even exist."

The disused lab glitters around us. Fluorescent light reflects off glassware through a mist of cobwebs. The boy swears he nabbed the only key from his professor. Whether that's really the only copy is anyone's guess; the danger is part of the fun. Like the pleasure of touch, the little pockets of freedom opened by the Hall School's imperfect chaperonage. But the occult pillow talk is the real point of the exercise.

Shirts are shed as he spins tales of volumes hidden deep in Crowther Library's restricted stacks. So far, no one's even gotten me in the door. It's fun to talk about powers that men know not, but the powers forbidden to women are more mundane.

I want these things to be real: the intelligences from beyond the Earth; the cities that rose in golden splendor millennia before our own histories begin; the scholars who consort with dark forces, who sacrifice air and light and their human forms in exchange for unimaginable secrets. I want to see them. I want to talk with them, to decide for myself whether that deal is worth taking.

But if those deals are anything like these furtive exchanges—touch for touch, safety for whispered rumor—then I think they must be well worth it.

The shallows around the Outer One lair were safe, and shiveringly strange. I discovered that the riotous spectrum of fungi that girded the place were a deliberate ward, better than any we might set ourselves. Within them lay a well-tended garden. Ribboning walls rose eel-like to mark clearings and grottos; swift lines of light darted along the paths between. The whole structure was bound through by multicolored filaments—I suspected the root system of the mushroom ward, and carrier of the alarm Mary set off when she took her sample.

Strange creatures followed those lines: serpents with hominid faces, crystalline spiders with too many legs, a spike-backed tadpole, a musk-scented blob that clung to a single point of air for long moments before writhing into blurred speed. Outer Ones walked here as freely as on our own plane.

"They're not dreaming," suggested Audrey. "They're in both places at once."

"Maybe more," I agreed. I felt my own mind's limits keenly, able to perceive only one aspect of reality at a time—at best.

New York's heartbeat was a distant rhythm, passed through a single thread of the Outer One's wards. My mind hewed close to that root, and waited for dawn.

≈≈≈

"Aphra! Child, wake up." The voice, a low, hoarse whisper from a throat not meant for whispering. A muscled hand on my shoulder, scales dry and rough against my neck.

Grandfather crouched by my cot, crest wilted, eyes veined red and dilated wide.

I sat up fast. "Don't shout."

His laughter was as muted as his voice had been, too low for airborn ears. "I wasn't, but thank you for the warning. I have more self-control than you seem to think."

My cheeks warmed. "You attacked Nnnnnn-gt-vvv. It gave you reason, but . . ."

"S'vlk attacked. I joined in rather than let her fight alone."

"S'vlk?" My own voice rose in shock.

He put a finger to my lips. "Old fears can be the deadliest. S'vlk has honed her hate for millennia—and though she's met them more often than I, it's been a long time since she needed to do so. I've dealt with them face to face all too often and all too recently. I remember the forbearance needed to come out with any advantage. We must practice it now—and convince S'vlk to do the same when their enchantment releases her."

S'vlk slept with her head in Trumbull's lap. Trumbull dozed over her, head shifting as she threatened to overbalance. Audrey often found her drooped so over her desk.

"They haven't threatened to hold us here," I said. "Do you think they will?"

"Not unless they have cause. But—" He lifted my hand, examined my palm, pricked it with one sharp claw. I winced, but didn't pull away. He sketched a quick sigil on my skin with the blood, murmured softly, then tasted the remnant on his fingertip. He nodded. "You seemed yourself, but best to check. The Outer Ones are artists of flesh, but they cannot change the nature of your blood."

"They can look like us?" I whispered.

"I doubt even an Outer One has enough artistry to make itself appear human. But I once spent two hours with a man I thought my ally before learning he was one of their thralls, wearing a mask of my friend's face and taught his manners of speaking and standing."

I looked around the room. I'd know, surely, if Charlie or Audrey were not where my eyes told me they lay. Trumbull had been in my sight until I fell asleep, then held down by S'vlk's weight. Neko . . . mistaking an ally was one thing, but I'd spent more time with Neko than any living being other than my brother. I knew every shade of pain and hope that shifted her shoulders, how she whimpered in the throes of nightmare. Surely no deception could be that good. But Grandfather . . .

He bared teeth in recognition of my realization, and pricked his own palm where the scales were thin. He drew the sigil on his own flesh, and offered me his claw-tip. Uncertain, I tasted. For a moment, I saw nothing, heard nothing, but felt around me the vast pressure and monstrous currents of the deep ocean. A sense of belonging suffused me, of connection with something huge and inhuman, and with schools of tiny human things that shared that connection.

The feeling faded, and I looked again on my grandfather. "A simple test," he said, "but it takes more study than you've accomplished on your own. As you learn more, you'll be able to taste more—health and age, even traces of memory. But if nothing else, you can be sure I'm an elder."

"Yes, Grandfather." I leaned against him and took comfort in his strength. The others were beginning to stir on their cots. "I want to get out of here. But the FBI agents will arrive soon, and we'll need to watch them as well. If they start trouble, I need to know."

"Agreed." But he stiffened against me. "Aphra Yukhl, do I recall that our cousin introduced us to a Mad One?"

"Yes. She says she's here to escape her body's madness. But she helped perform the experiments that created Audrey's family. Audrey's terrified of her, and I suspect she's right to be. I don't know what to do."

He snorted. "Gods save us from all creatures who can't keep to one shape. If we find the ghosts of ancient dragons down here, and a worm grown fat on a wizard's flesh, we'll have a full menagerie of dangers."

I blinked at the list of half-remembered legends. "Was that advice?"

He cuffed me lightly. "I think you're right—hopefully Khur S'vlk can be persuaded to stay here until nightfall. Then we'll need to find our way back to the ocean, not by the route we came. I don't trust Nnnnnn-gt-vvv's patience, nor S'vlk's. Can Caleb help? Is he somewhere you can reach him?"

"No—except through the most basic connection of our confluence. That's what I wanted to tell you. George Barlow and his team are in town, investigating disappearances that turn out to be the Outer Ones' doing. Virgil Peters insulted Miss Dawson, and Caleb wouldn't put up with it. We'd been arguing anyway, about whether to work with them or investigate separately. They left to get a hotel room on their own; that's all I know. I haven't even been able to tell them that we found Freddy."

"Tch. That boy needs to learn to make better use of his temper. But I'm glad he's elsewhere. Outer Ones swim in murky waters."

"*Meigo,* they are called." S'vlk rose from where she'd slept, and her glare was venomous. "Where is the slime-grown corpse-creature that tried to steal my mind?"

"Nearby, and well-protected," said Grandfather. "Sheathe your talons until the current holds us up."

"S'vlk." Trumbull's slender hand seemed too small to restrain the elder's muscled forearm. "Please don't attack it again. The result was terrifying enough the first time. I need—we need you here and whole."

S'vlk's whole body shuddered as she closed her eyes and drew a slow breath. Another then, slower and seeming equally painful. But she opened her eyes and nodded. "You're right. I'll control my temper until it's wise to show it." She sat on the nearest cot. Neko, stirring awake, curled her legs out of the way. She rubbed bleary eyes and examined the black-crested storm, clouds still roiling gray, at the foot of her bed. She bit her lip.

Even for me, it was hard not to see S'vlk in this mood as some natural force, a small god whose wrath I should sensibly cower from. But there was something younger in her eyes when she said, in R'lyehn, "My eldest daughter loved to clamber through the scree of the foothills. The elders swore them haunted, and forbade her to explore alone, but still I could do nothing to keep her in the camp. She always brought back fruit or nuts or a brace of game as excuse—until one night when we saw the sky full of wings. She would never hide from what she didn't understand. My brave, foolish child.

"The elders went with me to negotiate, and I saw her body still as death. Her mind was beyond any star we've named, and they swore

I'd go into the water before she returned. I saw her again many years later, unaged, and when I tasted her blood it was bone dry. She was no longer a child of the water. She claimed her journey worth the cost."

Grandfather knelt before her, and took her hands. "I mourn with you. I share your desire to avenge lost daughters. The sleeping god's lesson lies heavy, sometimes."

"Patience." In R'lyehn, the word was half-sigh: *yrahl.* "You've lived the blink of a mortal's eye, and you've never had to wait more than a few decades for anything."

In the hunch of Grandfather's shoulders, I saw my own bristling irritation at an elder's rebuke. But he said: "It's not my place to judge the difficulty of your wait—only whether we can afford a fight in this place and time. If you seek your vengeance now, you'll find death or enthrallment instead."

Trumbull understood R'lyehn better than she spoke it. In English, she said, "Your daughter is recorded in the Archives."

S'vlk released a softer breath. "Yes, she is. And in the Archives, my own life covers a few scant pages. I'll follow your counsel."

"Good." Grandfather rocked back on his heels. "For now we'll watch, and learn."

I heard shuffling in the hall, turned to see Freddy in the doorway. Amid all the strange noises down here, I couldn't be sure how much he'd heard before catching my attention. At least he didn't speak R'lyehn. He'd be unlikely to approve of either S'vlk's mourning or her desire for vengeance.

"Your G-men are here," he said.

CHAPTER 12

My scalp prickled. I wouldn't have chosen to greet Barlow's team red-eyed and sweaty, wearing the previous day's rumpled dress.

Fortunately they were distracted. I'd missed Barlow and Peters's first encounter with the Outer Ones—though it must have gone well since both seemed cognizant of their surroundings. (Would the talismans that protected them against the Yith also defend against the Outer Ones' mental arts? I made a note to ask Mary if we might bargain for extras.) But I did get to see them gape at the elders. Spector, who knew my grandfather already, nodded at him easily and proffered a bulging paper bag, smelling of yeast and fish.

"Thank you," said Charlie fervently. I took a bagel thickly caked with poppy seeds and garlic, and a slice of smoked salmon, artifacts of a sunlit world above where bodily needs were treated as commonplace.

Grandfather extended his hand and waited while Barlow made up his mind to shake it. Green scales enveloped pink skin. Talons scraped close. "I'm Obed Marsh. I've heard much about you." He bared his teeth. "You were impolite to my granddaughter, this past winter."

Barlow glanced my way. "I apologized."

"And so you should have." A gentler smile, though Barlow might not recognize it as such. Peters, he pointedly did not address.

"My grandfather and S'vlk came here last night," I told them. I hoped the others would follow my lead in omitting S'vlk's title. "They also wanted to meet the Outer Ones' companions."

"And learn more about this expansion of their territory." S'vlk wasn't trying to be menacing, but the men stepped back anyway. Kvv-vzht-mmmm-vvt and Nnnnnn-gt-vvv—I assumed, I still couldn't tell them apart—watched this interplay. They drew nervous looks, but never that easy dance of body language, negotiating for space and status. For all the difference between air and water, we apes understood each other.

"You gave us twenty-five names," said one of the Outer Ones. "Of those, twenty-three are among our companions, and seventeen are here today. We'll introduce you to them, and they can assure you of their well-being."

Our route avoided the room where the bodies lay, and I was grateful. In the conversation pit, the agents split up to speak with several humans, some accompanied by Outer Ones and some on their own. The room dampened noise, so that I heard only the occasional voice raised in anger or enthusiasm. One of the Outer Ones found me near the lip of the bowl.

"Speak with me," it said.

I looked for the elders, wondering why it would choose me when more experienced negotiators were available. I fell back on etiquette. "What can I do for you?"

"You understand the cities of the sea. Humans there live, if not in peace, then with the moderation and adaptation needed to preserve themselves in the face of change. You believe you'll survive so long as this world remains habitable, and it seems plausible."

"We know we will." But of course the Outer Ones didn't trust the testimony of the Yith—and, if they never went to the Archives, would never read the firsthand testimony.

"But you're also working with these state agents. You understand the drives that push them toward extinction."

"We know *something* will." *Understand* was too strong a word. "It doesn't seem fair to blame them for those drives. All species pass, sooner or later."

"We endure, because we change." A soft chitter, underscoring the ubiquitous buzz. "You don't recognize me, do you? I'm Kvv-vzht-mmmm-vvt."

"I'm sorry. I'm trying to learn to tell you apart."

"Yet you cannot bear to look at our wings."

There was no answer but to look at them. It felt like staring at an eclipse, too bright and too dark at once. My vision blurred, and I had to look away. "If there are clues there, my eyes aren't made to see them. I'm sorry."

"You haven't decided to be ready. But you needn't pretend—just ask who you're talking to. We're all different people, and I'd like to think that matters to you."

"I'm sorry. I'll ask." I shook my head. "You wanted to talk about men of the air?"

"Yes. I want to know how long you believe they'll endure."

I shook my head. "There are events we believe still lie in humanity's future. But we could be wrong—we could have missed them. Or they could be brief, empires that rise and fall in the space of a month, leaving a swift deep scar on history. There could be population crashes sufficient to drive us from the land—and once gone, we won't be able to return."

"I don't want an answer based on your patchy histories of the future. Based on your own observation."

It seemed hubristic to answer. "Men of the air are growing more dangerous to themselves. A moment of foolishness at the wrong time, or a moment of wisdom at the right, could decide between extinction and a million more years of history. But why are you asking me? You boast of seeing so many species live and die."

"It's *your* species. The Deep Ones are eternal observers—from your limited vantage point, you see much." A ripple of something painful on the edge of my vision. "The question is a point of contention among our colonists here. People on all sides cite the same points you do."

Freddy had told me to ask: "And what do you believe?"

"That humanity is at risk, but can be saved."

I thought the same—but couldn't believe we were in perfect accord. "Saved how? By whom?"

"That depends. Maybe you can do it on your own. Maybe you need help."

"What kind of help?"

Tentacles stretched and contracted. "What do you think you need?"

Perhaps they were asking me *because* I was unprepared. I had enough power to make agreements, but was too inexperienced to avoid the perils. If I got nothing else out of this conversation, I was gaining experience. I parried the question. "You call us observers, but you claim to have been on Earth since before we painted caves. What do *you* see, that we might miss?"

Kvv-vzht-mmmm-vvt's body seemed to settle among spindled limbs. "There are the obvious danger signs, of course. Fission weapons, and fusion soon. The immediate destruction isn't even the issue, so much as mutations to fragile genetic structures. Then there are the industrial scars: changes to air composition, temperature ranges, agricultural capacity. Humans can be responsible as individuals, but as a species you've no institutions to coordinate stewarding your ecology."

"We're capable," I said.

"*I* think so. But these are the obvious threats—any species that wasn't alarmed by them wouldn't be smart enough to build them in the first place. If a species survives carbon-based industries and city-killer weapons, it's by developing some method of stewardship. But that takes trust. And here, we *have* observed a pattern: you can predict such trust by how a species uses weaker magic. That's where humans, on their own, fail."

"Men of the air barely use magic at all." Perhaps that was the problem. For me, magical practice forced perspective, a patience that didn't come naturally. For Caleb, who scarcely remembered a community before the camps, the confluence offered a bone-deep trust that his bitterness couldn't smother.

"But we've seen how you use it when you do," said Kvv-vzht-mmmm-vvt. "Magic by its nature blurs the boundaries between individuals. The trapezohedron lets us share a thousand points of view, understanding that transcends any one set of senses. Every vision conveys what a real person sees, or once saw."

That view of R'lyeh, guards rising in response to . . . what? "One of you?"

"Yes, but not the way you mean. Freddy is one of us, and Shelean, and all our travel-mates. Species is meaningless to our community."

I should not have, but— "You make no distinction between Outer Ones and captive minds?"

"They're no such thing." I sought anger or amusement in Kvv-vzht-mmmm-vvt's mild tone, but could read its voice no better than its body. "We share our abilities and knowledge willingly—that's an end in itself, not just a side effect of some abstract search for knowledge."

"I'm sorry. I didn't intend any offense."

Kvv-vzht-mmmm-vvt bent its head toward me, and I froze as tendrils whispered against my hair and pricked my forehead. "Most of the water's people wouldn't have—they think being a Yithian 'captive' a great honor. You're more ambivalent."

I pulled back. "You were saying. About magic and boundaries."

"You illustrate the problem yourself. You flinch when I understand you too well—but I've been reading humans since long before you were born. You want to believe some boundaries too essential to blur. You choose to make the differences between us a barrier."

"You think humanity can't avoid another war . . . because you make some of us uncomfortable?"

"It's one example. The blurring of boundaries that magic requires can build trust or destroy it—depending on how it's understood, and used. After your first atomic explosion, we surveyed the species. Our standard practice. We sent emissaries across the world to study wizards skilled at sharing bodies or sensations, and witnesses of great and terrible workings. We learned that humans usually practice such arts to glorify individuals, not to understand each other. They break social bonds and fan paranoia."

"Wait." My mind raced; I struggled to parse the core of what it had said from the larger implications. In January, investigating rumors that Russian agents had learned the secret of stealing bodies, we'd visited the last surviving witness of the last such crime I knew. We'd found him in Pickman Sanitarium, grown truly mad from his years there. And he'd mentioned earlier visitors who'd asked the same questions. "Were *you* the ones who asked Daniel Upton about body theft in Innsmouth?"

"The name sounds familiar. Yes, among many others."

"That's . . . a relief, after a fashion."

"Why?"

"We knew someone had talked with him about it, but we didn't know who, or what they wanted. We were worried that someone wanted to repeat Ephraim's crime."

"And thus in trying to learn more, we added to your paranoia. I'm sorry. It's difficult to avoid, once a species starts down that path."

Kvv-vzht-mmmm-vvt's suggestions came perilously close to my own fears. Scant years after our latest world-shaking war, tensions were climbing again. Russia, once an ally, pushed into new territory; few other powers would countenance that for long. The mere suggestion of magical weapons in their arsenal had sparked answering American research. I still kept to myself the strongest evidence that their fears were well-founded. My people made body theft a capital crime for a reason: loyalty could too easily tear out its own throat, when every skin might hide an enemy.

I couldn't trust the Outer One. The oldest and wisest people I knew, whom I *did* trust, warned me against it. But like Barlow with his foolhardy experiments, the Outer Ones would act whether I offered them direction or no.

It had said something earlier . . . I realized I was chewing my lip. "You mentioned 'wizards.' More than we knew about. You had some way to find out who was practicing those arts." I tilted my head briefly toward Peters and Barlow. I suspected Kvv-vzht-mmmm-vvt could read my body language far better than I could read its. "Their paranoia runs deep, and it grows from a lack of knowledge. They see enemies everywhere if none make themselves obvious. If you have a spell, a device, that can tell for sure whether someone is truly themselves, that would be the best help you could offer. Barlow, and others like him, could *know* when they had nothing to fear."

Tentacles swept one direction, then the other—was it shaking its head? "We learn who practitioners are by long observation, and by reading minds. Our life-shaping arts are strong and well-practiced, but we can no more give you telepathy than wings."

"Oh." The answer was disappointing, on multiple levels.

"Those ones there—" Tentacles rippled toward Barlow. "You've spoken before of the power they wield in fear. If they're connected with leaders who share their fears, perhaps we can teach them better ways. I'd like to learn more—first from your testimony, and then I'll speak with them directly."

"What do you want to know?" I tried to balance my caution with the chance of gaining something from this strange, exhausting week.

"I want to share your perspective. The trapezohedron can not only provide understanding, but record it. What you've seen of these people's fears could be invaluable. We could know them better, and others like them. Perhaps with that knowledge we could offer something that would ease their terror."

My first instinct was desire: on the trapezohedron's altar was a chance to see R'lyeh again. My vision had been terrifying, compelling—and blood-deep reassurance that however difficult it might be to build Innsmouth, another home waited for me, solid and sure.

But my gut yearning faded before sensible revulsion. Memory is precious and perilous. To share our journals with the Yith was a sacrament. To share my own perceptions with any lesser creature—especially with someone who might use my experiences *now,* for practical ends that I could not control—seemed more vulnerability than I should risk. My memories were full of secrets. Things I'd promised Spector never to share—even if the Outer Ones already knew them. Other secrets I held close for the sake of the world, or for a single friend.

And yet, the dangers Kvv-vzht-mmmm-vvt described were real. Humanity walked a precipice. We tried to hold them back from the edge—as well as we could on our own, at great price. Weighed against the chance of giving my species another fraction of safety, almost any cost was meaningless.

"Neko should come with me. She doesn't practice magic herself, so she sees what we've done from a different perspective." I couldn't ask Kvv-vzht-mmmm-vvt about the threats Grandfather had mentioned—the suggestion of doppelgangers might infuriate them if mentioned aloud, whether rumor or truth. But I could ensure myself well-chaperoned, and by someone who wouldn't object to the duty.

I also knew Neko wouldn't argue with my decision. I didn't try to catch the elders' attention before we left the room.

The shimmer of the altar room was still disorienting, but easier this time.

"How do we do this?" asked Neko. She touched the altar gingerly. The metallic gray surface seemed an anchor in the shifting atmosphere.

"Think on what you wish to share," said Kvv-vzht-mmmm-vvt. It leaned its head over the carved box. "You need not visualize everything, only invoke the set of understandings. Let me know when you are ready."

I leaned back on the cushions and thought about Barlow and his team. An image came to me: polished shoes in the snow, as I lowered my eyes at gunpoint. Other flashes: Mary's voice dissecting my brother's desperate testimony, suggesting talismans for interrogation. The smell of Peters's breath as he accused me of treason. A room etched with glowing gears. The rush of airless cold.

Mary cradling a girl's dead body.

"I'm ready," I said.

I braced myself, but the nausea was worse than I'd remembered. Every sense told me that something was *wrong*. Acid coated my tongue, ears cringed against a piercing shriek, fingers rubbed the raw edge of a pustulant wound. Then all died but vision and sound.

I sat bound in a Miskatonic administrative office. A uniformed man tied a blindfold across my face. Fear and anger surged, muted by my absence of heartbeat and breath. I attended with all my effort to the voices around me, labeling for Kvv-vzht-mmmm-vvt's benefit the people who called me a spy, trying to explain their motivations.

Now I stood outside the library. A siren screamed. Around me, students exhaled fog into the night. By the great doors, Barlow approached the college president and head librarian. I thought about what he wanted in that building, how he'd exploit the commotion to steal books on forbidden arts.

Then Barlow, Peters, Mary—and their stolen students—arrayed around a vast diagram in a basement lit only by candles. They insisted I explain my presence. I could not move, and could not feel the cold I knew was there—cold without which this scene made no sense. I struggled for comprehension, pushed the dissonance away, and tumbled paralyzed—

To earlier terror, to guards training guns on a line of people with bulging eyes and thick necks, faces streaked by salt. One man wore a gold ring engraved with his wife's name; they shoved gun barrels against his chest, demanded he remove it now now now—

But the desert is nothing without heat, and I fell onto a beach, snow swirling around Trumbull and Mary as they discussed how to save my life. I couldn't feel the cold—

And then at last, wrestling with my own incomplete memories, I dove again into deep water. No city beckoned. Instead, through sight that drank in the least light and gathered heat, I saw the great vent. Hot-bright water streamed upward, a vast and deadly fountain. Life clustered: fungous cacti and lichen, poppy red. Long darting things with glowing spots along their sides, and fish thick with insulating fat. Scuttling crabs, utterly colorless, and an octopus with limbs like barren branches. Starry tentacles flowed from a conical shell.

And there were elders. Webbed hands and feet, muscled limbs, crests furled against skulls, gills flared wide. They moved like dancers. They eased their way around the strange forms, which they examined with lens and talisman. Wards glowed softly, flaring with the power needed to filter the vent's toxic gases.

At the edge of vision something moved, too vast to take in. An eye blinked and vanished, and an elder looked up. I heard: *kraken?*

Then I gasped with lungs suddenly real. Neko's floral perfume filled my mouth. She leaned against me, taking shuddering breaths, head pressed into my shoulder.

"I'm okay," she said. "I'm okay. Just need a minute. I was flying, I don't think . . ."

"That was unpleasant," I said. Except for the last vision, the memory that hadn't been mine. Had it been meant as trade? And if so, who had I traded with?

"I saw," said Kvv-vzht-mmmm-vvt. It returned the trapezohedron to the finely etched box, a hint of reverence in its movements. "Your FBI agents seem fickle allies, at best."

"It's more accurate to call them fickle enemies. They help us only reluctantly."

Anemone movements stilled. Wing-tips quivered. "We should go back now. Your elders are frightened by your absence."

CHAPTER 13

W here did they take you?" demanded Grandfather. "They said you went willingly."

"As they always say," added S'vlk.

"I did," I said. "I took Neko for a chaperone. And I came back. It's barely been half an hour."

Grandfather grabbed my arm, shark-swift, and scratched my still-sore palm with his talon. I stifled a shriek. He wanted to be sure of me, and I couldn't blame him. He tasted my blood and relaxed perceptibly. "It's been near an hour since last I saw you. Neko, here."

"We're fine, Ojiisan, I promise." But she offered him her wrist, and received a gentler version of the same test. I couldn't imagine how he'd distinguish her blood from any other man of the air, but the ritual seemed to reassure him.

In R'lyehn, Grandfather continued. "Aphra, we're among a pod of dolphins, smart and needle-sharp, and you swim off on your own. What were you thinking?"

In English that question would have been rhetorical; in our tongue it demanded a blunt response. "I needed to do something danger-ous, and knew you'd forbid it. So I made the safest choice I could and didn't ask permission."

He heaved a sigh, hoarse with his hours out of water. "Aphra,

I don't have grandchildren to spare. Can't you restrain your disobedience until you're grown?"

"The thing needed doing now."

"And this necessary, unspeakable danger . . ." prompted S'vlk.

I managed to keep my eyes from Barlow's team. They were still engrossed in conversation with a stack of canisters, but I didn't want to risk their notice.

"Our host wants to hold off humanity's extinction. In my judgment, if I told it we needed no help, it would still act on its own. It sees the state's fears as a threat. So do we. The Outer One"—I avoided names, assuming that any sapient would be attracted by their own— "asked to see my memories. They have a device—" S'vlk dropped to a crouch and hissed.

When my own defensive reflexes flared, I could intimidate most men of the air. Now *I* froze, and Grandfather stiffened. Neko's hands flew to her mouth. "S'vlk-sama," she whispered.

"You do *not* let them touch your mind," said S'vlk. "Yringl'phtagn, we must leave, now. Your granddaughter is in danger."

"But we—" I gestured helplessly at the conversation pit, where my confluence and the FBI agents sat engrossed in a dozen conversations.

"Khur S'vlk," said Grandfather. "It's full daylight out there, and a thousand mortals between us and the sea."

"We'll ford that current," she said, "after we escape their influence. I *am* being patient, I *am* biding my time, but we'll lose everything if I'm the only one who takes this danger seriously."

I stared, frozen now by uncertainty rather than fear. S'vlk had a long history with the Outer Ones. She might well know more about the trapezohedron than I did. She was also frightened and driven by rage. And in my experience—admittedly much briefer than hers— fleeing anything other than the immediate threat of destruction merely invited pursuit.

"We can leave," I said. "But not without a plan. You know how dangerous Outer Ones can be, but I know how dangerous modern men of the air are. Step outside uncloaked in daylight, and someone will shoot you."

"My stubborn granddaughter is right," said Grandfather. "Aphra, obey me this time. Gather your people, and we'll decide what's to be done."

This, at least, was easy, even if it took long minutes during which I constantly glanced at S'vlk for signs of erupting impatience. And, my own fear summoned by hers, at the Outer Ones for signs that they might object to our departure.

Considering where we were, and what we needed, I also gathered Spector. He sat with Charlie on one of the pit's broad steps, knees up and leaning toward a canister. The first time I'd seen him in that pose, I'd thought him a praying mantis, sleek and monstrous in his black suit. Now, surrounded by the uncountable limbs of the Outer Ones, all I could see was another human. I heard him mention Poland as I approached, some shared reference to the warfront there.

"Mister Spector," I told him. "The elders want to leave now, and not the way they came. Can you help?"

He looked over his shoulder. "I take it they refuse to wait until dark. Isn't patience supposed to be one of your virtues?"

Charlie stood, wincing and rubbing his back. "How well do most humans live up to their virtues?"

"Do you have any idea how to get them out of here in broad daylight?" I asked. "I don't have so much as a cloak." I wanted to leave too, now that the possibility was near enough to consider. I wanted a room with only people I loved and trusted, where I could beg advice or absolution, where I could safely submit to my family's judgment.

Frances appeared beside me. She hugged her chest, hunched her neck. "Are we leaving now?" Her voice dropped. "Please tell me we're leaving. I don't trust these people, and I don't know what to make of Freddy's . . . girl."

Spector answered. "As soon as we can figure out a way to get an eight-foot-tall—that is, Captain Marsh and Miss S'vlk—out of the

Bronx without attracting attention. I've always sworn there was no good reason to own a car in New York, but I should've been more imaginative. I don't suppose you own a pickup, Miss Laverne?"

Her lips quirked. "Or an ice cream truck?"

"Could we buy one?" I asked, then answered myself: "Not in the next hour." I wished, and not for the first time, that Trumbull's guest would suddenly reappear. She'd had a penchant for cutting easily through this type of obstacle, and could likely have simply hidden our presence on the street.

"Are you sure they couldn't get a ride back the way they came?" asked Spector. "I understand why they don't want to, but it does seem the easiest way."

"S'vlk is this close to taking her frustrations out on them *without* any further provocation." *Gods, we're going to have to stay here until it gets dark. I have no idea how to keep this under control.* I looked around for Audrey, and realized she'd been huddling uncharacteristically by the wall, as far from the canisters as possible. She caught my gaze, and hurried over.

"Oh god, can we go now?" she asked.

"That's what I'm trying to figure out. Have you got a brilliant idea for hiding the elders on the street?"

"Huh." It was worth asking just to see the distress fall from her expression, replaced by bemused thoughtfulness. "There's no way to keep them from standing out. But we don't need them to blend in, we just need them not to look like the sort of scary weird thing that would make people call the police. If these guys have fabric lying around, and maybe something to make a mask with, we could have everyone out of here in half an hour."

I threw my arms around her. "Audrey, you're brilliant." Then I drew back, thinking the plan through. "We'll have to ask *them*, won't we?"

"Awkward as this whole situation is—yeah, I don't think we're getting out of this party without saying goodbye to the hosts. You should talk to Freddy. He's the one you really want to make a good impression on, right?"

I would have rather sent Audrey. Men tended to do what she wanted without thinking too hard about why. But this was, in fact, my responsibility. And I suspected that the canister against which Freddy sprawled, deep in conversation, was Audrey's ostensible creator. I wasn't going to ask her to face Shelean again today, not when she'd so clearly been avoiding her.

I paused a few steps away, and considered Freddy. Except for our shared blood, he was nothing I wanted in a mate. He scarcely seemed the same species as the salt-wise scholars and sailors I'd grown up with. When I imagined lying with him, I felt hollow.

And yet a hunger for magic and home, kin to my own, must have driven him to this circle of *meigo* and Mad Ones.

"Freddy," I said, and stumbled as I tried to explain my urgency in a way that didn't insult his beloved Outer Ones. "We need to get Khur S'vlk and my grandfather back to the water. Acolyte Chulzh'th will fret more the longer they're away, and the dry air isn't good for them. Audrey suggested we pull together costumes so their natures wouldn't be obvious on the street, even if we can't make them blend in. I don't suppose there's any fabric around here, or leftovers from a masquerade . . ."

The cylinder laughed. "Clever girl! This city is full of unexpected things; they just need to lie about what sort of surprise they are. Sweet boy, there's a storeroom down the third hall over, second door on the left—no, fourth—that's full of clothes and masks. All you need for a night on the town, whether you've got gills or wings or a tail full of poky spikes! They'll want the tallest cloaks you can find, and big wide masks, and something for their hands, too."

"Maybe something that could make it look like they're on stilts?" I suggested, relieved and a little alarmed. "There are a few men of the air about Grandfather's size, but not many as tall as Khur S'vlk."

"Such *nice* bodies," crooned Shelean. "It's a shame to hide them."

Freddy flushed. "I'll see what I can find. You wait here."

While he went in search of the unanticipated wardrobe—one that implied an alarming number of winged, spike-tailed creatures wandering New York at the Outer Ones' behest—I returned to the elders.

"They may not be the most comfortable outfits," I warned. Imagining the vaguely described masks and gloves, I added: "Or the most dignified."

"I will dress like that great green statue in the harbor if it gets me out of here," said S'vlk.

Fortunately, that didn't prove necessary. Freddy returned with two vast cloaks, clearly intended to disguise a multitude of alarming anatomies. They'd been tailored by someone with a taste for the garish: one bore green and gold stripes; the other was a patchwork potpourri of velvet rags. S'vlk exclaimed over the latter, apparently having never seen the material before, which left Grandfather resembling a circus tent. Neko tugged at the rag seams and pronounced them likely to hold for the brief period we'd be outside and visible.

The masks were stranger. They were full headpieces, very nearly human looking. The skin was pale but tanned, the features broad under bushy hair. Under the cloak they might pass, or at least give the impression of a deformed or poorly made up man of the air. Yet something about the nearly-successful simulacra terrified. When S'vlk pulled one over her head, my stomach clenched with nausea. She looked as if some terrible magic had reversed her metamorphosis but warped her original form. No matter how she adjusted the mask, some part of the face bulged or drooped.

It would do what we needed, though. With the mask on and cloak pulled tight, and gloves as distressing as the mask pulled over her hands, a stranger might find her disturbing, but would pass on without guessing that her freak-show appearance hid something even less familiar.

"People will notice," said Spector. "They don't walk like they're on stilts. They walk like . . ." He trailed off. On land, elders either moved at full predatory rush, or the shuffling hop that made a more comfortable compromise for muscles and joints adapted to deep water.

"You're *looking* for weird things," said Audrey. "Most people, if what they see doesn't match what they know, assume it's their eyes that are off. But I was hoping for weird and *exciting,* like a mask for a dance, or Museum Night. If you have some cardboard, I could make tiger faces in a few minutes . . ."

"These will do," said S'vlk grimly.

While the elders prepared, Spector pulled me aside. "New York's a big place, with room for a lot of strangeness, but I'm not the only person who knows how to spot anomalies. I saw a little hotel about six blocks back toward the train—it'll be a pit, but if you've got a little cash you should be able to rent a room for the day with no questions asked. Once we're done here I can requisition a van to bring your family back to the water. They look like they need it."

"Thank you," I told him. For all my ambivalence about the state's involvement in this business, I was grateful for Spector's pragmatic thoughtfulness. "Are you getting the answers *you* wanted?"

"The missing people are eager to reassure us that they're fine, if that's what you're asking. But the whole business opens up a whole new kettle of things we need to find out. Later, I'd appreciate your coming over to the Ritz and talking us down from our mistaken conclusions."

"I can do that." Maybe we'd have a chance to sort out our own conclusions first.

Despite all my fears, the Outer Ones didn't try to stop us from leaving. When I thought about it, there was no reason they would. We had far more at stake than they did.

S'vlk stepped out into sunlight, a waxen figure in a patchwork cloak. I shut my eyes against the glare. For a moment, I felt myself a stranger, as foreign to this place as the Outer Ones. The vertiginous alienation passed, but a veil still seemed to lie between me and the world. I stifled a yawn. I hoped a safe place to sleep would help me finally throw off my exhaustion.

I helped Charlie down the steps. The block around the Outer Ones' stoop was sparsely populated, and we drew little attention. Trumbull hovered close to S'vlk, and the rest of us spread around her and Grandfather. Our bodies might further hide their un-stilt-like walk.

The masks and cloaks made expression difficult to discern, but both elders turned to catch glimpses of the inland city.

"You can't even smell the ocean," said Grandfather. "How far did they bring us?"

"About thirty miles," I said. "But Mr. Spector's van will cover it quickly."

S'vlk crouched as a car growled by, then straightened and peered after it. "Those still seem unnatural. Better than horses, though, and faster, even if they do have their own dreadful smell."

"Jumping at horseless carriages will stand out far more than our looks," said Grandfather. "Compose yourself."

"Yes." A pause. "The buildings here aren't that much taller than in Innsmouth."

"They get a lot more impressive further in," said Trumbull. "Maybe Mr. Spector can give us a driving tour."

"I'd like that." They shared a look through the mask's filmy eyeholes. "I'd like to see something cleaner than that place."

The Outer Ones terrified me, and I found their den claustrophobic, but the simplicity of her hatred upset me. "We've all seen worse."

The mask swiveled in my direction. "I know full well how monstrous humans can be. But when men stab you in the heart, you *know*. You can be in terrible danger among the *meigo* and never see it. You can escape their presence and never know whether that danger stayed dormant, or whether you had to fight. You can fight and *lose* and never know."

I thought, but didn't say, that a loss you could ignore was one you could survive. I knew she'd suffered a loss she *couldn't* ignore. I'd nurtured my own furies for a long time, and still held some of them tight; I'd no right to judge her grief.

And no time for it—as we continued toward the promised hotel, the street grew crowded. It was late morning now, the sun pulling sweat through my pores and picking out the pallor of the elders' masks. People noticed us. Perhaps that had been the goal, but the looks cast our way were not bemused. I recognized, though I'd forgotten until this moment, the loathing of strangers. Strangers passing through Innsmouth. Strangers in Arkham when we stepped off the bus, on the rare errand that couldn't be fulfilled at home. Our mother had never brought Caleb on those expeditions—but she'd started to take me. It was a skill to be learned, to refuse the silent provocation and move on swiftly before anyone could give it voice.

But in Arkham we'd been known, the subject of endless bloody rumor. Were the masks truly that disturbing? Or had these people already seen something more frightening than an elder, wearing similar garb? Both truth and libel might lead someone to hate what walked under those cloaks.

"This isn't right," said Frances through gritted teeth.

"Keep walking," I told my companions. I lifted my chin and walked as quickly as I dared, quickly as the elders' pace and Charlie's permitted. I wanted to run, or to turn and demand explanation for the glares. Neither seemed wise.

We hurried past whispering women in straw-brimmed hats. A hot dog seller crossed himself as we went by; a young man spat at us, wetting the concrete just short of our feet. Underhill, I'd yearned only to be surrounded by common humanity. Now, I remembered what that meant.

A bulb-barnacled sign embraced the corner of the building. Beneath its assurance that we'd reached The Pavilion, a smaller sign promised vacancies. Audrey blocked the elders from the door. "Wait out here while Aphra and I—no, Charlie and I—pay. Let's not tempt fate."

I took inventory of how we might appear to a curious clerk, and nodded. The pair went inside, emerging tense minutes later with a brass key. When we at last escaped the sun's glare into the cool lobby, the clerk had gone back to reading behind his ornately carved cherry counter. The desk, its wooden screen filigreed with birds and moss-dripping trees, seemed out of place on the unswept linoleum floor, illuminated by dingy fixtures. Someone had loved this place, a long time ago.

We trudged up narrow stairs and at last squeezed into a room that must have been their most luxurious, or at least their largest. The air cloyed, heat thick enough to catch in my throat. Faded gold fleur-de-lis marched across peeling wallpaper. We could all fit, if three or four sat on the bed. Neko pulled yellowed curtains across the window, and S'vlk immediately tore the mask from her face.

"Careful," I said. "We may need that later."

"It's an abomination. Smell it." She tugged off the gloves, only a little more delicately, and dropped them on the bed.

Grandfather followed suit. "It smells vile. What of it? It's been at the bottom of a storage chest for people who reek of rotting mushrooms. It could hardly be sweet."

I picked up one of S'vlk's gloves. It felt too soft for something that looked like a wartish pale hand, like finest quality kidskin. I lifted it to my nose. Above a whiff of S'vlk's sweated-in salt and oils, I caught something leathery and equally organic. I thought it almost pleasant, though there was a hint too of the Outer Ones' fungous swamp.

Then I realized why a glove that looked like a hand might smell of leather, and threw it on the blanket with a cry. I looked for something to wipe my own hand on. "It's skin. It's real skin."

S'vlk scraped hers on the curtain, grimacing as cobweb clung to her fingers. She pinched the threads gingerly between talon-tips and let them drift to the floor. "They're bloodless, I can assure you of that.

Not flayed from sacrifices, but grown from thralls who let their masters copy their bodies piecemeal. Once in a *meigo* den I saw their gardens: long pipes flowing with black fluid, empty hands and faces dangling like moss."

"Ugh." Audrey picked up a mask and examined it, nose wrinkled. "Not very good copies, I hope? Because I feel bad for the models, if so."

"Faces grow better on skulls," said S'vlk. Then: "Aphra Yukhl."

I'd wanted to surrender to the elders' judgment. I hadn't expected to enjoy the process. I rearranged myself, on my corner of the bed, into a semblance of respectful kneeling. "Yes, Khur."

"Tell us exactly what you perceived, while you and your sister-in-adversity were alone with the *meigo*."

"And what you thought worth the risk," added Grandfather, "now that there are no unfriendly ears."

I did my best. I resisted the urge to gloss over my memories, still raw from the trapezohedron's forced recollection. Grandfather knew the basics of our first encounter with Barlow, and had been there for the culmination of our efforts to salvage their damage. But the details would anger him, and rightly so.

More tentatively, I described the deep oasis of which I'd caught the briefest glimpse. I scarcely had words to describe something that must be as familiar to S'vlk as a streetlamp or manhole cover.

Charlie had put a hand on my shoulder, silent comfort as I recounted painful memories. Now he dropped back to lean against the wall, listening in fascination. On Neko's face I saw equal interest, mixed with yearning and frustration.

"And you?" S'vlk asked Neko.

"S'vlk-sama. I saw the same scenes Aphra did at the beginning, my own memory of them, though the lack of touch didn't bother me so much. I wish it had; I think I spent longer reliving each memory. Or they felt longer. I guess they did in real life, too—I just remember being scared for her, and for Audrey, and—" She halted abruptly.

"And for Sally Ward, yes," said Grandfather. "Go on."

"But then I saw something new. I'm not sure how to describe it. It was the strangest place: I was flying among shapes I couldn't quite see, and hearing music very far away. And I felt very calm, and very happy, because the flying was fast and smooth and I knew I was going somewhere wonderful. It was more like a good dream than a real memory."

S'vlk hissed softly, thoughtfully. "Only one of their memories each. Perhaps this will not be as hard as I feared. That was the first time they used their tools on you?"

I *had* glossed over something, after all. I closed my eyes. "No, Khur. The first time we went to their den, Freddy showed us the altar room. He invited us to join him in ritual. I was worried, but I wanted show respect, to listen to him so he'd be willing to listen in turn. Why . . . ?"

S'vlk shot Grandfather a frightened look—fear like I'd never seen in her before. She was tens of thousands of years old, an alumna of the Archives, but this disturbed her. "Tell me everything," she said.

I told her then about our first disorienting experience with the trapezohedron. Charlie and Trumbull joined in, but it was my testimony on which S'vlk focused. I forced words around the flashes of strange worlds. Sharing those memories felt wrong, raw and private. *You wanted their judgment.* "And then I saw—I think it was R'lyeh. There were enormous statues, and buildings as high as the canyon they filled. Deepwater fish, glowing with their own light. And guards. I suppose I must have been seeing through the eyes of an Outer One, and they chased it off."

"Or welcomed it," said Grandfather. "We do talk to their emissaries; things would be far worse if we didn't. But I don't like them sharing what they see with all their kin. And yes, that was R'lyeh." He gave me a long look, and bent to sniff my hair. "It will be rightfully yours, one day."

"But after the visions," said S'vlk. "When you awoke. What happened?"

"I felt ill, but it passed quickly. It was the same for the others—except Mary. She had a seizure, just like after our foray in the dreamlands. Dr. Trumbull's guest scarred her mind. She does everything she can—but she's not well."

"The Yith leave trails in the minds they inhabit, and cut deliberately when they see the need. But the Outer Ones cut deeper, never admitting their arts can harm. They can—" She sank into a squat, traced not-quite-idle patterns with a long finger. Her voice was bleak. "You should try the Inner Sea. Perhaps I'm seeing storms in an empty sky."

The Inner Sea was the first spell any student learned, and the simplest. It was the root of meditation, the easiest way to assess physical well-being, and the core that bound the confluence together. "Khur S'vlk, you've been talking around something all morning. I know *nothing* about the Outer Ones, save what I've learned the past few days. Your fear frightens me. Please tell me; it can't be worse than trying to imagine what would scare you."

"And if *she* has something to fear," added Trumbull, "what about the rest of us?"

"You're likely safe," said S'vlk. She brushed the professor's temple. "Men of the air rest lightly in their bodies, and a returned captive especially. But Aphra."

Grandfather squatted next to her. "Aphra."

"Water binds us," said S'vlk. "It gives us greater gifts than air or earth ever offer. Health and healing, long life, the ability to thrive for the span of the ocean itself. But our bodies and minds are tightly entangled, with each other and with the sea. Even dreamwalking, those threads stretch but don't break—an experienced air-born traveler can go further and deeper than we ever do.

"I told you earlier that their arts are dangerous. The device you describe, their sacrament—I know it. I've seen it, seen others who used it. It has a purpose beyond mere ritual: it prepares new thralls for the abomination of *meigo* travel. Those who look through it even once yearn to return. They grow to love its visions more than their own sight. And all the while—it breaks threads. It smoothes tangles. It makes it easy for the *meigo* to extract a mind, like a clam from its shell, and fit it neatly into the box they make for it."

"I—" A dozen moments from the past two days came clear. I'd been reluctant to lead spells. I'd hesitated to confide in the elders. And other moments . . . I pushed past inhibition grown suddenly salient, and reached for the confluence. Ordinarily a thought was enough to bring me their echoed senses, changes to heart and breath that carried joy or terror. Now I needed to push. They were there—hearts too quick—but the sensations were muted. "Gods."

Grandfather drew me up, wrapped me in storm-tested arms. His strength, surrounding me, still felt real. He asked: "What comes next?"

"Neglect your body, as their arts urge, and your blood will dry. Like my daughter."

When I first learned the Inner Sea, it had brought me unspeakable relief to feel the tide of my blood, still promising the form I would one day wear. The desert had tried to destroy me, but I'd endured. I'd held on to this one treasure through degradation and grief; could I have thrown that away in two days of poor judgment? I couldn't bear the idea of finding out. The spell that had granted me assurance now seemed a source of horrible suspense. I curled within Grandfather's embrace, not wanting to see what expressions of pity or anger might surround me.

"Can anything be done?" asked Grandfather. His bass rumble carried more emotion than I'd heard since the moment I'd told him his daughter was dead.

"I wish the archpriest were here," said S'vlk. "Or someone else with true skill for reading and healing minds. Chulzh'th's still an acolyte. And the two of us—"

"I'm a dilettante," agreed Grandfather. "And you've spent more time learning to read rocks than people."

"The math that guides the grinding bones of the earth is a worthy and joyful endeavor," she said. "Just completely useless here."

"She's only been exposed twice," said Charlie. "Is it really so dangerous?"

"I don't know." I heard S'vlk's talons scrape the floor, a shuffle of webbed feet. The room felt too close. "My daughter isn't the only person I've seen fall to them, but I've never had a chance to interrupt the change. Most people, once they've shared the *meigo*'s visions, can't stay away. Once, I brought guards along to show strength during negotiation—we don't often clash over territory, but there was a cave-riddled cliff face dear to us, that they wanted to use. I intended the guards as spies, as well. One slipped away while we argued, and found a stone like the one you described. He came back to the boundary waters that night, but his eyes were distant and he'd talk only of other worlds. A few days later, he vanished."

I'd been right when I thought Freddy was endangering himself among the Outer Ones. I hadn't considered that he could so swiftly pull me down alongside him.

"I could place a geas on you, to keep you from going back." Grandfather sounded reluctant, and well he should. Geassa were crude, and binding a complex mind with a simple compulsion could cause pain or even harm. Most elders would only use them on thralls and criminals.

"No." I disentangled myself from his arms, determined to show a dignity I did not feel. "I can resist it. I know what's at stake."

Warmth at my back, and a familiar touch. "I'll hold you back if you try to run off," said Charlie. "I know how hard you've fought to win your life back. You aren't alone."

I smiled through terror. "I know." My face was wet—and no jar in sight. I scrubbed fingers against cheeks, and licked the salt lest it be lost.

"Well," said Audrey. "We've got a few hours to figure out what we're facing. Let's take a look, and we'll decide what to do from there."

She bent to the bag we'd packed for summoning the elders: the bowl would be there, and the salt, and the knife.

"I'm exhausted," I said softly. "Can't we . . ." But I trailed off.

Audrey retrieved our tools, knelt before me on the bed, and took my hands. "I've never known you to look away from anything. Even when we were fighting the cold thing, and my—my blood-guards. We'll fight this, too."

I closed my eyes. My cheeks warmed, shame and anger only half logical. "It seems I'm not so brave when my own blood's at risk."

"You're full of hooey. But there's no point in putting this off."

"Yes," said Grandfather. Charlie and Audrey stepped back, letting him pull me back against his chest. He began humming; the vibration filled my lungs. As quietly as an elder could, he sang the hymn of endurance. I'd last heard it lying on an altar, offering my own blood and pain for a vital sacrifice. He must have meant to remind me, or himself, of my strength. I cried freely this time, sobs that stabbed my throat. But I *was* exhausted, and had only so much salt to spare.

"I want," I said. "I want . . ." What I wanted was the people in this room, and the family I knew and understood. I wanted to get away from otherworldly emissaries and heathenish mistblooded, and developers tearing down familiar houses, and all the overwhelming world that would not return my clean community and its familiar rules. "It doesn't matter what I want. You're right. Let's find out what the Outer Ones have done."

CHAPTER 14

I attended to every detail of the Inner Sea's basic spellwork, more mindful than I'd been for months. It was far easier to focus on what I was doing than to consider my reasons for doing it.

I sketched the diagram in minuscule on paper torn from my journal. I leaned close and held the pen lightly, tracing thread-fine geometries across the ruled lines. Knotwork twists delineated each participant; a single variant glyph protected the confluence from expansion. I remembered learning each one: the first breathless lesson on the cool wood floor of Charlie's back room, the Yith's clinical criticism in Trumbull's study. Frances watched closely. Her first Inner Sea should have focused on celebrating her own blood-born strength. No help for this inadequate initiation.

Grandfather traced a simple seal across the wall; in this small a space, there was no room on the floor. Either it would rub off, or the hotel wouldn't welcome us back.

I grounded, focusing on the connection between myself and my world, as the others also looked inward. *My blood is a tide,* I told myself, and for the first time I feared that I was lying.

Then the chant. This part was easy: Enochian swirled around my body, indifferent to my lack of confidence—I only needed perfect enunciation, surrendering my voice to blend with Grandfather and

184 • RUTHANNA EMRYS

S'vlk, Audrey and Charlie and Trumbull. Neko, who joined us so rarely, hummed descant.

Then finally, not daring to think: the knife handle against my palm, the sting of blade on skin, the blood dissipating in intimate ripples.

And I sank into my blood.

My blood, usually a river in full rush to the sea, ran slow. I couldn't yet mistake it for Charlie's blood or Neko's, but its power had waned. Worse, I sensed it through a vertiginous haze, as though I saw the world a half-second late in a cracked mirror.

That haze lay between me and something that should have been inseparable. I couldn't fathom it. And so I simply perceived, in fear and confusion and mourning.

Something touched my wrist: contact breaking through the time-less haze. I wanted to cling to the physical sensation like a raft, but for this ritual that touch was only the means to another, harder inti-macy. My grandfather had grasped my arm so that he could see my blood for himself—and I was swept up in his.

If my blood was usually a rushing river, Grandfather was the ocean. My blood intimated a stronger, surer form that might some-day be mine; his embodied that form in full. Deep waters surged around me, vast currents and crushing pressure. Salt filled my every pore, not respecting the boundary of skin. I wanted to drown in him. I wanted to become part of the ocean any way I could.

But the tide receded, leaving me gasping. I sat on a coarse cotton blanket. Grit stung my eyes and nose; the air was heavy with our ex-halation. There was no water save my own sweat.

Charlie's hand hovered near me. I should have said something, but reassuring him seemed too much effort. Audrey looked almost serene, though her gaze lingered on me as well. Trumbull gripped S'vlk's shoulder. Frances looked thoughtfully at her palm, more still than I'd ever seen her.

I found myself afraid to move, to react—as if the harm done by the Outer Ones' generosity might grow with any motion.

Neko shook herself from trance and glared at me. "Well? It must be bad—we can't fix it if you won't talk about it."

I summoned what bravery I could. "My blood isn't right. It's not . . . not a part of me, like it should be."

"Will she still change?" Neko demanded. I wouldn't have dared, and I caught my breath.

"She should," said Grandfather, too much doubt in his voice. "But Aphra, you must stay safe. You mustn't let the Outer Ones work their arts on you, perhaps not even near you." He shot S'vlk a questioning look.

"There are things we can try," said S'vlk. "You must practice the arts that bind your body and mind more closely. And perhaps—Khur Catherine, the things we know—perhaps there is some way to teach her. The Yith kept my soul knit through five years outside my body, or mended it themselves . . . but it's like your ally Mary. Some arts leave vulnerabilities that cannot be effaced. Aphra, every time you stretch your mind beyond its natural bounds you'll risk snapping the threads that hold you together. And yet, that stretching is probably the only way to make yourself whole again. You walk a cliff's edge. You may walk it the rest of your life."

"Couldn't we—" Neko stood. She was the shortest person in the room: stunted by her time in the camp, and her family not tall to begin with. "Can we just *ask* them? I know you hate the Outer Ones, but they aren't idiots. They can't be ignorant of these risks. Maybe they have a way around them, or a way to heal people who react badly. When Miss Harris got sick, they had a medical kit right there."

S'vlk shook her head. "They could as easily compound the damage. Remember that they see our bond with the Earth as a weakness. Something to *overcome*. Why would they learn to heal what they consider worthless?"

"Let Aphra decide," said Charlie. "It's her risk to take."

I closed my eyes, breathed, tried to compose myself enough to think clearly. "I'm sorry that I didn't consider the danger. The Outer

Ones frighten me so instinctively that it's hard to be wary of their subtler threats. I wanted to understand them better—I wanted to understand Freddy better, and bring him home."

"He's traveled with them in truth," said S'vlk. "Even if his blood started strong, it would be too late now. Like my daughter." Frances flinched.

"Does that mean—" I dropped my eyes. I wished there had been some possibility of coming to New York a month earlier, some choice we could castigate ourselves for not making. But by the time we'd known where to find Freddy, he was already lost. How much else was lost with him? "Could he still have strong children?"

S'vlk grimaced, baring sharp teeth. "I don't know anyone who's tested that question."

"I'm more worried about *you*. What about the ritual we did in January?" asked Audrey. "Could we share Caleb's strength with you through the confluence?"

"I don't think it's the same thing," said Trumbull slowly. Her fingers fluttered absently. "There, we had to force something out that didn't belong—and repress something that did. But if Aphra's mind won't bind correctly with her own body, the strength of another's blood won't help. I could work on the problem with Mary. If you're willing to bring this up with her."

"Absolutely not," said Grandfather. "The state needs no more ways to weaken us." I imagined the trapezohedron used as a weapon, and nodded.

"You're being paranoid," said Trumbull. "She could make the difference."

"She could," I said. "But Mr. Barlow and Mr. Peters still think us traitors. If they knew that the Outer Ones could attack us at our core, they'd want a version for their own."

"They're here," said Trumbull. "You're going to have to deal with them. And by this point they should be too busy worrying about the Outer Ones to fuss about other humans."

"That's not how it works," said Neko. "I hate to say it, because I want help from as many geniuses as we can find. But when people are scared, they form ranks against everyone they've ever thought an enemy. They're going to look at the Outer Ones, and start wondering who they can really trust. Especially since the Outer Ones make a point of recruiting disaffected humans."

"Barlow's team wouldn't be wrong to worry," I said reluctantly. I should have thought more carefully about how to answer Kvv-vzht-mmmm-vvt's demands, should have considered what I made myself complicit in. "Kvv-vzht-mmmm-vvt brought me in to the altar room, that second time, because it wanted a starting point for its efforts to rescue humanity—someone they could use as a lever to move the world. I was afraid of what it would do if I left it to its own imagination, and the first thing I thought of was to point it at Barlow's team. But now that I've had longer to think it through, I fear the Outer Ones' 'help' will only make things worse. Kvv-vzht-mmmm-vvt is eager to intervene, and sure it can move human governments to its will. Whether it's right or wrong, the results could be disastrous."

"And we've no way to stop them," said S'vlk. She hissed softly. "You ought not have cooperated."

"I know."

≈≈≈

We tried to sleep. We were all in desperate need by this point. Even the elders were too long out of the water and had gone too far on little food. They weren't the only hungry ones, but for me the most urgent need was to close my eyes, and my mind, against everything that had happened since Barlow's arrival.

Charlie sat back against the headboard and dozed. The others lay close on the bed or leaned against walls. The masks and gloves we swept awkwardly into the dusty cave below the bedframe.

I huddled in Grandfather's lap. I was far too tall to lie there comfortably, but I slept anyway with his scales digging into my side and catching on my dress, his hand cool on my forehead. He sang softly, in English:

> *"Stars that stand over you, earth that lies under you,*
> *Dagon and Hydra take heed of your birth,*
> *Salt that will comfort you, waves that will welcome you . . ."*

I almost cried again, shocked by memories of my mother singing while I lay burning with childhood fever. But at last I slept.

The city's heart thrummed against the wards we'd drawn. New York turned slowly with the bedrock beneath it, taking in the heat of the approaching solstice, woven through with the plans and paranoias of its resident sapients. Crowded, aching, grateful, our bodies sought the little repairs and recoveries that can only happen while the mind looks elsewhere.

When the world's shadow fell on the city, and its own light rose to occult the stars, someone knocked on our door.

"Visitor for Mr. Winslow," called a voice.

Audrey rubbed her eyes, but managed to sound awake. "Thank you—we'll be right down!"

Charlie took a washcloth from the bathroom and made an effort to clear the traces of magic from the walls. Audrey retrieved our ritual gear and put the pack in some semblance of order. I examined myself: how much of my earlier paralysis had been induced by the trapezohedron, and how much had been simple exhaustion?

I was still frightened. I'd reclaimed my body after the camp at great cost, and with long study. Our confluence, built on accidental intimacy, had grown into a worthy family. I'd do anything necessary to make them mine again. Somewhere in my sleep, I'd accepted the risk. Even if ordinary magic put my mind in danger, I wouldn't give it up. I'd restore my squandered strength, or lose what remained trying. Charlie and Audrey and Mary all fought with, and for, bodies that did not easily accede to their needs. I could do the same.

Caught up in my renewed determination, it took me long minutes to realize what was missing. "Neko! Where's Neko?"

"I thought she was in the bath," said Audrey.

"No, that was me." Charlie held up his blackened washcloth. "I was trying to clean this damned thing off."

"Did anyone see her leave?" I asked. An image came inexorably to mind: an Outer One wavering into existence in our crowded chamber, snatching Neko into the outskirts before anyone noticed the intrusion.

"Here—" Audrey held up a slip of paper, covered in Neko's neat script. "It was under the lamp. *'I'm sorry to run out on you—but like Aphra, I need to do something important without asking permission. I still think the Outer Ones can help with the problem they caused, and I'm going back to convince them. I'll find you at the beach tonight, or back at Tante Leah's.'*"

"We need to get her back," I said at once. S'vlk's words echoed in my mind, more frightening than the chimerical kidnapping: *Most people can't stay away.*

"You must not go near them," said S'vlk. "Not until you've restored the strength they stole."

"She seemed enthralled by their visions," said Audrey. "Neko's always wanted travel more than anything else. They could give that to her, but—"

"She always needs to feel like she's traveling for a purpose," I said. "They'll find one for her, and convince her it's justification enough, and put her on one of their altars." I imagined her young, gentle face twisted in agony, frozen and mindless.

"She's a child of the air, and will survive it," said S'vlk. "You, we can't risk."

"She's my sister."

"*We* can go after her," offered Charlie.

Neko in the mine, Caleb and Deedee somewhere in the depths of the city. I felt the weight of the millions outside, overwhelming swarms of humanity obfuscating the few I cared about. Absurd, selfish, to feel that those millions, each with their own circles of exquisite care, were a mere barrier to my own loves. "I'm sorry. I'm not going to let you vanish into the mine in trickles. Letting people go off on their own has just made things worse—we need to stay together."

"Then you need to wait and see if Neko comes back as she promised," said Grandfather. "They'll not harm her in a single day."

I was more afraid of how she'd harm herself—but my own judgment was demonstrably untrustworthy. I bowed my head, acquiescing to the elders' orders.

Grandfather and S'vlk retrieved their disguises, donning them with ill-concealed distaste.

"Come on," Trumbull told S'vlk. "If Mr. Spector's found a vehicle with windows, you'll be able to see New York properly."

"Through these." She prodded a rubbery eyehole. But with a rumbling sigh, she worked the mask back over her head, flattening her crest awkwardly before pulling her patchwork hood over the resulting lumps.

She examined the ceiling's bare bulb thoughtfully. The cord slipped through her gloved fingers, and it was Audrey who turned it off after giving the room a final once-over.

"It's not that humans have learned to call lightning that's impressive," said Sv'lk, her voice muffled and strange. "Containing it is the harder thing."

Spector waited in the lobby. I caught Charlie's unguarded smile, quickly swallowed. The FBI agent ran a hand through his hair and stifled a yawn, but smiled back. "I'm sorry—this is going to be a bit of a clown car no matter what." He paused and looked us over. "Where's Miss Koto?"

"She—" It wasn't as though I could hide it from him, and I wasn't even sure I wanted to. "She went back to the Outer One lair, to try and—negotiate with them. On her own recognizance. I don't suppose you saw her?"

"No, but that place is a labyrinth. Do you need me to . . ." He frowned. "What *can* I do to help? Do you think she's all right?"

I sighed. "Probably. The elders insist that we go back to Chulzh'th before I try anything else. They're right, too, I think—the Outer Ones aren't going to *harm* Neko." It was only her own duty and desire that were at stake. And for all that the Outer Ones could enchant minds and sap wills, a Neko who chose to spend her short life traveling would be serving her own true desires. *Even if I see her rarely, I won't lose her as soon.* Was that a sensible thought, or the remnant of my own temptation?

"If you're sure," said Spector. "Everyone should fit in the car, anyway. And I got you dinner."

"You're a good man," Audrey told him. My stomach rumbled, reminding me that my body was still my own.

My hunger lasted until we went outside and saw the waiting vehicle. I froze on the Pavilion's top step, then forced myself to continue forward.

Spector glanced back at me. "Is everything all right?"

"Yes," I said. "Thank you for finding something big enough to fit us."

After twenty years and a war, the government must have replaced its fleet any number of times. But the black police van parked by the curb looked little different from those that had taken us from Innsmouth.

The elders had found the town deserted at dusk, long after those vans left. They climbed willingly into the back of this one. The others followed easily. I took a breath of muggy air, trying to steady myself. *Spector's driving. He's taking us to Chulzh'th.* At last I forced myself inside. The atmosphere was close and hot. I shuddered, though the barrier to the driver's section was down and the holding area— scarcely smaller than the hotel room—smelled improbably of garlic and soy and cooked beef. I took a proffered tray, and tried not to hear my mother begging Dagon's intervention, or smell my father's blood staining my dress.

"Eat something," Audrey told me. I dug mechanically into a dish bright with broccoli and peppers. The long cross-country drive to the camp had been meagerly rationed; filling my stomach pushed back the memories. Spector had ordered some sort of baked fish for the elders. The windows were tinted, so they could eat unmasked.

Spector pulled away from the curb. "Traffic's going to be a bear," he warned. "But you'll get a good view of Manhattan on the way." He paused. "I apologize. I know you want to get back to the ocean, but my colleagues are worried about what they've seen today. So am I, to be honest. I think you'd better talk to them *now,* and let Acolyte Chulzh'th wait a few extra minutes. If we can get everyone to agree about what the threat is and what courses of action might be a step or two above complete stupidity, it'll save a lot of trouble."

I recognized his tone. "What's Barlow planning?"

Horns sounded, and Spector braked hard. I caught the beef and broccoli before it could slide off my lap. Lights played over us, red and green mixing with the wan yellow glow of streetlamps. "I'm not sure. Honestly, I'm as disturbed as they are. Something's got the Outer Ones scared, and they're likely to try . . . I don't know what. If I can't predict George when he's got a bullheaded plan into his head, what am I supposed to do about *them?*"

"It's not only for our sakes we need to return to the water," said Grandfather. But he rubbed his gills and winced. Coruscating light reflected from his scales. "Acolyte Chulzh'th told Aphra to report back last night. She's less prone to panicked overreaction than your friends, but she has every reason to believe we're in danger. Will your friends deign to come back to Coney Island with us?"

Spector twisted around again. "Is that a good idea?"

"No," I said. "But it sounds like the best we have." And perhaps their report would help us decide how to respond to the Outer Ones' ambiguous incursion.

CHAPTER 15

The van had grown stuffy, but a breeze rich with imminent rain followed Barlow through the open door. I clung to the petrichor reassurance as Peters and Mary clambered in.

"Ron," Barlow called. "What would you have said five years ago, if I told you you'd be driving a car full of mermaids with duck sauce on their faces?"

"I'd have said that sounds a hell of a lot better than getting lost on shitty French back roads, and have *you* eaten dinner yet?"

The agents accepted cashew chicken and fried rice. The van lurched. From the sidewalk the streets seemed like arteries, but from within the mass of vehicles moved irregularly or not at all. Every time forward progress seemed possible, another traffic light flicked red.

Barlow set his tray aside, the cashew chicken demolished. "Ron, what do you think? Have we solved our missing persons case?"

"Go out to Long Island if you want to drive like that, jackass! Excuse me, ladies. I think the Outer Ones have been very forthcoming in granting us interviews with *most* the missing people. All of whom say they're very happy to be there. Are you telling me you don't believe them?"

Peters snorted. "Don't be an idiot."

"Virgil, he's being sarcastic." Mary rubbed her temples. "They all say that, but no one can explain why some of them were in their own bodies and others were stuck in those creepy cylinders."

"If you've got legs, you can run," said Spector. "In one of those cages, what recourse do you have if you don't trust your keepers? When they tell you what to say, what can you do but go along with them?"

"Hard to stand up to an enemy who has your body hostage," agreed Barlow.

I thought of Neko, entranced by the stasis room spotlights, and shuddered. "You don't think they're all like Freddy," I said. He might not have known what he was sacrificing, but at least he was there willingly. "He adores them."

"Some of 'em do," said Peters. "That weird . . . girlfriend? . . . of his, for a start. But some of them—they tell you all about cosmic wonders, but sound like a carnival huckster. With someone digging a gun into his back, telling him he'd damn well better convince you to go see the egress. Then there are the ones they insist are out exploring the universe. Maybe they are. But it's funny that the ones who vanished quickest, with no talk about nasty new acquaintances, are more likely to be out of town."

"How many of them are like that?" asked Frances. "How often do they force people along with them?"

"Eight who weren't there at all, and six of those didn't give any hint before they disappeared," Spector answered immediately.

More quietly—quietly enough that I didn't think she wanted a response, Frances said, "Freddy should have noticed."

Barlow took a deep breath. He sat straighter, steadying himself against the wall of the cabin. His eyes were on S'vlk, and I realized he was nerving himself up. "You've been dealing with these guys a lot longer than we have. How much trouble are we in? At least with the Reds you know how much territory they have—and what they want."

Grandfather growled quietly—a sound I recognized as thoughtful, but Barlow flinched. The elder bared his teeth. "Are you worried they'll do to you what you did to Innsmouth?"

Barlow recovered and glared. "I joined up after Pearl Harbor. Are you really going to make this about a few people who got the wrong idea in their heads back in the '20s?"

"You can blame George for plenty of things," said Spector. "But in '29, I'm pretty sure he was learning about magic from beat-up issues of *Weird Tales*."

S'vlk's baritone sliced through the argument. "Men of the air have been at our throats for tens of thousands of years. And we at theirs. The *meigo* are like us, and therefore dangerous. They are different from us, in ways we don't fully understand, and therefore the danger is compounded. And they are older, their dangers more practiced."

"Older—as a species?" Barlow shook his head. "Age isn't everything. They say cockroaches have been around millions of years, but you can still step on them."

"Older as a civilization. They came to Earth aeons before humanity arose. They had weapons and tools even then that we still can't match. They claim an empire—if that's the right word—of uncounted planets, and uncountable further realms. And yet they fear what we can do to them. That gives them reason to threaten us as well."

"They fear *for* us, too." I still wasn't sure what I should tell Barlow. I had warned the Outer Ones against him—almost certainly a mistake. Trusting him could be equally fraught. But he already knew enough to make costly mistakes. "The biggest danger now is their desire to protect us."

"I know," said Mary. "One of them talked to me about it."

Barlow swiveled: "What did he say?"

"Kev . . . Kevashtem-vat? I don't think I'm pronouncing that right. He said they had tools that could help me with my fits. Asked about the situation in the Soviet Union and China, and whether we thought they'd have A-bombs of their own soon. And HUAC's Hollywood report. Said they could help with those things, too. I told them I wanted to hear more later, but I don't like it."

"I don't either," said Barlow. "When you meet Jacques in a café and he offers to help with your Russian problem, he's trying to compromise you. What do these guys want? And how did he know about your—your health?"

She shook her head. "I've been pitched by Jacques. This feels more like Boris offering to help out his fellow commies in Czechoslovakia—it's not *me* he's after, it's *us*. All of us." She patted his hand. "But there's no mystery about the fits—he saw one. After that hallucinatory ritual I told you about. I'm sorry; I didn't want you to worry."

"Mary, I'm already as worried as I can get." He put his arm around her shoulder. "The more we know about what sets these episodes off, the more we can do to help you."

She sighed, and let her eyes slip closed. But when she spoke, she sounded clear-minded and alert. "Let's focus on these Borises for now. If we don't agree to shill for them, will they try their luck with the Soviets? Or have they already? If what Miss Marsh says is right, they want to prevent open conflict—no matter what it costs us."

"They spoke to me, too." Peters sounded oddly subdued. "Kevizhtim . . . Kevin. I'm going to call the weird bug thing Kevin, damn it, because today's been hard enough without a sore throat. Kevin's pitch to me was different from what he said to Mary. Vaguer, and—more personal. He asked a lot of questions about how our team works together."

The van rattled over a series of potholes. For a minute it was too loud to talk. Faces flickered under the streetlights. Rain blurred the world beyond and lensed strange patterns across our skin. The swift intermissions of bright and shadow interfered with my night vision, making everyone seem half-invisible.

"What did you tell him?" asked Barlow.

"He asked what I thought of our fish—of these guys here. Mr. Marsh's people. I told him they were strange, but Americans like us." He inclined his head toward me. "I'm not about to air our differences to a bunch of bugs. I don't think they have the best interests of *anyone* on this planet at heart. Not even the Reds."

Every time Peters spoke, I felt a surge of disgust. His half-swallowed epithet, the way he dismissed attacks and accusations as "differences," even the way he insisted on addressing whichever of us he found least discomfiting regardless of seniority, galled me. Yet he'd assumed that in this thing we might be allies. I hoped he couldn't see my cheeks burn in the darkness.

It was a long ride. Barlow and Spector circled the question of the Outer Ones, wearing tracks in the conversation. Europe had taught them both how little sway the weak had over deals with the powerful—and what happened to those who tried to stay independent while their neighbors dealt with power. In what they didn't say, I heard the fear that this greater power might trip the wire-thin balance between human states.

I cared about those states only for their influence over Innsmouth. America was younger than Archpriest Ngalthr, the USSR younger than me, and we'd likely outlive both countries. S'vlk, born before such boundaries were ever set and accustomed to the deep waters that no military dared claim, might easily forget their existence in a few millennia. She'd remember them, though, if their conflict was the one that brought humanity low.

On my first visit to Coney Island, looking back over the park, I'd thought that New York wore a glamour of impossible permanence. But in the bright-lit darkness, with the city towering rain-cloaked and ghostly around me, the end was easy to imagine. Humanity would pass from the land like any other species, leaving behind only the cities of the water. Extinction, now or in a million years, was inevitable. And not only for humanity. The lobsters flooding our beach at low tide, the dogs and horses that shied from our presence, the frogs trilling in the bogs, and the moths that swarmed our candles would all be gone, replaced with forms as strange as any Outer One.

As long as the oceans survived, the Chyrlid Ajha would adapt. Our pets and predators, our beasts of burden, would not. *We will be lonely.*

To me, that was the true heart of the Outer Ones' allure. S'vlk's daughter might have given up millions of years of life and the comfort of her own people. She'd also walked away from that loneliness, and left behind all mourning embodied in the clenched gut and the burn of tears. I wouldn't make that trade willingly, but I wanted to go into the ocean knowing that life still thrived on land. I wanted to watch my friends and family grow there, for as long as they could. I wanted to avoid the loneliness for as long as possible.

So, clearly, did the Outer Ones. Equally clearly, it didn't occur to Kvv-vzht-mmmm-vvt that its own interference could magnify the paranoia that hastened oblivion. The few humans that they'd stolen, seeking a lever to reshape the species, might mean death for two billion.

"I don't know what we're going to tell their families," said Barlow.

We got to Coney Island late.

"Still more people around than I'd like," said Spector. I peered over the front seat. The rain had tapered off, and a few stragglers wandered the streetside booths. Most of the stalls were dark; others still illuminated spears of cotton candy and funnel cake. Beyond, bulbs delineated the swollen arcs of roller coasters and the Ferris wheel's great circle. They looked like a vast glowing diagram, summoning the day's visitors—and now releasing them. The wheel guttered out; the arches faded to retinal sparks.

"Do we want to brazen it out now, and try to avoid anyone noticing we're headed in the wrong direction?" asked Barlow. "Or wait and hope no one notices us at all?"

"We got in quietly last night," said Charlie. "Was that really last night? It was much later than this, though. And there were fewer of us."

"And less noticeable," added Audrey.

"How long must we wait?" The skin around Grandfather's gills looked raw and dry. The wind through the driver's side window, noxious with sugar and meat and rancid oil, drowned the nearness of the ocean.

"Could we find a less-used entrance?" I asked. "Somewhere less busy, or closer to the water?"

"If we go down West Fifth," said Spector, "we should be able to park near the beach. Hopefully government plates mean the car'll still be here when we get back."

We left the revelers trickling into the subway, and made our way to darker streets. We passed a hotel that might almost seem a grand old house, save that awnings and electric signs made it gaudy as any roller coaster. The boardwalk, though, was cool with shadows.

S'vlk, cloaked and masked, crouched to examine the planks. "They've destroyed the dunes. The ocean will eat this place soon." She shifted to gaze up at the nearest coaster, smaller and shoddier than those flanking Stillwell. "That thing is fascinating. How does it work?"

Trumbull helped the elder up. The rag cloak flowed to engulf her grip. "The car wheels interlock with the track. Get them up to the top of the slope, and gravity does the rest—they go around very fast. It's like riding in a dirigible when you've caught the wind."

"I miss that. The view here wouldn't be nearly as nice as over the Archives, though."

Past a row of bathhouses, rickety stairs descended to the beach. I wanted to tear off my shoes and feel the sand shape itself to my skin. But after our last trip, I'd had to pick too many glass shards from my soles.

Sudden tension stretched my spine. I couldn't say what caused it—some distant echo or change in the angle of the light. I looked around, saw nothing. But whatever it was had startled the elders, too.

"Under the walk, now," hissed Grandfather. I gave up my own search and did as he bid. "Silent and still."

We all found spots well away from the lamplight. I knelt, cautious of litter. S'vlk and Grandfather backed into the darkest part of the boardwalk's underbelly. With their hoods pulled close, they vanished save for a silvery square of S'vlk's velvet patchwork.

A flashlight played over the sand outside our huddling place. A man's voice called, "Who's there?"

Barlow and Spector glanced at each other. Something shifted and they became a pair, longstanding collaboration plain in their twinned stances. Peters frowned and half-rose; Barlow waved him back down.

"FBI," called Spector. "Sorry to startle you. We're coming up now with our badges out." He and Barlow stepped into the flashlight beam. The stairs muffled the staccato thump of their feet.

"What the hell's the FBI doing here? Don't tell me you guys give a fuck about these nonsense fish-man rumors?"

Barlow: "What's this about fish-men? We're in town trying to track down a couple of missing persons. We got a tip about a body under the boardwalk, but it looks like it's a bust."

"Bodies hell. We ain't had one of those for months."

Spector: "It was an anonymous tip. They don't usually come to anything, but we have to check them out."

"Well, good. You can keep an eye out for my fish monster, and I can go home to Greta."

Barlow: "I'm glad to help, sir; I'm a family man myself. Do you have a description for this, um, fish person? Aside from looking like a fish, I guess?"

The guard chuckled. "That's about what I heard. Either some joker dressed up like Solomon Grundy, or more likely our witnesses had a little too much to drink. But this kind of shit scares off crowds and attracts troublemakers."

Barlow: "If we see anyone dressed like a fish, we'll run him off for you. And if we don't, we'll say we did."

"You're a pal. Hope you don't find any bodies, though. No offense."

"None taken. We'd rather find our man alive."

The footsteps and the light retreated. It was longer before Spector and Barlow joined us again.

"Family man?" asked Mary as they approached.

Barlow smiled. "I have a family." The expression that passed between him and his teammates startled me, so much like something I might share with my confluence. It vanished beneath his usual mask as he turned to the rest of us. "Your friends need to be more discreet. What's a Solomon Grundy?"

"It's a comic book character," said Frances. "Fights Green Lantern—Freddy loves that stuff. I guess he might look a little like Chulzh'th if the light was bad."

I didn't like it. Even an unlikely rumor would prompt people to look for the monster. We went on, staying under the walk in case any other guards came along. Both elders strayed toward the water, but checked their steps.

A couple of blocks down, Chulzh'th stepped from behind a pillar. "You're here. Thank Dagon."

"We're well," said Grandfather. "Merely . . . blown off course. It was unpleasant, but they let us leave in peace."

"He means I lost my temper," said S'vlk. "And *we* are well, but Aphra is not."

Chulzh'th beckoned, and with relief I went to kneel at her feet. I closed my eyes, felt her talon graze my forehead in benediction. "Tell me," she said.

I sat back on my heels. "I will, I promise. But Grandfather and Khur S'vlk need water, and a park guard saw you. He was searching the boardwalk until Mr. Spector and Mr. Barlow chased him off. Did something happen?"

She snorted, less dignified than befit her station. "I misjudged when the throng would abandon the beach, that's all." She cast her eyes over our expanded group. "Miss Harris, you're welcome among us again. And you, then, must be Mr. Barlow and Mr. Peters. Will you greet me?"

Barlow offered his hand. "A pleasure to meet you, Miss . . . ?"

She laughed, flashing needle-sharp teeth, and he did flinch a little. "Cartwright, though it's been a while since anyone called me that. I'm Acolyte Chulzh'th, but you can use my water name alone if the title disturbs you."

Peters ducked his head, then with visible effort offered his own hand. "Acolyte."

She nodded appreciation. "S'vlk, Yringl'phtagn, I don't hear anyone near. Go wet your gills, then return. Aphra, you've delayed long enough. Tell me the dangers of your day, and then I'll speak to you of my own. I sought a vision; perhaps your story will help me understand it."

I couldn't bring myself to respond immediately. Instead, I watched the elders shed their bitter disguises and trot down the beach, shadows thrown long by the city and the waning arc of moon. They dove into the water, and I imagined doing the same. My hand rose unbidden to the side of my neck, where wrinkles and tender skin laid anticipatory outlines.

"Aphra."

"I'm sorry, Acolyte. It's a hard story."

She laid her hand once more on my forehead. I closed my eyes, focused on the tang of salt. The sea was near enough now to overcome the rot of sand-caked detritus. "The Outer Ones have a device. It shows visions of distant worlds—and of this one. I've used it twice, first for politeness and then for negotiation. Both times were misguided. I didn't understand what the device is capable of. S'vlk says the Outer Ones use it to weaken the connection between mind and body. For us—for me—that weakens the body's connection with the ocean. I'm not lost yet, but I'm in danger—not only from the device's direct effects, but because having marked me the Outer Ones may well try to claim me." I paused for breath. "They may have already claimed Neko. I need your guidance."

Her fingers curled against my brow, the prick of her talons a welcome reminder that I still lived in the physical world. "Come."

She led me to the ocean's edge. The tide lapped in and swept the flat wet sand blessedly clean. At Chulzh'th's direction I cupped water in my hands, frigid in spite of the day's heat, and drank. Salt shocked me awake, and the chill lit a line through my throat and belly. I dipped my arms to the elbows; if the FBI agents hadn't been waiting scant feet away, I'd have stripped and immersed myself entirely. My dulled and distant nerves ached for the water's touch.

Chulzh'th drank as well. "I've always attracted visions," she said in R'lyehn. "Trying to force them rarely succeeds, but I feared for Yringl'phtagn and S'vlk. This time the ritual worked—I saw something, even if I don't yet understand it."

She drew sigils in the sand—or perhaps she was merely fidgeting, for I didn't recognize the shapes. I waited, as I had with my own story, afraid of what might cause her to hesitate.

"The Great Race understands fully the principles that shape time. With those truths, they travel aeons and see through the eyes of others at will. Archpriest Ngalthr says our visions are a fledgling version of those arts. But we're a billion years behind what they know. We can't so much as direct what comes to us. You saw when you worked with Khur Trumbull's guest how little we truly know of magic. And worse than our primitive arts is our lack of *perception*. What they sense directly, we must translate for eye and ear and our own limited understanding. I cannot describe to you the frustration I feel, knowing my senses distort every vision before I'm even aware of it. When I first went into the water, I tried to push aside those filters. But without them, the signal devolves into pain. So I must work with moiré reflections of truth."

She dipped a finger, and sketched sigils around her eyes. "I saw the water full of disembodied wings, diving like whales. They faded and reappeared like octopodes, shifting color. Some were like the wings of the Outer Ones, but there were also wings of every color and form you can imagine, from skates to South Seas parrots. Their edges sliced one another as they passed. Blood fogged the water. Behind the fog, the wings formed ranks, and the blood grew darker. I heard them whisper: 'We will protect what we love.'

"That was all. It was simple, but it frightened me. The most frightening part was the frustration I spoke of. That whisper I heard, I could tell was radically mistranslated. Their true words were the most important thing in the vision. They would explain the wings' strife, if only I understood. And the reality of that strife was more complex—and more dangerous—than mere bloodshed."

She looked at me hopefully, bulging eyes wide. As if I might have some insight that she, with decades' experience interpreting her own visions, lacked.

In Miskatonic's library, Caleb had found one of her childhood journals. I remembered the pride she took in her visions when she was still too young to become Ngalthr's apprentice: she'd struggled for humility and patience. "Talking with the Outer Ones is like that. They speak English with casual fluency. From the words alone, you might guess they were men of the air. But when Kvv-vzht-mmmm-vvt tells me he wants to save humanity, what does he mean by 'save'? When Freddy warns me that they disagree passionately over whether and how to intervene, what options do those arguments compass? Spector and his colleagues think some of the Outer Ones' human 'friends' are really captives, while Kvv-vzht-mmmm-vvt takes talk of 'captive minds' as a grave insult." I caught my breath. "Acolyte, I'm drowning. I'm terrified of what I may have done to myself. I know my life is nothing compared to what's at stake, but I can't stop thinking about it."

I splashed water over my face, giving my useless fears to the sea. My nose and mouth filled with salt. I wanted always to stay this close, smelling and tasting nothing else.

Chulzh'th stroked my neck. "What happens to your mind, your body and soul, *is* important. The Outer Ones argue over the survival of men of the air, but your fate is *our* survival. Someone must be the last and youngest of the Chyrlid Ajha. We will live on after that, until the oceans boil. But something will die when we lose our tie to the land. Someday, we will welcome a newcomer to Y'ha-nthlei for the last time. Someday R'lyeh will cease to build new dwellings, will gather its people tight and prepare for the great extinction. If you lose the water, that day comes close."

I bowed my head. "I seek your guidance. Please."

"Oh, child. We can't answer prayers either. What did S'vlk tell you?"

"That any magic stretching the link between mind and body would be dangerous, and that I needed to practice those arts anyway to strengthen the link. And that until I do that, I mustn't return to seek Neko."

"I wish the archpriest were here, with his millennia of healing experience. But I've seen people injure their minds in other ways, through ill-planned magic, or summonings gone wrong by sheer bad fortune. From what I know, S'vlk is right. You need to stretch, and risk breaking yourself. If you avoid the risk, the break is certain."

My belly, still cool with salt water, twisted on itself. "I don't trust my own judgment—how much to risk, how far to go."

"I'll chaperone. But first we should deal with our new visitors."

I would have preferred to stay under the invisible stars, in reach of the water. But our gathering was large enough that a wayward guard or loiterer might see us a long way off. We returned to the dank pylons under the walk.

I heard voices raised, in excitement rather than anger or distress. Mary was waxing enthusiastic, Trumbull exclaiming counterpoint, with occasional notes from male voices.

My grandfather's descant: "That can't possibly be how they work."

"Look," said Mary. Whatever uncertainty she might have felt in the face of the elders was clearly overcome by interest in the topic at hand. "We *know* that mind and brain are intrinsically interlinked. Harm to one is harm to the other—my case alone shows that much. The Outer Ones' captives are our only example of minds surviving for *any* significant time outside the brain's lattice. They've obviously created some artificial structure that can support minds as well, or nearly as well, as their natural scaffolding."

"Then each canister would be essentially a body," said S'vlk. "And need a mind in it to survive—but they keep those things around empty."

"That's the other side of it," said Trumbull. "We've seen the people in stasis. They've found a way to preserve bodies without embedded minds. Perhaps they do the same thing with the canisters."

"These Outer Ones may be disturbing, but they have technology decades, probably centuries past ours." Mary proffered something. After a moment I realized it was one of the skin-masks, hanging shapeless like melted tallow. "We decide what advances are impossible based on what we can do *now*. But if they can grow human flesh outside a human body, so could we. They could teach us so much."

"Which brings us to the real question," said Barlow. "Can we afford to learn from them? When one side has better weapons or medicine, people take advantage of it. In war or at the negotiation table, it's not hard to guess who'll come out ahead."

Peters scowled at Barlow. "If there's one thing worse than trying to trade your beads for rifles without losing your shirt, it's being the next tribe over."

Barlow saw Chulzh'th. "Good, you're back. We need to make sure we don't trip over each other this time. We can't afford it."

Chulzh'th settled among them, cross-legged. "Mr. Peters is right to think about how European settlers treated this continent's natives. The Outer Ones keep their treaties, in theory. But it can be difficult to discern how they interpret their sworn obligations—nor are they above deliberately misleading language. It might be better, safer, to agree with your human rivals that you'll both refuse outside aid from greater powers."

"Humans *don't* always keep treaties," said Peters. "Russkies especially, if they think they'll get an advantage—and they won't believe that any power's bigger than them. Goes against their 'philosophy.' They think communism's the end of history, and they'll assume the Outer Ones are either 'comrades' or inferiors."

S'vlk paced between pylons. "You might be surprised how easily instinct overcomes philosophy. You were with the *meigo* all day. Were you thinking much about the philosophical advantages of how you organize your state, or were you thinking about how to protect yourself?"

Spector made a calming gesture, smoothing imagined clay with his palms. "We know too little. How we negotiate with the Outer Ones—and I don't see how we can avoid it—may be the most important decision anyone will ever make. And whatever knowledge we can gather now is probably the only advantage we'll have."

Peters spared a deeper frown for the rest of us. "You want to use your irregulars, of course. I suppose George is right that they know more about the *meigo* than we do."

"The *elders* know more than we do. As for my irregulars, it's clear the Outer Ones find them interesting. Miss Koto is talking with them already, and Miss Marsh and Miss Winslow both have relations among their captives who could be useful sources of a . . . a perspective that we can make sense of. I'm sorry, Miss Winslow, I know it's not a pleasant thing to ask."

Audrey shifted position to look at me sideways. She couldn't have seen much useful guidance in my face. "It sure as hell isn't. I wouldn't count on my 'cousin' for any useful perspective. Crazy people who've lived underground most of their lives, and only went aboveground to kidnap human test subjects, aren't too reliable."

Mary had been rummaging in her briefcase; now she returned with her face set in some decision. "Whoever we talk with, we want to learn more than they do. Use these." She thrust a small sack into my startled hand. Fine white silk threatened to slip from my fingers. Within, I felt the faintest shiver of magic. I spread it open, half-afraid I'd encounter the sting of her interrogation talismans. But I recognized the inscribed bundles within: I'd last seen one burnt black by Trumbull's guest's mental powers.

Shields for our thoughts. Something to stand between my will and Kvv-vzht-mmmm-vvt's powers of usurpation. And a token of how much the Outer Ones had unnerved Barlow and Peters, for neither contested the gift.

"Thank you," I said. Mary passed the rest around. Spector frowned at his and shoved it in his pocket. Was it too heathenish for his comfort, or was it simply the source that worried him?

"We can face them on a more even footing, while we decide how to handle the relationship," said Barlow. He sighed, letting fatigue slip through. "While we decide whether we can afford to have one."

"Whatever we do, they won't go back to ignoring us," said Charlie. "The U.S. may be small change to them, but they care whether there's another war coming. They won't just leave us to our fate. Even if we'd rather they did."

CHAPTER 16

F rederick Laverne—June 20, 1949:
 They're fighting. I can tell. The buzzing squall churns louder, breaking the harmonies that usually hum through the mine.

Embodied and encircled alike retreat to edges and corners—but not too far. We all want to hear, even if we can't understand. I set Shelean's canister down in the refuge we've claimed, and curl against the sleek metal.

"Does this happen a lot?" I ask.

"No, it isn't normal at all." She sounds worried, and I guess she should. It's not the first argument I've caught since we got back from Yuggoth. She goes on: "This is like bad days in the affection group where I grew up. Only Outer Ones don't banish people to the entertainment pits when they're angry. They know how to make up properly."

I wish she had a body I could hold. "I guess there's worse things than only having one parent around."

"Yes—your raiser seems nice, even if she doesn't like me much. None of them like me. Scary K'n-yan, scary mad girl."

Across the room, more buzzing voices join the tumult. "You're not scary."

"Oh, but I am. If you knew me like I was—Audrey has every reason to be terrified. They've let us run a long time, but they keep grudges. They might come any time with their capture wards and brands. You should breed with Aphra Marsh like she asked."

I scoot back and sit up. "I won't do that to a girl!"

Giggles from the canister. "You won't breed with a boy without a lot of help. Or with any of the Outer Ones, even if you can keep track of their genders."

"You know what I mean! I won't knock a girl up and then not marry her. And I don't want to marry Aphra Marsh. If I were going to marry anyone, it'd be you." *I flinch when I say it. I've known Shelean less than a month and if I do get to propose, I want to do it properly. But she giggles again.*

"Sweet boy. You're not going to sire babies on me. My body's too well worked to make children on its own, even if I could go embodied for that long. And you wouldn't have a very good time covering me, either." *Her voice turns sober.* "I'd get distracted."

I touch her canister below the camera, where her cheek would be if the camera were an eye. "I'd like to kiss you. At least once."

She laughs. "One of us would like it, anyway. Aphra doesn't want to marry you either. She's already got an affection group, with all the sordid little dynamics that implies. But I think they do love each other."

"I don't understand. She's got her brother and her friends. Or is she with Charlie? Getting between them wouldn't be any better than leaving her pregnant on her own."

"They're together, but I don't think they're fucking. Did you see how Charlie doesn't look at Ron? They're together and don't want anyone to know. And Audrey doesn't look at Aphra, because she wants to and she doesn't want Aphra to know. Aphra might be the sort who doesn't like sex at all. She isn't attracted to you, anyway, she just wants to breed."

"Shelean! You're not helping."

"I think you're beautiful. And you'd make good, strong babies." *She makes the little clicks that mean she's thinking, so I don't interrupt.* "If you won't cover her, would you cover Audrey? She has some of my blood in her, so it'd be like you were breeding with me."

"Shelean . . ." *It comes out as more of a moan. Sometimes I swear she does this stuff just to tweak me.* "Shelean, are you trying to distract me?"

"It's working. And it distracts me, too. I can understand their language, you know. Spend enough time here, and you'll pick it up too."

She's got a century's head start, of course. "What are they saying?"

"They're mad about your family coming here. Not at you, though. Mad at the people who thought they could grab so many humans at once and not get noticed. And they're worried about the government people, whether all the agents your cousin dragged in will make humans more unstable, and what the Outer Ones should do about that. Some of them want to make your visitors go away, and some want to recruit 'em." Another clicking pause. "I don't like it when they fight. Let's talk about sex again. Or philosophy."

"Right." She wants distraction, I can give her distraction. It's a better idea than obsessing over Mom and Dad's buzzing argument. "We were talking about how best to judge character . . ."

The FBI agents left the beach at last. Even without mutual trust, we agreed that we needed to learn more—and that we shouldn't promise anything to the Outer Ones without consulting each other. None of us were comfortable with that last part, but even Peters agreed it was necessary.

Watching Mary, I realized that she, like Spector, had come to straddle our divide. She'd worked alongside the elders on our rituals, accepted our word on the dangers of her research, and argued for her inventions without assuming our caution cowardly. I almost wished I could ask her for help. I needn't tell her why I'd used the trapezohedron the second time, or admit my race's vulnerabilities. I could simply say that the ritual had hurt me, because it had hurt her, too. If there were a better, faster way to heal, she'd find it.

But even if I dared, that would have to wait. She'd already picked her way through the sand leaning on Barlow's elbow, retrieved her heels at the base of the stairs, and followed him back down the darkened boardwalk. They'd soon be in their cushioned headquarters, comparing filed notes with Outer One reality long into the night.

"It's time," Chulzh'th said. My own reluctance told me she was right. Normally I found it impossible to turn away from frightening realities. Danger at my back was far more terrifying. Now something had sapped my urgency, and left me only the animal desire for a safe-seeming place to huddle. I dared not give in.

"Do you want me to come?" asked Charlie. I nodded mutely.

"What about me?" asked Audrey.

"Too many," said Chulzh'th. "I don't know this area, and we're not properly warded. I did preliminary scouting, though, before seeking my vision, and thought I smelled gaunts."

Grandfather sighed heavily. "I don't supposed you'd accept me."

"We'd shine like R'lyeh in the depths."

His hands lay heavy on my shoulders. "Ïa Shub-Niggaroth, zh'd Thulig'n'Uhy ich." *May the Mother of All protect you.*

As well as She ever does.

The hardest part was clearing space to sleep. Every time I thought I'd gotten the area clear, I found grease-stained cardboard or abandoned sunglasses or a jag of metal digging into my back.

"Maybe closer to the water?" suggested Charlie. "It's late enough that we probably don't have to worry about anyone watching." But the wet sand would leave him shivering even in the summer heat, and likely worsen his knee on the morrow.

S'vlk rose silently and retrieved the cloaks. "These will provide padding, as long as you don't mind the smell."

He buried his nose in the velvet. "I'll cope. Thank you."

In the lee of the tide, Chulzh'th drew symbols of protection and guidance more complex than those I'd been using. When she was done, they stretched from the bound of the waves' reach to where drier sand heaped in miniature dunes. Charlie folded the cloaks beneath him, and we lay on the damp slope. Chulzh'th nicked my finger. She drew a sign on my forehead, first in my own blood and then with salt water. She lay back beside us, and began chanting. I joined in. Every word felt off-key as it left my tongue, but at least they were the right words.

Chulzh'th's well-practiced magic pulled us swift and deep. I knew the truth of the English term: I *fell* asleep. Fatigued surrender blurred with vertigo.

Chulzh'th and Charlie were the only sleepers close enough to mingle their dreams with mine. I could not be surprised when my vision cleared on a nightmare of parched desert. Birds wheeled in a burning blue sky. Why starlings so often filled Charlie's dreams I couldn't say, but they were a comfort. There appeared before me an antique sink, stacked with grime-caked dishes but dry as the desert in which it stood.

"You can ignore that," said Chulzh'th from behind me. The dishes clinked; when I made the mistake of looking again, there were more of them. "I do. Let me see your threads, both of you."

I turned, and saw my companions. I tried to ignore the dishes, and the hot grit digging into my bare soles. "I'm sorry, Acolyte. I don't know how." Something already felt off, beyond the familiar nightmare. My awareness of time's passage kept slipping. I could barely sense my body's pull.

"Child, there's no shame in being new to the dreamlands. I'll show you." She beckoned Charlie closer, turned him so I could see the space between them. The sigils she'd drawn on our foreheads appeared as raised scars, long healed. She traced another, complementary symbol over the first. Her finger left a trail of sparks so that I could more easily see what she made. Charlie blinked hard in reflex.

Then, from his forehead (the image of his forehead, created by his mind in shadowed imitation of the armor it normally wore), she drew a translucent ribbon that trailed into invisibility as it neared her fingers. Poets and alchemists shorthand the link between mind and body as a "silver cord," but his was grass and emerald green.

"See here," said Chulzh'th, and I came closer. Charlie peered at the cord awkwardly, a rainbow's end trying to catch a glimpse of the whole. "Yours frays a little," she told him, "and is paler than it should be, but the damage from the Outer Ones' tool is already healing. It stretches easily—you'll see that more clearly when we dive deeper."

He nodded, cutting off the gesture abruptly as his ribbon undulated in response.

"Now you." He backed off, and I positioned myself so that he could learn as well. It was easier if I thought of it that way: just another lesson. But the ribbon she drew forth was palest blue and tattered along the sides. Worse, where Charlie's had been supple mine lay flat and brittle.

Chulzh'th brushed it with her finger (the image of her finger, created by her mind in shadowed imitation of the tools it normally controlled), frowning. "It still retains a trace of elasticity. But we should be cautious. Stretch slowly, and remind all the parts of yourself that they *can* be flexible. Are you ready?"

Risk breaking, or break. I nodded.

She drew a new sigil on the ether before us. Ordinarily, making the transition from shallow true dreams to the dreamlands was like pushing through a thick barrier. This time it felt both longer and easier. The desert faded slowly, not only from my sight but from my sense of reality. The starlings wheeled into fog. Part of me reached eagerly into the depths, while another part felt with dread the reluctant stretch of that pale cord, fracturing in tiny cracks that could snap as easily as heal.

From the beach's edge New York was bright; the spiderweb city was brighter. We stood perhaps a mile or two away—even from there minarets and bridges brushed the sky, each strand limned in dewdrops of light. But where New York blotted the stars to invisibility, this city rose toward a galactic sweep brilliant as midnight in the hills west of Arkham. I turned slowly, mindful of both this place's dangers and the inner dangers that I'd come to test. For the moment, my cracked cord held.

Behind us lay a wide plain. Rocks and rare spindly trees cast lumpen shadows. Nothing moved, though I heard something that wasn't a mourning dove: three deep, wistful notes offered into the night.

"What's in there?" whispered Charlie. I turned back around and, with pupils widened from peering into the plain, saw what I hadn't before. The low dark ridge between us and the city was riddled with the darker silhouettes of caves.

I inhaled, trying to pick out unfamiliar instruments from a symphony of scents: ozone like incoming thunder, amber resin, warm stone, pine, loamy dirt. All these were natural and pleasant, but something putresced beneath. Out of sight, meat rotted on the bone.

Then I smelled something familiar and unwelcome. Without thinking, I moved toward the cliffs. I should have let Chulzh'th take the lead, and taken the rear myself to protect Charlie, but the trail had a lure of its own. At the ridge's edge, I found what I'd feared: a patch of the Outer Ones' fungus, blossoming across the rock face in a luminescent spread. It had not grown into anything like the ward on their mine, but it was here and should not have been.

"Is this another of their hideouts?" asked Charlie.

"Maybe," I said. "But I don't see any sign *except* the fungus. And something doesn't smell right."

Cool air spilled from the nearest cave. Unmistakably, that was the source of the rotten smell. Something scraped in the darkness.

Chulzh'th pulled roughly on my shoulder, putting both of us between Charlie and whatever waited inside the cave mouth. A shroud lay over everything past the threshold, though the glint of galaxy and city fell on us plainly as moonlight. Chulzh'th planted her feet wide and bared her talons.

Something squealed, a painful high-pitched mewling that descended into a glibber of unrecognizable language. Chulzh'th exhaled, lowered her claws fractionally, and barked something in what I presumed was the same tongue.

"It must be one of the dreamland's intelligent species," I said quietly to Charlie—largely for the comfort of hearing a more familiar language. He'd read the same books I had, and neither of us had ever spoken to such a creature.

"A ghoul, do you think?" he asked.

"It would fit. They're supposed to be common at crossing points." I knew there was a warren in Boston, though I'd never seen any sign around Innsmouth. There were many language-using species in Earth's dreamlands, and a few with whom we had an "understanding"—less than a treaty, enough to avoid violence when we met—but ghouls showed the greatest interest in humans. In several ways.

Chulzh'th backed up a pace, and motioned us to join her. I heard scrabbling against unseen stone, and the ghoul crept out.

It was very nearly human, but it moved like a wild animal, limbs bent at unlikely angles and tensed to leap or flee at a moment's notice. It twitched and bared sharp yellow teeth—merely being near us set it on a knife's edge of fear or hunger. Translucent skin slid over unpadded muscle. It seemed made entirely of wiry sinew and arteries. It's—his, I thought, though I wasn't sure what cue I was picking up—his long narrow tongue darted out to lick his lips. He wore a short, kilt-like garment and a necklace of what looked like finger bones. Very *small* finger bones.

Chulzh'th said something else in the ghoul's language, then to us in English: "Good, you recognize the species. Have you met them before?"

"No," I said, "only read about them. And never studied the tongue."

"Lllugich Rrrriglit Rrrrilahn ee Engahlllsss Prrreel lllubr'til?" she said. It was nearly as hard to pick out words as with the Outer Ones; Ghoulish used more human sounds, but it seemed to roll L's and R's in several different ways, all of which sounded nearly identical to me. The intermixed coughs, spits, and clicks seemed likely to hurt my throat.

"English," said the ghoul. "Yes. Can speak. Polite." I could understand him easily, though he shortened most of his vowels and sounded as if he were forcing the words around a mouthful of rocks.

"These are my warren-mates," said Chulzh'th. "Aphra and Charlie. Our warren is the vast sea."

"Honor to meet." The ghoul licked his lips again and skittered sideways. "Glabri." Anglicized, the L and R sounded uncomfortably curtailed. "Warren of shining city and deep stone. Biggest north of Sarnath's grave pit."

"We're honored to meet you as well," I said. There was something compelling about Glabri as well as off-putting. Or perhaps I was simply relieved to meet a creature whose nervousness I could comprehend. "I hope we're not trespassing. We don't intend to stay long." I realized as I spoke that my internal clock, so carefully cultivated during our practice, had failed. I had no idea how long I'd been dreaming. I assumed Chulzh'th was tracking the length of our stay, but it was unnerving—on my own, I could easily miss the moment when returning to my body became urgent.

"Deep rock is territory. Plain is hunting ground. All hunt." He chewed thoughtfully on a blunt claw. "Explain holes?"

"I'm sorry, I beg your pardon." The only holes I saw were the black cave mouths. "What do you mean?"

"Holes! Ch'blllrl." He pronounced the Ghoulish word slowly and loudly, lingering on the trill, as if that would improve our comprehension. He crabbed suddenly sideways. We all jumped back, and he scrambled up the rock face, clinging with long fingers and toes. Hanging upside down, he loosed a hand and pointed at the bloom of mushrooms. He didn't, I noted, come close to touching them. "Holes."

"Oh. Do you know what Outer Ones are?" I asked. Chulzh'th translated.

That she knew the Ghoulish for "Outer One" answered my question, so it was no surprise when Glabri said, "Yes, they are marrowless clutch-thieves. In shining city too long already. But why *here*? Two nights ago, solid earth here. What *changes*?"

"We don't know," I admitted. "We just noticed the spread ourselves."

Chulzh'th cocked her head. She gestured in my direction, and the ribbon of my corporeal link wavered briefly into visibility. It shook with tension. "We need to go back soon. Glabri, is this a concern for all your warren, or just you?"

"All—warren creeps and digs and eats together. Marrow-less leave no bones."

I didn't fully understand, but Chulzh'th said, "We're trying to find out what's going on too, and stop it if we can. We'll share everything we learn, if your warren will do the same."

"Yes. Shared bones." Glabri scrambled down to crouch again on the ground, and lifted the loop of his necklace over his head. With dexterous fingers he unhooked the complex scrimshaw clasp, and slid off three of the bones.

Chulzh'th sniffed the offering. "Yes, these will come back with us. Wait a moment. Aphra, let me do this quickly. Hair is easiest, and yours is long enough." She combed her fingers through it, not careful of tangles, and came away with a few long dark strands that she braided swiftly into a rough ring. Glabri clasped the necklace back in place. My loosening braid tangled around sticks of yellowing ivory.

"We'll know each other," she said. "It's time to go back now."

The dive had been easy; ascension pressed the air from my lungs and dug thorns into my temples. I struggled for control of my body. I could sense, dimly, how it lay on the ground. I managed to twist onto my side, but pushing myself up set off a coughing fit. Spasms wracked my chest as I tried to drag in air by force of will. My eyes blurred.

Hands grasped my shoulders; cool water trickled against my throat. I managed a single wheezing breath, then another. My vision cleared slowly. Chulzh'th knelt in front of me, chanting quietly but urgently with her palm against my chest. The hands on my shoulders were Charlie's. I could feel him and Audrey breathing, trying to remind my lungs of their work. Even with my attention lensed onto reclaimed breath, I could tell that my sense of their bodies had grown clearer. I could even feel Caleb and Deedee more easily, yearn for their presence without a smothering cushion muffling that sharp desire. Nothing was as strong as it should be, but a spark of triumph flared in my chest along with breath and blood. I'd taken back a sliver of what the Outer Ones had stolen.

"I'm all right," I said, when I could speak. I wasn't, yet, but easing their breathing would aid my own. And I did feel as if I'd cast aside a veil. The lungs that ached, burning with the scar of the desert, were my lungs. The smell of salt water and garbage rose from a real place where I sat gasping. I wiped my watering eyes. Chulzh'th, satisfied, rinsed my hands in the receding tide.

"I'm all right," I repeated.

Charlie came around and sat beside me. "That ghoul. I hadn't expected that. What he gave us—those things can't be what they look like, right?"

"They can. Let's see if we managed to bring them back." Chulzh'th felt around the wet sand and retrieved three twig-slender bones, yellow and with holes drilled through the ends.

"What are those?" demanded Frances.

"Tokens of alliance," said Chulzh'th. At Charlie's expression of horror, she added: "If it assures you at all, ghouls are obligate scavengers. They don't kill what they eat, ever."

There were a thousand ways an infant could die. In those bones, I saw Ezekiel Gilman crying with desperate thirst at his mother's teat. I saw Clarissa Thornwright's stillborn girl lying in the dust while she scraped out a tiny, shallow grave.

"We don't have to carry them, do we?" I asked.

"You do if you want this ally against the Outer Ones," said Chulzh'th. "I don't like those mushrooms." And then, of course, she had to explain to the others how we'd come to exchange tokens with a ghoul.

"You're telling me those . . . things . . . live right next to us," said Frances. "Just watching, when they aren't coming through to eat dead bodies. How is that okay?"

"It isn't," said Charlie. He frowned at his hands. "The world isn't under any obligation to be 'okay.' That's why we have to take care of each other, because there's no greater justice waiting." He gave me a wan smile. He'd found Aeonism's insistence on an indifferent universe hard to accept, and it didn't appear to satisfy Frances now.

"I don't like the mushrooms either," said S'vlk, bringing us back to practicalities. "Why would the Outer Ones be spreading their marks? Or is it some sort of spore from Nnnnnn-gt-vvv's presence here yesterday?"

"Would we find the same if we looked elsewhere in the city?" I asked. Ragged leaves unfurled in a childhood memory. Left alone, I recalled, they stole the soil from whatever grew before. We pulled their early shoots, and they flavored springtime stews in tongue-puckering abundance. "Like garlic mustard. Could their wards eventually grow over the dreamland?"

"An excellent question," said Grandfather. "I suspect that the spread is a new phenomenon—else the invasion would have been complete millennia ago."

"But what does it mean?" Frances burst out. Her eyes were still on Chulzh'th's hand where she clutched the ghoulish tokens.

I counted on my fingers, trying not to think about the bones beneath the skin. "We know the Outer Ones are worried about humanity, and came to this city to learn more about our present state. We know they have internal disagreements, political and personal, over how to handle their relations with us. We know they care only a little what we think of their methods. Barlow *and* Spector think they're hiding something, that not all the missing people went missing willingly—that fits S'vlk's dealings with them, and Glabri's too. 'Clutch-thieves,' he called them. They're not hiding as well as normal, maybe because they're someplace new, or maybe because they're doing something different from what they usually do." I sat back, running low on fingers. "I don't know what all that *means,* though."

"Trying to predict how someone will jump, with six legs," said Grandfather.

"Ten legs," said S'vlk. "I think."

"We need to learn more," said Chulzh'th. "You're in the best position to do so, Aphra—you and Audrey."

"Oh no," said Audrey. "I told you, I don't want to talk with She-lean, and we couldn't trust anything she told us in any case."

"One could hardly hope to speak to a Mad One under safer circumstances," said Chulzh'th. "And she sounds loquacious, if nothing else. She must observe a great deal—more than Mr. Laverne, who's young and hero-stricken."

The elders weren't likely to show mercy on this. "I could talk with her," I said. "If you want."

"I'd rather we *all* stay away from her." Audrey shuddered. Normally she welcomed risk; it was painful to see something cut her so closely. "But if someone must—thank you, Aphra."

It felt easier to confront her awkward relative than mine. Perhaps Audrey would talk to Freddy in return. My breath eased as I considered the implications. "Acolyte—you think I can visit the Outer Ones safely now?"

" 'Safely' may be too strong a word—but I think you'll be ready soon. Not tomorrow, however. Whatever the Outer Ones are up to, it will keep while you honor the solstice."

"I can't!" I was shocked she'd suggest it, under the circumstances. "Grandfather said we weren't to risk being alone with the Outer Ones. The Summer Solstice is all about solitude, and we know they can appear anywhere. It's bad enough that Neko's among them now without giving them a chance at the rest of us."

"I said you should not *have been* alone with them." The rumble in his voice reminded me that I'd already disobeyed his edict. "Chulzh'th is right—you shouldn't shirk this duty, especially now. Now that S'vlk and I are safe and clearheaded, we can ease the risk of private meditation."

A shiver raised the hair on my arms. "You'll track me."

"We'll know if you're in danger, or not where you seem to be."

222 • RUTHANNA EMRYS

"The solstice ritual is about knowing yourself, and knowing your community," said Chulzh'th. "You'll need the strength of that knowledge when you go back to the Outer Ones' lair—to learn, and to protect your sister-in-adversity. This is no time to sacrifice a sacred rite to fear."

And that, I dared not argue with.

CHAPTER 17

Spector had waited late for us at Tante Leah's, hoping to check in without his colleagues around. Having promised to rise at dawn, I wanted to go to bed—but I owed him an explanation of where we'd be the next day.

"So you just wander around by yourself until sunset?" Spector sounded dubious. "I suppose not all your holidays can involve controlling the weather, can they?"

I laughed in spite of myself. "It's as different from the Winter Tide as you can get. The strongest magic for the longest night, and the deepest contemplation for the longest day." I sighed. "Finding solitude in New York seems hard, though. It's supposed to make you appreciate having people around more, when you return to them, but here there are people around all the time."

He shrugged. "You learn how to make a place for yourself in a crowd. The funny thing is, everyone cooperates. Go to D.C., or worse, out to the country in Virginia, and everyone on the street wants to stop and yak. But New Yorkers can't get away from each other, so we try to give what privacy we can. I guess . . . there are a lot of parks where you can get some solitude, but the places with no one around are more dangerous than crowds—not that you can't defend yourself. What about a museum?"

"Maybe." I imagined pacing an unfamiliar museum, avoiding

Audrey and Charlie while helpful docents tried to explain the art. At least New York's institutions wouldn't, so far as I knew, hold stolen artifacts from Y'ha-nthlei.

He took a deep breath. "I'll tell you what. I was there for your last holiday, I can do something for this one. I know you've got too many people to worry about right now—but when all this is over I'll talk with my family, and set up that dinner I promised Mark. It'll be a little late, but we'll have a local feast to celebrate. If that's appropriate. If you want to come."

It was another offer of trust, even if the meal would be awkward. And the promise of an "over," of an oasis from Outer Ones and agents, was comfort in its own right. "I'd be honored."

As we parted, I recalled a more urgent message. "Mr. Spector?"

His hand was on the door. "Yes, Miss Marsh?"

"Warn your colleagues: none of you should be alone with"—I was not fully confident in our lack of eavesdroppers—"*them*. They're better at disguises than you might suppose from the masks."

"I'll bear that in mind. And if you're not allowed in yet, I'll try to find out whether Miss Koto needs any help."

"*Thank* you."

I pounded up the stairs, relief warring with my awareness that I was about to face a solitary bunk. But when I entered the room, it *wasn't* solitary. Before I could summon shock, Deedee pulled me into a fierce hug. "There you are!"

"There *I* am? Where have you been? Where's Caleb?"

"Here." He swung down from the top bunk, hair disheveled from envy-inducing rest. "*We've* been fine. Your pulse has been all over the map. What the hell have you been doing?"

"Meeting Outer Ones in Hunts Point, and arguing with our new cousin, and losing track of Neko, and . . ." I sat on the lower bunk and buried my head in my hands, overwhelmed all over again with the thought of explaining everything to him, suffering his reactions to each new turn. "You tell me yours, first."

"Not that much to tell, I'm afraid," said Deedee. "We figured you had the weird fungus people covered. So we went back to Dr. Sheldon to find out if he could help with any other leads."

"He's exasperating," said Caleb, "but he really did want to help. And I suppose—I wanted to give him a chance to be less terrible than Peters. Which he was."

"He was very polite," Deedee assured him. "Mostly. He gave us the measurements he'd worked out, and had some suggestions for where we might look. G.I. records were his big idea—if we can find a way in."

"Mr. Spector might have access." I sat up. "It's a good suggestion, thank you."

"You're welcome. And now I want to hear about Neko—if you lost her, please tell me you found her again?"

"I know where she is. That's not the problem." In as much detail as I could bear, I sketched the two days since we'd last seen each other.

"We have to go get her," he said, when I'd finished.

"Chulzh'th says that after the solstice, I'll be ready to face them again."

Caleb shook his head. "Not *you*. We clearly need to keep you away from them. Deedee and I can go after Neko while you're off being spiritual. We know what to look out for, and to stay where we can see each other. Can you imagine telling Mama Rei that we couldn't get her back because we spent an extra day wandering the city?"

My relief at his presence was gone. For all that I'd missed him and feared for him, as long as he was away from the situation he was *safe*. "She *chose* to go back to them and worried as I am, I don't think they'll hurt someone who wants to be there. But you—I can't imagine telling Grandfather that I let you take this risk, when I'm already in danger. I'm sorry, but my vulnerability means we need you out of harm's way. Mr. Spector is going to check on Neko tomorrow, and we'll go after her as soon as we can."

"She's my sister too," he said.

"And my friend," said Deedee. "Our confluence needs to look out for each other."

"I beg you," I said. "Let me know that you two, at least, are safe while I'm doing what I promised tomorrow. After that I swear we'll meet the elders at Coney Island and we'll all go together to settle what's happening with the Outer Ones and Neko. I feel like you're all being peeled away a strip at a time. The idea of you going into danger without me—just please, don't. A few hours longer, and we can all face it together."

Still he hesitated. "Grandfather won't like that, either."

"If he wants to talk you out of going, he can do that himself tomorrow night."

By the time they left for their own hotel, I thought I had them persuaded. But still I feared.

I slept under my own wards, dreaming ordinary and anxious dreams. I woke sweating from a metamorphosis gone awry, where my finger-webs grew metallic and nerveless as an Outer One canister. Gray light seeped through the window slit. I rubbed my fingertips against the blanket's cotton weave, the wall's rough plaster, the join of wood at the corner of the bunk. I prodded my upper arm where Grandfather had scratched his rune. An ordinary cut would be barely visible by now but the white skin still puckered, edged in swollen pink. Close by, faded by months of healing, was the spot where a similar mark had connected me to Sally Ward. Surely I imagined that the skin around my new link swelled cold, that the blood beneath it stilled. I wished the weather could justify long sleeves.

In the hallway, Audrey yawned and grinned at me, and Charlie nodded. But outside, we separated as soon as we could. I walked alone—except, of course, for early-rising New Yorkers opening stalls and hawking papers, and those who staggered home bleary-eyed on the trailing edge of a late night. A small dog scampered across the

street. It twitched, whirled on the sidewalk, and barked at me. I
backed up, hands placating. It darted forward, stopped abruptly, and
keened distress before racing again into an alley. I shuddered: dogs
never liked us, and the encounter was not a good omen.

But the day brightened, and no one else intruded on my path. At
home I would have carried saltcakes made the night before: hearty,
contemplative food for the day's meanderings. I'd gotten back to the
hostel too late, and risen too early, to request anything from Tante
Leah's kitchen. She'd have wanted to talk in any case, breaking my
ritual silence. Instead, I chose a bakery with its door ajar and the smell
of fresh bread wafting through. I pointed at a small loaf, nodded when
it was offered for my inspection, placed my hand on my heart in
thanks, paid with cash from my skirt pocket. The proprietor, unfazed,
must have assumed me unversed in both English and Yiddish, reluctant to mangle either for this simple interaction. She fell back on
Yiddish, so I understood only the friendly amusement of her pros-
ody. If I followed custom strictly, I shouldn't have let anyone speak to
me either—but our interaction seemed a better omen than the dog.

I found a small park, and a bench where I could break my fast.
The morning was warm but humid, and the tang of ozone promised
rain. I offered crumbs to birds. I prayed, feeling much less certain and
much less grown-up than when I'd last done this. *Ïa, Yog-Sothoth, Gate
and Key. Open the way for me to see myself, to know what I am without others
to support me. And keep the gate open, the key in sight, for me to return and
be again enmeshed with my family, my community, my confluence.*

*Ïa, Dagon, Ïa, Hydra, show me what I can be for Innsmouth. You guarded
us in life and did not prevent our deaths; can you lead us toward life again?
Or do you only watch?*

*Ïa, Nyarlathotep, you've had your laugh. Now let me recognize when others
seek to lead me astray.* No. *Let me recognize when I'm about to lead* myself
astray.

At first, I tried to pretend I was truly alone. I tried to focus on the
proper subjects for solstice meditation as I had learned them: myself,

my family, the full community of the water; expanding circles of connection with each concentric ring fully encompassing the lesser rings within.

But that was no longer my life. So much of my family now fell outside the compass of the water. The Kotos, who had welcomed me and Caleb when we'd lost everyone else, when they were raw with their own mourning for father and husband. I'd been so glad of Neko's company these past six months and missed the others desperately. I loved the confluence, but I'd never wanted to leave Mama Rei and her proud and dutiful caretaking, sharp kindness that pierced and bound all at once, like her sewing needles. I hadn't wanted to leave Anna, as comfortable following her mother's advice as Neko was conflicted, or Kevin, still exploring his first freedom. I hadn't wanted to leave San Francisco, where rain and mist soothed my skin every day, where the hills strengthened my legs and mountains cast long shadows on rocky beaches.

And yet, if I'd stayed in San Francisco I would have missed my newer family. They were stranger to me than the Kotos, who built their community in a shape much like my own. The Nihonmachi was an Innsmouth of a sort, an oasis of shared understanding and culture. The confluence was different. Deedee avoided her family for reasons she would not name. Charlie spent uncomfortable holidays with his parents, who disliked everything they knew about his life. Audrey was close to her family, and yet I'd never met them—and never would, for we were none of us the sort of friends they would approve. Whether my friends welcomed or repudiated these bonds, they didn't extend to me. Still the confluence connected us.

I realized, though, that I *had* met one relative of Audrey's, this very week. And she had approved of me.

I'd met relatives of my own as well, people of the water who weren't part of that greater circle. Frances, initially reticent, seemed drawn to our offer of community. She'd asked how she could celebrate the solstice herself, and would meet us at Coney Island tonight. We needed to create a ceremony, when we had the time, to welcome her to the family she'd never known. Very few mistblooded children had ever been reclaimed before their metamorphosis, and we'd never needed such a ritual before. But gods willing, the Lavernes would not be the last.

Freddy. Part of me wanted to interpret his choices, made in ignorance of our connection, as simple self-destructive delusion. But through him I'd seen another tight-knit community, strange and dangerous and utterly at odds with our blood. The Outer Ones and their companions were another ripple spreading outward, intersecting with my own.

I thought then not of concentric ripples, like a stone dropped in a pond, but of rain on water. Each drop left a mark, some spreading almost invisibly while others grew into waves that would cross the ocean. I stopped trying to ignore the crowds around me, and started watching them, trying to understand the lives that intersected so briefly with my own.

A young boy, red hair flashing beneath his skullcap, chased a ball out of an alley. Two more boys followed; they scuffled around the ball before retrieving it and racing back between the buildings. A woman beat a scarlet rug over the side of a balcony. I heard a baritone singing in an unfamiliar language.

I walked south, mindful of the network of trains undergirding the city, and where I had to be at sundown. Neighborhoods shifted and blended—as they did in San Francisco but larger, louder, more multitudinous. Alphabets and chords of scent, line of cheek and tone of skin, flavor of language: these differences marked each cluster of blocks unmistakably, showing where communities settled together to share comfort in an unfamiliar place. But each permeable pool spread rivulets into the surrounding pools, as people intermingled for food or friendship or business or simple curiosity. Without that flow, they might have grown stagnant. With it, they became a thriving wetland of shared strength.

Those rivulets were the veins carrying the pulse I'd felt since I arrived. I could feel it now, speeding my own heart and making my fingers tremble. It fascinated and overwhelmed me. Even those who lived here sometimes seemed discomfited. An ice cream cart minder shouted at a boy: "Talk English! I ain't got time to figure out what you want!" A pale man, gangling in a tweed jacket, walked hunched as if against blistering wind, arms tight across his chest. He caught sight of an awning marked in Chinese characters and shuddered, hurrying on.

Innsmouth, England, had been truly isolated, clinging to the tip of a peninsula that high tide cut completely from the mainland. When nearby towns swelled toward us and brought suspicion with them, we'd sought similar solitude in America. We'd settled for a patch of land girded by bogs that discouraged the Puritans who claimed territory nearby. We'd traded with native towns as well, trying to keep them as a buffer between ourselves and those who knew us better. I recalled our history from faded lessons: decisions treated as inevitable in the schoolroom. What would we have been like, if we'd come here instead of the Massachusetts coast? If we'd given up secrecy for the camouflage of a hundred other mutually unfamiliar cultures?

I mused, imagining a few blocks claimed beside the ocean. Awnings marked with Enochian runes, carts serving saltcakes and fried fish on skewers. A temple squeezed into a narrow storefront. Perhaps we would have been safer.

But we'd have been very different, by now. Children on the street shouted in mixed tongues, and most merchants seemed more forgiving of crossed boundaries than the ice cream vendor. In spite of each demarcated oasis, I saw mixed heritage in many faces, and clothes that told nothing of their wearers' origins. I watched a young Chinese woman, whose dress would fit perfectly among Audrey's fashionable friends even if her skin would not, argue enthusiastically with a gray-haired negro woman whose peacock-blue skirt flowed past her ankles. Our little oceanside haven would have had permeable edges as well: neighbors sharing apartment buildings for cost or convenience, children playing comfortably alongside men of the air, moving across town to be closer to a job or a lover. We would have gone everywhere in the city, sooner or later. Talked to everyone.

We would not have lost as much as we had in reality—but we'd have argued endlessly over the trade-offs we'd made. Now, with what little we had left, those trades were unavoidable.

Neko Koto—May 1949:

Audrey finds me on the beach, trying to figure out how to skip pebbles. I was never any good at it in San Francisco, and the Atlantic is no more cooperative. Deedee and Charlie both have the knack, and Aphra's grandfather is good enough that I suspect chicanery. Or just a century of practice.

Audrey finds a sea-polished pebble and turns it round in her hand. She crouches and splashes water over her face—then winces at the salt in her eyes. Aphra's customs don't always suit the rest of us, I think, but I can see Audrey finds it comforting in spite of the sting.

"What's wrong?" I ask.

"Nothing." She tosses the pebble from hand to hand. "Do you miss your brother?"

My stone sinks to the sandbar. I think about Kevin, full of life and energy, occupying all parts of a room at once. Of his cries in a small cabin. "Sure, sometimes. But I'd rather be here." And I think of why Audrey would ask. "Do you miss your father?"

"Sure, sometimes. But he's close by. And . . . I know how to ask him for things, you know? But not how to ask him about things." She dips her hands again and runs them across her face, pausing with the pebble against her forehead.

"Your brother," I say gently. I know he died in the war, little more. I've never asked what theater.

"I've been thinking about him. Because he didn't know—what I am, what he must have been. I don't see how knowing could have made a difference, but I keep thinking somehow it might have."

I've imagined miracles to save my father, sent alone to a dissidents' camp and dead of flu the first winter, a thousand times. I sit beside her. Around Aphra, I've grown used to damp dresses. "Does your family talk about it? I mean—his passing. We talked so much about my father, we mourned him, but without a body or a funeral it all felt unreal. Except when it didn't at all."

She nods. "We had a funeral, of course, but no body either. My family's not great with funerals, but at least my parents would say his name. I had friends whose fathers and brothers vanished into these big empty spots in conversations, holes you could fall into." *She frowns at her rock, and spins it out over the water. It skips once, barely skimming, and disappears. I think of the prayers we said over my own father—no chance for a funeral, in the camps, only stolen moments for remembrance. Aphra and Caleb guarded our moments of contemplation and mourning, as we guarded theirs.*

Audrey goes on: "Mom and Dad were almost eager to get me out the door for Hall—not because they didn't want me around, but I think they didn't want to have something happen to me, too, before I got to live my life. I'm grateful, but . . ."

But she almost died on this beach, a few months ago. I need to remember that. Audrey wears confidence like a diamond necklace, and yet she walks the site of her nightmares every day. Mine are safely on the other side of the country, and it doesn't feel far enough. Sometimes I just want to pick a direction, and keep going until I find that distance. "You can't tell them that something did happen."

"They have pretty narrow ideas about what kind of life I should live. It would never even occur to them that I wanted something else. And even if the circumstances weren't impossible to explain, it'd kill them to think my life was in danger."

"Mama knows. But we've been through danger together; I don't think she expects me to avoid it. To be able to avoid it." *I need to remember that too— however constraining I sometimes feel Mama's expectations, she knows what my real life is like, and doesn't think it too strange to bear.*

CHAPTER 18

The sky had darkened while I walked, and now as the morning waned the sidewalks smelled of petrichor. Clouds lowered tendrils of slate and softest gray, rich with the promise of rain. As the sky prepared for storm, the eddies of the land cleared. People retreated from stoops, and restaurants helped those lingering at sidewalk tables bring their meals indoors. Umbrellas blossomed. The first drops came, and I moved aside so I wouldn't impede the people whose steps sped in response. Water fell cool on my brow and bare arms, and soothed skin rough with the city's grit.

The rain quickened, blurring the world's edges. In the silvering air, a flash of blue caught my eye. Across the street, a woman had retreated under a grocer's awning. She bent her dark head to examine a box of grapes. It was her skirt, blue as a cloudless noon sky, that had attracted my attention through the rain.

I'd seen that blue before, peacock-bright, as she argued with a young Chinese girl a dozen blocks past and an hour earlier. Had we both come this way by coincidence? I'd seen thousands of people already today; surely some must have kept walking in my direction. The woman twisted half around. Her eyes met mine briefly before skidding away. She stretched her fingers past the awning's protection, as if to test the rain, then frowned at the result and returned to inspecting produce.

Audrey would have been subtle, but I was not Audrey. I crossed the street as soon as traffic permitted and strode to the grocer's. At the last moment, though, I shied away. Suppose I were wrong? I'd make a fool of myself and likely frighten her as well.

I steeled my nerves, gathered what dignity I could in a dress rain-plastered to my frame, and released with regret the solstice's gift of quiet safety. "Excuse me, ma'am."

She wasn't much for subtlety herself. She flinched, and turned to me with an effort that mirrored my own. "Yes, miss?"

As gently as I could, I asked, "Were you following me?"

She sighed, and brushed her hand over her pouffed hair. "I told the man this isn't what I'm good at. But I suppose he didn't have much choice. He's got trouble, and he wanted me to track you and find out if you might help. I was trying to decide if I ought to just ask. You'd better come along back, then."

She had an umbrella, broad and red, and tried to hold it over both of us. Droplets splashed our shoulders.

"I don't mind getting wet," I said. I wanted urgently to know what was going on, and was willing to follow her as long as she didn't seem a threat. My hand drifted near Grandfather's rune. He couldn't provide reinforcement at this time of day, but I didn't want to simply vanish traceless. "Who's 'he'?" Perhaps she was a friend of Freddy's.

"Nnnnnn-gt-vvv, of course. Not an ordinary sort of man, but it's as good a word as any." She looked around nervously. "I'll take you back to my place. He'll explain the whole thing better. Unless he's still running scared; then I suppose I'll do it. This ain't normal. I've known them since I was a little girl. They're good people. Peaceable."

"Are they being . . . not peaceable?" With effort, I kept from rubbing the rune. *Neko.*

"I'm afraid so. He'll explain." She pushed back her hair again. "I'm Clara Green. His friend near forty-five years now, and travel-mate just this last year."

"Aphra Marsh."

"I know. And I know you don't like them—he told me—but he thinks you can help. For sure no one who does like them seems capable, so maybe he's right."

I was glad of the rain in my eyes. "How did you find me? I'm sure I'd remember if we'd met."

She laughed. "During your first visit to the mine? It's a wonder you remember *any* of us two-legged folk. But you've been part of our rites, and you're bound in with us a little now. Nyarlathotep knows your mind through the trapezohedron, and so do they. None of us is ever hard to find." She sighed and sucked on her lip. "Except that he's done something to hide us. He isn't sure how long it'll work."

Another thing to hold against them. "I wish they'd told me everything the trapezohedron did. I have bonds already, ones I've chosen. It's good Nnnnnn-gt-vvv knows I'm upset—they weakened those bonds without asking my leave. They must have known I'd refuse, and they didn't care."

"That's not what they're like. When they fail, it's just the opposite—they assume anyone would want their gifts, so they don't need to ask. Nnnnnn-gt-vvv's better than most. He doesn't always remember to ask, but he listens when I warn him off."

I thought of S'vlk's stories. "You're lucky."

"I was just a little girl when I met him. People who come to them older know enough to be awed. I was just excited to go play with the fairies."

A friend for forty-five years, and traveling for just one. "They didn't take you on a grand tour of the universe?"

"We'd better catch the train back to Harlem, unless you want to walk all that way again. I thought you had to stop some time for sure, but you just kept going!" She led me down between copper posts, into a station. Her umbrella spattered the floor as she slid it shut. "I wanted to go with him, but I warned him off. My papa needed me—and then my babies needed me. I couldn't very well leave these old bones"—she slapped her arm cheerfully—"lying in bed while I skipped around the stars. I told him I had to wait. But as they grew I told my Nellie and Jack, you find people who'll take care of you and stick by you. Now they're both grown and married and have their own babies in tow, and I can finally travel a little."

"I wouldn't have guessed the Outer Ones would put up with that."

"Maybe you don't know them as well as you think."

From the stories I'd heard, the Outer Ones *didn't* normally respect human duty. Was Nnnnnn-gt-vvv different, then? He'd given her exactly the chance most men of the air never got, to have a second life after she'd fulfilled her obligations. Perhaps I shouldn't have, but I felt safer in her company, knowing she understood what it was to serve duty first. She seemed closer kin to us than Freddy.

"I'll talk to him," I said.

Clara's walk-up was three flights above a tiny pharmacy. The building squeezed rail-thin between its neighbors. If people had to raise children in such places, it was no wonder they ran as rambunctious in alleys and sidewalks as Caleb and I had in the open labyrinth of the bogs. I wondered if she'd find our wetlands as overwhelming as I did her concrete and brick, or if all of Earth's offerings now seemed as narrow to her as these apartments.

She knocked, and waited for the muted rattle of the deadbolt.

Nnnnnn-gt-vvv backed away from her door, pressing against a bookcase to let us in. Clara Green's narrow living room did not easily accommodate a creature the size of a small horse, and the Outer One hunched its uncountable limbs tight. Wings fogged against the edge of the photo-crowded table and the record player in the corner. Shelves of paperbacks crammed us in tighter: science fiction pulps and romances, and ragged volumes of popular science and history, most of which I'd seen pass across Charlie's counter.

Clara buried her fingers among Nnnnnn-gt-vvv's tentacles, and it buzzed louder and pushed against her like a cat. It wore a brass pendant indented with an ornate pattern of spiraling dots, which swung hypnotically as it moved. Clara chuckled. "How're you doing, old man?"

"You found her."

"And then she found me. She says the trapezohedron messed with her—" She *hmmmed* and buzzed with her tongue between her teeth, something in the Outer One's language that I didn't catch properly.

"I'm sorry for that," said Nnnnnn-gt-vvv. "Kvv-vzht-mmmm-vvt isn't always . . . communicative . . . about our rites. It doesn't trust our human compatriots as we should; I'd rather let you make your own decisions, even if they're wrong. Our small philosophical disagreement has cracked the mine apart. It isn't right. I must speak with you, and with your allies in the government—no matter that we're mates thrice over, I can't countenance what Kvv-vzht-mmmm-vvt's faction is planning."

"Which is what, exactly?" I tried to sound more sympathetic than impatient, but my tongue was dry.

Nnnnnn-gt-vvv shuffled limbs and said nothing. It backed as far as it could, claws scraping the floorboards between couch and record player.

But sound crackled from the pendant: a familiar, almost maniacal voice. "Kvv-vzht-mmmm-vvt thinks it knows what's best for us, of course it does. So old, so wise. We children need some discipline before we play with fire, that's all."

I suspected my shock showed all too clearly on my face before I got it under control. But to meet with Shelean under these circumstances—*what did she have to do with this? Is their conflict her doing?* My hand stole to where Mary's shield lay under my collar. "What are you doing here?" I asked sharply.

"Oh, I'm not *here*. I'm at Freddy's side, and Kvv-vzht-mmmm-vvt's, learning about its plans and making a few small suggestions. This is just an encrypted projector. It's like talking through a long metal tube—it all *echoes*." Her voice turned sober. "You've heard terrible things about the K'n-yan, and they're all true. Believe, as your cousin won't, that I know the harm done when only the powerful are trusted to choose their lives. When the weak are protected from every danger *except* those powers. Better to risk letting us burn the world. But Kvv-vzht-mmmm-vvt thinks I'm being silly. Of course the Outer Ones are better stewards than the Mad Ones. Better than men of the air or the water. They're old, after all, and wise, and they've survived their own wisdom for a long time."

Nnnnnn-gt-vvv rattled—a sigh? "Shelean speaks the truth. Kvv-vzht-mmmm-vvt wants to take a more active role in human affairs. To guide your species in this time of hazard, so you can pass through the crucible of your technology and join us among the stars. You may have all the potential it perceives—but conquest isn't supposed to be our way. Nyarlathotep leads us along the void's edge, and tests our wisdom and—"

"And watches to see whether we keep our balance or plunge in screaming," said Shelean cheerfully.

"My point," said Nnnnnn-gt-vvv, "is that humans deserve the chance to make their own way across the cliff. I think you'll fall—so many species do. Most of you are insular and provincial and paranoid and prone to making terrible decisions in crises. But if we shape you to fit through that narrow gap, we'll shave away everything that makes you yourselves. Better to save the few who yearn to travel with us, and offer your leaders what wisdom they're willing to take freely, and let you own your risks. I love you as much as Kvv-vzht-mmmm-vvt, but if we believe everyone has something to contribute to the great conversation, we can't silence you to keep you safe."

"I—" I sat on the couch, though it brought me close to Nnnnnn-gt-vvv's shifting limbs and diaphanous wings. Before I spoke I breathed, in and out, slowly, feeling something shift inside me. I looked at the Outer One, pushing through the strangeness, through the nausea of senses that rebelled at its presence. For the first time, I understood in my gut why Freddy would take such people as kin. "I fear for humanity's future too. And I'm very grateful that you respect it as *our* future. I'll do what I can to help."

"That's about how I feel," said Clara. She settled beside me—she still looked nervous, but some of the tension had left her. She gave me the same considering look I'd given Nnnnnn-gt-vvv.

"Tell me—" I took a deep breath. "Tell me exactly what happened. I need to understand where the danger lies."

"But first," said Clara to Nnnnnn-gt-vvv, "*you* come out of the corner and sit down like a civilized person. And pull in your wings before the neighbors ask what I'm smoking. You know you're leaving trails. You're going to drive me crazy with all your fuss."

Nnnnnn-gt-vvv slunk from its retreat. It hunched on the rag rug in the center of the floor, even more out of scale. Crab-like claws flexed against the spiraled fabric; tentacles brushed the floor. Abrupt jerks punctuated their anemone ripples. Its wings contracted to ordinary matter in a gust of cool air. The eternal humming buzz rose and fell, resolving into words as the wings condensed into bat-boned leather.

"It's hard to speak against them even now. It's always hard when our debates grow bitter. For aeons we've honed our instincts toward cooperation, but sometimes it's still not enough. The interventionists have closed the mine to dissenters—my faction's in exile now, dispersed and seeking shelter so we can regroup.

"Kvv-vzht-mmmm-vvt told you that we left our hills to learn more about humanity's crisis—what danger you posed to yourselves, how soon you might face extinction. That's true as far as it goes, but it didn't tell you that while we came to New York, made our visits to Arkham and New Orleans, each was trying to prove our view of the answer. This argument isn't confined to Earth, either. Many believe, like Kvv-vzht-mmmm-vvt, that we've been too passive in mining the universe. That we should teach more species to be like us—it would say 'teach'; I and my faction would say 'force.'

"Our own flirtation with ecosystem-breaking technologies is aeons past, fallen into legend. In the generations since, we've developed weapons subtler and safer and far more powerful. We use them to defend ourselves and our travel-mates; no one would argue against that! But now Kvv-vzht-mmmm-vvt's belief-mates say they've learned enough, and they think we should use those weapons to bring humans similar safety. If it works here, they can influence their fellows across the cosmos to do the same wherever the opportunity arises."

"What kind of weapons?" I asked.

"You've seen what the trapezohedron can do: showing people more of the universe changes how they think. Then there are the cylinders. Removing people from their bodies makes them less subject to visceral fears, or to instinctive disgust at strangers, even after they return. These are tools if used on the willing, weapons otherwise. There are the arts I used, at their weakest setting, to calm your elders. We have all manner of methods for controlling and shaping minds, for insinuating subtle influence where it won't be suspected. Kvv-vzht-mmmm-vvt thinks these will save humanity, but I know your paranoia. We saw it in Arkham, and I know that if they once find a hint of our influence they'll suspect it everywhere. Kvv-vzht-mmmm-vvt is too confident. Fail or succeed, the interference it plans will lead to catastrophe."

Now my mouth was bone-dry. "And it wants to start with Barlow's team." A chill went through my bones. "And mine. Why did you follow me for so long instead of telling me my people are in danger? I have to let them know!" I rose from the couch, but sank back as I realized the problem. "They were going to spend today in the—the mine. I warned Mr. Spector that they needed to watch each other, but it may not be enough. And Neko's there, too. Can I still get in? Kvv-vzht-mmmm-vvt . . . it has reason to think I'd go along with it trying to . . . influence Barlow's people. I could try to get them out . . ." But I felt sick with the suspicion that my testimony had spurred Kvv-vzht-mmmm-vvt to do everything it wanted. I'd aimed its ambition at people who, for all their faults, didn't deserve to fall under its sway, and who could be used to inflict terrible harm.

This is the same mistake I made in January. Treating people I disliked as problems to be solved, instead of seeing them as people. I should have refused to answer Kvv-vzht-mmmm-vvt's question. Ïa Cthulhu, please don't let my mistake cost lives this time. As useless as a prayer could be.

"You mustn't go back to the mine," said Nnnnnn-gt-vvv. "Kvv-vzht-mmmm-vvt wants your support very badly, and doesn't fully trust you. It will use our weapons to control you if it can. It perceives you as *zzzzz'v'ck.*"

"Oh, high praise!" said Shelean.

"What does it mean?" I asked. I clamped my hands in my lap, nerves threatening to descend into useless tremors.

Shelean: "It means you're a hub and a lever. You know people who'd otherwise never meet, you link them to each other, and they listen to you. If you were an Outer One, you'd be hailed as a great leader— but you're human, poor thing, so you'll just get leaders who want to use you. Kvv-vzht-mmmm-vvt first among them."

I wanted to pace, but there wasn't room. I clasped my hands, nails stinging flesh. I hated to admit it, but the Outer One was right: going to the mine on my own was no better an idea now than it had been last night. Worse, knowing that Kvv-vzht-mmmm-vvt sought to draw me in. But to avoid the place entirely—that I could not countenance. "My sister—Neko Koto. Do you know where she is, what Kvv-vzht-mmmm-vvt intends for her? Can you get her out?"

"She came to the mine a couple of days ago," said Clara. "I remember her—we always pay attention to newcomers, even though there have been a lot lately. But they were treating her normally, introducing her around, teaching her our ways."

"She asked about differences between air and water," said Nnnnnn-gt-vvv. "She seemed worried, but she was there willingly. It's those who wouldn't willingly cooperate whose minds are in danger."

Can't I fear what my sister does to herself willingly? I forced my thoughts from that track. "Let me think. Most of us are supposed to meet at Coney Island tonight. The elders should be able to detect any new interference, maybe even treat it." *If Barlow cooperates.* "The rest of us who used the trapezohedron—are you looking for them as well? Will Kvv-vzht-mmmm-vvt look for them?"

"Are they also alone?"

"It's the Summer Solstice." *Why today? Did they know?*

"I don't observe holidays based on orbital patterns. It seems presumptuous to pretend they shape our lives as they do those of the planetbound. Kvv-vzht-mmmm-vvt celebrates them, of course. Your celebration involves isolation?"

"Yes—Charlie and Audrey will be on their own. So will Frances, but she's never been involved in your rituals." Trumbull was exploring the New York Public Library in spite of her disdain for their collection. Better not to mention Caleb and Deedee, perhaps still unknown to the Outer Ones and not included in their plans.

"Kvv-vzht-mmmm-vvt may be interested in your companions, but it has other priorities—your agents who visit the mine unwitting are the most vulnerable."

"Okay. The fastest way to reach them is probably to wait at their hotel room. Whatever's happened to them during the day, we'll deal with it when they return. Would you be able to help? Tell if something's off?"

"I . . . may be able to."

"What it isn't saying," said Shelean, "is that it's gone to a lot of trouble to hide what it's doing and where it's gone, and Kvv-vzht-mmmm-vvt's work could be just as well-hidden."

Arcs of pain in my palms, to keep me focused on moving forward. "Then that's what we've got to work with. I'll take the train to the Ritz. Can you make your own way there?"

"Yes." Its buzz rose in pitch, painfully, then fell again. "I'd feel happier if you'd come with me. Anything could happen, traveling the long way."

"With all due respect—I saw how your shortcut treated Grandfather and S'vlk. I don't care for it."

"I startled them, took them without asking. I've already said I shouldn't have. If you don't try to claw my joints open, I promise I won't suppress your emotions. And if you insist on traveling on the street again, I'll let you—but I think it's a terrible idea. We've tried to be discreet, but any of us could have been tracked."

I didn't want to see more of how the Outer Ones traveled. But if Kvv-vzht-mmmm-vvt really was after me, I'd probably like what it had in mind even less. "Will it have the same effect as the trapezohedron? Will it dissociate me from my body, or do anything else that would make it easier for you to"—I had no polite word, but recalled Freddy's term—"encircle me?"

"No. During sidestepping, your body and mind travel in tandem. Someone skilled in dreamwalking stands a chance of finding their way home if they pull away. Otherwise there's no relationship to any art of separation."

If that was true, then the last remaining question was Nnnnnn-gt-vvv's own trustworthiness. My judgment was demonstrably faulty: I should not have sacrificed Barlow's team to Kvv-vzht-mmmm-vvt's benevolence. But Nnnnnn-gt-vvv wasn't asking for targets, or probing for vulnerability. I could work with it, at least for now.

"All right." My nails still dug into my skin; I mustn't let them draw blood. "Let's go, then."

"She's not used to giving directions in the outskirts," said Clara. "How are you going to know where to go?"

"Can you explain it to her?" Tentacles swiveled in her direction. "You should stay here, in safety, while she takes me to the hotel."

"But I'm not gonna. First, because I'm your travel-mate. Second because Kvv-vzht-mmmm-vvt could send someone to find me as easily as you found Miss Marsh here. This place isn't 'safe' anymore." Nnnnnn-gt-vvv's hum sounded distressed, but it didn't argue further.

"What do I need to do?" I asked.

"Even without equipment Nnnnnn-gt-vvv can—not exactly see your thoughts, but perceive the shape of your mind. If you think about

244 • RUTHANNA EMRYS

where you met these people, not just what the place looked like but also how you got there, the map of the world around it, he should be able to get close. From the outskirts you can look at the world and point out the right room."

"It's easy," said Shelean. "All you have to do is not get distracted by getting yanked out of physical reality for the first time."

"You shut up for once," suggested Clara. "What are they doing back at the mine now?"

"Aphra's secret agents just left. If Kvv-vzht-mmmm-vvt did anything big to them, it wasn't while I was in the room—but it hasn't exactly been carting me around. There was a lot of negotiation behind doors."

"One at a time?" I asked.

"They stuck together, as far as I could tell. But again, I'm basically planted in the conversation circle listening to gossip, and trying to get Freddy past"—she mimicked a child's distressed whine— "'But how can they be *fighting* with *each other*?' Poor boy, he so wants them to be better than humans."

"Do you love him?" I asked abruptly.

She sighed, exaggerated as a heartsick youth. But her voice turned sober again. "I'm getting there. I still feel the wonder of having people I can really talk with, and I see that in him, too. He basks in ideas like he's standing in the sun for the first time. I can't fault him for naïveté while he's still blinking at the light."

CHAPTER 19

Clara filled a bag with clothes and such supplies as she thought we might need. Nnnnnn-gt-vvv stood and shook itself. It rubbed its limbs together, as if it were cold or stiff; I tried to fathom the gesture. *Am I making another mistake? What am I missing?* Nnnnnn-gt-vvv's respect for Clara's worldly duties, like nothing I'd seen from Kvv-vzht-mmmm-vvt, was all the difference I had to go on.

I put aside doubts about the decision I'd already made, and considered how much I should tell Barlow and his team, when I finally saw them. If the Summer Tide was supposed to make me appreciate the people I could truly trust, I was certainly learning that lesson in full.

Clara slung the surplus army duffle over her shoulder. Nnnnnn-gt-vvv wrapped its limbs around her, and she slipped her own arm among them, grasping something shoulder-like, comfortable as a child with a favorite doll. She looked at me expectantly. The golden pendant tittered.

The air beside the Outer One was cool. Sweat shivered from my skin, and static tickled the hair on my arms and scalp. The touch of its limbs, chitinous and yielding at once, jolted me into a strange awareness: my body felt closer and clearer, while the rest of the room seemed to fade from importance. Its buzz vibrated through my bones.

246 • RUTHANNA EMRYS

"Show me your map," Nnnnnn-gt-vvv hummed.

I forced myself to think about where we were going. Clara had said the shape of the space was more important than how it looked, but it was easiest to start with vision. The glittering lobby, the stares as we made a path to the elevator. Barlow's suite, ostentatiously roomy. Their papers and books everywhere. Trying to keep my eyes open while they worked their rituals. By now the room must be rich with the track of their efforts. The blocks around the hotel, bright with plate glass windows and rancid with traffic . . .

Nnnnnn-gt-vvv's wings snapped wide past the limits of my perception. Wind, gusting mint and ozone and formaldehyde, whipped my face. We rose; my eyes blurred with sparks, and I felt myself falling in all directions. I clung to the insectile limbs that held me fast.

"Focus, kid." Clara's voice, improbably clear. My vision swam when I turned my head, but she looked normal. "Focus on where we're going."

"And on not losing your lunch," added Shelean. "Even *your* fancy body has disadvantages."

"You be quiet," said Clara. She was half the K'n-yan's age, I realized. Growing up, she'd have come to know Shelean as a harmless if eccentric aunt.

I tried to pull my thoughts together. I closed my eyes against the improbable winds through which we flew. I imagined the suite, the table and the candles and the file that must now be thick with notes. I imagined George Barlow and Mary Harris and even Peters, brute that he was, living in that space and shaping it. It was a good exercise, nearly complete in its distraction.

"Now." I felt Nnnnnn-gt-vvv's words as much as heard them. "We're getting close. Show me where we need to go."

I cracked my eyes, then forced them open. Shifting layers of reality lay dissected before me. The Ritz shimmered within diaphanous walls, ghostly floors and furniture. Will-o-wisp guests shone like candles. I tried to recall, exactly, the elevator with its supercilious attendant. I counted floors.

"Eight levels up. There should be a room with more books and papers than normal."

We drifted closer. We passed through brick and plaster; I might have imagined the moments of pressure against my skin. A maid gathered towels strewn in mad profusion beside a bath; I turned my head away from three people twined naked on a broad bed. They took no notice.

"Is this it?" asked Clara.

"Yes, that's the one," I said with relief. The room was unoccupied, but piled with books and files. Diagrams still covered their floor slate, now pushed to the edge of the carpet.

"Very good." Nnnnnn-gt-vvv flapped its wings hard, braking, and the scent of rotting fungus overwhelmed everything. We broke from the wind's grip into the ordinary warmth of summer. I felt as if I could breathe again, as though whatever passed for air in that strange between-space hadn't filled my lungs.

"Whew," said Clara. "Your friends have nice digs. Are we gonna get dirt on the carpet?"

Limbs folded back to release me at last, and I stretched cramped muscles. "They need room for their work."

Nnnnnn-gt-vvv turned slowly, stretching as well. I tried again to count its limbs. The effort was irresistible; I felt as though, if only I could nail down this one detail, I'd be able to understand it as well as any human stranger.

You needn't pretend—just ask who you're talking to. Kvv-vzht-mmmm-vvt had told me that, but it was still sensible. "I hope it's not rude to ask, but how many limbs do you have?"

Clara snickered, and Nnnnnn-gt-vvv's buzzing stuttered a little. Laughter? Anger? Sympathy? "It's not rude, but it's not a question I could answer without a great deal of theoretical physics. Have you studied the field?"

"Never mind." Maybe I could get Trumbull to ask, later.

"They've got terrible pictures of you. Look at this." Clara had found the Outer One file, still lying on the table.

I was tempted to explore, myself. It would be good to know more about their current obsessions. "Leave that alone. It'll be hard enough, when they arrive, to convince them we haven't been ransacking their files." It only now occurred to me how displeased they'd be to find us here. There was no help for it; we could hardly wait in the lobby. And my stomach rebelled at the thought of hovering outside reality for hours.

Grumbling, Clara consented to join me on the couch. Nnnnnn-gt-vvv folded low on the rug in front of us, trying to look slightly less intimidating. *This is the longest day of the year. After it gets dark, we can tell the elders. They'll know how to handle this.*

Minutes passed. The room was nearly silent. Only a faint blur of machinery, traffic, and distant conversation made it through the walls.

"Last night," I told them, "Acolyte Chulzh'th and I walked the dreamland near Coney Island. We found some of your . . . mushrooms? The things you make your wards from—growing there. Is that normal? Do they grow wherever you go?" I didn't mention Glabri; it didn't seem necessary and the ghoul would probably prefer discretion.

"No, that isn't normal." Wings shifted and furled. "How far had they spread?"

"All along part of a cliff face. Perhaps a few dozen feet."

"That must have been deliberate—and the spores must have been planted a day or two beforehand. They could provide the seed of a new mine, or a safe place to hide if the old one needed to be evacuated. Kvv-vzht-mmmm-vvt must have been planning for the interventionists' exile, if they failed to take the mine."

It didn't surprise me to hear that the interventionists had so carefully considered contingencies. But it did make me more worried about trying to move against them. It would be a challenge to come up with a strategy they hadn't prepared against.

When I wasn't mulling Kvv-vzht-mmmm-vvt's possible plans, I tried to recover the shreds of the solstice. I tested the strands that bound the confluence, plucking at the echoes of Charlie, Audrey, Caleb, Deedee. They remained fainter than they should be, and vaguer— and still more than I had of Neko. My anger at Kvv-vzht-mmmm-vvt burned in my chest, low and steady.

The lock rattled. I started to stand, then sat down again. The knob turned. George Barlow stepped inside. He saw us, inhaled sharply, and drew his gun.

"We've got company," he said. He stepped aside, keeping his aim steady. Virgil Peters and Mary Harris followed, their own pistols drawn. I'd expected them to be angry at finding us here, but I hadn't expected *this*. I tried to remember what I'd wanted to say. I tried to remember to breathe.

"You've got some nerve," said Mary. "I'm not even sure I want to hear your explanation."

"I do," said Peters. "I'm pretty sure that's the dissident Kevin was talking about. What's he doing here? And who's his pet?" Clara bared her teeth but had the sense not to respond.

"Let's take it easy," said Barlow. His aim didn't waver. "Kevin didn't tell us anything about these guys that we shouldn't have guessed earlier."

Aware of every shifting expression, I saw Mary swallow and blink hard. *She's more upset than the rest of them.*

"You tell me." Mary looked directly at me now. "You tell me how you could stand there and ask for my help, and act sympathetic, and imply it was *my fault* for writing a bad equation, when all along you knew exactly what Catherine's *friend* did to me. You tell me, and then you tell me why I should believe you *now*."

Nnnnnn-gt-vvv's tendrils spread wide. Its ubiquitous buzz filled the room and made my teeth ache. I tried to focus, to pull together an answer that would have been hard even without the image of my father's broken body interrupting every thought. *She deserves to know.* It was probably impossible to say anything she'd accept; raw honesty was the best I could manage.

"I was terrified of what you'd do if you knew about the Yith," I said. "They don't like people getting in the way of their studies. And they can travel through time. If they thought your government, our civilization, our species, was a threat to their archives, we wouldn't have a chance. By the time we saw you again, it had fled home and left Professor Trumbull to deal with the outsider you'd raised. She was still trying to understand what had been in her head and why. I'm sorry. I wish I could have trusted you with the knowledge. I still don't—what are you going to do, besides threaten to kill me for not telling you?" My voice was rising, breaking; I stopped before it broke entirely.

Nnnnnn-gt-vvv spoke for the first time. "And just as important, what did Kvv-vzht-mmmm-vvt actually tell you? I wouldn't assume it was the pure truth either. We came here to warn you that it wants to infiltrate your government—starting with you. It sounds like it's well on its way."

Peters barked a laugh. "You thought that if you didn't break into our hotel room, we might decide to trust someone who looks like a crab glued to a squid? Don't worry about it."

"Nnnnnn-gt-vvv," I said warningly. I'd seen it react precipitously when provoked; I didn't want to see its temper pitted against Mary's.

"We do, don't we?" said Nnnnnn-gt-vvv. "You look like someone tried to re-sculpt a melted *vbbrllt'zaa*. People worth talking with can look like anything. Kvv-vzht-mmmm-vvt doesn't need to win your trust, only to get you alone. As I told Miss Marsh, we have many arts to control the mind and body, fine weapons if you don't worry about the ethics."

"These guys jump bodies too?" demanded Barlow. "How many damn monsters are wandering around passing for human?"

It was a question I could answer, at least. I was sick with the weight of further secrets that would destroy all chance of cooperation between us. Part of me ached to release it, and to tell them now that Kvv-vzht-mmmm-vvt's interest in them was my fault. "As far as I know the Outer Ones don't jump bodies." I glanced at Nnnnnn-gt-vvv.

"We don't," it said. "Body-theft is a Yithian perversion."

"But they do," I continued, "mimic them very well. Far better than the masks they lent the elders. They can mold their servants to pass as anyone they like. And they can bind people to them, make people think more like they do, the same way they prepare them for travel. Miss Harris, the trapezohedron that made you so ill was one such art. The single time you used it shouldn't do too much harm, but you probably don't want to try a second ritual even if they can avoid triggering your seizures."

"Charming," she said. She kept her aim steady. "I'm tired of people treating my mind like their playground. What was her name?"

"Beg pardon?" I said.

"The creature that did this to me. What did it call itself?"

"Oh. It called itself Catherine Trumbull. Professor Trumbull—the real one, I mean—knows its name, but not how to pronounce it with a human tongue."

"Figures." She waved her gun, and I flinched. "George, unless you need these jerks for something, I want them out of our suite. I've had a long day. I want to be alone with people I trust."

"You heard the lady," said Barlow. "Oh, and to answer your question, I'm going to do what I need to maintain American security with *all* the powers we find ourselves surrounded by, however many there turn out to be. And I'm going to do it without your help. Whichever of these guys is telling the truth—and I've no reason to believe either of them more than the other—no one gets to lie to me more than once." With his own gun he gestured toward the door.

"I'd rather leave the way we came in, but I don't want to startle you," said Nnnnnn-gt-vvv.

"As long as you don't attack us, I don't care whether you take the elevator or slide down to the street on a rainbow. You're leaving now." Nnnnnn-gt-vvv stood, and took hold of me and Clara.

"Thank you for your hospitality," said Clara. She grinned without humor.

The Outer One spread its wings—slower than before, I thought— and we fell back until the hotel room looked like a tissue paper dollhouse, glowing invitingly with warm bodies.

I looked out Clara's window at the sky, still stubbornly bright. Behind high and fraying clouds, a translucent glow told of a sun still far from setting. I wished the rune on my arm could pass messages more complicated than my location and continued existence.

I wished I had some way to contact the others, not only Grand-father, before evening. After Neko, it was Spector who worried me the most. Why hadn't he come back to the hotel with the other agents? Did they know that *he* knew about the Yith? That would be enough to cost him his job—and discredit anyone who believed, as he did, that my people were worth cooperating with. He was, as far as I knew, the fiercest advocate among his fellows for treating Aeonists with respect.

I should never have risked bringing Barlow to New York.

Kvv-vzht-mmmm-vvt, at least, didn't know that Spector had met Trumbull's guest. If Spector kept his head and lied as well as he usually did, he'd be fine. I had to believe he'd be fine. I sent pulses of my worry out through the fragile connections of the confluence: *careful, careful, careful,* coded in breath and blood.

"Well, that could have gone better, couldn't it?" Clara sifted through her record collection. She pulled something out. "You know Alberta Hunter's stuff?"

I shook my head; Caleb had picked up a phonograph and Deedee was "educating" him on the past two decades of popular music, but I hadn't joined those lessons—the books seemed far more important. Clara slid the engraved disk from its sleeve and laid it on the turntable. She kept the sound quiet: a woman's voice, low and rich and soothing.

"I've heard about the Yith," she said. "They sound like nasty work. What happened back there?"

In spite of my frustrations, my first instincts were still to defend them. "They *can* be nasty. I've met one, and I've seen that firsthand. But they also make sure that nothing we do is forgotten. That legacy means a lot to us—more to me now. When my mother was young she met a Yith and had a conversation about . . . the sorts of things a kid would ask if they met someone who could answer any question. The state killed my mother in the camp, but that portion of her life is recorded in the Archives, and will be read when Earth is a cinder." I sighed and turned from the window. "Mary Harris put together a summoning spell to call one of everything within reach, without any safety precautions. One of those things was . . . you know what an outsider is?"

"Zzzzmmm'vvv-rrrt," said Nnnnnn-gt-vvv.

"Oh," said Clara. "Those things. In *this* dimension?"

"Not for long. The Yith who was wearing Professor Trumbull's body banished it. In her fury she cursed Miss Harris—she can't read now, or use any symbols at all—so that she wouldn't do it again. I was there. Miss Harris and her colleagues don't remember. The Yith said their minds were 'scabbing over,' but she helped that along, too."

"You try and stop her?"

"I don't think I could have, but no. I was terrified and angry. The summoning had grabbed me up, too, and held me there while that thing tried to sink its claws in me—" *Cold, so cold, and no air in my lungs, praying to be remembered*— "And just before it showed up, they'd been explaining that the summoning caught me because I wasn't really human. At that moment, I wouldn't have minded if she'd shredded their minds to scraps. Even after the Yith had gone home and Miss Harris helped us banish the piece of outsider that they'd missed, and we got to know her better—I didn't trust Barlow with the knowledge. So I kept quiet."

"Huh. And they just found out."

"Kvv-vzht-mmmm-vvt figured it out when the trapezohedron made Miss Harris sick. It confronted me, and I told it *why* she didn't know. Now it's using that to keep them from listening to me . . . how did it know I'd be in a position to warn them?"

Nnnnnn-gt-vvv hummed. "I doubt that was its main concern. More likely it was trying to gain their trust by telling them a secret. It thinks it can control their reactions."

"Everyone *always* thinks that." Shelean's mad singsong held an edge of fear, or bitterness. "Everyone's wrong."

Clara was running her hands over a row of paperbacks. She pulled out a ragged Doc Smith with a bubble-helmeted man on the cover, thumbed the pages without looking at them. I understood wanting these symbols of civilization close when danger threatened. Songs and written words.

I sat on the couch, breath suddenly dammed in my throat. I tried to swallow past it.

"You okay?" asked Clara.

"Yes. I just . . . noticed something. That I'd missed. Mary and— my people, in 1929, there was a raid on Innsmouth, and they brought all the landbound to a camp in the desert."

"A camp. Like Germany? Or like here, with the Japanese?"

"Japanese Americans. Nikkei," I said automatically. But I was surprised—I hadn't met many people outside the Nihonmachi who would have made the connection. "I shouldn't like to compare it with either—though they brought some of the Nikkei to our camp, toward the end. It was convenient. The camp was already there, and it was . . . mostly empty, by that point. A lot of bad things happened there, but one of them—" I paused, trying to collect disordered thoughts. "The soldiers had some vague idea that we could do magic. There had been libelous rumors that we sacrificed children, and consorted with demons. They knew that whatever we did required books, writing. So they forbade us even a scrap of paper or a stub of lead. They beat us for drawing in the dirt. It's not the same thing the Yith did to Mary: she has people who can read to her, we could still hold letters in our minds. But . . ."

Clara sat beside me, and handed me the Lensman novel. My breath loosened in the perfume of dusty ink. She nodded. "Seems like a lot of people want to keep that power to themselves, when they're in charge. My grandma, she came up from Maryland in the '50s. She meant to go all the way to Canada, but there was a little town of freedmen in Vermont and she met my Gramp there. He taught her how to read."

We drifted into less consequential topics: favorite genres, favored authors, the reassuring rhythm of readers everywhere. We might have been at Day Books's old quarters in San Francisco, warm and dry, mist drifting in with every chime of the doorbell.

Clara was fond of the pulp science fiction series, like the volume she held. "They're absurd," she explained. "But I always liked to read them, knowing I'd get to see the *real* universe. And that there'd be humans out in space, and they wouldn't be these square-jawed white guys at all, and no one would be able to tell anyway. The universes in these books are too well-controlled. The real thing is wild and beautiful and untamed, even for Nnnnnn-gt-vvv's people."

I wasn't as enamored of the genre—so many of those authors pulled resonance from stray bits of misunderstood myth. Tripping over fragments of Aeonism distorted by Greek or Aztec cosmology always put a bitter taint on my reading. I preferred Westerns, where problems were always unnaturally simple, and spy novels, where problems were always unnaturally complicated, and the sort of ornate "realistic" novels that gave seemingly intimate glimpses into the ordinary exotic lives of men of the air. Clara hated the first, enjoyed the second, and recommended a few of the third that I'd never heard of.

To my surprise, Nnnnnn-gt-vvv had opinions as well. I wasn't clear on whether it saw in the right frequencies to read a book directly, but apparently Clara had read aloud to it from a young age, sharing whatever held her fancy at the moment. The Outer One particularly enjoyed human poetry, without distinction between Ogden Nash and Keats. "I like the way you describe emotions," it said. I managed to dredge from memory most of the elegy for the *Hydra's Third Daughter,* lost at sea in 1633, and a couple of pieces by Yone Noguchi that Anna was forever quoting.

The sun arced low.

CHAPTER 20

From the vantage of the outskirts, Coney Island was an eldritch tangle of tracks and gears and levers, generators and engines, layers of wood and cloth and metal darted through with living lights. We watched those lights trickle out to cars and subway. After long minutes, the last stragglers left the knotwork infrastructure dark and still. The ocean lapped gently against the shore, untouched by the wind howling outside the world. Miniature waves shimmered under starlight.

"There," I said. A small cluster of lights emerged from beneath the boardwalk. Three more came from the water.

Nnnnnn-gt-vvv furled its wings and dropped to the sand.

Chulzh'th and Grandfather both shouted when they saw me. I wanted to fling myself into his arms, kneel at her feet and beg advice. Instead, I mutely held out my hand and suffered them both to check whether I was indeed myself. Then my friends surrounded me, Charlie and Audrey and Trumbull and Spector, asking questions too quickly for me to answer. Nnnnnn-gt-vvv and Clara hung back, waiting out the flurry of concerned family.

"Enough." S'vlk's voice cut through. "Aphra, explain. Unless this *meigo* would like to."

"I would like it," said Nnnnnn-gt-vvv, "if you wouldn't use that word. What are we supposed to be an 'abomination' against, anyway?"

"Khur S'vlk," I said. "Please be at peace. Nnnnnn-gt-vvv is an ally for now, and it sounds as if we need one."

The explanation took a while. Holiday food, simple picnic fare brought in anticipation of a happier feast, circulated while I talked. I hadn't expected to have an appetite, but found myself craving the physicality of salmon and peaches and tarragon bread. The taste of oil and the texture of grain reminded me of myself, and of the hands that had prepared them, and the connections between us.

A few minutes in, the elders' heads swiveled, and Grandfather stood up. "Caleb Nghadri!"

When I looked out from the boardwalk I saw him, and Deedee. A thread of my tangled emotions eased loose.

Caleb's expression was grim, though, as they sat among us. "What's *that* doing here?" he asked of Nnnnnn-gt-vvv.

"Helping," I said briefly. "The situation with the Outer Ones has changed, and Nnnnnn-gt-vvv and Clara came to tell me about it." I nodded at the two of them in brief if belated introduction.

"Well, that explains . . . something," said Deedee.

"You'll be furious, I'm sure," Caleb told me, "but we tried to go back for Neko. It wasn't right to make her wait, and I thought—"

"We thought," said Deedee, "that sometimes a person needs to be *told* that they're missed. Or needs to be rescued from something they thought they could handle on their own."

Grandfather growled deep in his throat. "What must I do to keep my grandchildren from casting off in hurricanes?"

Caleb bowed his head. "Pull people from the water before the storm starts."

"Which is what we hoped to do," said Deedee. "We figured out the general location of their mine from your description, and we searched until we saw their guards. But when we got there, it felt . . . I can't explain it, and maybe we were just imagining things. The Outer One lair felt *wrong,* and not only the wards you told us about."

"She told me that if your plan doesn't even survive going near the enemy, you regroup," said Caleb. "So we're here, regrouping. Now we need to *do* something, no more waiting for everyone to be ready. Do your new friends know what changed?"

Reluctantly I explained the conflict in the mine. Caleb's jangling eagerness for action, much as it matched my own, made the Outer Ones' civil war no easier to talk about, and gave me no insight into how to appease Mary's anger.

"She knows, now," said Trumbull. It was half statement, half question.

"Yes. I tried to explain why we didn't tell her, but she wouldn't listen. I can't really blame her. If someone hadn't trusted *me* with something that important . . . but no matter how I examine my choices, I come back to the fact that they *weren't* trustworthy, and still aren't." I checked Spector's reaction—he'd agreed with my judgment, originally, but that didn't mean he'd be happy to hear me express such a blunt opinion of his colleagues. But I found no disapproval; he simply watched me curiously.

Trumbull stood. "I have to go to her."

"Professor," said Audrey, "that doesn't sound like a great idea."

"They didn't want anything to do with *any* of us," I said. "They held me at gunpoint. If anything, they have more reason to be upset with you."

"No. I need to talk with Mary about this. I've wanted to from the start. What happened to her was done with my body and my brain."

"Yes," I tried. "But what your guest did isn't your—"

"No. It was done with *my* body and *my* brain. *I'm* the one who's studied in the Archives, and who's been trying to recover what I learned. If anyone can actually help her, it's me. Now that she knows what happened to her, we can finally work together on the problem. You all can figure out the diplomatic and sociopolitical issues, and I'm sure you'll do the right thing, and I'll help however you need. But right now, I'm going to find Mary and pay the debt I've owed her for six months."

I couldn't argue. "Go carefully."

S'vlk gave her a respectful nod and made a sign with her fingers. Trumbull blinked in surprise, smiled, and made an answering sign before heading toward the train.

I hoped Mary would forgive Trumbull for her guest's actions. Turning to Spector, I asked: "What about you? They can't have decided you're complicit, or you would have said something."

"No, they haven't. I looked as surprised as they did. But they *were* extremely upset, I think George even more than Mary. And very grateful to Kvv-vzht-mmmm-vvt for telling them."

"Which is of course one of the reasons it told them." I remembered Kvv-vzht-mmmm-vvt's original affront at Mary's injury. "I think it's acting on real principle, too."

"Kvv-vzht-mmmm-vvt is an idealist," said Nnnnnn-gt-vvv. "That's never in doubt." There was a pause while we pondered this.

Clara Green had been staying close to the Outer One, but looking curiously at my companions. She broke the silence: "I know there's a lot going on—but is that you, Dory Dawson? I didn't expect to see you again any time soon."

Deedee started. Caleb gripped her shoulder. After a moment she sat up straighter, taut with tension. "It's me. Good to see you, Miss Clara." There was a trace of real pleasure in her forced smile. "Not many people I'd say that about, but it's good to see you."

"You know each other?" I asked stupidly.

"Millions of people in this city," said Deedee, "and you had to drag the social hub of Seventh Avenue to our beach."

Clara shrugged. "We go everywhere. We talk with everyone. Some of us just do it in a smaller neighborhood, that's all."

"So you do," said Deedee. "Have you been traveling with these guys all this time?"

"Wouldn't have been fair to my Nellie and Jack, now, would it? Just this past year I finally got free to go my own way. But we've been friends since long before you were born. You know your ma finally left that Clark fellow?"

Deedee leaned back into Caleb's arms. "Did she? About time. Maybe one of these days I'll let her know I found a *good* white boy." She squeezed his hand. "Pale, at least."

"This is all so charming!" said Shelean. "But could we maybe catch up later? You're as scattered as an affection group house meeting."

Audrey half-rose, interrupting whatever Deedee was about to say. "You didn't tell me *she* was here."

I sighed. "I was getting to it. She isn't, technically—she's still back in the underhill, spying and trying to convince Freddy to leave."

"Spying which way? How do you know she isn't reporting all this back to her minders? Or just chatting about us to Freddy with no regard for who *he* might tell?"

"Cousin, if there's one thing you learn among the K'n-yan, it's never to trust anyone who wants to make all your decisions for you." A theatrical sigh. "But I'm a terrible spy. No one's saying *anything* interesting in the conversation pit today. It's all rushing back and forth, getting things done in the back rooms, and stopping by occasionally to tell us that everything is perfectly normal. Freddy's flipping out, but he still trusts Kvv-vzht-mmmm-vvt. He doesn't want to think his new tribe could be as screwy as the people he left behind. I've barely seen your friend, either—maybe they're keeping her where Freddy's nerves can't scare her off, or maybe they want something from her."

"Huh." Audrey sat, but watched Shelean's pendant through narrowed eyes.

"The Mad—Shelean—is correct," said Grandfather. "Let's focus on the immediate crisis, and how we must respond. If there's anything we can do, the opportunity may not keep. Nnnnnn-gt-vvv, how large are these factions?"

"And what do you think Kvv-vzht-mmmm-vvt has planned for my

colleagues?" added Spector. "Difficult as they are, I don't want to leave them in danger."

The Outer One buzzed and shifted its limbs. "The question of humanity's survival consumes all of us on Earth. Until today I would have said there were dozens of factions, all arguing and trying to come to an understanding. But now several have coalesced around this idea of direct interference with the great political powers. And great technological powers: it's the combination of dangerous invention with political volatility that they hope to dispel." To Spector: "I don't know what exactly it wants with your colleagues—but clearly it's trying to gain their trust. It might work on them slowly, molding them until they're willing to take advice. But given how fast it moved to expel dissenters from the underhill, I think it has something more drastic in mind. I just don't know what."

"Not necessarily," said Spector thoughtfully. "It could simply want to present a united front while opening diplomatic relations. But I don't like it either way—I need to let my superiors know what's happening. If you were in Kvv-vzht-mmmm-vvt's shoes . . ." He trailed off, looking at Nnnnnn-gt-vvv's crab-like claws, and shook his head. "—in Kvv-vzht-mmmm-vvt's place. What would you do? As 'something drastic,' I mean?"

"If I didn't honor your right to make your own mistakes? I would offer to help heal Miss Harris, and use treatments that compelled their loyalty. It's easy to tweak a mind as you move it."

"Or *by* moving it," said S'vlk grimly. "Your 'travel' changes people. It makes them pliable and passive."

Clara stood. She walked over to S'vlk and lifted her chin to meet the elder's gaze. "I waited forty-four years to go to the stars, and now I've finally done it. I've been out of my body six months this year, and I dove through the hole in the center of the galaxy and listened to the music of the spheres and had the best conversations of my life. Want me to show you how passive I am?"

S'vlk stared down at her. Deedee chuckled. "She doesn't sound any different from when I knew her, that's for sure."

"But Khur S'vlk is also right," said Nnnnnn-gt-vvv. S'vlk's head whipped around, and the Outer One lowered its own. "Clara, you were as prepared for travel as anyone could be. And like anyone I would invite to join me, you wanted to go. But it's not hard to force someone into it, and you don't have to be gentle. If you *want* to break someone that way, it's easy."

"You're saying Kvv-vzht-mmmm-vvt would . . ." Clara shook her head. "I know you're no better than humans, really. Of course some of you would hurt people like that."

"It would happily break a few humans to save your whole species. Our consensus has always been that learning too much about the universe would destabilize your societies—you might grow into that truth someday, but for now you're far too provincial. There's plenty of room for variation within that consensus, though. If Kvv-vzht-mmmm-vvt puts our allies in positions of influence, no one off Earth will interfere. Barlow is a start. It could use his team to draw in others, create a web of people following its lead towards peace and cooperation." Nnnnnn-gt-vvv's claws made long furrows in the sand. "This plan works very well, if you assume no one among your remarkably paranoid, xenophobic species will notice the infiltration."

I could all too easily imagine Mary Harris torn from her body, imprisoned in a canister. I recalled my own nightmare desperation in the touch-impoverished visions of the trapezohedron. "Spector's colleagues can do enough harm when their paranoia is unfounded. If they see creatures from another world trying to take over, they'll gather all the forces you could dream of—especially if the USSR is involved. Which you said Kvv-vzht-mmmm-vvt wanted."

"Yes, its mates in Eastern Europe are trying to do the same thing there."

I sat back, digging my hands into the cooling sand. They were sticky with peach juice, and grit crusted under my fingernails. The moon was an austere slice of light. *Are they up there, too? Looking down, making plans for people they only half-understand?* Behind all my fear for my world, my species, seethed fear for my sister, who only wanted her freedom.

Spector, who of all of us was most comfortable thinking at this level, frowned and stared at his hands. Charlie watched him anxiously. Deedee frowned at him as well, but focused on Nnnnnn-gt-vvv. "And what are *you* doing? You said you're part of a faction that's been kicked out of the mine—are you planning to take it back? How many of you are there? Do you have a plan for how we can help, or is this just you running?"

"We're . . . considering."

"What kind of an answer is that?" demanded Deedee.

"Take it easy on him," said Clara. "What you've got to understand is that this is really confusing for the Outer Ones. Their whole society is built around cooperation. They're taught how to fight other people, but not their mates. Kvv-vzht-mmmm-vvt is probably just as shaken, but his faction can distract themselves with the business of running the mine and working on their plans with the government folks. These guys—the hands-off-humanity group—they don't have anything they can do short of challenging their mates directly, and they don't know how to do that."

"Are they *willing*?" asked Grandfather. There was a rumble in his voice, deeper and more dangerous than usual.

Tendrils swiveled in his direction, iron filings to a magnet. "Before we do anything else, we have to survive our exile."

CHAPTER 21

Nnnnn-gt-vvv—*June 21, 1949, 4 a.m.:*

I'm monitoring the stasis room, listening to the reassuring harmony of well-tuned systems, when the alarm goes off. The wards assure me at once that it's a drill, and I settle into the practiced rhythm of emergency procedures. Fortunately this is one of the minor exercises: only embodied need evacuate, and the emergency protections raised by the skeleton crew are minimally onerous. That doesn't prevent me from wishing myself off-duty. If I hadn't taken tonight's shift as a favor to a travel-mate, I'd be waiting out the tedium in the comfort of the outskirts.

Halfway through the required checks, I notice an oddity. By now, my own repair procedures should be synchronizing with those in the ward room. Instead, the monitors report discord. I force my cilia in the same direction and explore more closely. I find the guards deep in the ward controls, making changes too swift and consistent to be error. My wings spread reflexively in search of safer dimensions. They're reprogramming the wards to keep the evacuees from returning. No one will get back in without explicit approval.

The records confirm my sick intuition: Kvv-vzht-mmmm-vvt arranged the drill.

I've long since outgrown the childish terror of being outside homespace, but I feel it now: the irresistible, irrational awareness of how my body violates local physics, and of the thousand artifices preserving my existence in the face of that violation. Core among those artifices is the haven of the mine itself, enough like home to restore coherence between trips. Without its protection, those outside will languish swiftly.

Kvv-vzht-mmmm-vvt meant me to be outside now, with the other dissenters. I'm no ward-writer; I can't reverse the changes they've made. My mind recoils from the thought of what they'll do when they notice me. I have minutes at best.

I set the monitors to automatic. A projector pendant hangs just outside the stasis room. With moments to choose, I key it to Shelean. When I examine my choice later, I'll realize that of all my travel-mates, she's the one with the greatest experience of betrayal.

"Don't say anything through your canister," I tell her.

She doesn't question, doesn't squeal or argue. "I won't. But I'll watch."

I snatch Clara from the street outside the mine, where she waits sweating, into the outskirts. She shrieks at the unexpected transition, then laughs and clings to me. For a moment she assumes this one of her childhood games, the fairies come to pull her out of the world for another adventure. But she sobers quickly as I explain the drill's true nature. One at a time, I find and confer with the evacuees who share my opinions. We slip away still immersed in somber discussion.

We came to New York to resolve a vitally important debate, with civilizations hanging in the balance. Until now, I thought we'd find a way to do so peacefully. This schism is like nothing I've experienced before, and I can only hope Kvv-vzht-mmmm-vvt is as disoriented by its actions as I am.

It had been easy, Nnnnnn-gt-vvv told us, to hope the bloodless coup a local aberration. But when the evacuees sought refuge at the Vermont mine, they discovered that parallel revolts had taken place elsewhere. Messages to Yuggoth had received no response. A few people had set off toward the edge of the solar system to learn what was happening there, but they feared the worst. The rest had scattered, searching for safe places to call their brethren back into congregation.

The number of Outer Ones was small but influential: fewer than a hundred across the planet, with perhaps two dozen in the hands-off faction. And of course, there were many more humans, some loyal to one of the factions and some simply trying to understand their patrons' rift. Most of the nonhumans were in canisters, and therefore under the control of the interventionists regardless of their actual political proclivities.

"So the first thing you need is a safe place to regroup?" I asked. I thought of the tunnels under Innsmouth's temple, the ones we'd never made it to during the raid. "What constitutes safety?"

"Somewhere we can put down wards, for a start," said Nnnnnn-gt-vvv. "They scaffold our survival in this space. If we can't grow new wards, and the interventionists have taken Yuggoth, we'll soon need to surrender or die." It paused. "I'm tempted to try to exploit the mine seed you found earlier. But they may have built in the same restrictions they're using to keep us out of the full-grown mines. I don't know if that's possible—I'm not a deep ward-writer."

"What's the risk of trying?" asked Spector.

"More than you might think," I said. "Those caves are already inhabited." Glabri's token burned dark in my mind. I knew its precise location in my pack. I hesitated—but Kvv-vzht-mmmm-vvt could not have missed the colony's existence when it planted its seeds, and Nnnnnn-gt-vvv wouldn't miss them when it went to look. Better to forestall the potential for conflict now. "It looks to be a ghoul warren."

"Nor were they pleased," added S'vlk. "What was it they called the Outer Ones, Acolyte Chulzh'th?"

"Clutch-thieves," said Chulzh'th, with somewhat less relish than S'vlk.

"They were quite upset about the mine seed," I said. "Maybe we can convince them to help stop the people who planted it."

"By letting Outer Ones stay in their caves?" asked Charlie. "They seemed awfully territorial. Do we have anything to offer them, aside from the chance for revenge on the interventionists? Not, ah, food, I hope."

"That's traditional," said S'vlk. "Invite ghoulish aid in battle, in exchange for leave with the dead."

Charlie shuddered, and Deedee said, "Ick," more cheerfully than was perhaps warranted.

"Will it come to that?" asked Caleb.

Nnnnnn-gt-vvv's hum edged into a high-pitched keening, resolving again into words. "I hope there won't be corpses. There haven't been so far. We must talk with the ghouls if they hold the mine seed. It's just like Kvv-vzht-mmmm-vvt not to care whether its reserve site is inhabited."

I had an unpleasant thought. "Did it plant the mine by the ocean because of us? You said it was interested in me, because I'm—" I paused, trying to retrieve the term.

"Zzzzz'v'ck," said Clara. "Someone who connects people. Like me—the 'social hub' of whatever street you happen to be on."

Shelean's voice echoed from the pendant. "Oh, yes. If you have to run away, you want someone strong at the other end to help out. Especially if you think you're strong enough to make them help you, even in retreat."

"That wouldn't be his only plan, though," said Clara.

"Such a cautious creature," agreed Shelean. "If I were him, I'd put little seeds all over the city. But we don't exactly have them on a map, do we?"

I thought of the fantastic skyscrapers and ethereal bridges beyond the cave ridge, marble plazas and tumbled ruins, skies swarming with gaunts and dark caverns sheltering ghouls. And among them, spreading tendrils through all the levels of reality, scarlet fungus taking root. "The people who have to live where the seeds are planted, they'll know. We'll ask the ghouls what they've found."

It wasn't simply a matter of dreamwalking and calling for Glabri. Chulzh'th settled in to demand details from Nnnnnn-gt-vvv: how many Outer Ones it needed to house in the cave, what they might have to offer, and whether the ghouls would be stuck with them as permanent neighbors. I should have stayed to help, but I felt over-whelmed. The solstice's opportunity for contemplation had frightened me, but I'd needed it. That contemplation shattered the moment I saw Clara. The shared revelations that should have been my reward at the day's end had been replaced with all-too-pragmatic planning.

"Go wash your face," said Chulzh'th. "We'll be here when you get back." Advice for a child, but at the moment I didn't mind.

The quiet moonlight glinted sparks on the ocean's shifting con-tours. Salt and seaweed overpowered the smell of the beach's debris. Cool water cleared my head and throat. I lingered with fingers trail-ing in desultory waves.

It was easy to get caught up in the urgent tide of great powers in conflict. What did I want out of this? Or rather—letting the sol-stice remind me of my community—what did *we* want and need?

The Outer Ones, in their fear for humanity, risked awakening my species's basest instincts. We wanted to be better—but that was long work and had little to do with the Outer Ones. If S'vlk was any indi-cation, it might be *very* long work. She was old and wise, but no less prone to blinding hatreds than any man of the air.

What we needed from the Outer Ones was the time to do that work. If the interventionists had their well-meaning way, they could send us spiraling into xenophobic wars. We needed Nnnnnn-gt-vvv's passivist faction to reassert their influence and to hold sway over what their species did on Earth.

But it was harder to fathom what form the relationship between our species might then take. Barlow already knew about the Outer Ones, and now about the Yith. He'd almost certainly pass that intel-ligence on to his masters. Would some treaty now be needed between the state and the Outer Ones? Promises of aid to soothe newfound fears? By deceiving Mary we might have forfeited our ability to influence that process.

We had too narrow a place to stand, and too little we could do to stop cities from burning. But as long as humans survived there was something for us to save. *And even after we lose the fight to save them, we'll still have work to do.*

All I wanted, in that moment, was for my family and species to survive this moment, this year, this decade. Millennia felt too painful to plan for.

The faint crunch of sand made me turn, and Charlie and Audrey joined me by the water. Audrey knelt to anoint herself. Charlie began the awkward process of lowering himself to the sand, and I hastened to offer him a handful of water so he could cleanse himself standing.

"You don't have to do this," said Audrey.

"Do what?" I was still thinking about preventing atomic war.

"Dreamwalk to talk with the ghouls," said Charlie. "Chulzh'th can do it, and we're good enough to go along without you."

"You tried for a few minutes yesterday, and it was really hard on you," said Audrey. "You may have to keep stretching, but you should wait 'til that can be the focus. We've got no control over how long this is going to take—and we have other people who can do the negotiating."

I thought about it, and about whether I could bear to stay behind. "That's very sensible."

"I've known you to be sensible, sometimes," said Audrey.

Charlie glared. "Do you mind explaining why this can't be one of those times?"

"I . . ." That was harder. "It's my fault that Mary and her team were so vulnerable, and my responsibility that Neko's caught up in all this. And Nnnnnn-gt-vvv came to me. And Freddy's my cousin, in danger from Kvv-vzht-mmmm-vvt even if he refuses to realize it." And, if I admitted everything to myself, I wondered if there was something to the way the Outer Ones saw me—as someone with a talent for connecting people who wouldn't otherwise have met or spoken. If that were true, I might be able to help in ways no one else could. "I can come back to rest as often as I need to. But I'll do what I can."

Charlie twisted his cane, drilling into the wet sand. "What happens after these negotiations? We aren't ready to pull through another world war, let alone a war with *other* worlds."

"That's what I'm afraid of. It's why I can't just wait somewhere safe. Hold back, and there may not be anywhere safe to go."

As we returned to the others, Audrey tugged at my elbow.

"Do you trust her?" she asked.

I didn't need to ask who she meant. Her usual mask wavered, revealing a glimpse of apprehensive bewilderment. Her inner trembling echoed hazily through the confluence.

"I don't know. I believe what Shelean's saying—but that's different from trusting her. Usually I trust people because of their actions. But Shelean can't act, only speak. I don't know how to judge that. Except for the way she talks—and I think Neko's right about that—she's not what I would have expected. I never thought about how *they* must suffer."

"Neither did I." She leaned against me, and I stroked her hair as one might a child. She went on: "After I found out—I thought maybe we were conceived in a star-crossed romance. But more likely they kept some poor woman prisoner and forced her to bear children . . . I pictured cackling scientists, but I never thought . . . She's a victim, but she thinks what they did to us was a good idea. And I can't *argue* with her, because I wouldn't exist otherwise. I don't know how to talk to her."

"I think deep conversations may be more than we're ready for. But she doesn't like what Kvv-vzht-mmmm-vvt is doing, and I'm provisionally willing to believe her and Nnnnnn-gt-vvv—they're the only window we have into what happened."

Back under the boardwalk, Chulzh'th was drawing the necessary diagrams. Deedee was talking to Clara, looking more comfortable than I would have guessed from her first reaction; Caleb stood behind her massaging her shoulders. Spector watched everyone, looking worried and disconnected. When I passed near, anxious and uncharacteristic sweat underlay his familiar cologne. This must have been a very strange day for him; I resolved to arrange some opportunity for him and Charlie to be alone. Chulzh'th finished the last geometric swirl of her work and stood, brushing sand from her hands.

"You insist on going, I assume?" Grandfather asked me.

"You know her so well," said Audrey.

Chulzh'th looked me over with a rumbling sigh. "You'll go back when I tell you it's time." I nodded. She could have ordered me not to go; either of them could have.

The three of us who'd already met Glabri—Chulzh'th, Charlie, and I—would go again, joined by Grandfather. The elders judged the greater show of strength was worth the risk of drawing attention.

"If this goes well," said Chulzh'th, "we can tell the ghouls that we have an Outer One who'd like to negotiate, and complete the discussion on our native level of reality. Ghouls can walk here comfortably enough."

"I thought they could only travel through gravestones," said Charlie. I remembered reading that as well. My mind wandered the shelves of our collection, seeking the source. *Encyclopedie du Pays Dormant,* that was it.

"A story the Puritans told to comfort themselves," said Grandfather dismissively. "Graves have meaning to us, not to the universe."

"But men of the air believe it," said S'vlk. "Everywhere I've gone ashore, you find such stories about the places people leave corpses. Ghouls may not *need* to come through in those places, but it's where they have regular business. You might just as well suppose elders can only come ashore near where our descendants dwell."

This time, Grandfather sang the lullaby. His bass voice vibrated in my chest, carrying the cadence of sea shanties into even the gentlest song. It was as much a thing of flesh as of mind. I couldn't imagine losing track of my body, with that song guiding me.

CHAPTER 22

Our dreams were calmer today, though I'd expected any number of nightmares. We stood on the deck of a ship. It was a trading vessel, hard-worn by wind and salt, but clean and painted in the sand-and-bark colors that marked every ship out of Innsmouth. I recognized Grandfather's hubristically-named *Kraken's Journal*. Sailors, oddly difficult to focus on, moved among too many sails.

Chulzh'th tugged me from distraction. "Let me see your cord."

I turned obediently, a little frightened. "I keep losing track of time, forgetting to count. You'll watch over me?"

"Stubborn child. Yes, since you insist on coming along, I'll keep time for everyone." She frowned. "You too, Yringl'phtagn."

He returned from the rail. "My apologies, Acolyte. I haven't seen her in a while."

"Is this your ship?" asked Charlie.

"It was," said Grandfather. *"Kraken's journal, written in the script of sails across the waves.* Abiel liked the poem, but he never liked the name."

"I remember," I said. My eldest cousin had inherited the ship when Grandfather went into the water. "He was superstitious about it. He always swore he'd change the name to *Obed's Terrible Handwriting*." Grandfather's laughter boomed across the deck.

Chulzh'th drew the blue ribbon from my forehead. It looked smoother than before, though the edges were still ragged. It bent, but stiffly. "It's healing, but still brittle," she told me. "You must be careful. As with a half-healed bone, you'll be tempted to move as if you were whole, but you could shatter it easily." She hesitated, and I thought for a moment she'd finished speaking. "Ghavn Yukhl, it's proper for the eldest-on-land to have a place in these negotiations, and I respect your knowledge of the air's politics. But speaking solely of your own well-being, this is a bad idea. You should have delegated to your brother."

I started to duck my head, thought better of it as the cord wavered. "Thank you, Acolyte. I know the risks. And I know the politics better than Caleb."

As carefully as we could, we pushed through. The city rose in a cascade of shining towers, shadowing the ridge. I took a cautious breath, testing the cord between mind and body, as much *me* as the things it connected.

Figures scrambled across the face of the ridge. My eyes adjusted despite the city lights: sinewy ghouls clambered over the rock like monkeys, in sudden fits of movement, circling the fungous growth without touching it. Withered scarlet stalks lay scattered on the ground. One ghoul hung almost upside down, held in place by its fellows. It wove its fingers in a cat's cradle and spat between them. The droplets sizzled as they hit the mushroom ward, and more stems and caps shriveled and fell.

The ghouls looked different from each other, but the things I'd marked about Glabri were things they all had in common. They were all raw sinew and muscle, skinned corpses in obscene motion. Yet they varied in the contours of their flesh, in height and sickly shade and blotches that mimicked wounds and rot. On a battlefield, interrupted in their feast by a living intruder, they might fall motionless in an instant, perfectly camouflaged among their meals.

I held up the string of tiny bones. "Glabri! Are you here? We've learned more."

One figure broke from the herd and crabbed his way to the ground. I could see now that he was tall and lithe for his kind. His well-muscled legs were spotted with greenish discoloration, and his ears came to sharper points than most of the others.

"We learn," he said, drawing himself up. "Can fill holes. Explain holes?"

Chulzh'th glanced at the uprooting in progress on the cliff face. Our negotiations weren't likely to be as simple as we'd hoped. "I yield to you in this," she told me. Grandfather nodded, looking stern and reassuring in his quiet support.

I took a deep, steadying breath, but had to disguise my reaction: the ghouls' camouflage included scent as well as appearance. I stepped forward. "One of the Outer Ones came to me, seeking help. They've split into two factions, fighting each other. One faction planted the holes here in case their attack on the other failed. The ones they chased off need a place to retreat if they want to continue to fight. If you're willing to come back with us, they want to negotiate for the holes."

Glabri scratched his leg, looked back at the cliff. "Dead clutch-thieves good—safer for clutches. But clutch-thief battles useless. No bones, no marrow. Why should we bring them here?" He shrugged and cocked his head. "But you want to help—why? You hate clutch-thieves too."

"The attackers want to interfere in human wars. The defenders want to stop them. We want to stop them too—our wars are our own business." But would Glabri care? Perhaps it would matter to him that atomics left no corpses—though merely the thought of that reasoning turned my stomach.

"Interfere how?" He added something in his own tongue, and Chulzh'th responded.

"I'll translate," she murmured to me. "He understands English better than he speaks it, but . . ." I nodded.

"They're worried that we'll destroy ourselves," I told Glabri. "That we'll fight too hard and go extinct. We're worried about that too, but we think that if they try to help they'll make things worse. We're helping the faction who agree with us." Up on the ridge, the other ghouls had stopped their weeding. The corpse-crowd watched us with silent, black eyes. "Do you care if we destroy ourselves? You eat our dead, but I suppose you can eat something else when we're gone. What matters to you, besides keeping Outer Ones away from your den?"

He laughed—a surprisingly normal-sounding laugh, where most of his speech darted like his movements. "Humans. So superstitious. We taste death—same stuff alive. Can like alive, still eat dead." He nibbled his finger, which disturbed me unreasonably. *Superstitious.* Familiarity with death had never reconciled me to it. In the camps our captors had studied our corpses, turning atrocity to practical use and supplanting the sacred rites we should have been able to offer. I tried to think of the ghouls' diet as something other than desecration— but it was hard. Glabri continued. "Clutch-thief guests near our den, chased by enemies? Too dangerous."

"If you'll talk with them, they might have more to offer," I said. "They might even agree to stay away from your clutches forever." I didn't think Nnnnnn-gt-vvv would be thrilled by that. It was too attached to letting individuals go where they willed without any authority's leave. But it might have little choice.

Glabri snorted. "Clutch-thief promises? Llllirrap murrrrt."

"He doesn't believe it," said Chulzh'th. "Roughly."

Charlie touched my back, a shock of warmth. "Aphra, I'm starting to feel queasy. We've been here a while. Are you okay—do you need to go back?"

"This isn't a good time," I said.

"Excuse me," said Chulzh'th to Glabri. She added something in Ghoulish, and once more drew my cord into visibility. She hissed. "Yes, you need to go back. Yringl'phtagn and I will finish the discussion. My apologies, Glabri."

I sighed. I *had* promised to be responsible. I didn't want to leave the thing half-finished—or worse, let it fail without me—but I'd do no good if I collapsed. "My apologies as well, Glabri. I have . . . an illness . . . and I can't stay long in the dreamland. I'll have to let the elders take over. Unless you'd be willing to come back with us, and continue our discussion there even if you don't want to speak with Nnnnnn-gt-vvv?"

He snorted again. "Better here—no clutch-thieves. I'll talk to scaled lords." He wiggled his fingers impatiently at the staring ghouls above us, and they laughed and returned to their work, tearing out Nnnnnn-gt-vvv's hope.

"All right. Thank you." Perhaps when I got back I could convince Nnnnnn-gt-vvv to offer an initial concession, a show of good faith that would convince the ghouls to be more cooperative.

I released my hold on the dreamland and cast myself back toward my body—or tried to. Instead I gasped and stumbled. There's a moment, exhausted and drifting at day's end, when you seem to fall suddenly onto your bed, jarred awake by sleep's approach. So I fell now. I—my image of myself, created by my mind in shadowed imitation of its sustaining form—lay on my imagined belly in the dream-dirt, aware at my core that I wasn't in my native reality. I gasped out a sob.

"Is she all right?" Charlie's voice, and Grandfather's behind it: "Is her cord broken? Chulzh'th!"

Chulzh'th's voice, not as calm as it should be, and dream-talons against my dream-forehead. "It's still there, but it's cracked. I don't know how to get her back safely." My confidence in my own form wavered vertiginously, and I teetered on the brink of dissolution.

Feet scratched lightly in the dirt. The gut-wrenching stench of rot pulled me back to the illusion of my senses.

"Ghouls walk that path whole. Could carry a human mind—maybe." He bent and sniffed my cheek. I almost gagged, and was grateful. I pushed myself to sitting. The movement made me feel worse physically, but more like I *had* a physical self to do the feeling.

"Could you carry her mind back into her body?" asked Chulzh'th.

Glabri shrugged. "Never tried. But shorter walk, safer than your way?" He chewed his finger again. His nails were dark and ragged. "Clutch-thieves *good* at minds alone. Bring stupid fleshless thing here. We will allow, long enough to help carry lost mind."

"Thank you," said Grandfather fervently. "Next time I have a carcass, I'll bring it to you in thanks."

I breathed, concentrating on the ghoul's rot and the warmth of Charlie's hand.

"Don't go," I told him.

"I'm right here," he promised.

The dreamland grew nebulous around me, or I within it. One of the elders must have gone for the Outer One. I had no idea how long it took. A jag of ashen silver etched the blue of my cord.

Ghouls chittered alarm. Tentacles brushed the dream of my head, raising static.

"Can you help?" asked Charlie.

"Yes, I see the problem. I can't heal it, but I can hold it steady while we move her. Like a cast on a broken bone. Miss Marsh, focus. Don't let yourself drift."

"Sorry," I said. "I'm trying to hold still."

"Hold still. But focus. This will feel odd."

It did feel odd—not painful, but like someone wrapped a scarf around one of my limbs and I couldn't tell which one. Then as if, wrapped in this inexplicable fashion, they pulled me through a narrow pipe for a very long time . . .

I tried to concentrate on myself, my wholeness, and not to question these incomprehensible sensations. I tried not to think about how frightened I should be.

Then I lay crouched on real sand, coughing with my real lungs.

Every smell, salt and garbage and sweat and cologne and ghoul-rot, cut through fear and dissociation to bind me again to myself. I breathed the warmth of confluence and family.

Because I could, I counted seconds. I didn't try to focus on anything outside myself until I reached one hundred, and knew my heart was counting on its own. Then I looked up. Charlie and Grandfather still attended me—Grandfather checked me over as if seeking some outwardly visible wound, Charlie simply stayed near. The others watched me anxiously, save for S'vlk. Her vigilance was all for Nnnnnn-gt-vvv and Glabri—as theirs was for each other. Rigid attention thickened the space between them.

Chulzh'th squatted in front of me. "I was foolish. You will not have your way in this again."

"I . . . think that's a good idea." I hadn't considered how my diplomatic efforts would distract me from stretching precisely as far as was safe, and no farther—or how my safety might distract all of us from the task at hand. I hadn't really believed my limits so inflexible. I didn't want to confess that weakness in front of Glabri and Nnnnnn-gt-vvv, grateful as I was for their help, but Chulzh'th could see my hubris clearly enough.

Nnnnnn-gt-vvv swayed and said something to Glabri in Ghoulish. I wondered how many languages it spoke—and how long it would take Deedee to learn this one. Chulzh'th, still crouched before me, translated in a low voice.

Nnnnnn-gt-vvv: "Your people travel well."

Glabri: "We travel between home and feeding ground. Not out to the stars, away from meat and bone."

(I should not have been surprised, to learn that the ghoul was more poetic and fluent in his own tongue. It shouldn't have been so easy to dismiss him as a mere scavenger.)

Nnnnnn-gt-vvv: "You're angry with us because some of your people make a different choice. Because we welcome those ghouls who want to join us."

Glabri: "Children are more than their own choices."

Nnnnnn-gt-vvv: "They're more than yours as well. You think we don't understand family, but we do. We recognize many kinds of family, many kinds of connections that matter. We understand duties beyond obedience, and loyalty that can transcend species. We're not the demons you think, tempting children away from the safe shadow of the gravestone. We serve a greater purpose too. We can aid you, if you'd take what we have to offer."

Glabri: "That's a very nice speech, but there's no flesh on you. Nothing to trust."

(I looked for some clue in Chulzh'th's expression. Should I try to mediate? But sitting upright still took all the effort I could muster. At least I'd succeeded in my first goal: convincing Glabri to speak with Nnnnnn-gt-vvv.)

Nnnnnn-gt-vvv: "I can't help being made of different matter. Our homespace is a long way away, but I promise there are creatures there who'd love to feast on my corpse."

Glabri broke into barking laughter. "Maybe I ought to talk with *them*."

Nnnnnn-gt-vvv: "If they recommended our carrion, would you be willing to offer us shelter? We'll die here without a mine, with no one to honor our bones."

Glabri: "Too close to our clutches, alive or dead. Why not take a hole with you and plant it somewhere else?"

Nnnnnn-gt-vvv: "Because I don't know how to start a new mine growing—I don't think any of my faction-mates do. I know just enough to turn what you've left intact"—it had, a few seconds before Chulzh'th's translation, waved tendrils at the cliffside growth—"into a crude shelter. We won't have the means to encircle minds, or any other comforts. Just a place that mimics our homespace, where we can rest. I can't ignore Nyarlathotep's command, but . . . I can promise that if any of your young come to us asking to join our travels, we'll bring them to talk with you. They won't disappear."

Glabri chittered thoughtfully. "Your enemies will attack. They'll make a mess of our den, and leave no bodies."

Nnnnnn-gt-vvv shuddered all over, wings and tendrils drawing inward. "If they wanted to attack us directly, they wouldn't have gone to such trouble to trick us into leaving the mine peacefully. They'll focus on their own plans and leave us in peace."

As I listened I realized that I'd been thinking like a human. Of course, I'd assumed, Nnnnnn-gt-vvv's allies would want to attack those who'd exiled them and retake their lair from the usurpers. Of course such passionate disagreement must come to blows. I'd assumed we would join them in battle. And with them beside us—or more realistically, beside the elders with their warriors' experience—we could prevent the interventions that might otherwise break humanity.

But from all I'd seen, the Outer Ones hated direct conflict. With each other they found it nearly unthinkable. Nnnnnn-gt-vvv's passivist faction would dig in to their new shelter and think of slow, subtle ways to regain their place while the interventionists—gently and without ever drawing blood—did their best to control humanity.

And Neko, and Spector's colleagues, would remain unwittingly vulnerable.

"Very well," said Glabri. "I'll speak to the warren. I'll tell them we should give you shelter so long as you keep your word about our clutches, and leave when we say. And you'll owe us flesh when you have it to give, and protection one day when *we* need it." He bared ragged teeth. "Always good to make alliances with strange people— you may be creepy, but your strengths complement ours."

He solemnly offered Nnnnnn-gt-vvv another bone from his string. The Outer One bent low, took the offering, and brushed tendrils over the ghoul's shoulders. Glabri hissed and shuffled back, but the agreement appeared sealed.

I should have been pleased at our success. But I'd risked life and mind not merely to gain Nnnnnn-gt-vvv its refuge, but to oppose

Kvv-vzht-mmmm-vvt's plans for my family and species. In all the ways that mattered to the people in danger *now*, I'd failed.

I was ready to sleep for a week, but didn't dare give in yet to exhaustion. Waves splashed against sand, and I clung to the sound. I reached deliberately and carefully for the confluence, and was rewarded by the syncopation of four hearts supporting my own. "Before you go, Nnnnnn-gt-vvv, we need to know how you plan to stop the interventionists. When will you move against them? We need urgently to reclaim the mine before their interference with human governments turns disastrous. We want to help."

"We want to get my son out of there," said Frances.

"Freddy chooses to stay with Kvv-vzht-mmmm-vvt," said Nnnnnn-gt-vvv. "That's his right."

"He's being an idiot," said Shelean. "I've tried to talk him out of it, but he trusts the creature. I used to. It *means* well, of course it does."

"Have you learned anything new?" asked Nnnnnn-gt-vvv. Spector watched intently.

"Not much," she said. "They've talked about whether they can fix Miss Harris's brain, and how much risk they should take in the treatment. They really do intend to help her, but they also think that it'll give them more influence over her team. And they've talked about getting Russian government people into the Carpathian mine, but I haven't been able to figure out who's actually there."

Nnnnnn-gt-vvv hummed thoughtfully. "Keep listening and try to find out. And if you can get one of them alone, try to give the American government our side of the story. Maybe one of my faction-mates knows someone in Moscow as well. In answer to your question, Ghavn Marsh, we need to reclaim influence so we can demand our place in the mine. Shelean, if any of Kvv-vzht-mmmm-vvt's faction-mates sound amenable to our perspective, we may be able to siphon off some of its strength. But that will depend on having a stable anchor in this space, where defectors could join us."

Spector leaned forward. "Are you sure it wouldn't be better just to talk with Kvv-vzht-mmmm-vvt yourself? I don't like how it treated your faction, but it seemed willing to engage openly with the government today, regardless of all this talk about espionage. If they want something from us, we may be able to get concessions, for humanity and for your faction."

"You must not," said Nnnnnn-gt-vvv. "Even during the most aboveboard negotiation, it could undermine you surreptitiously—it's been practicing such artifices for longer than your country has existed. It would love the chance to influence more of your people." Tentacles swiveled in my direction. "You especially must stay away. It wants you; that's why it tried to draw you in through the trapezohedron."

I wished it hadn't mentioned the trapezohedron. Sharp and fresh, memory of R'lyeh mixed with awareness of my new fragility. "I can't just hide. It's used me already; I have to help stop what I gave it the means to do. And Neko is there. She may have chosen to go, but she didn't know *this* was coming. She didn't know about the trapezohedron's influence." I'd waited too long already; whatever my vulnerabilities, however I'd strained them already, I needed to see this through.

"I agree with Nnnnnn-gt-vvv," said S'vlk. "Not that we should work subtly and slowly—this isn't sea floor mapping—but that open negotiation is a good way to lose. They hate fighting, so that's our best option."

"Makes sense to me," said Caleb. He looked ready for that fight. I wasn't the only one to inherit Grandfather's impulsive streak.

"They might *prefer* to talk," said Spector, "but they can certainly outclass our spears and guns. If they don't like violence, it's for the same reason humans should have learned—their weapons have grown too deadly. The Outer Ones have probably had atomics since we were swinging in trees."

"I've seen them fight," said S'vlk. "I'm not suggesting we rush them with tridents. Just that we *act*. Go in, sabotage or steal what we can, and try to reset the wards so they answer to Nnnnnn-gt-vvv's faction instead."

"You've been complaining that the interventionists will act rashly, and get the opposite effect from the one they intend," said Spector. "You could easily do the same. More easily—you've had less time to plan than they have. Let us *try* negotiation—it costs nothing and could save a lot of bloodshed."

"It risks everything," said Nnnnnn-gt-vvv. "And S'vlk's plan is even worse. I beg you, give us time to work our own way."

Audrey watched this exchange with unreadable eyes. I thought she'd been quiet because Shelean was present, but now she turned to Spector, smiling brightly. "I assume you reported this whole thing to your superiors—I know you don't have the same boss as Barlow. What did they say? Is this whole negotiation idea theirs, or yours?"

"Both," he said. "They didn't even know this species—this political power—existed until a few days ago. They want to learn as much as they can, and you do that by talking."

"What do they think about the Outer Ones talking to Russia?"

"Obviously they'd prefer these people as American allies. They're willing to offer a lot to make that happen, and I agree with them. The safety of our country may depend on it." He nodded at me. "Aphra, I know you have every reason to be upset after how you've been injured, but it may not have been intentional. If the Outer Ones value your diplomatic abilities—as we do—your help could go a long way toward making this work out in our favor."

I stiffened. It had been a long time since Spector had so cavalierly assumed I'd cooperate. Even with the day's stress, I expected better of him. "I do have every reason to be upset, yes."

Audrey stood and stretched. "I'm just gonna point out that it's past 2 a.m., and none of us have slept well in days. Unless you have?" She smiled at Spector, and he smiled back and shook his head. She paced around the circle, stopping near him to stretch again and then clear a smooth seat in the sand beside him. His gaze tracked her movements. Deedee's did too, more thoughtfully. Audrey put a hand on Spector's arm. "What do you think we can get from them, if we play our cards right?"

"Well . . ." He didn't pull back. My pulse surged, but I forced myself not to show any reaction. He went on. "We can convince them that we're a power in our own right, one worth treating with respect. I think it would be better if we could treat with them openly—being the first country with public diplomatic channels would give us a great advantage."

I recalled Audrey, smug with the information she'd wangled from Barlow, admitting cheerfully that she could never do the same with Spector. *"Your brain is always going, even when you're talking to a girl."*

Spector was among the few men who could go armed around me without raising old terrors. Now I stared fixedly at the sand to avoid looking at his holster. What should I do? Who would react quickly enough, if I said something? I felt Charlie's breath quicken, the chill that squeezed his chest.

Audrey smiled more broadly and slipped her arm around the man beside her. At last he started to draw away—but the gun was in her hand, and she pushed herself back as he gasped. She trained the weapon on him. "Thank god. I was afraid you knew how to look after this thing. But you were just wearing it because he does."

My veins stung with the speed of her pulse. Charlie stared, breath tight in his throat. Spector—whoever he was—raised open hands. "Audrey—Miss Winslow—what are you talking about?"

"Mr. Spector would never be so familiar," she said. "It's sweet, really. Plenty of guys act the gentleman with young ladies, but they're not *respectful*. Nnnnnn-gt-vvv, I don't suppose you recognize this imposter?"

I turned on the Outer One abruptly. "Did you know? That he was one of your doppelgangers?"

"No!" Nnnnnn-gt-vvv approached the man from the side, not blocking Audrey's aim. It brushed his face and hair with tentative feelers. The man pushed them away—but he seemed accustomed to the Outer One's uncanny presence. "Body sculpting, done right, leaves few traces. And I met Mr. Spector only in passing."

I glanced at Charlie. Every line of his body was rigid with tension. His lips moved silently.

"It doesn't matter who you are," I said to the man. "Where is *he*? What are they doing to him? Why do they have to hide his absence even from his colleagues? Aren't they supposed to be working with you?" Barlow's team didn't know; I couldn't imagine that they knew. *I told him never to be alone with them. He promised he'd be careful.* But if the Outer Ones had this double ready in advance, it would have taken only a second of distraction, a colleague's back turned while swift dark wings dragged Spector away from the visible world. Leaving a cuckoo in his place.

Had he argued, where they'd been persuaded?

Dear gods, had the people I'd spoken to in Barlow's hotel room been who I thought they were? Trumbull was alone with them now.

"You're talking nonsense," said the man who wasn't Spector. His eyes focused on the gun, as anyone's would. I didn't know whether Audrey could shoot. I didn't want to imagine what it would look like if she did. My traitor mind colored the sand with blood and bone.

"Were they all replaced?" I asked. "Was Neko?"

"No one's been replaced," he insisted. "I swear I'm myself—I can prove it. I don't know why you've got this idea into your heads."

Fury roiled in my throat. "Stop telling me you don't know what we're talking about. You're not a good enough actor, and we know Mr. Spector better than you thought. You've failed—the best thing for you now is to cooperate, and hope your masters will take you back in exchange for our friend."

"You may have suddenly decided not to trust me," he said. "My own supervisors will know me when they see me—and they won't be happy that you threatened me. They'll be even less happy if you actually hurt me."

He sounded even less like the man I knew—but he was right. If Audrey did shoot him, we'd have the corpse of an FBI agent on our hands, indistinguishable from the original. Even if we hid the body, everyone knew he was with us. The state would gladly mete out punishment to what remained of Innsmouth, and what remained below it.

Audrey's aim wavered, and I knew her thoughts followed the same logic.

"Let me," said Grandfather. He stalked toward the man, and Nnnnnn-gt-vvv backed away to make room out of Audrey's line of fire. I expected him to put claws to the intruder's throat, another visceral threat. Instead, he stopped an arm's length away. "If you run, we will kill you and deal with the consequences. The stakes are too high for us to do otherwise. If you sit down, we'll know you can't do anything sudden or rash, and I'll tell the girl to lower her gun."

Deedee spoke up. "Check him for weapons first. Mr. Spector only carried a service pistol, but this fellow might have something extra from the Outer Ones."

"Good thought. Do that, then—you know how, and your palms are more sensitive."

Deedee patted him down efficiently and without any particular delicacy, then nodded. "He's clean—though I assume they can track him."

"Unlikely," said Nnnnnn-gt-vvv. "For this kind of replacement that's often considered too risky. Especially now, when they want to fool their own kin."

The man looked at us all, and sat.

Frances tugged at my arm. She'd been smoking steadily since Audrey grabbed the gun, and my fear-shortened breath grew rougher as the smell rolled over me. "Are the elders going to . . . hurt him?"

she whispered. "I know we have to—we have to do whatever's necessary, to find out how to rescue him—them—everyone they've taken prisoner. I just need to know what they're going to do, so I can brace myself."

"I don't know," I whispered back. I'd seen Grandfather threaten people before. I knew he'd hurt people, killed when he thought it needful. I tried to tell myself that torture for a purpose wasn't the same as what the state had done to my mother. But then, her captors had thought their study reason enough.

Grandfather heard us, of course. "Pain makes men talk. It doesn't make them honest." He looked the man over, searchingly. "Some men will confess as soon as I bare my teeth. They've never seen anything like me before, and they're convinced I must command storms and spirits or hunger for human flesh. You can get almost anything out of someone who's just learned their orderly cosmos is an illusion. But I don't think that's you. You're not the sort to be shocked by men with scales—you've traveled the stars, met people who make me and Miss Winslow look like twins. You go everywhere, and you talk to everyone."

The man was nodding along. I recalled my own relief when I'd heard my gods named in a strange place—I couldn't fault him for that instinctive response to an adversary voicing his own truisms. But in a moment he jerked still.

"There, you see," said Grandfather. "This will be much easier if you tell us your name. Something to call you, so we can talk like civilized people. I'm Obed Marsh." His child-name would be more comfortable for most men of the air.

"How is *he* civilized?" demanded Caleb. His voice was stiff with anger. Grandfather gave him a quelling look.

The man looked at us, more nervous than when Audrey had threatened to shoot him. His shoulders slumped, then rose with reclaimed dignity. "I'm Nick Abrams. And this isn't as nefarious as you're making it out. When Kvv-vzht-mmmm-vvt presented his case, the agents agreed that Mr. Spector should travel to Yuggoth so he could report on the truth of their claims. Shaping someone as a 'replacement' is standard practice when a person can't vanish even briefly without arousing suspicion. It isn't meant to fool the government, only his acquaintances."

Charlie gritted his teeth. I shook my head. "No. We aren't just acquaintances—he would have told us. He wouldn't try to fool us this way."

"*Not* hurting him doesn't seem to make him honest either," said Caleb.

"Patience," said Grandfather. He put his hand on Nick's wrist. The edge of one talon lay a hairsbreadth from his skin. "Mr. Abrams, give some credit to our intelligence. You wanted us to negotiate with your—travel-mate, is it? We won't do that without full understanding. We know Kvv-vzht-mmmm-vvt's done things he doesn't want us to know about. But you can't expect us to sail in without a map. You have to give us something, to get what you want. Where is Ron Spector, really? And where are his irritating colleagues?"

The man didn't answer right away. For once, no one jumped in with a sarcastic jab or impatient demand. There was silence save for the ocean's endless whisper, ten people breathing, and the creak of shifting metal in the distance.

"No one else has been replaced," he said finally. "That's the truth—your friend Miss Koto has been in the mine for days with no need to hide her absence. The other agents were willing to listen to Kvv-vzht-mmmm-vvt, and it spoke honestly with them." I breathed gratitude—Mary's anger had rung true, but I'd been frightened still. Even if Abrams was lying, if Barlow or Peters had quailed at cooperating with the Outer Ones, Trumbull wasn't alone with three doppelgangers. He went on. "Mr. Spector didn't trust it, and argued both with Kvv-vzht-mmmm-vvt and his colleagues. But he's vital—a voice for peace in a government of wolves. You know that yourself. He advocates for the worth of many kinds of people, just like we do. Once he sees how we live and travel together, he'll understand that we're alike. We can help him convince his colleagues to work with people—like you—who they'd otherwise treat as enemies. He'll be back in a few days, no worse for wear."

I imagined Spector stripped of all but his voice and vision. Spector's contorted body lying on an altar to a god not his own. "But his colleagues don't know," I said. "They'd never have gone along with it."

"You've hidden things from them before, to prevent them from starting wars. If you don't want them picking fights with the Yith, you don't want to turn them against the Outer Ones, who actually care enough about humans to notice if they're attacked."

"Credit Barlow with some intelligence as well," said Grandfather. "He knows Spector at least as well as my granddaughter does."

"Your granddaughter didn't notice. *She* did." He glared at Audrey, who smiled demurely back. He blinked rapidly and flushed.

"Be that as it may," I said. "They know him very well." I hoped it was true—in Barlow's case, I was sure of it. Trumbull walked among her colleagues as an eternal stranger, so her replacement with an ancient and inhuman intelligence had drawn no comment. Spector made himself known. "You're no better an actor than I am. But if we go to them now, you still might salvage your masters' desired alliance."

"And then what? If I confess to them, will you talk with Kvv-vzht-mmmm-vvt?"

"No!" said Nnnnnn-gt-vvv.

"I know what *you* think of it," said Grandfather. "Help Miss Winslow guard our prisoner while we confer."

He beckoned me and Caleb, S'vlk and Chulzh'th, and, after a moment, Frances. Charlie levered himself up with his cane and followed, uninvited. Deedee stood as well.

"He's my colleague," she said.

Audrey smiled at me and patted the gun. *I'm needed here. I trust you.* But I could still feel her heartbeat, only a little slower than when she'd first pulled the gun.

We walked down the beach, where only the sea could hear us plan our assault on the mine.

CHAPTER 23

Mary Harris—Solstice 1949:

George's hands cut through my exhaustion. A decent back rub's no trade for the ability to take notes, but it's far better than nothing. I hate being tired—fatigue blurs the little mnemonics that keep my thoughts in order, the walls that keep me sane and focused and distracted from how much I yearn to read myself to sleep. But tonight the sleep won't come, and the walls can't keep out my useless desire. George and Virgil, bless them, won't leave me up alone.

Virgil's reading Gaudy Night aloud while George works painful knots from my muscles. It's one of my favorite books, and I don't have the heart to tell him that tonight it's the opposite of a distraction. I'm almost grateful when someone knocks at the door again.

Virgil peers over the chain. "You've got nerve, showing up here."

Catherine's voice quickens my heart. I can't sift fury from terror, anticipation, pleasure. "I've wanted to talk to Mary about the Yith since I came back. Now I can. Please, let me help."

"You've done enough already."

"I haven't done anything, and you know it. But I've studied with the people who did."

So tired—too tired for Virgil's well-meaning, vicious defense. "Let her in."

Catherine's hair frizzes from its bun. Her dress is wrinkled. Her dignity infuriates me even though she's done nothing to deserve my anger. She enters, *ignoring George and Virgil: her eerie attention focused entirely on me. She sinks to her knees, and my own awareness narrows to the point where our gazes meet. It feels like we should be able to touch our strange shared history, manifest it between us with the force of our absorption.*

"My guest did a terrible thing to you," she says at last. "I take responsibility for her work, and for agreeing to hide it from you. I'm sorry."

"And you came here to apologize?" I ask. Virgil says something; I wave him back. George is still there, his touch a welcome intrusion from another universe. His hand rests lightly on my shoulder.

"I have to apologize before I can do anything else. But I came here to help." She raises her chin, meeting my eyes. "You and I, the couple of times we've been able to collaborate, we've made incredible breakthroughs. And I have studied in the Archives, even if I only remember a little. It doesn't have to be tonight—for once we're not on a life-or-death deadline—and you don't have to decide right away, but I couldn't wait another day to offer. S'vlk could help too."

I blink. "Why S'vlk?" I stumble, trying to wrap my tongue around the elder's name. Not for the first time, I wish I could see it spelled out.

"I'm sorry, of course you don't know. She's like me—another captive in the Archives. We've been working together to interpret my guest's notes."

"Oh." I have so many questions. I hunger to write them down, hand her a numbered list and study her answers with the grim focus of a late-night study session. "What are they like? The Outer Ones say they're arrogant, that they believe themselves worth more than every other race, that they destroy peoples and civilizations for their own convenience. But we barely know the Outer Ones—it's easy for them to throw around someone else's secrets. You said you were the Yith's prisoner, you must have opinions on them."

She sits back on her heels, uncharacteristic humility giving way to the glint of academic passion. "Not a prisoner, a captive. They can't exactly ask permission before they yank us out of our lives, to keep us millions of years in the past while they take our bodies for their own. Everything Kvv-vzht-mmmm-vvt told you is true, and incomplete. The Archives are the most important thing you can imagine. The Yith record every civilization that rises on Earth, and preserve them after the sun is a frozen ember. We captives have the honor—the grace—to add our stories to those records. The Yith give mortal humanity a legacy." She stops for breath. *"You know how rare it is to have true colleagues. In the Archives no one cares about your sex, or what family you come from, only what you bring to the conversation. The Yith do terrible things, and I can't help but love them. I still care for those they've dismissed. All the sacrifices they demand for their great mission—I'd willingly lie down on that altar myself, but it would be my choice."*

Virgil glares at her. "Listen to you go on. You're completely mad."

She isn't offended. "I've seen live dinosaurs. I've read books written a billion years after my death. I've argued theology with Cleopatra's handmaid. You can as easily go mad from too narrow a life as from one thrown outside human experience. I know which madness I'd choose."

Abrams came with us; what choice did he have? Even with Nnnnnn-gt-vvv carrying the willing elders through the outskirts, there were enough of us to surround him on the subway. He looked hopeful for a moment as we transferred between lines—two short flights of stairs that seemed miles long—but Audrey still had his gun in her purse, and her tight smile was enough to keep him close. Clara wore Shelean's pendant, ready to pass along any updates on Kvv-vzht-mmmm-vvt's subterfuge. Charlie swallowed hard when he looked at the imposter, nausea welling through his veins. I could tell how hard it was for him to stay close.

We'd spoken of logistics, agreed that having Barlow's team at our backs was worth trying to appease their anger. Our own anger, we hadn't discussed.

I had long ago admitted that Spector deserved my respect, even my trust. Now I had to admit that I liked him. As with Clara, I felt kin to anyone with so strong a sense of duty, whether or not I approved its object. That was Spector: loyal to a state he knew didn't love him, determined to drag it into worthiness. He served with his whole body and mind—he had no long life to lose, no future trans-figuration to risk, but he'd hate as I would to be severed from his perceptions, his ability to act, his hands and lungs and steadfast back. Freddy and Clara and Shelean found freedom in that lesion; we could not.

I wanted Neko back—or barring that, to speak with her face-to-face and know that she'd chosen to leave me with her whole mind. I wanted Freddy out of there too, away from Kvv-vzht-mmmm-vvt and its faction and their overweaning paternalism toward humanity. But he wasn't being deceived. However foolishly, he'd chosen them, and he'd had plenty of time and cause to make that decision. When I thought of Spector, though, I wanted to tear apart the mine with all my half-grown strength.

Since he was likely somewhere sideways of Jupiter at the moment, strength and anger would not be sufficient. We needed as many people on our side as we could get, and we needed to break the nascent alliance that Kvv-vzht-mmmm-vvt was counting on.

Mary let us in, looking calmer if not yet friendly. She and her team were awake and dressed, but her eyes were bloodshot. Trumbull looked up, pen paused mid-note.

"Nnnnnn-gt-vvv and the elders will be here in a moment," I said when we were inside. "We need to talk."

"Why are you here *again*?" demanded Barlow. "Don't you people ever sleep?"

Outer One and elders broke through into visibility. The elders wore their cloaks from the mine, though their faces and hands were bare. A shiver escaped Abrams's facade. Unsympathetic, I pushed him forward.

"What the devil are you up to now, Ron?" asked Peters. He sounded as much tired as upset.

"This isn't Ron Spector," I said.

"What?" Barlow glared at Abrams, and at me. He stalked forward and frowned at the man. "Let me see your ear."

Abrams turned obligingly to the side. "I haven't shaved since this morning, but the scar's still there. Avignon, and that guard we weren't expecting. George, *you've* got to believe me. We were in the middle of a perfectly normal conversation when these idiots pulled my own gun on me! They've been insisting I'm some sort of doppelganger—I don't know how to convince them otherwise."

"Are you going to try this *again*?" demanded Audrey.

"I'm going to keep telling you I'm *me* until you believe it."

Barlow looked between us. "I've always hated this part of serials. I like knowing who people are. But you idiots—" He rubbed his forehead, wincing. "You wouldn't be this ridiculous unless you really believed what you were saying. You'd never make up this kind of byzantine story, you'd just show up begging to talk. Again. And you—" To Abrams. "I think I'd know you anywhere, but I've seen some crazy things these last couple of days. Where'd we meet?"

"Fort Belvoir. I asked about the books in your duffle—we were both on special duty within the month."

"What was the password to get back behind lines, the day you got that scar?"

"How the hell am I supposed to remember a thing like that? . . . Oh, but I do. I won't say that in mixed company, George."

"You wouldn't even say it in front of the soldiers, with your cheek still bleeding. You were always a prude."

"You do know me. What goes well with canned beans?"

"Truffles and chardonnay. Obviously. *You're* fine. I don't know what's wrong with the rest of you."

I'd taken Abrams's confession for granted. It hadn't occurred to me that he'd know all of Spector's secrets and in-jokes. But it was reflex that had betrayed him to us, not his conversation. And the tricks we'd used on the beach wouldn't work now—he'd be braced to speak more civilly to the women, react with cooler blood in their presence, hold himself still if we invoked the things he found sacred. "He admitted to us that he was an imposter."

298 • RUTHANNA EMRYS

"I might do the same if you held a gun on me. You're wasting our time—and you, Ron, maybe you've learned something now about trusting your irregulars?"

"I still think . . ." he said. His pupils were wide with reluctant disappointment; in that moment I might have doubted what I'd seen.

"Vi s 'deyn eydish?" asked Deedee abruptly.

"Nisht shlekht. Vi s dayner?" One corner of his mouth quirked in pleasure at passing the test, where Spector's colleagues couldn't see.

"Your questions are useless," S'vlk told Barlow. "The Outer Ones steal thoughts as easily as people, and hand them to their favorites as gifts."

"Then how did *you* know?" asked Peters, exasperation overcoming fatigue. "Mary, you seeing anything we don't?"

"I don't know him as well," she said. She looked at the rest of us. "I'm sorry. I trust George's judgment."

My eyes felt caked with grit. I was exhausted, furious, and every course of action seemed too costly. I knew what I *should* do: with so much at stake it was time to explain plainly what difference we'd seen between Spector and Abrams. But S'vlk's words had put a horror in me. The Outer Ones had left Spector no privacy, no thought or memory that wasn't shared. How could I compound that by exposing his most precious secret to colleagues who would hate him for it? I saw the fear in Charlie's eyes too, and knew I couldn't do it.

"I can see it was stupid to come here," I said. "We'll leave now."

"And let an imposter infiltrate your government?" asked Nnnnnn-gt-vvv.

Barlow and Peters moved instantly to stand between them. "We know what *you* are," said Peters. "We're not letting you near him."

"Let it go," I said tiredly. "We've lost this one."

I half-hoped Nnnnnn-gt-vvv would ignore me and pull Abrams into the borderland, though Barlow would probably grab as many of us as he could in retaliation. But the Outer One simply spread its wings, drawing claws in tight. "Have it your way. My mates are wait-ing for me."

It left, alone. I considered the elders, considered the FBI agents, and hoped that at this time of night no one outside the room would look at us too carefully.

"Out," said Barlow.

In the hall, Audrey burst into tears. "Goddamn hell! I'm sorry . . ."

"Don't apologize," said Charlie. "We're all right there with you."

Deedee nodded. "It's awfully late to be ladylike."

"I'd better, though." She wiped angrily at her eyes. "I think we're going to have to go down and get a room. If someone finds us in the hall like this, I don't know what's going to happen." The elders had pulled their cloaks over their faces, but the overhead lights were un-forgiving. A luxury hotel had little place for the exotic mysteries of the streets. I couldn't be angry at Nnnnnn-gt-vvv, though. It had de-layed rescuing its faction-mates to bring us here. Their lives depended on what it had accomplished with Glabri, and there was only so long it could wait.

Deedee looked the rest of us over with cold calculation. "Charlie, you're the most respectable gentleman we've got right now. Caleb, give the man enough to cover an absurdly expensive hotel room. I hope we've got the cash."

Caleb grimaced, but dug out a wad of bills.

"I've got a little walking money if that'd help," said Clara.

"Don't worry," said Deedee. "We can swing it. He's being frugal, but I think we're past that."

We huddled in the hall while our ostensible upper-class white couple (mascara streaked, shoes filthy with sand and subway grime) went to procure a private space. We'd have no recourse if a maid came along; our only hope was that it was far too late, or early, for housekeeping. I settled against the wall, head against my knees, eyes heavy.

I leaped awake at the sound of voices, on my feet and ready to fight before I realized that it was Charlie and Audrey returning. My relief nearly overcame the surge of terrified wakefulness.

"It's even on this floor," said Charlie, and Audrey smiled pride over this small but vital triumph.

I didn't fully relax until everyone had crowded into the room and I'd heard the deadbolt clank solidly closed. I examined our surroundings: no suite like Barlow's, but more room for our elbows than the closet where we'd stayed after leaving the mine. Two beds beckoned, but I imagined Spector lost in the dark beyond the sun's reach, and Neko eagerly preparing to lie down on one of those altars, and decided sleep could wait.

It wasn't only Spector's and Neko's fates that gave me urgency. "Mr. Abrams will try to report to Spector's masters as quickly as possible. He knows we know what he is, and he'll try to spread the Outer Ones'—the interventionists'—influence before we can counter it. Spector needs his body back, and we need the passivists back in the mine before Abrams brings more feds into their trap. Only we don't have any passivists with us, and don't know when we'll be able to reach them."

"We're here," said Clara. She patted Shelean's pendant.

"*She's* here," said Shelean. "I'm in the mine, which would be even better if I weren't shuffled off in a corner. But we've as much right to the place as an Outer One does—if we can make it stick. Once we do that, we can call Nnnnnn-gt-vvv's shiny new mine and let it know we've done its dirty work."

"Do you know how to change the wards?" I asked.

"If someone gets me in, I *think* so," said Clara. "I've been looking over their shoulders for decades."

"I helped set the things up," said Shelean. "As long as I look over *your* shoulder, I can make sure you do it right."

S'vlk pulled back her hood. She sat heavily on one of the beds and dug talons into the quilt. "Aphra Yukhl, are you suggesting a frontal attack?"

The mattress looked blissful, but I refused to make any concession to my fatigue. I tugged at my dress, as if straightening it could restore my body as well. Was I suggesting an attack? "I don't see any alternative."

Grandfather rumbled amusement. "Even in disgrace, I have people who could help. But without Nnnnnn-gt-vvv we have no way to bring them to the mine."

The Outer Ones' lair spilled across dimensional barriers. There were many potential directions to get in—all guarded and warded. But only through our native sliver of reality could we safely travel. Especially me.

My restless hands found a familiar, and disturbing, lump in my pocket. I withdrew the finger bone, cradled it in my palm. "We have other options for troops. If we can persuade them to aid us."

"I, too, have a terrible idea," said Shelean.

"How terrible, precisely, do you have in mind?" asked Audrey. Her voice was light, but her eyes were hard.

"Depending on what you do with it, anything from perfectly reasonable to excitingly catastrophic. If you play with a couple of safety settings, the altar room can recall minds almost instantly into their bodies."

"Then we *can* rescue R—Mr. Spector," said Charlie. My chest eased a little.

"It's painful," warned Shelean. "And dangerous. If he's lucky, he'll just get his mind scraped up, like climbing naked over sharp rocks. It's meant for *real* emergency evacuations. But I was thinking that calling *more* people back, especially the new ones who don't all want to be there, would make a great distraction."

"And we could rescue them too," said Deedee. "So much the better."

"What about Freddy?" asked Frances. She seemed calmer than the rest of us, awake and determined.

"We'll get him if we can," Caleb said. "We can't force him. Or Neko." That last so quiet I couldn't swear that anyone else heard.

"Of course you can," said Grandfather. "The idea that children should be allowed to make any mistake they fancy, no matter—"

I held up my hand. "We'll do what we can." I swallowed, and said reluctantly, "I *will* prioritize rescuing those who want it over those who don't."

"And what counts as 'excitingly catastrophic'?" asked Audrey.

"My body's there too. If you need a bigger distraction, or someone to walk through a wall—I can hold on to my sanity for a few minutes, if I need to. There are tricks the K'n-yan know that no one else does." There was a shudder in her voice, and I remembered stories of Mad Ones warping flesh in fits of pique, of their cruel art transforming men into animals and air into poison.

"Let's try and avoid that," said Audrey.

"Believe me, no one wants to avoid my embodiment more than I do."

Grandfather stretched and bared his teeth. "That's a reasonable range of tactics," he said. "I suggest we plan strategy."

After intense discussion, we reluctantly concluded that the best way into the mine was to offer the interventionists what they wanted. But Grandfather would not countenance Caleb risking himself along with me.

"This isn't just about men of the air," said Caleb, his voice rising. "This is a battle for Innsmouth. We need Freddy, we need a safe place to spawn—you would never have let anyone hold you back from fighting to defend our people! You'd never have sent your sisters into battle alone."

"If you both sacrifice yourselves to save the spawning grounds, we lose more than Innsmouth. Aphra has already thrown herself too far into this idiocy to avoid risk. You and your lover will wait here, safe."

Deedee bridled. "Ron Spector is my colleague, and Neko's my friend. I respect you, but I don't owe you obedience."

Grandfather bared teeth, humor stretched wire-tight. "True. You could leave Caleb here alone to prove the point. Do you think your courage in doubt, in this company?"

"I'm not trying to prove anything to *you*. I've got a duty."

"Deedee, he's right," I said. I didn't like it; I wanted her keen eyes and chameleon speech beside me. "If you got hurt going along with us, I'd never forgive myself. *Caleb* would never forgive me."

"That would be stupid of him. Never's a long time."

"Deedee?" Caleb's anger had dropped away. His eyes begged. He took her hand. "Just because I have to breed with others doesn't mean you're replaceable. Please stay?"

She gripped his hand, sighed, and said in R'lyehn, "Ich d'luthlu, ri ich ngevh. Ph'chlit nge y-ngavn." *You're an idiot, but you're mine. I'll stay.*

Clara couldn't come in the front way either, too recognizable as Nnnnnn-gt-vvv's partisan. "Like I said, Miss Marsh needs companions who'll show off how many groups she's made connections with. To the Outer Ones, it's how you prove strength. Like a human strutting around flexing muscles. Extra people will just look like you're trying too hard. It'll look suspicious—and he's already gonna be inclined that way."

"I won't take more people than I need," I said. I felt the abyss of action opening before me. It was time to talk to Glabri, and see how much risk *he'd* countenance to rid himself of his Outer One neighbors.

CHAPTER 24

"Kvv-vzht-mmmm-vvt wants to see me."

The guards at the mine's entrance were more obviously guards, though still miscellaneously dressed. I had brought both Audrey and Charlie—my excuse that they came from different communities even if they were both part of my confluence—along with Frances. All three branches of humanity, symbolically at least, stood at my back. I'd left Trumbull at the hotel, reluctantly, fearing she'd be interpreted as a representative of the Yith. Clara swore my little entourage was as good a show of strength, by Outer One standards, as the trident-bearing warriors who once accompanied my grandfather.

We waited a long time while messages were carried beneath the earth and answers returned to the crumbling stoop. At last some of the guard—the bearded negro man who'd been there on our first visit, and three more people new to me—led us below. I was exquisitely aware of the balances between us: we had them outnumbered, but we walked through their place of power. They moved among uncounted allies; I had only who I'd brought with me. For now. I moved carefully, afraid to reveal the protective talisman Mary had given me when she thought she could trust us—or worse, the token of Glabri's dubious alliance. Both lay hidden beneath the collar of my dress.

I was necessary bait, since we needed Kvv-vzht-mmmm-vvt's

people to take us in, but I was also a vulnerability. I hadn't Audrey's or Deedee's skill in deception. I could only mask anger and fear with cold dignity; my lies were brittle. *I only need to fool them for a few minutes. And I can let them see my fear.*

We passed through the obfuscatory rubble of the mine's upper corridors, down rickety stairs unworthy of what lay below. The crumbling plaster walls, unspeakably mundane, made me shudder at how pervasive this kind of scenery was. Like the hills under which they normally dwelt, New York's untenanted buildings provided endless crannies where these creatures might hide.

Unfair, to find that disturbing. In the twenties frightened policemen, soldiers, mothers, neighbors, had shuddered to think that Aeonists might whisper our gods' names anywhere or everywhere. The fault wasn't in the Outer Ones' species; I had come to know Nnnnnn-gt-vvv as well-meaning and thoughtful, its fits of temper and flightiness no worse than many humans. Yet I still needed to brace myself to look at it.

This time, less entranced by my newly discovered cousin, I felt the claustrophobic depth of our descent. Perhaps Shelean found the underhill homey. I could only compare it to my imagined ocean, where the swift pull of arms through water and the kick of strong legs would carry me down amid Y'ha-nthlei's cool hearths, or bring me up through the surface into starlight. For the Outer Ones, of course, this place was precisely that: material barriers wouldn't stand between them and their native element.

An Outer One was waiting for us. And with it—Neko. She threw herself into my arms. I staggered to keep my balance, returning the embrace reflexively even as my mind churned with relief and suspicion. The way she shifted from toe to toe, was that her ordinary enthusiasm? Were her flushed cheeks and wide pupils what I would expect from my wayward little sister? I shuddered with anger at the mere thought that they might have made mock of her face, and hoped she took it for some more appropriate emotion.

"Oh, Aphra," she said. Her voice sounded like her voice, but Abrams had sounded like Spector. He'd *said* the interventionists had no reason to make a doppel of her, but he'd also said they wanted a hold over me. "I'm sorry I left the way I did. I knew you'd argue if I asked, but it seemed like the best chance of helping you."

With the Outer One watching, I couldn't afford an honest conversation, but I couldn't bring myself to any carefully considered response. "You wanted more of their visions. And to see the real thing, even if it meant leaving yourself behind."

She pulled away. "I'm right here. And yes, I'd like to see other worlds—but I wouldn't have run away to satisfy myself. Kvv-vzht-mmmm-vvt says they can help you, if you'll let them." Her voice dropped. "But they've got problems here, too. And they want our help. Some of their people want to push humans into another war."

It would make sense, if they'd told the humans here that the passivists were trying to start a conflict—a neat contrast with the interventionists' desire to prevent one. Part of my mind leaned into the story, into the comfortable lie that Kvv-vzht-mmmm-vvt's benevolent intent would lead naturally to benevolent effect. A more nuanced, wounded part of me wondered if it *might* have been Nnnnnn-gt-vvv who lied to us. But then there had been Abrams.

"That's why we came," I said, to the Outer One as much as to Neko. "We're here to help."

"I'm glad. I've missed you."

She led me to the Outer One and, remembering its instruction, I asked, "Kvv-vzht-mmmm-vvt?"

"Yes. I'm glad you came."

"I'm not, but you've left me no choice." A sliver of truth, enough to explain the bitterness in my words. It was easy to try and hide it, easier to fail. Charlie and Audrey stayed close, their warmth and postures bespeaking confidence that I drew in like oxygen. It wove through the confluence in steady breath and tense muscles. I tried to ignore the connection's fragility.

"What do you mean?" asked Kvv-vzht-mmmm-vvt.

"You took our friend. Nnnnnn-gt-vvv contacted me, but it has no plan to get him back. It doesn't like your ideas about how to handle humanity's peril, but doesn't have an alternative. I'm not sure I like your idea, but I know you want my help and I'd like to have some say in my people's future. I just need to see Spector, to be sure he's all right." The lie fell like rocks across my tongue. I hoped Kvv-vzht-mmmm-vvt would only hear fear for a comrade in my stumbling speech.

"Whatever Nnnnnn-gt-vvv's people told you, your friend Ron decided to travel with us willingly." Limbs shifted. "You met Nick."

"Audrey saw through him." Another sliver of truth, that they'd hear soon enough from Abrams himself: "Barlow, Peters, and Mary Harris didn't. They still think they're talking with Mr. Spector."

Kvv-vzht-mmmm-vvt lowered its head to examine Audrey, tendrils weaving. "You're perceptive. More gifts from Shelean?"

She shrugged. "I pay attention. Some humans do. How is she, by the way?"

"With Miss Marsh's cousin. She appreciates what we're doing—she knows what a species can do to itself, left alone. Would you like to speak with them?"

"Mr. Spector first," I said.

Around us, the instruments still glowed purple, and Outer Ones and humans still moved quietly around them. I tried to sense some change in the tenor of the room, some hint of tension, but felt nothing. If it was there, perhaps Audrey could see. If I couldn't sense their distress, I hoped they would miss mine for these few crucial minutes.

"Mr. Spector is on his way to Yuggoth," said Kvv-vzht-mmmm-vvt. "He's beyond reach of communication until he returns—it will likely be a day or two."

Shelean's pendant, I realized, put lie to their insistence that so many of the disappeared could not be reached. Unless the projector worked only on Earth? But Shelean had sworn that the emergency retrieval system worked over any distance—if they could do that to an entire mind, surely they could transmit speech. I almost said something, a disastrous slip caught before it left my throat.

"My cousin, then," I conceded. "I want to see for myself that he's okay. And Shelean, if she's with him."

"Gladly," said Kvv-vzht-mmmm-vvt. It began to lead us back among the purple umbrae. "And then we must talk. You have many connections, and you understand what frightens humans. You know what pushes them to risk their own survival. And you can translate the lessons of your tribe's long memory. We need your perspective, if we hope to make this work."

I eyed the instruments. Nothing looked familiar or even comprehensible. Where buttons or levers might sit on a human machine, these had childish scribbles and strange asymmetric protrusions.

Our plan depended on Glabri not only for distraction, but to crack the wards so that Clara could slip through. Familiar with the logic of her old friends' technology, she might be able to puzzle out the ward controls. There was no way I could operate them alone, even with Shelean's aid.

"Aphra!" In the conversation pit, Freddy rose grinning to greet us. My frustration broke against that grin, wide and near-lipless. For a moment, I saw only a man of the water. I wanted to take his hand and drag him from this cave, to show him Innsmouth's unpaved dunes and gambrel roofs and the view of Union Reef from my widow's walk. I wanted Grandfather to grant him a boat bought with Y'ha-nthlei gold, show him how to coil a rope and set a sail, teach him how to be a man of our people. But he had only a tourist's interest in Innsmouth's humble beauty, or even in its glorious reflection below the reef.

"Cousin!" Shelean's delighted exclamation gave no hint of how recently she'd spoken with us.

"Cousin." Audrey's tone was perfectly controlled, a believable mix of reluctance and acknowledgment. She reached out gingerly, a wary second's brush against the canister.

As if the idea had just occurred to him, Charlie asked, "If we can't talk with Ron—with Mr. Spector—can we at least see his body? Make sure he's well?" It could have been my line, but if Spector's secret affair lay dissected for the Outer Ones we could at least take this small advantage.

"Oh, can I come too?" squealed Shelean. "I've been sitting in the conversation pit all day, and I'm bored!"

Kvv-vzht-mmmm-vvt buzzed at another Outer One nearby, who waved cilia at us before scurrying off. To us, it said, "Will you not take my word for his well-being? I know you find the stasis room disturbing. Many newcomers do. It won't provide the solace you seek."

"Nevertheless, we want to see him," I said.

"Hmmmvvvv. Very well, if you insist. Come on."

I did not permit any hint of relief to escape my close-lipped frown. I followed, moving closer to Neko. Even now, when I couldn't be sure of her, I wanted her near when I faced my newest source of nightmares. Freddy tagged behind with Shelean. We'd earned our first success.

As we entered the glaring light of the altar room, I straightened my collar. The tip of my finger brushed the little finger bone beneath. *We're here. We're ready.* Lips motionless, I prayed that our actions today would add some meaning to the brief life of the bone's original owner.

Then I made myself look at the bodies. I knew how long it had taken me to cross the room before. There could not reasonably be more than a couple dozen figures laid out on the rough stones, but I could not count them. My gaze snagged on the wide pupils of a dark-skinned young man, the rictus smile of a pale woman with tangled curls. Yet Freddy trailed his fingers casually against a platform, smiling fondly.

Informed by Shelean's descriptions, I could see—after forcing my eyes from the waxen bodies—the lumpen shapes of controls on each altar. She kept up a stream of commentary now, names and gossip and introductions for each terrified face. I could imagine how that babbling narrative had served her well among the K'n-yan: not merely a sign of madness but a cloak over whatever honest emotion might attract a peer's cruel whim.

"Oh," she squealed, interrupting herself. "There's mine."

"You're beautiful," said Freddy, in the tone of someone who'd said the same thing many times and wasn't yet tired of doing so.

"*It's* beautiful," she corrected. "*I'm* here."

"You're beautiful, and your body is beautiful."

"Sweet boy."

Shelean's body was small. Awake, she might have come up to my shoulder. She was brown and slender, and the proportions of her limbs matched neither air nor water. Tattoos ran across her skin: strange beasts and vining helixes, unfamiliar runes and one ancient symbol, a stylized comet trailing fiery seeds, that stood for Shub-Niggaroth's fertile bounty long before humans rose from Earth's dust. In the entire room, her face alone was serene. Her empty eyes met the fierce spotlight with pupils relaxed; her frozen smile showed only tranquility.

"Here's your friend," said Kvv-vzht-mmmm-vvt. I made myself look away from the oasis of Shelean's face.

Until that moment, I discovered, I hadn't quite believed that Spector had been stolen. I'd spoken with Nick, knew he wasn't what he claimed, but I'd seen Spector's face and left him at the hotel. Yet here he lay, stripped bare and captured in an instant of fear and fury such as I'd never seen on his waking face. Charlie's nails dug into my palm.

"It's hardest the first time," said Freddy anxiously. "You shouldn't read too much into the expressions—it's like getting a shot. It hurts, coming out of your body, but what you get after is *good*."

I nodded distractedly, looking for the shapes Shelean had described. Kvv-vzht-mmmm-vvt still lingered, and I could do nothing under its full attention.

Normally, awake and outside ritual, I could ignore the worlds that waited a breath away. But now I felt something stir in the dreamland. Kvv-vzht-mmmm-vvt's wings flexed, and its tendrils went rigid. "Excuse me. Something is happening, I must—" and it vanished, gone to whatever layer of reality Glabri had chosen to invade the mine.

"There," said Shelean. "That squiggly bit—no, the other one. The *long* squiggly line. Tug it straight."

"Aphra?" asked Neko.

"What are you doing?" demanded Freddy, but I'd found the protrusion from Spector's altar. Stone writhed beneath my hand like a living thing. I dug in my fingers and pulled it slowly, painfully, taut. Something clicked and went still.

"I'm bringing him back," I said. "He's not like you, Freddy. He *didn't* want to be here." I watched, willing Spector to motion, but his body remained arched and frozen.

"He did," said Neko. Her voice diminished to an uncertain thread. "Kvv-vzht-mmmm-vvt said he did."

"Why isn't he back yet?" I asked anxiously.

"The further away you are, the longer it takes," said Shelean. "No emergency's worth the risk of pulling someone back too quickly."

"You helped her betray them," Freddy accused her.

"I told you, sweet, I know what happens when you force gifts on someone. We shouldn't be doing that, *they* shouldn't be doing that, and I can't allow it. They can save their generosity for people who want it."

Neko pressed her fist against her mouth, a little-girl gesture of horror. Above her hand, her eyes narrowed with grim outrage.

"Kvv-vzht-mmmm-vvt was right to doubt you." A hum from the room's edge modulated in displeasure. An Outer One crouched, and lifted the object it bore. I saw with sudden dread the vessel holding the trapezohedron. The intruder bent its eyeless head, and lifted the lid tenderly. "You need to understand us better. Just as he did."

I couldn't look away. I felt the painful, rasping strain on my azure cord, still half-shattered. But something held me back from the trapezohedron's abyssal vision. Mary's talisman knew that siren call as an assault on my mind, and gave me a chance to fight.

I knew I should seize that chance. And yet I wanted to look upon R'lyeh again, to dive beneath waters that might otherwise be decades away. The talisman warmed against my breastbone.

Freddy lowered himself to the floor, entranced, steady in the throes of the familiar sacrament. Neko cried out and collapsed. I should have worried; all I could think was that she, too, sought the visions. Still I pulled back, recalling vaguely that the pain in my head would get worse if I gave in. It was hard to remember. The pain must *fade* if I gave in, mustn't it? The pain only lasted a moment, like a shot . . .

"Aphra. Aphra!" I became aware, distantly, that Audrey was tugging my arm. "Your cord, Aphra, you have to stay here." I couldn't answer. The world around me began to fade. Through the fog, I saw her pull off her own talisman and thrust it over my neck. She pressed the cloth bundle against the skin beneath my collar. The ribbon caught on my hairpins, but my sight began to clear. I remembered that I must fight, could almost recall why. I couldn't make my body move, but I swam against the trapezohedron's undertow, fighting a swift and deadly current.

It was Audrey, seeing only the surface silence of my struggle, who said to Shelean, "You gave us the strength to resist because that's what *you* wanted, isn't it? To be safe from anyone who tried to twist your mind? I can feel that thing's pull, but I can hold it off." As the Outer One stalked toward her, she added, "I hope to god your judgment's still that good." She flung herself down beside her cousin's altar, and grasped the line that would call her home.

CHAPTER 25

Spector's mind was long light-hours away; Shelean had only four feet to travel. Even through the pain of trying to hold myself together, I felt the shock of her presence. She swung to her feet and whirled to take in the room with an expression of pure and terrifying delight.

"Oh, what an awful idea! Everything's a weapon to you, Audrey, even people—you *are* one of us. The Outer Ones' improvisations are so much more civilized." She stretched out her hand, and I stumbled as the trapezohedron released me. The backlash sent me to my knees, temples squeezed by blinding agony. When it cleared, I saw that the trapezohedron itself had vanished. The Outer One backed away from a cloud of glittering dust. Frantic buzzing resolved into frantic English: "Shelean, lie back down! Shelean!"

Audrey knelt, retching.

Freddy's eyes widened at the sight of his lover. "Shelean?"

"There you are!" She dragged Freddy to his feet. "Just a moment. I have to do . . . something, what am I supposed to do?"

She shrugged, then swept Freddy into an embrace. She kissed him deeply, twined fingers in his hair, dragged sharp nails down his neck and spine as if to gather in an instant all the sensation she'd forbidden herself for decades.

Neko groaned. Frances stooped to help with trembling fingers. Her eyes never left Shelean.

I squatted beside Audrey. "Audrey, are you . . . ?" I wasn't sure how to finish the sentence.

She caught her breath. "I had to do something. He was going to break your cord."

"I was fighting it."

"You were losing. It was all I could think of." She gasped, and I held her shoulders as her throat seized up again. Only a moment, then she forced another breath. "I'm sorry. I can feel them, the things in my blood. They're not coming out, not yet, but they're awake. They recognize her as a threat. Wasn't that smart of her?"

Through all this, Charlie hadn't moved. Now he whimpered, so softly only someone who knew him well might notice. Audrey and I both looked up. On his stone slab, Spector struggled upright. Self-control had begun to veil his face, but rage and horror still held sway. He patted himself cautiously, and his expression grew bland. I recalled him urging a coat on me as I emerged naked and dripping from the ocean, and wished I'd brought one of the cloaks.

Shelean clung to Freddy, watching Spector with pride and pleasure as if he were some Frankensteinian monster brought to life through her will alone.

Charlie could not, I saw, move to help his lover first. I did my best to ignore Spector's nakedness. I wanted to touch him, to give Charlie the excuse, but he wouldn't appreciate the further assault on his dignity.

"Mr. Spector," I said, giving him what refuge I could in formality. "How are you feeling?"

"How am I . . . ?" His laugh stretched thin and ragged. "I feel like someone grabbed my brain and pulled it out through my ears. It's so hard to concentrate. What's going on? What did they do?"

Tentatively, I took his hand. "I know it's hard right now, but

Professor Trumbull says that at times like this you have to pay attention to your body. Get up, move around, shake your mind back into place."

"She'd know, wouldn't she?" He obeyed, rubbing his hands together and then pushing himself to stand, colt-like, on the floor.

I felt overwhelmed myself—by the aftereffects of the trapezohedron, by Audrey's nauseous dread and Neko's confusion and Spector's blurred anger. Thanks to the ghouls' distraction, we'd rescued Spector. Now we had to provide our own distraction so the ghouls could slip Clara through to reset the wards. Unless her memory was better than she thought, she needed Shelean's guidance to make that possible. The K'n-yan still had an arm wrapped around Freddy, but she was staring at her empty slab with her mouth in a fascinated O.

"Shelean," I said sharply. She looked at me and blinked, and I felt suddenly that her casual attention might be the most dangerous thing I'd ever faced. "Can you still see what Clara's doing?"

"Don't be daft, of course I can't. The projector's tied to my canister, not my body. You want me to go check on her? I remember how to do this . . ." She held up her hand, smiling oddly, and her flesh began to blur into muscle-red fog.

"Oh god, stop!" Audrey cried. Her eyes squeezed shut, and she trembled violently.

Shelean looked at her in mild surprise, but her hand re-knit itself. "Oh, cousin-child, there you are. It's hard the first time, isn't it?"

Freddy broke through his own shocked silence. "Shelean, what are you doing? You destroyed the trapezohedron! Why are you treating Kvv-vzht-mmmm-vvt like the enemy?" He edged away from her, his flinch adding the unspoken: *is this the madness you warned me about?*

Her voice filled with sudden, sane pity: "The trapezohedron's only a sacrament till it's defiled. Look at Ron, there. He didn't *want* to travel with us. Aphra doesn't want the universe, just the ocean. But the interventionists won't let them go their own way. They think what's right for us has to be right for them. Pick your side."

Freddy glared at me, at his mother. "This is the first place in my life where I've fit in. Kvv-vzht-mmmm-vvt gave me that."

"I know," I said. I imagined trickling sand in an hourglass: Glabri's troupe forced into retreat, Clara stranded with no way to carry out her task; the Outer Ones rallying to extract us from the altar room. "As much as we want you in Innsmouth—if this is your place and your family, you get to make that choice. But Kvv-vzht-mmmm-vvt's people tried to take that choice from me and Mr. Spector, and they'll take it from our whole species if they get the chance. Nnnnnn-gt-vvv's faction wants to protect our right to make our own choices, even if they might be dangerous. You can help."

He looked between us, shaking his head. "This isn't right."

"Pull yourself together, kid," said Frances, irritation breaking through. "Did I ever tell you doing the right thing always felt good?"

"You never found us a home to feel good in. How would you know?"

"You think I haven't been looking?"

He pulled farther away from Shelean. "You're all wrong."

His lover shook her head. "Stupid, beautiful boy."

"If you won't help us," I said, "then go." My face felt hot and dry.

He stared at us for a long moment, hands flexing. The ache in his eyes, haunted and overwhelmed, reminded me how young he was, how little he'd seen of his own world before leaving it behind. He turned away with that silent misery etched across his body, and flung himself from the room.

"I should—" said Frances, looking after her son, then at me. "No. We need to do this thing. He'll be okay?"

"Kvv-vzht-mmmm-vvt wouldn't hurt him," said Shelean. "Freddy wants what it wants him to want."

Neko watched Freddy go, but didn't move to follow him. "They lied to me."

"I'm sorry," I said. "I know what you hoped to find here."

"I hope for a lot of things, and they don't always fit together. But I still trust you. I'll figure out the rest later. What do you need us to do?"

"We don't have much time," I said. I felt that with certainty: whatever Glabri and Clara were doing, it couldn't have gone right. Clara didn't know how to fix the wards on her own. She needed Shelean's guidance, and had depended on getting it through the pendant. We needed Spector's experience as well, and quickly—with both the violence and the negotiations to follow. "Mr. Spector, you need to know what's happened so you can help us deal with it. They've made up one of their people to look exactly like you. He's fooled your colleagues, and he'll urge your masters to go along with Kvv-vzht-mmmm-vvt's terms. If we succeed here, it won't matter—the interventionist faction won't be in charge anymore. But if we lose, you're going to need to convince them to break with the winners."

He nodded. There was a soldier's determination in the set of his lips. I tried not to notice his hollow eyes.

"This is ridiculous," said Charlie. "Aphra, give me a hand." I took his cane, and he leaned on me while he unbuttoned his shirt. "Ron, you have time to cover up before you save the world."

Spector laughed, and his eyes cleared a little. "Thank you." Their hands brushed as he took the shirt. It was too small, but he tied the arms around his waist. The impromptu loincloth seemed to help.

"Shelean." I took a steadying breath. "You said before that you could hold yourself together for a few minutes. Are you still in control?"

She stared at me wildly. "He left! He was supposed to stay with me, and argue philosophy, and he left! Where did he go? I should never have let him run away!"

"Shelean," I said again. I took a step toward her. I kept my voice soothing, singsong as I would with a child. "Freddy's not angry with you, and he isn't gone forever, but right now I need you to focus.

Can you help us get you back in your canister? I know you like it there, you've said so. You can lie down, and tell me what to do, and then you'll be able to talk to Clara again."

Anger gave way to confusion. "Oh, but it won't work. When you call someone home, the whole system cycles to clear itself out. I won't be able to go back for, oh, minutes. Lots of them." Tears welled in her eyes. "I don't like this body." She drew a finger down her arm, and blood bubbled through the skin like some strange ichor.

"Shelean, please don't." The Outer Ones probably had an emergency procedure for this. Likely it involved snaring her with the trapezohedron, or binding her in the apathetic trance that Nnnnnn-gt-vvv had forced on Grandfather and S'vlk. They would be here any minute to do just that, saving us from her shifting whims—and making it impossible to reclaim the mine.

"Neko, Mr. Spector, I need you to guard the doors. Shelean, I've got a—a gift for you. It'll help you feel better. But I need you to work with me and do exactly what I say."

Shelean stared at me hungrily, childishly. "Okay. What should I do?"

"You're of the rock, right? I'm of the water. More than any other kind of human, we're at home in our bodies. I can share a little of that stability, for the few minutes you need to wait."

"Oh no," said Audrey, looking up.

"I've kept you stable," I said.

"Yes, but when my blood-guards came out that first time, keeping me safe almost destroyed you. And she's—" She bit her lip and shuddered. "I'm only going along with this because it might save the entire human race."

Spector took his post by the door, frowning. Charlie watched him, eyes shadowed with worry, before turning the same expression on me. "All right, let's try this."

"I'm going to start with Grandfather's way," I said. "It's faster." And protected the rest of the confluence, a little, from the risk I was taking. "But I'm still . . . wounded. Charlie, Audrey, I need you both to concentrate on our connection, hold me together while I try to help Shelean."

"We're here," said Charlie.

Candle-faint at first, I felt their warmth. Pulses swift, breaths heavy, but sure of me and of each other. By their light, I could more clearly see my own weakness, the rivulet cracks in what should have been whole as the ocean. But I could also see, through our bond that didn't distinguish mind from body, the parts that were still strong.

My anger flared: this connection, this family rooted as deeply in my own flesh as I was in the stuff of my world, was what Kvv-vzht-mmmm-vvt would have me cast aside. I forced down my temper. Whatever Shelean needed to borrow of my nature, surely it wasn't that.

Grandfather had shared the ocean in a taste of his blood. Even then, I could see that it was a deceptively simple spell. Still, I knew the principles, and thought I recalled the sigil and words he'd used. *Last time you rushed an unfamiliar spell, you nearly drowned in it.* There was no Yith this time to rescue me, so I'd have to do it right.

I sat Shelean on the floor in front of me. She watched intently, but didn't try to hurt herself again. Nor did she summon my blood to the surface in a fit of helpfulness. Lacking talons, I pricked my finger with my knife, and slowly and carefully drew on my palm the symbol I'd seen Grandfather make every time he'd tested my selfhood. Enochian flowed from my mouth, words for deep water and deeper understanding. I'd paid them only casual mind when Grandfather said them, but now I could see their logic. And their danger.

I put my bloodied finger to Shelean's lips. Her tongue, neat as a cat's, darted out to claim it.

Grandfather had probed my awakened blood gently. Shelean grabbed hold of it and pulled tight. I felt how that connection could become a leash, in either direction, with a moment's concentration. I stood in perfect and terrible balance between the confluence's bracing stability and Shelean's wild strangeness.

"Oh," she said. "That's nice. You're all *solid*. I mean, liquid. But you don't scatter."

"No, I don't. Can you follow my lead?"

She nodded slowly.

"We need to reset the wards. I don't think Clara can do it on her own."

"No. I know how. I think." Her voice sounded steady, but murk hovered around her thoughts. The defenses she'd designed into Audrey's blood had once gone to bay faced with older, cleaner power. But I'd dived into the ocean itself to force the confrontation. My blood knew what I'd someday become, but it wasn't there yet. So with that weaker strength I held Shelean above an abyss of anger and chaos.

I tasted her madness. "Insanity" was a poor description. She wasn't confused about the world around her; she understood it too well. I couldn't allow that understanding to infect me, or worse Audrey. But I caught unwanted glimpses. In her eyes, every molecule hung on the brink of change. She saw, every moment, how she could transmute skin to gas or gold, all the potential waiting for release. That matter should not answer to her whims felt blasphemous.

I focused on my own faith in a deep, ever-changing world, immune to anything beyond the most tenuous control. I let it spill into my blood. She clutched that faith hard, and left bruises.

Slowly I led her toward the door. She gripped my hand, as her mind gripped my mind. My skin crawled. I could only hope the sensation was fear, and not Shelean considering all the things my hand might become. Audrey followed close. Neko came behind. I hadn't asked her to come with us, and I wanted her safe—but I didn't stop her.

Charlie cracked the door to the ward room, and I discovered why we'd been left alone. Clara might not have been able to complete her task, but Glabri had carried his out admirably: ghouls flooded the control room. They flicked in and out of the level of existence I could see, and Outer Ones followed. The distraction was thorough and alarming.

"Ooh," said Shelean, bouncing on her toes.

"Stay focused. They aren't going to hurt us."

"But they need bones to crack. I can help!"

"We'll worry about that later," I said firmly. How Shelean might produce a cracked bone didn't bear thinking about. "Focus on the wards. Where do we need to go?"

Trumbull's guest had treated magic as a practical system of well-understood components, where I saw memorized patterns. But the Chyrlid Ajha had learned our patterns from the Yith—perhaps some from S'vlk's guest when they'd deigned to join our hunts and campfires—and Yithian magic followed comprehensible rules. The Outer Ones' ward controls were as different from my diagrams and chants as their bodies were from earthly lifeforms.

Shelean smiled as she rested her hand on a random spot of color. It shifted out from under her hand, and I felt her reaching for it with her mind. Then she pulled away as if burned and flung herself against my body's oceanic regularity. "No no no no no no!"

"Shh," I soothed. Her grasp on my blood was starting to hurt. I didn't think the spell, which Grandfather had always used for brief diagnostics, was intended to last this long. My fragility made this even more dangerous, and I didn't dare let her see lest it feed her own. Audrey's support was fickle; I had to shield her from Shelean's perceptions as much as she shielded me from breaking. My blood's strength, and my own concentration, were crumbling barriers. We needed to finish this swiftly. "Tell me what's wrong."

"I don't have enough hands. And I *can't* use magic to hold everything at once—I mean, I can, it's easy, but then it will all get very bad."

The crawling on my skin intensified. When I glanced down, the back of my hand was thick with inky vines. Her tattoos, creeping across the gossamer barrier between us. I wanted to scream, to drop the spell, to pull away as hard as I could. Very calmly, I said, "You don't need magic. We have plenty of hands. All we need is your memory of what to do."

"I remember. I know how *everything* works. But the memory is in my mind, not in *you*."

The backs of my hands stung. The sensation began to creep up my wrists. I didn't look down. "Shelean, I want to help. But I need you to keep your magic out of my skin." Nauseous terror thickened my words. As I spoke, I felt the abyssal force of her attention: my body was only molecules, their current arrangement a trivial coincidence. I had to deny that deadly awareness. I concentrated on the truth of my skin: how it sweated in the summer humidity, reddened under the hot sun, grew supple with the soothing touch of salt water. *Ïa, Dagon, who gives flesh the gift of change. Ïa, Hydra, who gives flesh its limits.*

"Oh." Her eyes widened. I felt her attention ebb, from the maddening consciousness of molecular drift to the merely nightmarish consideration of my body's malleability. "But it's our skin. I can feel it."

"No. I need you to remember whose skin is whose, or I'll need to take the ocean back. And I need you to stop playing with anyone's skin. I need you to focus. Can you tell us what to do? Like you were going to tell Clara?" The stinging sensation, like a fistful of nettles, didn't go away. But it didn't continue its journey up my arms, either.

"I can try. She knew what things were called. But it wouldn't have worked—she didn't have enough hands. I'm not sure *we* do. No tendrils."

"For people who claim that all travelers are created equal," said Audrey, "they sure design their dashboards for themselves."

"You noticed!" Shelean grinned. Then she picked up my hand. My palm flared with a thousand pinpricks. "Hold it right here. Then move your fingers like that . . ." She manipulated my hands into the precise position she wanted. I tried to ignore the pain, to be flexible as a child's doll. "Audrey, I need to touch you."

Audrey's eyes widened. She stared not at her cousin, but at me—at my fingers where Shelean had touched them. Her legs twitched, but she didn't move. She shook her head. "I'm sorry, no. No, I can't. I'm sorry."

Neko took a shuddering breath. "I'll do it."

Shelean blinked at her rapidly. "Yes, you, that's good. Come here."

When she gave direction, I heard a hint of old authority in her tone, a breath of connected thought. And yet, I was afraid to look at my hands.

Shelean pulled Neko to the other side of the console. She posed her fingers precisely, shifted them by fractions. "No, it's not enough. You have hands, but I can't explain it right. You aren't tangled with us the right way. I need, I need, I need . . ." Her longing gaze fell again on Audrey.

Soon, the Outer Ones would contain Glabri's invasion. Soon, someone would notice us. I forced myself to look down.

Monsters writhed on the backs of my hands, and ink-stain vines twisted. At the edge of every hoof and thorn and sharp-tipped tooth, blood welled to the surface. Beneath my skin, I felt improbable needles of bone thrusting upward.

"Shelean," I said quietly. "Can you feel my blood?"

"Yes. It's beautiful. So wet and deep and old. It's holding me up— please don't take it away!" Her voice rose in panic.

"Shhh. I'm not taking anything away. But you're scaring your cousin. My blood holds me up, too. If you pay attention, you can see my true shape in it. I'm not malleable. I *am* my body, and my body knows what it's supposed to be doing. So I need—" My throat dry with fear, I breathed in the stuffy air of the underhill. "I need you to look at what you're doing to my hands, and make it stop. I need you to put them back the right way. If you do that, maybe Audrey will let you touch hers, too."

Shelean stared hungrily at the blood. "But everything changes."

"Yes, I know. I'm going to change in my own time. I promise."

She drifted back around the console, licking her lips. Her eyes fixed on my hands. Her own tattoos were less animate than mine. Even so, the beasts seemed to kick in the corner of my vision, or grab hold of spiraling lines with their too-human hands. She drew my fingers from their careful placement, knelt, and pressed her face against them. Her mind's grip on me tightened, and I braced myself against the pressure. I felt something wet and warm: her tears, or my blood, I couldn't tell. I smelled salt, sharp and unlikely as if the whole ocean attended our work.

Then the stinging vanished, and when she released my hands they felt as cool as if I held them under the inflowing tide. The pain in my bones, too, had vanished. With exaggerated care—or perhaps not exaggerated at all—she placed them back where she wanted them on the console, just so.

"Audrey. Cousin. You've every reason to fear me. But the Outer Ones' folly can warp far more than I can. Please. I can keep control a few more minutes, I promise."

Audrey looked at Neko, and then at my hands again. My skin was as clean as if Shelean had never touched it, marred by nothing more than flaking patches of sunburn. I felt Audrey's heart pounding. She offered her hand to her grand-creator. "All right, let's do this."

Shelean placed Audrey's fingers with the same deliberation. Finally she set her own on the other side of the console, beside Neko. "The easiest way is to set everything back to default, like a seed ward instead of a full mine, so it lets us all in. You have to do exactly what I say. Aphra, move your little finger left just its own width. It has to be on the green blotch . . ."

It was hard, slow work, in the midst of chaos. The ghouls were trying to create as much confusion as possible, frightening the mine's defenders and dividing their efforts rather than aiming for any specific target. I worried that one of them would jostle my elbow, or that Kvv-vzht-mmmm-vvt's allies would realize what we were doing or simply notice Shelean's presence. And I worried most that Shelean would misremember a critical step, or we would misunderstand her instructions, and call down disaster. The connection between us helped; I could dimly sense what she imagined as she tried to direct minute physical movements, and feel her startled alarm if our attempts didn't match her desires.

"Perfect—hold it just like that!" She bounded around, darted in to prod a knob, and swiped across an inscrutable display. "Now let go!" We stepped back. The world shuddered, and the scent of rotting greenery grew overpowering.

The ghouls froze in their paths, lifting their faces to sniff the fungous air. The change at last drew the attention of the two Outer Ones in the room.

"Shelean!" said one. It began to gesture. Shelean gasped, reached again for the console. As something in the unfathomable machinery twisted and changed color, I felt her drop our stabilizing connection.

Then the mad energy drained from Shelean's eyes, and serenity pressed hard against my shields. Audrey, still protected only by her own native willpower, took my hand and dug nails into my palm: one more goad to help me hold fast to anger and fear.

"You don't need to do that to us," said Audrey. "We'll come quietly without the poppies, thanks."

The pressure eased. "What did you do?" demanded the Outer One.

"Sent out an open call," said Shelean. Her voice was dull, but I heard the barest hint of triumph. "To tell your exiles that they're free to come home."

The room began to fill as wavering air coalesced into uncountable claws and membranous wings.

CHAPTER 26

We were Kvv-vzht-mmmm-vvt's prisoners, or perhaps guests. The distinction was subtle, and we hadn't yet tried to leave. Nnnnnn-gt-vvv had brought a dozen or so passivist compatriots, along with Clara. They didn't fight as humans would to reclaim the building. Simply by being there, they prevented the interventionists from taking dominion again—but until they came to some agreement, they couldn't leave without surrendering.

The two factions' mutual interest in returning Shelean to her canister eased their awkward reunion. Placid, she lay willingly back on her stasis table. Audrey and Charlie and Neko and Frances clustered close around me. Spector, with a glance at the still-empty platform where he'd been held, stayed within our protective orbit. He'd always kept himself a little apart from us before, a welcome intruder among our friendships. Now . . . I knew he must have been thinking about the imposter, about what was being done in his name outside the mine. Or perhaps simply about what had been done to him here.

I felt adrift. I kept checking my awareness of the confluence and my body. They remained intact. Whatever was causing this feeling was less tangible, an ordinary vagary of emotion. We'd achieved every goal we'd sought when we entered the mine—and I could see now how little that was. Kvv-vzht-mmmm-vvt still held the upper hand.

Its agents, Abrams not least among them, still held positions of perilous influence. It still would not trust humans to save ourselves.

Humanity must pass from the earth someday—but we faced a dangerous pivot in our history *now*. Outer One interference would only make us less stable, and it didn't seem avoidable.

Humanity had never truly lived in isolation, though. Besides the Yith, what I'd said to Spector was true: other species, from our own world and others, constantly passed among us. And our own variation—not only among rock, air, and water, but among the thousand languages and races and nationalities that daily brushed skin in New York alone—meant that we were always surrounded by alien beings. Even at its most provincial, Innsmouth had traded and negotiated and seduced. Strangers were a constant.

"Kvv-vzht-mmmm-vvt," I said. Then I hesitated. With so many crowded around us, I was afraid that we'd both shape every word around a dozen possible reactions. "Can we talk somewhere private?"

I took Audrey with me as chaperone, confident in her protection. It found us a nook off the conversation pit. I wanted to pace the cramped space, or jitter like Shelean, but I forced myself to stillness. Even more than Audrey's presence or the shield of Mary's talisman, I needed my mother's dignity. I needed also an elder's blunt honesty, though I had less practice with that. *Nyarlathotep, guide me to say what is true and what is needed.* "You wanted me because of my connections. Because I speak to many different kinds of people—like you do."

"Yes. I hoped you would introduce us into the councils of the air and water. Instead you've taken the passivists' part."

I pressed on. "I took their part because I didn't trust you to save us. I want humanity to continue a little longer, at least as much as you do. But the cliff we walk means that the smallest error of judgment could end us in an instant.

"You've been at this only a few days, and already humans have reacted to you in ways you didn't expect—and not only me. It took

Audrey minutes to expose Spector's replacement. Even this first part of your plan has failed. Do you still believe you can manipulate us into survival?"

Kvv-vzht-mmmm-vvt rubbed claws, a chitinous rasp against its usual buzzing. "You have something to propose."

"Yes. Let me mediate between your factions. I can help you come to a true accord in place of the détente you have now. After that, I want you to treat my species like adults. Talk *openly* to the states you want to influence. Come as you are, instead of trying to deceive them with doppelgangers and trapezohedrons. I don't want them to discover your secret influence and grow even more paranoid."

Kvv-vzht-mmmm-vvt's expressions were still unreadable, but perhaps some part of me was finally learning the language of its emotions. In the shift of its limbs and the eye-watering furl of its wings, in the weave and swing of cilia, I detected a trace of thoughtfulness—and perhaps, from someone who claimed to talk with everyone, a willingness to listen.

The short night had begun to fade into dawn when we knocked on Barlow's door yet again. I didn't feel tired, but the aftereffects of fear and excitement jangled through my veins, sticks borne on the flood. I covered my mouth as if stifling a yawn and surreptitiously licked sweat from my wrist. It helped.

It was late enough for the suite's inhabitants to have gone at last to bed, and etiquette dictated waiting until a more reasonable hour—but etiquette didn't know what Abrams might accomplish in the interim. We knocked a second time before a bleary Peters opened the door. His half-buttoned shirt didn't look much more put-together than the ill-fitting jacket that Spector had scrounged from the mine's wardrobe.

Peters stared at Spector, then twisted to stare at one of the bedroom doors. Barlow emerged in a bathrobe. He, too, stifled a gasp and looked back at the door.

Why would Abrams sleep here? But of course, the real Spector had been staying with people who'd known him his whole life. Our unmasking had shaken Abrams, and he'd found an excuse to remain with those he'd already fooled. Easy enough to claim that he feared our ambush if he left.

Mary emerged too. She wore a long flannel nightgown and a holstered gun, and her gaze followed the same track as the others.

"What now?" she asked, tone perfectly flat.

"This is the real one," I said.

Mary turned to Barlow. "Get him out here."

Barlow disappeared into the bedroom, steps jerky with anger. He emerged dragging the doppel clad in boxers and a slept-in shirt. The color drained from Abrams's face when he saw Spector in the doorway.

"What are you doing here?"

Even knowing which one was which, seeing them together made me shudder.

"Pulled home early." Spector sounded dangerously bland. "I always said you didn't know me as well as you thought you did, George, but I didn't really believe it until tonight."

"But he knew—you! Where'd we meet?"

"Fort Belvoir, bonding over Von Juntz and Damascius, as any fool with a mind-reading machine thousands of years ahead of human technology could tell you."

Abrams yelped as Barlow's grip tightened. Barlow asked, almost apologetically, "Where have you been?"

Spector grimaced. "Halfway to the edge of the solar system, or so I'm told. They don't show us passengers the map. Fortunately, those canisters turn out to have an emergency eject button. You can thank my irregulars that I'm not stuck shivering on Pluto about now."

With a cry of anger, Barlow threw Abrams to the floor. Mary drew her gun.

"Stop that," I said, though I could feel no sympathy for the imposter. "He's still the Outer One's representative here—and we've come to bring you their terms for a more honest relationship."

"Why should we trust them?" demanded Mary. "Or you?"

"I'm not asking for trust, and neither are they. But the last few hours have convinced them that infiltration won't work as well as they thought. From where we stand now, it's impossible to avoid a relationship with the people who share our world. It's in your interest, as much as ours, to make it as aboveboard as possible."

Neko handed Barlow her neatly transcribed notes on the negotiations we'd mediated. Both factions of Outer Ones had agreed, point by carefully argued point, to work directly with the United States government on the common goal of avoiding human extinction.

Abrams eased himself into a sitting position. Glancing at Mary, her gun still trained on his chest, he didn't attempt to rise further. He rubbed his arm where he'd fallen and addressed Spector. "I hope you enjoyed your trip, however abortive. There are wonders out there."

"I wish you joy of them. I'm sure they're beautiful when you've chosen to see them. And when no one's using your face to double-cross everyone you know."

I tried to imagine what emotion Spector's flat expression masked. How would I feel, talking with someone wearing my eyes, my arms, the sagging skin of my neck that whispered the promise of gills?

Barlow looked through the notes, frowning. "It's one thing for us to interview a bunch of tentacle bugs as part of an investigation. This is the next thing to a treaty. It's big."

Mary glared at Abrams, who hunched smaller. "I'm tired of being lied to," she said. "I'm definitely not ready to be diplomatic with the liars."

"I don't trust the Outer Ones," said Peters. "And I don't trust these guys. Can we please make all of them someone else's problem?"

"They're someone else's problem," said Barlow firmly. He put down the papers and stretched. "Plenty of people in D.C. have been sleeping soundly all week. Let's wake someone up at State."

≈≈≈

Peters took over guard duty on Abrams, whose status wavered between hostage and potential emissary, and whose sculpted face was a constant reminder of how dangerous it was to work with the Outer Ones—not only for the people of the water but for all humanity.

You can fight and lose and never know. But avoiding the fight wasn't an option. The conversations would happen, openly or in secret, lies passed through agents with stolen faces or amid the glitter of diplomatic parties.

Before we went our separate ways, Mary cornered me. "It wasn't your place," she said. "What happened to me—I had a right to know."

"I'm sorry," I said. I resisted the urge to explain my reasoning again. She knew, and repetition wouldn't make her forgive me. "What will you do, now that you know?"

"You really thought we'd provoke a war over this." She chewed her lip. Her nightgown ought to have made the scene absurd, but she held herself aloof from her dishabille state. "You once talked me out of what you claimed was a dangerous line of research. But now I can't trust your warnings about where not to look. I wish I could—I suspect you know where all the world's ends are buried, don't you?"

"If I did, I'd feel a lot more sanguine that we weren't about to hit one now. Miss Harris—" She nodded. "I have a strange favor to ask."

"Really. Now, after all this?"

"It's a favor that goes both ways." I took another deep breath, and offered up another precious drop of truth. "You wanted to know about world's ends. Ask your friends at the State Department to tell you if they hear about a place called Fángguó. Or Cān Zhàn, or the Protectorate—it's got a couple of different names."

"What's Fang Gow? Not a chop suey place, I'm guessing."

"The Yith keep their secrets, but they drop hints about the future.

The rise of the Fángguó Empire is the last event that we know about in human history. It could be large or small, could last a thousand years or a few months. It could be an empire in name only. It's not the most reliable reference point—but if no one's heard of it, then the current tension might not be how we die." I paused. "Of course, if the Yith get involved, that safety is meaningless. They don't *like* to change history, but they will if we cross them too badly."

She rubbed the back of her head, where her night's braid clung against the nape of her neck. "The end of human history. Of course you don't care about preserving the United States. You don't even see it, do you?"

"It killed my family, of course I see it. And I care, in spite of that. We live here still, and every time an empire falls, it takes our young men with it." *Caleb. Freddy.* "But I haven't the luxury of imagining America will last forever. The Yith didn't bother to tell us about Innsmouth, and they won't tell you how your state will die either. They won't tell you how to overcome their curse, nor anything else you'd want to hear."

"You still want us to leave them alone. After what they did."

I sighed. "I wish I knew what to say. I don't blame you for being upset with me. But I'm warning you off for a reason."

"And the Outer Ones?"

A few doors down in our own rented room, S'vlk waited to learn what we'd done. She would not be pleased. "We've been arguing and negotiating with them for fifty thousand years. Nnnnnn-gt-vvv says they've got thick skin when it comes to human insult."

"I wish they'd been honest." Her lids slid shut, flew open again, and I saw a glimpse of bloodshot fatigue. "I liked how they treated my condition as a problem to be solved, not just a weakness. Like Catherine."

Barlow came over and squeezed her shoulders. One finger fell against the bare skin of her neck rather than the flannel collar, and she turned to brush his knuckle with a thoughtless kiss. He frowned at me, halfhearted. "Mary, you should get some rest—Virgil can watch that fellow till backup arrives. State's going to have an embassy here in the morning."

CHAPTER 27

atherine Trumbull—Date not noted:
    I raise the window and welcome the humid night air into the hotel room. The buildings beyond send out beacons of light, and from the street rise scents of metal and sweat and smoke. A thousand organic compounds tell of the vast living city around us. S'vlk joins me, pushing aside the velvet curtain to let it drape across her back. I should warn her that people below can see us in the brightly lit room. But doubtless any who look up will assume prop or costume or sleep-deprived misperception, and I want her company.

"This is always the way, that youth charge into dangers out of our reach," she says.

"I don't like it either. I'd want to help even if the stakes weren't so high."

"Or the enemy so dangerous."

"I'm sorry about your daughter." It seems inane, and yet such losses transcend time as well as the Yith do.

She puts her arm around me as she looks out at the city. I try not to stiffen. I should pull away, but fatigue tugs at my body. It makes my mind heavy, jumbles my priorities. It makes it hard to think of the room full of witnesses behind us.

"I always think of what Thwg'ri could do," she says. *"My 'guest.' I heard so many stories of how they helped our tribe—no deliberate heroism, just the*

casual way they solved any problems that interfered with their studies. Every time a challenge arises that I can't surmount, I wish I could be like them."

"I'm glad it's not just me," I admit. "I worry that the others feel the same—that they look at me and wish she—they—were here in my stead. At least you know your guest's name." This last envious non sequitur is not quite unrelated. My new friends call my guest "Trumbull," when they forget.

"They introduced themselves to some of my family. Yours didn't tell anyone?"

"No." My hands rise of their own accord, the familiar frustrating dance of amnesic fumbling and physical dissonance. "I remember it from the Archives. I just can't make the signs well enough, with these hands, to transliterate it into spoken Enochian."

She releases my shoulder. "Let me help. I might recognize even poorly formed signs, as someone who's never seen the original couldn't." She holds out her own hands, tapping fingers talon against talon, wrists winding. In her more practiced approximations I can see the flow of tentacled limbs and the click of broad claws.

"Yes! Let's try it."

When we sit together with our equations, it feels like studying in the Archives. This is the same: slow efforts toward understanding, the patient urgency of the hunt, brute force trial and error where reason and intuition prove insufficient.

"Did you ever see the name written down?" she asks, and I shake my head. That would be easy: their language is designed so that a single alphabet can be pronounced easily in any body. The same written word precipitates into a thousand forms of speech, sounded out by human tongue or signed with ancient claws. My precious knowledge of my beloved Saujing's name comes from deliberate effort on a shared scratchboard. S'vlk and I must work click by click and sound by sound.

"Nlith'phui," I say at last. "Their name is Nlith'phui."

S'vlk laughs, teeth bared in delight, and pulls me to her.

I should retreat from her kiss. I can't let our companions see this flagrance.

But the elder tastes of oil and fish and salt, and sharp teeth scrape gently against my tongue.

When I look up at last, summoning the fear that should have been my first reaction, only Miss Dawson looks at all startled.

"It's about time you got around to that," says Caleb, slipping an arm around her.

Chulzh'th grins at us and tells Yringl-ph'tagn: "Thejh V'zgu-pt'a ng'rtil khur." They continue their conversation, giving us what little privacy the room affords.

"This can't be appropriate. What about our lifespans?" I whisper to S'vlk. If I'm lucky, I have a few decades remaining before this body crumbles to dust; Deep One orthodoxy would make what I'm feeling taboo for that reason if no other. "Our—"

She puts a talon to my lips and laughs, a burbling rumble. "Both our lives span aeons—what matter the years? We are captives of the Archives. As the acolyte says, we make our own rules."

For once, my hands feel like my own. I imagine a young, dark-skinned African woman walking north, imagine claw and tentacle amid ancient books and dark stone balconies. And as I imagine, I run my fingers over the scaled muscle and sleek, bony crest that my lover wears now.

In our own hotel room, our companions too had slept. Grandfather answered the door. He shepherded us in and embraced me. Behind him Chulzh'th dozed in a chair, eyes slit. S'vlk curled around Trumbull in one of the beds, Caleb around Deedee in the other.

"You are well?" Grandfather buried his nose in my hair, inhaling deeply. "You smell like mushrooms, and yourself. Let me check you, though."

We crowded in. "I may taste a little of Shelean," I warned him. "It's a long story."

He snorted. "I expect to hear it. But first, what do we need to know?"

"We rescued Spector. The passivists are back in the mine, and the interventionists were forced to compromise. Someone will come by before dawn to take you three back to the beach. The Outer Ones are opening diplomatic relations with the United States. I don't know how strange that's going to get, but it's less risky than the alternative." I leaned my head against him and breathed. Scales pressed against my cheek. I remembered the deep tidal force of his blood, and wanted to cling to it as Shelean had to my own shallows. "I don't know what I'm doing. Someone like me shouldn't be standing between great powers and trying to shape their interactions. It's hubris. It's not my place."

"Great powers surround us. If we don't choose to shape them, they'll shape us unopposed—we cannot let that happen again. Besides, you're a Marsh twice over. Gambling against the tempest is as much your inheritance as the ocean itself."

I choked on my laughter. I remembered sailors playing little games of chance on the docks, blaspheming at snake-eyes. "I don't think the storm rolls fair dice."

"Of course not. That's no reason to let it tear your sails without a fight."

Fatigue pressed in, but responsibilities lay on me still. The night's grand work was done, but everyone who'd stood with me deserved a word, a touch, a moment of attention. My father, a quieter leader than Grandfather, had been good at such things. He could pass through a room and leave behind him a trail of gratitude and thoughtful focus—or earn the same respect from a class of squirming students. I didn't have his skill, but it was work I liked. I liked it better, though, when I hadn't been awake so long.

Neko leaned against the window. I joined her, watching the shifting patterns of the waking city. Cars slid through the street below, moving more smoothly than during ordinary hours. There were probably more people awake in New York right now than asleep in Arkham.

"I was looking forward to it," she said.

"I know." I wanted to believe she'd made her choice, that her place by my side was secure. But that wouldn't be fair to her. "The Outer Ones have exactly what you want."

She pressed her hand to the glass. "Not exactly. I *like* having a body, and I'd rather take it with me everywhere. And I like being useful, wherever I go. But the things I saw in the trapezohedron, the stories Freddy told—I liked the thought of traveling safely in places that impossible. But after what they did to Mr. Spector, I don't think I could stomach it. Everyone I talked to, I'd wonder if they really wanted to be there. It'd feel like another prison."

I touched the back of her hand. She was warm and solid. Since the first day she'd joined us in the camp, she'd been there to soothe me when I awoke from my nightmares.

"You could still go. So many of their travel-mates *do* want to be there. Nnnnnn-gt-vvv respects our choices. He waited decades for Miss Green to be ready. I . . . don't think it would be wrong of you."

She turned to look at me, dark eyes drooping with the hour, pupils dilated. "You think I should go."

"I think you should do what you need. Do all the things you couldn't, when we were locked up together. Like I am." I looked out into the waking city. "I want you close. But that shouldn't hold you back."

"I don't want to go away forever. I just want to *see* things."

I shouldn't pull away from my sister out of fear she would pull back first. I put my arm around her shoulders. "I don't know whether it has to be distant galaxies, to make you happy. If it doesn't, I wish you'd just let us know when you want to spend a few days in Boston or something. You haven't even given yourself that much. We can call it reconnaissance if you'd like. Look for people who fit Dr. Sheldon's skull measurements, or find the closest hotels to the beach. If you were willing to consider playing tourist on other planets, surely you can countenance a trip to a museum a hundred miles away."

"You're probably right." She sighed. "I did some thinking yesterday, in the mine. About what I want, and what I owe my family. And what you said about family obligations. I think it'd be easier for me to meet some of Mama's expectations, if I didn't place all these artificial limits on what *I* want. Maybe if I go ahead and do what I need for myself, I'll bump into a nice Nikkei boy who needs the same things." A sly glance. "We can always leave the kids with you while we travel the universe."

"Any time you like." I hesitated. "You were right to be upset with me. Freddy's——" I tried to think of a good way to describe him, his idealism and rigidity and brittleness and simple youth. "He's made me *understand,* in a way I didn't before, that shared blood by itself can't make you compatible with a mate."

"No kidding. You deserve better."

I looked around the room, taking in my family. Thinking about the ease of sharing a home with Charlie and Audrey and Neko, even though we'd never breed together. "I've *got* better. If I can convince Freddy to sire children for me, I'll still accept it happily—but I'll raise them with the people I love. Even if duty comes first, it doesn't have to swallow us up."

She elbowed me. "Watch out. You're turning into a libertine."

I laughed, but the truth was precisely the opposite. Over the past few days, I'd nearly lost the water—something I hadn't known was possible. Freedom from the camps, studying magic, seeing the strength in my blood—I understood now that none of it was a guarantee. To put my happiness first, sometimes, rather than waiting on my metamorphosis, was to admit that the universe could still take everything.

EPILOGUE

September 1949

Our work in Innsmouth went on as before, less changed than I would have hoped. Frances, at least, had joined us there. Caleb took gallant pleasure in showing her around, and she and Deedee seemed to dance through some complicated negotiation over his time and attention. Freddy visited every few weeks, and we'd exchanged awkward pleasantries. He wore Shelean's pendant, but things seemed strained between them. Even she hadn't brought up the possibility of breeding.

Dr. Sheldon's inquiries brought reports of a few more scattered families. Three months of correspondence drew some of them to visit, and it seemed likely that more of our old houses would soon need repair. But even if every newly discovered family joined us, we'd still be too few. The empty houses filled steadily with young families who saw the town's rumor-tainted history as mere urban legend. The problem ate at me constantly, a distraction from every other activity. In the Crowther Library, I turned pages without reading them. At home, carrots were chopped or nails pounded by habit of arm; my mind poured through scenarios for repopulating the town with undiscovered cousins, or even with people of the air who could be trusted near the beach.

I worked with Archpriest Ngalthr, cautiously stretching the cord between mind and body as I slowly healed. But it was hard to feel whole, when I couldn't keep my physical and mental lives aligned in everyday life.

Frances had brought a small television in her meager carload of possessions. Our population was still far from supporting a movie theater, but her living room attracted elders—and the rest of us—with evening glimpses of the outside world. Static often drove Caleb onto her roof to adjust the antenna, an equally diverting source of entertainment.

I didn't like the grainy black-and-white images on Frances's set as well as the others seemed to. But I watched anyway, for the company and for the commentary, and in hope that some solution to my ruminations would present itself. And, of course, to search for hints about what had come of our time in New York.

From Spector, we'd heard only that negotiations were progressing— he wasn't permitted to say more, and I suspected that the people in charge of the negotiations didn't tell him much either. No Outer Ones appeared on the nightly news. I was just as glad. Revealing another species in our midst might distract the world from merely human conflicts, but it would more thoroughly embroil us in greater ones. The least of which was that once people knew to look for such secrets, the tenuous existence of the men of the water could not long remain hidden.

On September 23rd, we settled around the television with a batch of Neko's oatmeal cookies. When the picture and sound came clear, the announcer was reading from a sheet of crisp paper. His expression was somber. One hand rose to smooth hair already perfectly set.

"—Truman's statement continues, 'We have evidence within recent weeks an atomic explosion occurred in the USSR. Ever since atomic energy was first released by man, the eventual development of this new force by other nations was to be expected.'"

I sat back, staring, as the announcer went on. I tried, as he must surely be trying, not to imagine. At least they didn't have footage. Scientists had read the explosion in the vibration of the earth itself.

It was a scant week later when Spector knocked on my door.

I hadn't seen him since the belated dinner with his family. I'd liked his mother, found his siblings somewhat intimidating, and sympathized with Trumbull's status as his suspected lover. Spector had taken advantage of his family's presence to be friendly without talking about anything of substance. He'd run back to D.C. as soon as he could.

He'd grown thinner, flesh strained across his bones. Evidence of an early morning shave shadowed his face; he'd not stopped at a hotel before visiting. "May I come in?"

"Of course you can." I sat him on the couch, got him tea and a tin of saltcakes. "Charlie's in the study; I'll get him."

"Oh, you don't have to bother—I mean, that is—"

He still didn't know that I knew. "Unless you needed to talk with me privately?"

"Need, no. Though you're the other one most—" He caught himself again. I swallowed. This awkwardness was new, and worrisome. "Of all the people on whom Kvv-vzht-mmmm-vvt chose to . . . demonstrate . . . its politics, you suffered most directly. I hope you're recovering?"

"Yes, even if more slowly than I'd like. Archpriest Ngalthr has seen this kind of thing before, and is consulting with other elders who've treated similar injuries." I shaped my hands as if pulling something from the depths. "Thousand-year-old medical arguments bubble out of the Atlantic. But the exercises he's given me seem to help."

He nodded. "If you have any tips, I'd appreciate them. Every time I move, I feel like my body's about to slip off."

"I'm sorry. I'll do what I can to help."

He nodded again. "I want you to know that I listened, when you said not to be alone with them. I stayed in sight of George and his team. And then . . . George had turned around for a moment, and it seemed natural to walk away down a hall. I'd put Miss Harris's shield in my pocket—stupid, but wearing it made me uncomfortable. I saw myself coming the other way, and I gave him my jacket and holster without really thinking about it. Then I heard myself talking to George. They put me on that table, and told me they needed to demonstrate why my cooperation was so urgent. And then—I don't suppose you've ever been under ether?"

I shook my head. "Our healers use other techniques."

"I have—needed my arm sewn up once. Doctor did a great job, but for me reality just drained away, and then drained back in with my shoulder aching. Being encircled was the opposite. My body went away, but my mind was still there, out of its shell. Like being naked in a gale force wind. Maybe that's the wrong analogy to use with you." He smiled ruefully. He'd seen me go comfortably unclothed in a blizzard.

"I can imagine the vulnerability. Clothing, and flesh, provide more than one kind of protection."

"Exactly. Maybe it feels different for those who choose it, those who go willingly through the preparation. They like to talk—dear lord, the one carrying me nattered on for the whole trip—but they didn't like what I had to say. And still I could feel it working on me: I began to feel glad of their protection. Getting pulled back into my body hurt worse than getting shot. But I want you to know how grateful I was, how grateful I *am*. Thank you."

"What they did to you was vile. And—you're a friend. You've done a lot for us, even if *I* haven't always been grateful."

"A lot of what I've done has been double-edged. And I've asked for plenty." His hands flexed in his lap, fingers interwoven.

"Are you—" I took a deep breath. I wanted to believe this disclosure simply a sign of the friendship I'd acknowledged. I thought it was, in part. "You open up when you mean to apologize. You always have. What are you about to say that requires an apology?"

Another rueful smile. "When I first met you, I couldn't have guessed how well you'd get to know me." He rubbed his wrists. "I really would appreciate any suggestions your archpriest might have. I want to be at home in my body again."

"He'll be at the temple after moonrise. Meanwhile, does the FBI want something again? Dear gods, please tell me they don't want *us* to mediate with the Outer Ones."

"More than that."

I waited. "Mr. Spector, I am not going to shake it out of you. But I can find someone who will."

"I'm sorry. I like you liking me, and I know you'll be upset. Justifiably. But what I have to say will solve some of your problems. Double-edged, like I said." He squared his shoulders, and looked a little more like himself. "The negotiations are going well, or as well as we can expect when the differences in territory and power are so great, and the other side is so hard to understand. State, and the other agencies involved, are looking to settle into a longer-term relationship. Something stable. Especially with what just happened in the USSR, they want to get as much out of this as they can. They want a base within reasonable travel of the Outer Ones' Berkshire outpost. Somewhere relatively isolated, where people from different planes of reality can take long strolls together to work out politics, and no one will come around a corner and start screaming about monsters. And they'd rather not have to expel too many potential screamers to do it. Someplace where the government already has property, especially property they aren't already using, would be ideal. Easy access to the world's most experienced Outer One cultural experts would be a nice bonus."

I felt the shiver of desert sun, or the burn of frozen vacuum. "You're talking about Innsmouth. They want those things wandering around our town. State agents and soldiers and diplomats in our streets every day."

"People who're ready to face Outer Ones, and wouldn't scream when they saw Archpriest Ngalthr, either. The idea is to purchase everything they can back from the developers, and use eminent domain to reclaim the houses that have already been sold to earnest young couples who like long walks on the beach. They'd offer your community a hundred-year lease on the whole lot—you could use however much you needed, but the unfilled space would house the cadre negotiating with otherworldly superpowers."

It solved our worst problem—at the cost of our comfort in our own homes. The dream of remaking Innsmouth as it once was would be gone. "That's very generous. What if we refuse?"

"I pushed hard to make the deal as generous as it is." He leaned forward, hands on his knees, and didn't make the plea I could see in his eyes.

Another raid, I didn't say. If we refused, they'd scarcely need soldiers to force a street's worth of families from our homes. Audrey might pull in a few favors through her family, but they'd be outgunned. Out-lawyered, more likely, a clean and bloodless displacement. As long as we didn't fight back.

"I suppose I should thank you."

"I'm sorry. I know what you wanted to make here. I know how hard you fought for it."

I closed my eyes and leaned back in my chair. I should have been angry, should have railed and argued and cursed his masters. But what he proposed felt as inevitable as the fall of humanity itself, the natural consequence of battles lost decades past. "It wouldn't have worked, even if the state had left us alone. We're too few. There are still people on land with our blood, but none who share our culture. To walk down the street and see only people like us—it just isn't possible. I suppose we might as well have the soldiers, who at least won't look like they *ought* to understand."

"I know the tension. If you'll forgive me another confidence, you saw St. Mary's Park. My parents grew up surrounded by people who prayed the same prayers, spoke the same language, wanted the same things for their kids. But they wanted their children to go out into the world, and fit in there. Sometimes I want what they had, and sometimes it feels like the most closed-off, insular life I can imagine. If you can find any balance here, it'll be something worthwhile."

Charlie came out then, drawn by our voices, and joined Spector on the couch. Neko found us and insisted on adding to the small spread of food I'd put out. Soon Audrey would be home for the weekend, ready to tease out all the risks and possibilities she could wring from Spector's offer. The elders would come up from the water at dusk, eager to argue or approve. And I'd have to tell Caleb.

I was surprised to find myself picturing the Innsmouth that Spector proposed—and not finding it completely dreadful. Even while I'd yearned for the comfortable insularity of my childhood, I'd been building something more cosmopolitan. Perhaps Kvv-vzht-mmmm-vvt was right to say that was my true talent, where pulling together a likeminded community was not.

And much as "the state" still felt a monolithic horror in my mind, its representatives ranged from Peters to Spector himself. Perhaps some of their young officers would turn out to have bulging eyes, or an interest in studying Enochian. I'd decided that men of the air were worth trying to save; it followed that many of them must be worth talking to. *Go everywhere. Talk to everyone. Build with the materials you're able to gather.*

This world wasn't the one I wanted, but it was one I could work with. For however long we could keep it whole.

ACKNOWLEDGMENTS

Winter Tide was written in a rush of creative desperation, against an immovable deadline, while my pregnant wife slept exhausted beside me. *Deep Roots* was written in much shorter bursts of creative desperation, shoehorned into the cracks between unsleeping infants and the thread-hung weight of branching timelines that was 2016—and then the plummeting weight of the fixed timeline that was 2017. In the face of an uncaring universe, I hardly know what power or muse to thank for the shield of inspiration amid such events, but I thank them.

And I thank my wife, Sarah; my children, Miriam and Cordelia and Bobby; and householdmates Jamie and Shelby and Nora, for the entirely perceptible shield of their love and support (and in the case of the adults, extensive child-wrangling).

Lovecraft's sandbox remains an excellent place to play, even as his fears seem more relevant than ever. I thank him for leaving it open for the monsters to join in the fun, and offer in exchange however much exercise one can get by spinning in one's grave. Thanks are due as well to his collaborators Zealia Bishop, co-creator of the K'n-yan, and Hazel Heald, who hinted that Mi-Go brain canisters might be even creepier than they looked at first glance.

Lila Wejksnora-Garrott, Marissa Lingen, and Anne M. Pillsworth provided terrifyingly useful beta-reading feedback on an absurdly tight deadline. Anne is also my co-blogger on *Tor.com*'s Lovecraft Reread series; I'm indebted to her and our posse of squamous commenters for ongoing insight into the Mythos.

My social media fans and followers remain an excellent source of quick answers and quick thinking. Thanks in particular to John Cardoso, who suggested getting S'vlk out of the mine in a Statue of Liberty costume, and Mara Katz, who suggested trying to pass her off as a stiltwalker. Never let it be said that Twitter is merely a distraction from writerly productivity.

My father, Bob Gordon, could easily have been one of those boys chasing a ball across Aphra's path during the Summer Tide. He shared with me his memories of New York City in the '40s and bemusedly answered my questions about Brooklyn neighborhoods. D. W. "Lemur" Rowlands, infrastructure geek extraordinaire, provided historical subway directions. All errors are my own.

My wonderful agent, Cameron McClure, continues to provide feedback, guidance, and hand-holding—all much-needed during the creation of this book. My wonderful editor, Carl Engle-Laird, patiently (and sometimes impatiently) pushed me to make *Deep Roots* better, creepier, and more true to itself. I just cut an extra "and" out of the previous sentence because I knew he wouldn't like it, and anxiously await his judgment on the repetition of "my wonderful X" two sentences in a row. [We're good.—Ed.]

Belated thanks also to my *Winter Tide* audiobook pronunciation rescue squad: Alex Shvartsman for Russian, Janetta Lun for Cantonese, Shelby Anfenson-Comeau and T. J. Donahue and Lila yet again for Japanese, and Sarah Emrys for R'lyehn, Enochian, and Latin. Bella Wang helped me name Catherine Trumbull's girlfriend and translate Lovecraft's "Tsan-Chan Empire" into something sensible, and then kindly provided pronunciation help for the Mandarin and Cantonese.

Above and beyond everything else I've mentioned, Sarah continues to provide alpha reading, moral support, child care, a shoulder to scream on, and an endless willingness to gossip about the strange people who live in my head. Without her there would be no books, and a great many fewer sanity points.

ABOUT THE AUTHOR

RUTHANNA EMRYS lives in a mysterious manor house on the outskirts of Washington, D.C., with her wife and their large, strange family. Her stories have appeared in a number of venues, including *Strange Horizons, Analog Science Fiction and Fact,* and *Tor.com.* She is the author of the Innsmouth Legacy series, which began with *Winter Tide.* She makes homemade vanilla, obsesses about game design, gives unsolicited advice, and occasionally attempts to save the world.